NATURAL BORN LEADER

A Tribute to the American Political System

Ryan,
I hope this delivers as
many laughs as you can
stand. This is fiction but
sometimes too real.
Let's make politics fun again!

ROBERT L. SCHMIDT

authorHOUSE®

AuthorHouse™
1663 Liberty Drive
Bloomington, IN 47403
www.authorhouse.com
Phone: 1 (800) 839-8640

Published by AuthorHouse 10/14/2016

ISBN: 978-1-5246-4537-3 (sc)
ISBN: 978-1-5246-4538-0 (hc)
ISBN: 978-1-5246-4536-6 (e)

Library of Congress Control Number: 2016917242

Print information available on the last page.

Because of the dynamic nature of the Internet, any web
addresses or links contained in this book may have changed
since publication and may no longer be valid. The views
expressed in this work are solely those of the author and do
not necessarily reflect the views of the publisher, and the
publisher hereby disclaims any responsibility for them.

To my wife Marcia, my co-pilot in life and my co-pilot for this book. Your love and support inspires me. It's time to start our next collaboration.

CHAPTER 1

THE DYNASTY

William Barry "Tex" Flowers led a charmed life. The third-term senator from Texas was the latest link in a political dynasty that started in the 1930s when his great-grandfather Joseph "Pappy" Flowers tormented FDR as the leading opposition Republican in the House of Representatives.

Pappy was a Republican back in the day when most Southerners were Democrats. The Republican Party's popularity in the South suffered because of Abraham Lincoln and the Civil War, and it continued suffering through Reconstruction. When Pappy first entered politics in the 1920s, his selection of the Republican Party had nothing to do with his political ideology. Pappy's problem was that there were just too many incumbent candidates on the Democratic ballet. This made the Republican Party the path of least resistance. Pappy got on the ballot and said enough of the same things the Democrats said to get himself elected, first as a state senator and eventually as a US representative. Then national politicians like FDR and JFK came along, alienated the South, and turned it into Republican country. Pappy lived into the 1980s, and by that time, his choice of party seemed visionary. Of course, Pappy wasn't about to admit that it was all pure luck.

"They said I was a Republican because I was lazy," Pappy joked just before he died. "I wasn't lazy. I was smart. I knew the Democratic Party started to go to hell back when they nominated Wilson."

One thing was for certain: the Republican Party had been good to Pappy and the next three generations of his offspring. Bill's grandfather Horace "Teddy" Flowers did Pappy one better: he became a senator. Then Bill's father, George "Herbert" Flowers Sr., ran and won Teddy's seat when Teddy retired. Finally, Bill ran for and won George Sr.'s seat when he retired. This meant that the Flowers family continuously held a seat in Congress stretching from FDR's first term to the current day. The Flowers family was a Texas version of the House of Windsor.

As was befitting a southern gentleman, politics was not Bill's primary source of income. Bill's father, George Sr., may have retired from the senate, but he had his fingers in more pies than J. R. Ewing. While a poor man could and often did get rich in politics, a rich Southerner used politics as a mechanism to expand his power and convert his opinions and attitudes into laws that benefited himself and his friends. The Flowers political dynasty was mirrored by a business dynasty that was deeply embedded into Texas oil, real estate, and ranching. Their political, social, and business roots gave them access to the most powerful people in Texas. The Flowerses had evolved to a point where they didn't need to use these connections often. Instead they were the connections used by others.

Bill earned the nickname "Tex" because he'd grown up on the family ranch outside of Houston. He could ride a horse, and the childhood pictures of him in a cowboy hat, chaps, and spurs didn't hurt his popularity in a state where half the population thought they were cowboys and the other half wished they were. The cowboy represented a Texas history steeped in personal freedom and rugged individualism. The six-shooter and the open range were the Texas that existed before the liberals and the Communists came along and tried to ruin it.

The truth was that Bill wasn't much of a cowboy these days, and nobody had called him Tex for years. He attended private schools in DC while his father was in Congress, and then he attended Princeton and Georgetown Law School. If not for his Texas roots and Flowers name, it was difficult now to distinguish Bill from one of those liberal Yankee Democrats on the opposite side of the congressional aisle.

On paper, Bill was an accomplished academic, but he wouldn't have made it into Princeton or Georgetown without that family name. He was the hardest-partying student at Princeton and the only one they called Tex. His fraternity brothers at Beta Gamma treated Bill like the house mascot. They'd tell house party guests, "Welcome to Beta Gamma. Just remember, you can't be leaving until you see Tex heaving."

The Thetas were the sister sorority house of the Beta Gammas. Tex developed such a reputation with the Thetas, they'd even written a house poem for him.

We're Princeton Tigresses from Theta,
Always on the prowl for hot sex,
But if we can't find sex that's great-a,
We can always settle for Tex.

There was a standing joke the Thetas told each other the morning after they'd attended a Beta Gamma party. "You'll never guess who passed out on top of me last night!" a Theta would say. The punch line was always Tex. It became an old joke—and if you knew Tex, it was especially funny.

Bill had his share of hard bounces negotiating law school too, and he would have been out several times if his father hadn't been the dean's golf partner.

"You know I appreciate all you've done for Bill," George Sr. told the dean during one round.

"We appreciate all the Georgetown Law students you've hired or selected to intern," the dean replied. "I just hope having Georgetown on Bill's law school diploma doesn't come back some day and bite me in the ass."

When Bill first ran for George Sr.'s senate seat, there was a small minority of the Texas media who remained independent and outside of the influence of the Flowers dynasty. There were some unflattering accounts of Bill's college exploits, and one paper went so far as to publish an editorial cartoon that made some of the national wire services. The cartoon showed a college-aged Bill with a beer in one hand and a suspicious, hand-rolled cigarette in the other. The caption read, "I'm running for US Senate, dude. How gnarly is that?"

Because they were sure Bill wouldn't be able to hold the seat, the Republican Party tried to talk George Sr. out of retirement. They were wrong—but not by much. Bill managed to squeak out a win in that first election.

But after a few terms in the senate, the college stories had all faded away. This was partially due to Bill's popularity in Texas, but it was mostly because he had developed into a model, mature, and dedicated husband and father. After graduating law school and first failing but eventually powering through the Texas bar exam, Bill began to date Miss Maryann Simmons. Maryann was Houston's most eligible debutante and the daughter of Sanford "T-Bone" Simmons, a Houston retailing tycoon and powerbroker. It was as if the crown prince of Prussia was courting the princess of Austria-Hungary. Bill still occasionally ended up passed out at a Houston strip joint or nightclub, but he eventually proposed to and then married Maryann. Most political pundits agreed that Bill's marriage to Maryann just before his senate run was crucial in getting him over the last few inches of his election hurdle.

Just after Bill proposed, his future father-in-law invited Bill to his ranch and drove the two of them deep into the brush. T-Bone told Bill he wanted to show him a herd of his mustangs, but the drive was more about bonding with his future son-in-law and welcoming him into the family.

"If I ever hear about you cheating on Maryann, the two of us are going to have a problem," T-Bone told Bill. "Are you listening to me, son?"

Bill gave a tepid response that was too unenthusiastic for T-Bone's liking.

"You better listen," T-Bone explained. "If I find out you aren't, I'll cut off your ears, hang them in my shed to dry, and use them as skeet-shooting targets."

Bill had listened, and he'd managed to keep his ears— but it wasn't because Bill was faithful to Maryann. He'd pretty much hopped onto anything that wore a skirt and a smile. He thought he'd made sure it never got back to T-Bone, though. Maryann had her doubts about Bill on several occasions, but she had never expressed any of them to T-Bone, either. The better Bill got to know T-Bone, the more carefully he hid his dalliances. Bill was convinced that if T-Bone ever found out about any of his romantic escapades, he'd start by cutting off Bill's ears before he worked his way down to lower-hanging fruit.

Maryann didn't go into the marriage with blinders on. She knew her husband's reputation, and some of the stories she heard about Bill were fresh. She was betting on a hunch that Bill would grow up and ultimately honor the Flowers family name. Maryann was attracted by Bill's charm when it was focused on her (and she tried not to think about what happened when it was focused on someone else). She was also attracted by the concept of being a senator's wife, and Bill was the only person she was dating with that type of potential. She could live with a senator who had some minor hell-raising flaws. She was familiar with what it was like to live in the same home with a flawed but successful man. He was named T-Bone.

Maryann's hunch paid off. The family plan worked out perfectly. Bill and Maryann had a ranch home outside of Houston and owned a two-story brick colonial in one of Georgetown's prime neighborhoods. They had a son and a daughter in one of Houston's best private high schools. Fortunately, the children had their mother's sense of responsibility, intelligence, and beauty—and their father's social skills.

Despite Bill's flaws, his political career soared after his first election. There were no serious contenders for Bill's seat for the foreseeable future. He could continue to be Senator Flowers indefinitely, easily becoming the longest-serving Flowers in congress. If his physical and political health endured, he could even conceivably serve longer than the congressional record holder, Robert Byrd.

Bill might not want to serve that long, though. The Flowers *modus operandi* was to develop the next generation and hand over the reins. Bill could keep his Senate seat warm until his son, Justin, or, to be conservative but equal, his daughter, June, reached the point in their lives where they were ready to become the fifth generation of congressional Flowers.

There was one other thing that might affect Bill's Senate future, but it also had nothing to do with his physical or political health. Over the past several years, a new political plan had begun to take shape. It began at the Republican Presidential Convention. Bill was the most popular politician in Texas, and Texas was always important in national politics. Bill was invited to give the keynote address on the last night of the convention. Bill delivered a withering condemnation of incumbent

Democratic President Howard Randolph Smith and a strong endorsement for Republican nominee Imus Michael Whiteman. Unfortunately for the Republicans, I. M. Whiteman lost badly to Smith in the election, but Bill's speech continued to resonate with Republicans. The next presidential election was just over a year away, and this time the Democrats didn't have a popular incumbent candidate waiting in the wings. Early straw polls placed Bill at the top of the Republican candidate pool. Of even greater significance, he was easily outpolling any of his potential Democratic contenders, including Vice President Andrew Samuel Jackson.

George Sr. had already made a significant first move when he lined up Don Chambers to be Bill's campaign manager. It was no surprise, because Don and George Sr. were lifelong friends and political allies. Chambers had cut his teeth during the Reagan years, and any of his Republican rivals would have sold their souls to the devil or slept with the ghost of Eleanor Roosevelt to have him. Chambers was organizing a press conference for the following week. The plan was to have Senator George Flowers Sr. introduce his son. Next, Bill would announce his intention to run for president. Maryann, Justin, June, his mother, Betsey, and his younger brother, George Jr., would stand beside Bill to show their support.

Bill couldn't imagine a better showing. Don Chambers gave his campaign instant credibility. People would associate Don with the Republican Party's salad days, when Reagan won the Cold War with Russia, freed the Iranian hostages, fixed the economy, and kept the Democrats from invading the White House. Bill's family couldn't have been any better if they had been developed by a voter focus group. It would have been a little better if Justin and June could have been as young and cute as Caroline and John Jr. were in the Kennedy administration, but Justin and June were the pair of over-achieving,

All-American teens that every delusional father or mother thought they had. Maryann was as popular in Texas as Bill, maybe even more so. George Sr. and Betsey were American political royalty and could have passed as a pair of aging Hollywood movie stars.

Bill had asked his father whether it was really such a good idea to bring his younger brother, George Jr., to the press conference. George Jr. shared the striking good looks of his father and brother, but he wouldn't be doing much campaign stumping with Bill. George Jr. was one of God's special creations, a secret that was tightly guarded within the Flowers family. As soon as George Jr. was old enough to walk and talk, it became apparent that the Flowers political dynasty was solely in Bill's hands. George Jr. was destined to be a footnote in the Flowers encyclopedia of political history. Bill loved his brother and his brother loved him back, the same way they had when they were nine and seven years old. For George Jr., a seven-year-old's love was still the only love he knew how to give.

"George Jr. is part of the family," George Sr. told Bill. "He'll smile, but he won't say anything. Focus on your speech. You need to come out strong. If your numbers show you can't be beat, it'll keep others from announcing."

So if Bill played his cards right and avoided what Don Chambers called "downside behaviors," there was a good chance he'd be living in the White House with Maryann and his kids eighteen months from now. That thought fluttered through his mind briefly as he reached across the bed and stroked the upper thigh of the woman lying next to him.

Dorothy Landers rolled over to Bill, and they kissed. It lacked the passion of a few short minutes ago because they were both spent, even though it was barely mid-afternoon on a Tuesday. Bill planned to lounge naked with Dorothy for a while, have a few drinks, and then order in some food. By that time, he would be rested and ready for the next round. They were in an apartment Bill's office kept for staff members who worked late and needed a place to stay. It was vacant most of the time, but lately Bill had been diligent in making sure his constituents weren't paying for an empty apartment. Even though Maryann and the children were back in Houston, this wasn't the type of entertaining Bill could do at his Georgetown residence. The apartment was the only place Dorothy and he would meet. Dorothy was phase three of Bill's life plan. Phase one was to have the perfect family. Phase two was to leave a political legacy. Phase three was to have as much fun as he used to have when he was unmarried and in his twenties. Maryann's life plan only had the first two phases.

Dorothy Landers was a perfect phase three partner. Bill met her at a DC fundraiser, and there was an immediate spark between them. Bill was always careful about violating T-Bone's edict, though, and he was extra careful now that he was a potential presidential candidate. Bill didn't make a move until Dorothy had told Bill all about herself. She was married, and her husband was an international businessman who traveled all the time. When she made it clear she was interested in Bill but not interested in leaving her husband or getting into something serious, Bill's defenses went down. Bill and Dorothy were looking for the same thing—casual sex with a casual but attractive acquaintance. Bill hadn't been much of a student, but he had an appreciation for the lessons of history. Bill's standards had been lower up to now, but if he were in a presidential race, he'd have to become more selective. Dorothy wasn't an intern, a campaign volunteer, or a publicity-seeking gold-digger. He knew enough to avoid the pitfalls of his predecessors.

With Maryann in Houston and Dorothy's husband circling the globe over Europe and Asia, it was a testament to the manufacturer that they hadn't worn out the apartment's bedsprings in the six weeks they'd known each other. On the Senate's slow days, Bill did his best to know Dorothy three or four times a day.

"Can I get you a drink?" Bill offered as he rolled off the mattress and stood up. "I'm having bourbon."

"Make mine a cognac," Dorothy replied.

"I prefer to drink American, but the French did bail us out during the Revolutionary War," Bill joked. "We've been paying for it ever since."

Bill stood naked in front of the small bar cart along the bedroom wall as he took two highball glasses and added ice and a splash of their liquor of choice. As he started to walk back to the bed, there was a knock on the apartment door. Bill looked at Dorothy with raised eyebrows, put the glasses on the nightstand, and slipped on a pair of shorts and a golf shirt. There had never been any interruptions at the apartment. He left the bedroom and walked through the living area to the front door. He peeked through the spyhole and saw a man in the hallway holding a package and wearing a jacket and hat. The emblem on the clothing identified him as an employee of a courier company named DC Postal Express.

Bill wasn't expecting a package, and he thought about not answering. The deliveryman knocked again and waited. Bill looked around the apartment. He couldn't see into the bedroom from the front door, and there weren't articles of clothing strewn about or any other signs that this was a den of sin. Bill elected to find out what the man wanted.

The courier greeted the senator with, "Senator Flowers, I have a package for you."

Bill was startled. Nobody knew he was at the apartment, and the man had hardly looked at him long enough to have recognized him.

"You'll find a DVD inside," the man continued. "If you don't have a player here, you should watch this right away. It's a sampling of the shows you've been putting on with the young lady in the bedroom."

The deliveryman looked past Bill toward the bedroom and shouted, "Hey, Dorothy, grab your stuff and let's go."

The courier put extra emphasis on Dorothy's name, which sounded peculiar. Bill saw Dorothy emerge from the bedroom fully clothed, travel bag under her shoulder. It was obvious she knew this man and planned to comply with his orders.

"Dorothy, I don't understand," Bill said in confusion. "Is this your husband?"

"Sorry, Bill. I'm not married. He's more like my boss. My name's not Dorothy, but I'll keep answering to it," she explained.

"Not married?" Bill said to himself.

"This is kind of what I do, like how you're a senator," Dorothy tried to explain. "I make films, some hard but mostly the soft stuff, no penetration or anything. I didn't mind doing it with you. You weren't that much work."

"You're a professional?" Bill said to himself again.

"Hey, buddy, we're all professionals at something if we're getting paid for it," the man clarified. "Wait for me in the car, Dorothy."

"See you, Senator," Dorothy said as she left. "You've still got my vote."

"She doesn't quite get the big picture here, but I need to make sure you understand what this is all about," the courier began. "You won't be hearing from either of us again, and this isn't about money. It can stay our secret, but it's going to be up to you. If you announce your candidacy for president, your wife and the press will get

11

the DVD you're holding and about twenty others. As long as you take a pass on running, this DVD and the rest stay in our private collection."

"Who are you?" Bill asked.

"You can call me the deliveryman," he replied. "But I don't deliver pizza or flowers."

CHAPTER 2

THE RONALD

Ronald Tripp and Malcolm Warren sat in Tripp's office on the eightieth floor of the Tripp Universal Hospitality Hotel overlooking Central Park. They were watching DVD number sixteen.

"So he doesn't take any boner pills?" Tripp asked Malcolm. "He must be half jackass and half jackrabbit."

"We agreed to pay Miss Fontaine a tidy sum for the job, but she insisted we agree to an extra $250 every time she consented to have intercourse with the senator. She was an astute negotiator. By the time we paid her for all the extra sex, she made more than double what we planned to pay her," Malcolm offered.

"So what happens if Miss Fontaine talks?" Tripp asked. "She doesn't have the DVDs, but she could still spill the beans. A scandal with a high-profile senator would give a huge boost to her film career."

"There are layers and layers between Miss Fontaine and us," said Malcolm. "The DVDs got passed through people who didn't even know what they were. This never gets back to this office. If Flowers doesn't run but a scandal still rains down and hammers him, who cares? He's out of the race either way."

"I thought so." Tripp leaned back in his chair with a smirk. "It almost gets boring being so much smarter than everyone else."

Ronald Tripp was a New York real estate magnate worth over a billion dollars. He owned Tripp Universal Hospitality, the world's largest luxury hotel and resorts entity. The top floor of his New York hotel could have generated millions in bookings or rent, but instead he'd built it out into his personal suite and office complex. He held investments that reached far beyond real estate. They included investment services, retail chains, newspapers, television, and radio. He was a corporate board member for scores of companies and a silent, if not invisible, owner of others that operated at higher profit margins. The latter group included a holding company that owned a quarter of the San Fernando Valley Adult Film Industry, a publications company that owned two adult magazines and a shell company that imported and distributed counterfeit goods produced in China. The magazines were called *Amateur Gynecologist* and *Too Young to Bleed*. Despite the promises made in the second magazine's title, all of the freakishly late-blooming models were required to provide ironclad documentation that they were at least eighteen years of age.

Malcolm Warren held the title of Tripp Universal Hospitality director of security, but he was so much more. He was the only person on the planet who understood and was involved in all of The Ronald's enterprises, be they wholesome, marginal, barely legal, or black ops. The blackmail of Senator William Flowers was Tripp's number one black-ops project, and it was the most important one he'd ever undertaken.

Ronald Tripp was a Republican, although his New York background and flamboyant lifestyle didn't always mesh with the Republican Party's Midwestern and Southern conservative core. Then Tripp began to criticize President

Howard Smith in a fashion that was more relentless and focused than any other active Republican politician. When it started, it was just Tripp's way of venting his feelings, having some fun, and keeping himself in the eye of the media. Some of his remarks were far off the mainstream, but Tripp didn't care what other people thought or if they disagreed with his views. He was getting plenty of attention, like the class miscreant sitting in the back row making farting noises with his hand and his armpit. Then, though, he began to hear from people who thought the same way, or at least agreed with what he said. Tripp was smart enough to realize that some of the people expressing their support were crackpots, social misfits, or worse. Whatever you called them, they were an important part of his growing constituency. The same early polls that told Bill Flowers he could win the Republican nomination were telling Ronald Tripp he could place or show.

The Ronald planned to announce his own candidacy that month. Unlike his competitors, he didn't plan to just raise money, give speeches, go to campaign events, and then leave the decision to the will of the American people. "The will of the people" sounded a lot like a communist slogan. In Tripp's capitalist world, important decisions were made by powerful men with money. Tripp had decided to use some of his money to take out the lead dog. He wasn't looking for a level playing field. If he ran his election the way he ran his businesses, he'd be the last man standing.

Malcolm glanced above Tripp at a life-size bust that fit into an alcove above The Ronald's desk. The bust was an excellent likeness of a younger Tripp, except that it was inspired by Roman sculptures of Julius Caesar. The Ronald wore a tunic, light armor, and a crown of olive branches. Tripp had the bust commissioned in the eighties, when he still had his own hair, which he wore in a curly blond perm. Malcolm found the image majestically disturbing. Fortunately, Tripp's office was off-limits to all but a few.

"So, no news concerning Senator Flowers is good news?" Malcolm asked. "Do we think he'll just stay silent about the election?"

"The Republican Party and the media are waiting for him to announce his candidacy," Tripp told Malcolm. "He's got to tell them something. Whatever that news is, it'll be good news for us. He's either going to tell us he isn't running, or he'll be an idiot and tell us he is. If he goes with the second option, Senator Flowers will become the world's most famous movie star."

CHAPTER 3

NO WAY OUT

Bill Flowers was miserable, and this meeting was only making him feel worse. He'd flown to Houston and was sitting in his father's study with the old man and Don Chambers. Bill had a flashback to another time he'd sat in this same chair, sitting in front of his father's desk. Bill was a junior in high school, and his father had given him a new Corvette for his birthday. Bill went drinking in the country with a few friends and clipped a giant Texas oak tree trying to negotiate a curve at too high a speed. That was almost twenty-five years ago, but Bill didn't feel any smarter now than he did then. The exasperated look on his father's face hadn't changed much over the years, either.

"You're sure they recorded all this filth?" George Sr. asked for nearly the hundredth time.

"They gave me the one DVD, but said they had a lot more. The one I watched was about a week old," Bill repeated for nearly the hundredth time. "The number they have isn't important. You can see me and the woman clear as day. It was—how can I put it—a before, during, and after sequence."

"The number is important because it shows it wasn't a single lapse or a compulsive act. The number of hours they claim to have recorded does sound like overkill. Where was the camera?" Don Chambers asked.

"I didn't find it after they left, but I figured out where they hid it when I watched the DVD. It was shot from the top of the dresser. The woman always placed her travel case on the dresser. She must have brought the camera in and out of the apartment with her."

"That makes sense," Don said. "They didn't have to worry about planting it at the venue, and they probably started recording right away, during your first meeting. They couldn't have known how many chances they'd get."

"Of course not," George Sr. groused. "Who'd expect a senator to behave like a frat boy?"

Bill didn't answer. The truth was that Bill had been doing the same thing with different women for as long as he'd been married. He was a victim of this track record of success; he never expected to get caught.

Even a common stick-up man knew better than to tell the judge he'd robbed the ABC Liquor Store because he'd gotten away with robbing dozens of others before it. Bill had a law degree and helped write legislation, so he knew better than to try to use the victim-of-his-own success argument with his father.

"So," Don interrupted, hoping to avoid refereeing a family squabble, "they said they'd release the DVDs if you announce for the presidency. If they're telling the truth, you can go on in the Senate and nobody is the wiser. It could be worse. If they wanted to ruin you, they'd have just released the DVDs."

"Ack," George Sr. said dismissively. "We have a real shot at the White House."

"We *had* a real shot at the White House," Don reminded the senators.

Bill was meeting with two of the best political minds in the country, but in the end there was no way out. They couldn't debate whether to pay any blackmail money because an offer wasn't on the table. There was a ticking bomb somewhere, and it would automatically detonate if Bill announced he was running for president.

"I'm going to go home and see Maryann and the kids," Bill said glumly. "I don't plan to tell her anything yet. It'll kill me if she hears about this."

"There's a good chance of that," George Sr. replied. "I know T-Bone and his gun collection isn't just for show."

Bill involuntarily reached up and felt his ears. He'd never told his father about T-Bone's threat if he ever caught Bill in this exact situation. Everyone knew the consequences with T-Bone would be extreme; it was just a question of which body part T-Bone would hack off and how much of it he would take.

After Bill left, George Sr. stared at his drink in sad silence until Don had to speak.

"We don't even know for sure if this all would have worked out. He might not have won the presidency, or even gotten nominated. Running for president can be a long, painful, and uncertain journey. It's a lot different than a senate race," Don said.

"We'll never know. I just might have ended up with a son that got elected president," George Sr. answered glumly. "I was looking forward to the race. Don't tell me you weren't, too."

Don nodded. It had been a while since he'd been active in anyone's campaign. The networks called on him for sound bites and commentary every four years, but analyzing wasn't the same thing as managing. George Sr. and Don were both tired of the elder statesman role. It got George Sr. a prime table at Cattleman's Steakhouse, and they both got invitations to all the fundraisers they could attend—but it was low on excitement. Watching

Bill give speeches on C-SPAN wasn't the way George Sr. hoped to spend his golden years.

"I always knew he could blow it any time," George Sr. went on. "He's got Pappy Flowers' nose for trouble. The problem is that we're not in the thirties or forties anymore. In those days, if you drank and whored around the men loved it, the women didn't vote, and the press didn't write about it. This age of information is hard on politicians that are functioning morons."

"Any man could have made the same mistake," Don rationalized.

"Not every man. It's a shame she didn't proposition George Jr. He wouldn't have even realized she was making a pass," George Sr. said.

"That's true," Don laughed. "George Jr. would be the perfect candidate. He would never wander astray, he has Bill's good looks, and I've never seen him get angry or utter a negative word about another person. He doesn't have a political or work career history to dissect or attack. If he could give a speech as good as Bill, I could get him elected."

"Speeches? Who cares about speeches? Politics today is about a ten-second TV spot or just a video of someone smiling and waving. Then there's Twitter. Twittering is the only thing that idiot Tripp does, and people know all about it. Tweet, tweet, tweet, like some kind of venomous canary," George Sr. complained. "If Bill drops out, that son of a bitch could be our nominee."

"You know, this whole deal with Bill stinks. Have you thought about who benefits the most if Bill is out? I'm going to ask my people to check Tripp's tweets to make sure he isn't already hinting Bill won't run. This has his dirty paw prints all over it," Don said.

"Good luck proving that. He's going to use better people than Nixon did," George Sr. said. "That settles it.

We'll announce George Jr. as a candidate before it's too late."

"It sounds like a plan. I'll do his tweets, and you write his sound bites. He just needs to look into the camera and wave," Don joked.

George Sr. laughed and stared into his drink. He might be in denial, but he was still fighting the notion of giving up the presidency. He still couldn't think of any options that would get Bill back into the race. They had assembled the team, they had the money, and they had the window of opportunity to see a Republican back in the White House. The only thing they lacked was a candidate.

Then a thought hit George Sr., and it scared him. When he pictured his death, he'd always assumed it would be a heart attack because of all the beef he ate. If God was trying to use atherosclerosis as a way to tell man he didn't want him to eat the creatures God had created, it wasn't working, especially in Texas. A better approach would have been to make a medium-rare rib-eye steak taste like broccoli. The Texas obsession that eventually killed them would have ended right there.

It looked as if George Sr. no longer had to fear keeling over from the big one. This plan he'd developed in the back of his mind told him he was well down the road to Alzheimer's disease, because he must be experiencing the first signs of dementia.

CHAPTER 4

WEANING THE LAMB

Don Chambers watched George Sr. closely, a concerned look on his face. He didn't see any signs of facial drooping or tics, but that didn't guarantee the Senator didn't have a mini stroke. It could have been a host of other disorders. Don wasn't a physician, and even if he was a doctor with X-ray vision, a brain scan wouldn't detect most forms of psychosis.

"I was just kidding, the same as you," Don repeated. "If this is your idea of a joke, you're really overselling it."

"No, listen to me. You just agreed with me that politics today isn't about elegance. It's about perception. We can create perception," George Sr. argued.

"We can at first, but when the debates and the press conferences start, perception gets replaced by reality," Don countered.

"Reality," George Sr. sneered. "Good campaign managers create their own reality, and you're the best."

"I've been able to make the most out of my candidate's abilities," Don agreed. "But every one of them possessed at least the basic qualifications. They were college educated, they had some political experience, and they could give a solid speech without reading it. I couldn't even get some of *them* elected."

"Think about what you've got," George Sr. said. "You've got one of the best names in politics. You've got the best campaign team. You've got a candidate with the kind of looks that'll have women voters salivating."

"Until they hear what he has to say. Then they'll be gagging," Don said. "Listen, George Jr. is a great person, and we all love him. But this country isn't going to elect somebody with the mental capacity of a first grader. I can't believe we're even debating this."

"We're debating this because I know it'll work," George Sr. declared stubbornly.

"All right, I'll humor you. Let's imagine for a minute that getting elected president is as easy as winning a beauty contest," Don proposed. "What happens next? How is he supposed to survive the job?"

"That's the easy part. He'll have Bill, myself, and the best cabinet ever assembled. A very, very loyal cabinet," George Sr. said.

"I'm sure loyalty will win the day. They'll all resign and write books about him at the end of the first term, if he hasn't already been impeached. There's no way this doesn't explode in our faces," Don said.

"There may be a risk-free way to ease into this," George Sr. said. "I don't want a scandal, either. Besides, we could have a little fun with Ronald Tripp. He thinks he's knocked the Flowers out of the race. Imagine the look on his face when he finds out we aren't gone, we're just a little different."

"We're a little different, all right," Don commented. "Tell me about your risk-free plan."

George Sr. described the first tiny step on the road to a George Jr. presidency. They'd create George Jr.'s backstory, steal Bill's platform, and publish a qualifications and positions dossier. At the same time, they'd use their media and political connections to create media buzz. After a few weeks of buzzing, they'd conduct some polls to see if the George Jr. hype was registering in the minds of voters.

"If the numbers say no, we go back to hunting, playing cards, and sipping scotch together. If they say go, we figure out the next step," George Sr. encouraged. "It'll be a hoot."

"Aren't we forgetting something? The public expects a Flowers to run for president, but it's natural for them to assume it's the one who's already a senator. How do we explain that we're running George Jr. and not Bill? That makes no sense," Don said.

"It'll be part of the buzz," George Sr. explained eagerly. "Before we do anything with George Jr., Bill holds a press conference. Everyone thinks he's announcing he's going to run. Instead, he tells the press that he has news but that the news is not good. He's seriously ill, and he can't run for president. We don't tell people what he has, but we drop a doctor's name—someone associated with M. D. Anderson. I paid for a wing. They owe me. People will assume he has cancer. In six months or so, he announces he's in remission. There's no impact on his Senate seat. That creates the perfect scenario for George Jr. to run. He's stepping in for his older brother. It's a great story, and it gives George Jr. an instant sentimental edge."

Don Chambers listened carefully. George Sr. was still crazy, but it was a creative crazy, like a villain in a Batman movie. George Sr. might just give Ronald Tripp a run for his money in the game of political espionage. But there was still one very large hole in the plan.

"How do you spin this with Maryann?" Don reminded George Sr. "She thinks she's going to be First Lady. You plan to tell her she's going to be a widow."

"She'll be relieved, like everyone else, when we tell her Bill's in remission," George Sr. shot back.

"Are you serious?" Don asked.

"I suppose not," George Sr. conceded. "I could make Bill believe it, but Maryann is way too smart. She's the wife of a senator, and she's the wife of Bill. That means she's doubly capable of keeping a secret."

"Bill needs to figure out what to say to Maryann, whether George Jr. runs or not. She expects him to announce in a week," Don pointed out.

"I was hoping you could help with that. If Bill handles it by himself, I'm worried he'll say the wrong thing and T-Bone will actually shoot him."

"I'll work up something. Do you want to release Bill's story first or start on George Jr.'s dossier?" Don asked.

"Better do them together. Bill can't tell the world he isn't running until after he tells Maryann. We can't start to promote George Jr. until Bill's status is resolved," George Sr. decided.

The next morning, Bill was back in his father's office with George Sr. and Don. He expected another round of criticism for his poor judgment, but his father had moved on to a dimension that was two or three solar systems beyond their own. Bill's reaction was even stronger than Don's.

"George Jr. is going to run for president?" Bill kept repeating. "I love my brother, but we couldn't even attend the same grade school together. He still couldn't go there, and it isn't because he's too old now."

"We'll come back to this. You have a problem. A lot of people expect you to declare for the election any day now, and one of them is Maryann. What do you plan to tell her?" George Sr. bluntly asked.

"I thought I could tell her that we've been thinking about the election, and we've decided conditions might be better four years from now," Bill tried, with hesitation in his voice.

"She's too smart for that. She's seen your polling numbers, and everyone knows you don't wait so you can run against the incumbent who ends up winning this election. If it's a Republican, you won't even be able to run against them," George Sr. scolded.

"Maybe I should tell her the truth," Bill said.

"That's your call," George Sr. replied. "The Senate does throw one hell of a funeral. You might not be there, though, if T-Bone buries you so deep they never find you."

"Do you have a better idea?"

"We've come up with an alternate idea," Don intervened. "We wouldn't ask you to lie, but hear us out."

Don told him the account they'd devised for Maryann and the one they'd devised for the rest of the world. It didn't sound any better to Bill than their plan to elect George Jr. as president. At first he thought they were joking, but they didn't offer him a punch line. They were giving him their best idea.

"So my friends and colleagues will think I'm sick one way, and my wife will think I'm *very* sick in a different way," Bill complained.

"We discussed our options, and we thought this was better than telling Maryann you were being blackmailed because you were with another woman or because you were involved in some type of criminal behavior," Don said. "We also allowed you to play the youthful indiscretion card."

"What was your second-best idea?" Bill asked.

"My second-best idea is to let you figure it out yourself. Let me hear your best idea right now, or else come back at lunch with Maryann and we'll get this over with. We can help you explain it to her. Your mother will be here, too," George Sr. said.

"I don't want Mom to hear this," Bill protested.

"Don't worry. Your mother and I don't keep secrets. She knows about the blackmail. She'll help with Maryann," George Sr. said.

"Oh, God," Bill groaned.

"Son, when you let your penis do your thinking, it'll find you a ton of tail, but it doesn't give two cents about your dignity. That bimbo may not have charged you for sex, but you'll have to ante up a little bit more of your self-respect before you're out of this mess," George Sr. lectured. "We'll see Maryann and you at lunch."

At twelve-thirty, Bill was back in the study for the third time in two days. The ranch had prettier rooms, but George Sr. told the group they had business to discuss, and business was always conducted in the study. This time, Maryann and Bill's mother, Betsey, were in the room. Once everyone was seated on something covered in dark leather, George Sr. got down to that business.

"There's no easy way to say this, so I'll just say it," George Sr. opened. "Bill is not going to run for president."

Maryann and Betsey both had looks of shock on their faces. George Sr. had told Bill his mother already knew, but her appearance said otherwise. When Maryann turned away from Betsey to question Bill, Betsey shot her son a scolding frown for his benefit. Mother was quite the actress.

"Why aren't you running?" Maryann asked Bill. "And why couldn't you tell me this yourself?"

These were two perfectly reasonable and equally difficult questions. Bill was familiar with the pre-fabricated answers, but Don stepped in to help lay down the landscaping.

"Bill was too embarrassed to tell you," Don began. "He received a video tape in Washington. It shows something that happened when Bill was at Princeton. George and I watched it, and it was silly, really, but also embarrassing. It was something that goes on at fraternity houses. It's something I'm sure Bill wished had never happened, but when you're nineteen you don't think that you might end up a senator someday. There was a letter with the tape, and it said that there were copies and that the tape would be released to the press if Bill announced he was running."

"So he's being blackmailed?" Maryann asked. "What does the video show?"

"Yes, what could be so awful?" Betsey asked, glaring at Bill.

"Not awful, silly and embarrassing," Don corrected. "I'll let Bill tell you about it. We're concerned it would hurt him in the presidential race and might even damage his reputation in the Senate. We advised him not to run."

"I need to know what's on the tape before I tell you how I feel," Maryann declared.

Don and George Sr. nodded to Bill. It was show time.

"You both know I was a Beta Gamma at Princeton," Bill started.

He sounded nervous, which was believable. Maryann didn't need to know he was nervous because what he was about to tell her never happened.

"I was a pledge, and they had an initiation rite all pledges had to pass through called 'weaning the lamb,'" Bill went on. "A lot of frats have the most stupid, sadistic, and gross initiation rites, and this was ours. It wasn't dangerous to the pledge, though, and we never hurt anything. It wasn't in the best of tastes, though."

"Weaning the lamb?" Maryann asked. "Was there an actual lamb?"

"There was," Bill indicated slowly. "Again, there was no harm to the animal. No biblical or pagan sacrifices or that kind of thing."

"I would hope not. What did the lamb do?" Maryann asked impatiently. She got a sour look on her face. "Did you have sex with it?"

When Bill hesitated, Maryann blurted, "You have got to be kidding me."

"No, wait," Bill shouted back. "It wasn't sex, not real sex."

"Real sex?" Maryann picked up on the qualifier.

"Yes, Bill, what kind of sex isn't real?" Betsey asked her son.

She wasn't being as helpful with Maryann as George Sr. had promised.

"Okay, so we had to put baby formula on ourselves and let the lamb lick it off," Bill finally got out.

"You put baby formula on yourselves?" Maryann repeated. "On yourselves means on your penis?"

"Yes," Bill replied succinctly.

"How long did you have to do this?" Maryann asked.

"You had to finish," Bill answered.

He might have gotten by with less information, but it was the version of the answer he'd practiced.

"Oh, my God," Betsey chimed in.

"So one of your fraternity brothers took a video of you being orally pleasured by a sheep?" Maryann confirmed.

"Not a sheep, a lamb. Apparently someone there took a video. I don't know who recorded it or who has it now. I don't remember anyone taping, but we were pretty drunk," Bill tried to explain.

"What kind of twisted pervert thought this up?" Maryann asked.

"The head of the house was English," Don informed her. "I did some research, and this has a history in England, especially Oxford and Cambridge. I guess sheep were always readily available."

"So the smartest people in the world get oral gratification from sheep," Maryann mused. "They're smart enough to avoid getting recorded while they do it, I bet."

"Anyway, I hope you see why we don't believe Bill should run," Don summarized.

"So I've shared my husband with a farm animal," Maryann murmured. "I knew he'd explored some dank places before we were married, but I'd assumed they were all human."

Maryann noticed Betsey and changed the subject. She wasn't sure what to ask that wouldn't be a painful experience for all of them.

"What do you plan to tell your supporters?" Maryann asked.

Don smiled inside that she was already thinking ahead.

"We think his health is the only credible reason he wouldn't run," Don said.

Don reviewed the cover story for Maryann. Bill had a significant health problem that would compel him to forego the election. Most people would think it was cancer.

"Does he plan on surviving, or do I need to think about eventually dating again?" Maryann asked. "The way I feel right now, I'm fine any way you gentlemen want to play it."

"The treatment will be a total success," Don added quickly. "You should plan on a long and happy life in the Senate."

Maryann ignored the speculation on their future happiness and prosperity. She asked when the announcement was planned and was told it would be soon.

"What do you expect me to tell Justin and June?" Maryann asked. "I won't have them grieving for a father when he isn't even sick."

"You can tell them the truth," Don said. "They're old enough to be insiders."

Maryann would tell Justin and June the truth, at least as she knew it. They decided it would be better if Maryann handled it alone. It was too embarrassing for Bill to try to explain it. They didn't tell Maryann about their plans for George Jr. that day. She had heard enough for one day.

They'd need to make sure she kept up, but it didn't need to be in real time.

Don's fable of Bill weaning the lamb was an outrageous and distasteful lie, but it was also a brilliant lie. The account was too embarrassing and odd to be made up. Maryann asked Bill some more questions about the election over the next several weeks, but she didn't ask him anything else about the ritual or the videotape.

Don had provided Bill with more details if he'd needed them. The pledge weaning the lamb was required to wear a bonnet and hold a staff like Little Bo Peep. They called the animal Lamb Chop. Don knew it was these sorts of details that could make the story seem even more real. It had sounded real enough already to Maryann. She had heard enough, and she hoped she never heard it again. She especially hoped she would never hear it through the press if the blackmailer decided to go ahead and release the video anyway.

CHAPTER 5

FIRST LADY

Recalibrating Maryann was the only task that required immediate attention. Once that was accomplished, they began to more leisurely develop George Jr.'s dossier and campaign strategy. As George Sr. and Don brainstormed, they immediately hit a fresh snag.

"George Jr. is in his forties, but he isn't married and he doesn't have a girlfriend," Don pointed out. "This is normal for the George Jr. we know, but people are going to wonder. Is he some kind of player, or is he just gay?"

"He can't be gay," George Sr. said dismissively. "Log cabin Republicans aside, straight is part of the party platform. He isn't a Democrat running to be mayor of San Francisco."

"No arguments from me," Don said. "We also know he can't be a player, for obvious reasons. George Jr. needs a girlfriend, and she can't be fictitious. How do we deal with that?"

They'd been so focused on George Jr.'s political platform and policies that they'd forgotten one of the basic attributes of a strong candidate. His personal life and his political agenda had to align. Before George Jr. could talk the Republican family values talk, he'd need to show the voters he could walk the family values walk. George Sr. came up with another idea.

"I know just the girl," George Sr. declared.

"When you say you know a girl, do you mean some little grade school girl George Jr. can relate to intellectually, or do you mean a girl like you still call Ann Margret a girl? It would be better if she fit somewhere in between." Don pointed out.

"I know this woman," George Sr. clarified. "She and George are about the same age."

"I could tell you a list of things we're looking for, but the first question is, can she be trusted?" Don asked.

"She can be trusted," George Sr. assured Don. "I don't know if she'll do it, though. Give me a day."

Martha Wilson's mind spun as she drove to Brennan's to meet Senator Flowers for lunch. He had asked her to immediately drop everything she was doing for the meeting. He was exceptionally mysterious about the topic.

Martha had grown up in the Houston suburbs. Her father worked for NASA, but Martha developed a taste for business, not engineering. She went to college in Austin and then went north to get a Wharton MBA. She returned home to Houston and began to shake up the good-old-boy corporate hierarchies at several major Houston companies.

She currently worked for one of George Sr.'s divisions as his vice president of corporate real estate. When George Sr. hired Martha, he knew she was smart, but George Sr. was also used to having people do exactly what he asked them to do. Martha was a tall, attractive blonde who played volleyball at UT, but she wasn't always a lady. George Sr. modified his own style so he could work with this young, strong-willed, and opinionated woman because Martha's opinions were almost always on the money.

"Senator," Martha greeted her boss. "I'm working up the final numbers for the Minute Maid Place proposal tomorrow. I'm afraid you'll have to drink alone."

That was bad news for George Sr. It was a pleasure to share drinks with Martha; in fact, she could hold her scotch or bourbon better than most men he knew. A few drinks also might make George Sr.'s offer sound less ridiculous. He couldn't argue her excuse, though. The Minute Maid Place development next to the ballpark was a significant project that included hotels, restaurants, and shops. George Sr. ordered top-shelf bourbon and began to describe the urgent business he had vaguely referenced. He was an expert political strategist, but his strategy usually didn't come with a side order of matchmaking. It took some time to gather momentum behind his sales pitch.

George Sr.'s first move was to garner trust by sharing inside information. He told Martha that Bill wasn't going to run for president. When Martha asked George Sr. why not, she received more information than they had shared with Maryann.

"He can't keep it in his pants," George Sr. glibly explained.

"Is he a flasher, or are we talking about adultery?" Martha shot back.

George Sr. chuckled. One thing he liked about Martha is you never had to slow down so she could keep up with the story. She would make a fine fake future daughter-in-law, if he could convince her to try it. George Sr. told Martha about their plans to run George Jr. instead. Martha knew there was a George Jr., but like everyone outside the family, she had never met him and didn't know anything about him. George Sr. admitted George Jr. didn't have much political experience. Then he told Martha that George Jr.'s plan to run for president was the reason he wanted to meet with her.

"Do you want me to help with his campaign?" Martha asked. "I'd be glad to be one of his volunteers."

"I do need your help, although as more than a volunteer," George Sr. responded. "Much, much more."

George Sr. briefly laid out the campaign plan for George Jr. Then he described the elements in George Jr.'s personal life that would restrict George Jr.'s appeal to family-values Republican voters. George Sr. finished by describing what Martha could do to help limit those restrictions.

"Senator, I run one of your businesses," Martha protested. "I'm not an escort. There are websites and magazines that are full of women offering that kind of help. I'm afraid none of them are volunteers, though."

"We're talking about a woman dating a potential president," George Sr. explained. "She has to be incredibly smart, beautiful, personable, and, maybe the most important, incredibly loyal and trusted. You're the only person I know with any of those attributes, never mind all of them."

"My parents taught me that when the flattery gets this thick, you need to watch out for either your virtue or your wallet. Why don't you have George Jr. work on getting a girlfriend the old fashioned way? Have him date. There are some fantastic women who are sure to go after him," Martha suggested.

There was no reason for George Sr. to hold back on explaining to Martha George Jr.'s special qualities. If he could talk Martha into this, she'd find out about them soon enough. When George Sr. told her the specifics about George Jr., it became clear why he hadn't addressed his relationship issues on his own.

"Senator, pardon my language, but have you gone totally horseshit crazy?" Martha struggled to keep her voice down. "You're asking me to pretend to date someone I don't know because he's mentally challenged and he's running for president? So I'm there to make him look normal and keep an eye on him when you can't? What made you think I'd ever do this?"

"Martha, I admire your work very much," George Sr. began the real sales pitch." It's time for me to step down and let someone else lead the company. But we both know there are people in some of the other divisions with more experience, who have been with me a long time. If you do this, I'd owe you a tremendous favor. The only reward that is nearly good enough is to make you the new CEO."

"CEO?" Martha repeated. "If any of the other division heads hear about this, it'll be a cluster."

"If anyone figures any of this out, either inside or outside the company, that'll be the least of my problems," George Sr. assured her.

Martha motioned for their waiter and told him, "I'll have a double Glenlivet, rocks."

The next morning, George Sr. called yet another family meeting in the study. It included Don Chambers, Bill, Maryann, and Betsey. There was a sixth attendee waiting in the foyer, but George Sr. needed to provide some information to the rest of the group before expanding the roster. Maryann assumed they were meeting to discuss Bill's upcoming press conference. She was partially correct. George Sr. told them the press conference was set for Wednesday.

"Do you want me to wear black, or is that jumping the gun?" Maryann asked.

It had been a frosty week between her and Bill.

"Wear something upbeat," George Sr. suggested. "I also wanted to talk about some things Don and I have batted around. We can make our announcement and get out of the way and let the current candidates fight it out, or we can try to come up with a new plan. We've elected to come up with a new plan."

"Does this plan keep Bill in the race?" Maryann asked hopefully.

"There isn't any option for that," George Sr. answered. "With Bill out of the race, we plan to run George Jr."

"What?" Maryann said with an odd smile on her face. "He can't run for president."

"George Jr.?" Betsey feigned disbelief. "How could that work?"

Don answered, "Why couldn't he run? He's a citizen, he doesn't have a criminal record, and he's old enough. Everything else is about attracting voters."

Don described their plan to test the waters, establish his candidacy, and proceed with caution.

"President?" Maryann repeated. "He can't even live on his own."

"Stranger things have happened," Betsey threw in.

Maryann looked suspicious and demanded from Bill, "Did you know about this?"

"I'm as shocked as you, but I'll support my brother," Bill lied.

George Sr. told Maryann there was one more piece of news. George Jr. had a girlfriend; in fact, she was at the house waiting to meet them.

"Has she met George Jr.?" Maryann asked.

The answer to the question was no, but George Sr. ignored Maryann and left the room. He returned with Martha. Maryann was momentarily surprised by Martha's beauty, but she recovered and began to grill her.

"I'm Maryann," she said. "Welcome to the family. What's your name, and what's your deal?"

"I'm Martha," the tall blonde woman replied. "My deal is the same as yours. It's hard not to love those Flowers men."

"If you say so," Maryann responded. "Martha? That's a little too similar to Maryann. People are going to get you and I confused."

"I agree, Maryann and Martha are too close," Martha agreed. "What do you want us to call you from now on?"

"You've got some nerve," Maryann shot back. "Which online dating service did George Jr. and you meet on?"

"None of your business," Martha returned the salvo. "And from now on, you can call him George. We don't want people to get in the habit of calling the next president Junior."

"George and Martha," Maryann said to the group. "How colonial. I guess you've got a good name for a First Lady. One thing's for sure, you're the first lady who ever took an interest in George."

"George is an amazing person," Martha explained. "I'm going to be by his side through thick and thin."

It didn't take a genius to see that Maryann and Martha were not on the road to becoming best friends, but George Sr. took note when Maryann left off the Junior. Martha was strong enough to handle Maryann, which meant she was strong enough to handle most of the challenges in their path.

George Sr. wasn't sure yet how wise a decision it was to enter George Jr. in the race. On the other hand, he already knew that selecting Martha as his copilot was an incredibly smart decision.

CHAPTER 6

RIFF RAFF

George Sr. and Don finalized their plans for the next three weeks. First, they'd hold the press conference where Bill would disclose his illness and tell the public he couldn't run for president. Next, they'd float the idea that George Jr. was the best alternative. Finally, if the feedback was positive, they'd hold a press conference to announce George Jr.'s candidacy.

"I wish there was some way to announce George's candidacy at the same time Bill announces he's dropping out," George Sr. told Don. "The time it'll take to vet George allows the vultures to try to scavenge Bill's supporters."

"Most people don't know this, but I was a genetics major at Stanford as an undergrad," Don informed George Sr.

"That's nice, but what does that have to do with anything?" George Sr. asked. "Are you planning to clone a new candidate?"

"There's a bedrock theory in genetics called the 'one gene, one enzyme' concept," Don explained. "In politics, I developed a similar theory called the 'one message, one press conference' concept. The concept is that the press and the public can't process more than one idea at a time. In this case, let them get past Bill's illness before you make them accept George as a viable replacement."

"You don't have much faith in the voters," George Sr. observed.

"And I'm rarely disappointed as a result," Don advised. "The other thing that drove the theory was that by the end of Ronnie's second term, one coherent message at a time from him was the best we could hope for."

George Sr. didn't comment. If anyone heard them blaspheming the Chosen One, they'd end up in Republican Siberia. There was a second aspect of the press conference that worried George Sr., though. Maryann had been a bit of a pill since they'd told her about the weaning of the lamb, decided to pull Bill out of the race, and introduced her to Martha.

"I'm worried about Maryann," George Sr. warned. "We may have to rub an onion in her eyes if we want her to look like the grieving wife."

"Hopefully they'll think she's angry at God and not at Bill," Don agreed. "How'd she do with T-Bone?"

"He bought the story that Bill was ill," George Sr. replied. "Maryann told me T-Bone asked her if it was AIDS. She said he looked disappointed when she told him it wasn't."

The media turned out in force for Bill's press conference. Everyone knew Bill was planning to announce he was running, and they naturally assumed this was the big day. George Sr. suggested that they needed to take some of the shine off Bill's rosy complexion. Maryann was a former debutante and a current socialite, so she knew her way around a makeup bag. She worked on applying a layer of illness to Bill.

"What do you think?" Maryann asked Don.

"Better scrape off a couple of coats," Don advised. "He looks like he's auditioning for the role of Riff Raff in *The Rocky Horror Picture Show.* We just want him to look like he's sick. We're not trying to convince the coroner to pronounce him."

Maryann eased back, but when Bill, Maryann, George Sr., and Betsey walked in front of the press, there was still a murmur in the room. Bill's appearance coupled with the funereal shuffle of the participants made it clear this was no celebratory announcement. Justin and June weren't in attendance. The press thought they'd hear from Bill, but George Sr. was the one who walked up to the microphone.

"I realize you were anticipating an announcement on Bill's plans to run for president," George Sr. began. "This press conference will solidify Bill's plans, but I'm sorry to announce that it isn't the news our supporters and the American people were waiting to hear. My son is ill, and he needs to focus all his energy on returning to good health. Under these circumstances, he will not enter the current presidential race."

There was an eruption when George Sr. paused from his initial statement, a barrage of questions about the nature and extent of the illness. George Sr. held up his hand to quiet them down.

"I'm sure you can all understand that what Bill needs now is rest and excellent medical care," George Sr. continued. "Bill won't be making a statement. It's a testament to his strength of character and his determination that he's even with us here today."

George Sr. hesitated and put his hand up to his eyes. Betsey let out a sob and collapsed into her eldest son's arms. She took care not to knock the frail unfortunate off what the crowd imagined were his disease-ravaged, pencil-thin legs. Maryann stood stoically as if in a trance. She looked as if her overwhelmed brain couldn't comprehend the gravity of what was taking place.

"I'd like to introduce a man who I'm sure will become the most important person in our lives. This is Dr. Devdan

Gupta from M. D. Anderson," George Sr. managed to get out before he was overcome.

Dr. Gupta had not examined Bill up to this point. All he knew was what the patient's father had told him. His son was very sick. He looked at the man's face. He'd never seen a patient that looked so pale.

"I promise you our institution will do whatever it takes to diagnose and treat Senator Flowers," Dr. Gupta added.

Senator Brown from Arkansas was one of Bill's closest friends in the Senate. He and a few of his staff members watched the highlights of the press conference on the news.

"My God, I can't believe it," Senator Brown told his staff. "Look at the poor bastard. I just played golf with him last week, and he kicked my ass. I don't know what he has, but it looks like he's failing fast."

There wasn't anything else to say, so George Sr. closed with, "Please, I implore all of you to pray for Bill. Pray for my son."

Maryann had spent the entire press conference standing stiffly by Bill's side while her mother-in-law swooned. George Sr.'s words must have finally delivered the weight of the moment because she was profoundly affected. She began to cry like the rest of the family, and then she uttered the press conferences' last words.

"This is just so unfair," she wailed. "This is all so unfair to me."

The Ronald and Malcolm also watched the televised coverage of the press conference. They were the only other people besides the Flowers' insiders who anticipated the message.

"It looks like we can call it," The Ronald bragged. "The Republican presidential race officially ended today. The leader came down with a sudden illness, and I guess you'd call it a venereal disease. It was caused by having sex."

"I'll finalize your announcement plans," Malcolm said. "We want to catch Flowers' supporters while they're still in shock."

"I'll put out my statement offering my best wishes to the lying son of a bitch," The Ronald told Malcolm. "Not that he had much choice. All in all, I've got to give my compliments to Don. Given the hand they were dealt, they kept their guy out of the sewer and kept him in politics. I must be getting soft."

"Did you see that makeup?" Malcolm laughed. "It looks like they're going to keep him under wraps until he has to run again in the Senate."

"I hope it was makeup," The Ronald added. "It would be a shame if this scandal shakes the guy up so hard it actually kills him."

The Ronald and Malcolm both had a laugh at that thought. If it happened, The Ronald might take out a full-page newspaper ad to eulogize the senator and make another appeal to try to steal his former supporters.

CHAPTER 7

FLY-FISHING

George Sr. and Don met again a week after Bill's announcement. Don usually carried the responsibility of gathering and presenting data during a campaign, but today that burden of proof fell to George Sr. Don's role was to look at the information George Sr. presented with an unbiased, if not skeptical, eye. It was up to Don to decide whether a case had been made for George Jr.'s chances.

George Sr. had privately contacted all of Bill's heavy contributors. He had given them the positions and background pieces and assured them George Jr. would faithfully represent his brother's positions.

"We have a solid commitment from over ninety percent of the whales," George Sr. said.

The whales were the big money contributors. They'd stolen the term from Vegas.

"This next set of data is right out of the latest polls," George Sr. went on. "These numbers are from after Bill dropped out. It's a four-way split. Tripp leads, but by less than five points. Senator Martin, Senator Ramirez, and Governor Hastings are right on his ass and dead-even with each other. Bill had a double-digit lead, but now there's no clear frontrunner."

"Tell me something I didn't already know," Don told George Sr. "What happens when you add a Flowers name back into the mix, but it's not the same Flowers name?"

"Confusion," George Sr. replied. "Glorious, wonderful confusion."

"What was the methodology?" Don asked.

"We did focus groups and presented the candidates' position pieces along with their pictures and dossiers," George Sr. told Don. "They knew it wasn't Bill, but it hardly seemed to matter."

"Are you telling me people can't tell the difference between Bill and George?" Don asked. "That doesn't say much for the job we did promoting Bill."

"We did fine," George Sr. dismissed. "Do you fly-fish?"

"Do I look like someone who has time to fly-fish?" Don asked.

"I haven't done it many times myself. I prefer fishing for snapper on the Gulf. You get in a big boat with a cooler of beer, and you throw out a line with some hunk of something on it. If you don't catch anything, you've still got the view and the beer," George Sr. admitted. "I used to go fly-fishing with a senator from Wyoming. I commented to him one time about how the artificial lures were beautiful works of art, but they don't look much like real flies. He told me they were even better. The shapes and colors drew the fish, and they were hooked before they ever realized it wasn't a real fly."

"So you're saying voters will vote for any Flowers we run, and they might prefer George?" Don clarified.

"I'm saying the Flowers name carries weight, especially in Texas," George Sr. said. "They'll eventually find out that George isn't the same person as Bill, but by that time they might not care. They'll start to listen to George, and before they know it they're hooked."

"You said they'll listen to George," Don pointed out. "Isn't that what we're afraid of?"

"What happens when they listen is up to you. You just asked me for feasibility," George Sr. reminded him.

George Sr. slapped the last and most important report in front of Don.

"This report says that if George were in the race today, he'd be even with Tripp. These aren't as good as Bill's numbers were, but I'd call that mighty damn feasible," George Sr. announced.

Don picked up the report and examined it. His emotions ran the tracks of the world's tallest, fastest roller coaster. He shared some of George Sr.'s hunger for the hunt, but common sense kept interfering with his sense of adventure. He'd promised his old friend, though, that he'd pitch in and help his son if he didn't think it was time wasted or a disaster in the making. It was still an idea that could go wrong and waste them all, but Don tried to stay objective. If a qualified candidate had shown him these polling numbers and then asked Don to manage their campaign, he'd have accepted. He was only hesitating because he knew too much about who that candidate was.

"I think you're right. These numbers tell me he can win, and we haven't even campaigned yet," Don finally concluded. "I may end up hating you for it later."

"I'm usually right," George Sr. answered. "And plenty of other people have hated me for it."

CHAPTER 8

GOOD PEOPLE

The contrast between Bill's press conference announcing he wouldn't run and The Ronald's announcing he *would* run was like comparing a Protestant funeral to an Indian wedding. The Grand Ballroom of the Tripp Universal Hospitality Hotel was covered with posters promoting Tripp for president and massive images of The Ronald. Tripp hired a professional events company that specialized in corporate rah-rah sessions for the likes of Microsoft and Apple.

The press might look on at all the theatrics with a cynical eye, so Tripp stocked the event like he was throwing a lavish dinner party in the suites. He bought in champagne, hors d'oeuvres, and lovely parting gifts. The Ronald didn't always see eye-to-eye with the media, and it was bound to get worse, but he felt he should glean as much goodwill as he could at the start of the race.

Tripp's wife, Natasha, was joining him on the podium, and she was getting some coaching on what to wear. Natasha was originally from Russia, so her English wasn't always perfect, but she'd perfected Western fashion. She showed Tripp a sharp number from the hip New York boutique Gaspillage d'Argent.

"Find something else," The Ronald instructed. "You need to show more leg."

"If I be First Lady, I got tone it under," Natasha protested.

"Worry about your English, not your wardrobe," Tripp commanded. "I bring many things to the race that the other candidates don't have. A smoking hot wife is just one of them. Besides, I plan to turn things on their head. I'm going to do the opposite of what the Republican establishment expects from us."

"You might want votes from some them establishments," Natasha pointed out.

"I'll get the ones I need," Tripp assured her.

The press conference began to the beat of tremendously loud dance music that made the poured champagne pulse and vibrate in its flutes. Besides the press, nearly every one of Tripp's available employees was in attendance at the show. Their attendance was mandatory, and how well their next performance review went depended on how loudly they clapped and cheered. The Ronald and Natasha strode out onto the stage to thunderous applause. Tripp's employees displayed a level of enthusiasm that rivaled that shown by want-to-be contestants on *The Price Is Right.* Natasha's outfit looked like something a high school girl changed into for the party after she'd escaped her parent's house.

"I am here," The Ronald announced, "to save the Republican Party."

The applause was synchronized to the light show so that there was a strobe effect. The Ronald looked like Clark Kent, but he talked like Superman.

"I'm announcing today that I am a Republican presidential candidate," The Ronald continued. "I know what you're thinking. What took you so long? We could have used you the last eight years."

He paused again to let the energy in the room flow.

"Most candidates start off by telling you about the coalition they're planning to put together," he went on. "They talk about how they're going to draw in this group and that group, and before you know it, we're all one big mess of a happy family. I'm here to tell you my plan is just the opposite. I'm forming a coalition of good people. It's all we need. I don't want the support of people with ideas that hurt this country. Let me show you some examples, and you tell me if they're a good person. Is this a good person?"

The screen behind The Ronald displayed a picture of Democratic President Howard Smith, and the crowd uniformly shouted, "No!"

"Is this a good person?" he asked, and the screen went to a picture of vice president and probable Democratic presidential nominee Andrew Jackson.

"No," the crowd responded.

The chain of not-so-good people continued. A member of the New York Yankees named Otis Thomas, who was African-American, made headlines recently when he turned down a twenty-million-dollar-a-year contract extension offer. Otis felt he wasn't worth a nickel less than twenty-five. An athlete asking for more money wasn't news, but how he said it caused a stir.

"I ain't playing ball for no plantation master for no twenty million," was the quote attributed to Otis.

The screen showed Otis in his Yankee uniform at the plate striking out with his eyes closed and his helmet flying off his head. "Is this a good person?" The Ronald asked.

"No!" the crowd roared.

Hector Gomez made the news on sheer determination. He was Mexican, but his wife had immigrated to the United States with his young son. Hector had illegally entered the country three times to see his son, and he had been arrested and deported back to Mexico all three times. He was a hero father to some and a criminal to others, depending on their ideology.

"Is this a good person?" The Ronald asked when an image of Hector was shown on the screen.

"No," the crowd confirmed.

Rick Hudson was a famous actor who made a popular series of action movies. He had an actress wife and a promising film career in front of him. He had just come out of the closet, divorced his wife, and moved in with the actor who played his faithful sidekick Steel. He was a hero in the gay and lesbian community but boycotted by most of his former fans.

The screen showed Rick, and The Ronald screamed, "Is he a good person?"

"No," the crowd screamed back.

Violet O'Connor was a New York–based network news political analyst who constantly butted heads with The Ronald, to the point where it had gotten personal. Ronald commented negatively about her Rubenesque figure on Twitter and his blogs at every opportunity. Some of his quotes were infamous. When an unfortunate whale beached itself on the Jersey Shore, The Ronald had to tweet about it.

"Somebody needs to haul Violet O'Connor off that beach and out to sea before she starts to smell worse than she already does," he wrote.

When one of The Ronald's companies launched the world's longest supertanker, he had it named the *Violet O'Connor*.

"I felt it was only appropriate that the world's two largest floating objects be called the same thing," The Ronald posted.

To be fair, Violet O'Connor made it clear in her commentary that she was no fan of The Ronald. She had taken to calling him "the billionaire troll" on her newscasts. She didn't receive an invitation to the press conference. They posted an image of Violet on the screen next.

"Is this a good person?" The Ronald asked.

"No," the crowd replied.

"And she's still repulsive," The Ronald added.

This not-so-good people segment could have gone on for many hours. In fact, it could have turned into a global tour, but The Ronald moved on to two last pictures.

The screen showed a picture of Ronald Reagan, smiling and waving to the crowd.

"Is this a good person?" Tripp asked the audience.

There was a moment of hesitation, and a few people almost said no until they realized it was a transition point. The feedback that Reagan was a yes was finally delivered loud and strong.

"He's the best person this country has ever produced," Tripp told them, "up to now. Is this a good person?"

The screen showed a picture of The Ronald, and this time the audience was ready for it. The affirmative response was as loud as the one they'd provided for Reagan, and without the hesitation.

That ended the quiz of good and not-so-good people. Tripp went on to review his qualifications, which were many.

"In good faith, I should also disclose my weaknesses," Tripp told the crowd.

The crowd waited, but Tripp just stood at the microphone and didn't speak.

"I think that should cover them all. I don't have any weaknesses," Tripp explained.

The crowd applauded The Ronald's perfection. Then Tripp listed the country's current problems, which were everything.

"I don't plan to just fix this mess," The Ronald declared. "I'm going to tear down this government, toss away the rusty parts, and not replace most of them."

The Ronald finished his speech, thanked them all for their future support, and closed the announcement. He and Natasha walked down into the crowd of employees and press to mingle with the little people. He stopped and talked to every member of the media he recognized. If he didn't know them, they couldn't be that important yet. They were all drinking his champagne and eating his food. He spotted the senior analyst for the *Times* and walked over to test the waters. Peter Cline wasn't enjoying himself as much as the others.

"Peter," The Ronald greeted him. "Join the party. Someday you'll want to tell your grandchildren you were here when Ronald Tripp started his journey to the Presidency."

"I already have grandchildren, but I don't think they're interested in politics yet," Peter replied. "I'm sorry, Ronald, but loud music and character assassinations aren't what I look for in a president. I don't think I'm alone."

"I'm sorry you feel that way," The Ronald told Cline. Then he called to his henchmen, "Malcolm, Peter isn't having a good time. Help him find a cab."

Cline was a little surprised that one remark was sufficient to get the boot, but he'd been covering Tripp for some time, so his surprise was gone in an instant.

"You can't silence the press," Peter told Tripp. "That has never happened in America, at least not up to now. If you get elected, I'm sure you'll give it your best shot. Just remember what happened to Nixon and Agnew."

"I only need good people," The Ronald reminded him. "That includes the press."

Two of Malcolm's men stood on each side of the *Times* reporter and escorted him out of the ballroom, out of the hotel, and onto the street. Some other reporters took notice, but in general the party atmosphere survived the moment. The Ronald discussed next steps with Malcolm once he tired of the press.

"I'm going to start by hitting the South harder than Sherman, except instead of hiding their daughters, they'll be trying to have me meet their daughters," Tripp told Malcolm.

"Is Natasha going with you?" Malcolm asked.

"She won't like campaigning, and they won't care for her accent. She'd better stay in New York," The Ronald decided. "It's bad enough I'm a Yankee. I'm going to need to eat a lot of fried chicken to get in their good graces. I think they'll enjoy what I have to tell them."

George Sr. and Don watched the announcement on television. They anticipated it would come as soon as Bill dropped out, but it still seemed fast. They were still working to prepare George Jr.'s campaign launch.

"Look at that mob of people trying to dance. They're all white. That's a waste of a lot of expensive music," Don commented.

"I agree," George Sr. added. "It's like inviting a bunch of vegetarians to the world's biggest barbecue. Ronald has drawn the line on who he plans to appeal to, and it's a thin white line."

"We knew that going in. Unless he changes his rhetoric, his bed is made, and the sheets are white. Anyone who wants to support him that doesn't fit his definition of a good person would have to have a screw loose to vote for him. The minority factions are going to flock to us," Don said.

"That may be true, but we'll do better than just winning the minority Republican vote because Tripp won't take them," George Sr. told Don. "We want them to stay with George and the Republican Party after he's nominated."

"Amen to that. Don't get too overconfident about how much exclusion is going on in the Tripp campaign, though," Don advised. "There are a lot more out there like Tripp than you might think. You don't have any idea until you start to count their votes."

CHAPTER 9

MEET GEORGE

George Sr. met with Martha privately on the ranch to begin to prepare her for her role as George Jr.'s lover. But before they talked first dates and first kisses, George Sr. showed Martha the background they'd prepared for George Jr. As Martha read the document, her facial expressions told George Sr. this wasn't going to be one of their better one-on-ones. It almost ended the mythical George and Martha romance before it got started.

"This is a fascinating piece of paper," Martha said when she'd finished. "If I need to update my resume, you've saved me a lot of time. I'm reading about myself."

"Don and I felt it gave George an impressive yet verifiable business pedigree. The beauty of it is that you and I are the only two people who can attest to it," George Sr. tried to explain. "You should be proud of what you've accomplished."

"Don't you dare try to flatter your way through this," Martha shouted. "Now I know how a plagiarized author feels. Talk about identity theft. If I try to get another job, I'll have to resort to spicing up my resume with fancy paper and exotic fonts. All my content has been stolen."

"You should play the teamwork card," George Sr. advised. "You and George can share the credit."

"We're not sharing the credit. I'm giving my achievements away. George was my boss, so that makes these his ideas. I'm just the tactician," Martha protested. "This makes him responsible for the stadium project, the business parks, the Galleria expansion, and everything else I did."

"The only boss you should care about knows the truth," George Sr. reminded. "Just remember, that CEO title will build up your resume in a hurry."

They moved on to the other backstory that might be just as important in the election. They had to recreate a fictional romance.

"So we met at work, obviously," Martha said. "I've been meaning to ask you, what kind of a place do you run, anyway? People will wonder whether I dated George of my own free will or if I was coerced. Even worse for me, they might think I slept my way to a VP position. You're lucky I don't sue for sexual harassment."

"You both knew the relationship was improper, but you were seduced by his saintly charm just as he was seduced by your beauty and demure nature," George Sr. ribbed. "George came to me when you first started dating, and I immediately had you report to me directly."

"I guess you weren't as inspiring to work for as George. According to my resume, as soon as I started to report to you directly, I ran out of ideas," Martha groused. "There's another thing. You're lucky I'm having a dry spell. I'd get messy if I already had another boyfriend."

"Your pathetic personal life was a godsend," George Sr. agreed.

Martha asked George Sr. how they planned to make George Jr.'s employment story credible.

"Don't candidates usually provide tax returns? What happens when George shows the world he had no income?" Martha inquired.

"I've been paying George a salary since he was twenty-five," George Sr. explained. "He doesn't make as much as you, but you'll be pleasantly surprised when you see his finances. Even if he doesn't get elected, the two of you can afford to get married."

Martha shook her head. The man had all the answers.

They continued to pitch relationship ideas back and forth. Martha needed to get her hands on an engagement ring because George had proposed the month before Bill's announcement. They'd had the vacation of their lives in a remote part of Arizona, and their hobbies were gourmet cooking, hiking, and anything else they could think of that didn't involve other people. George Jr. and Martha had long, thoughtful discussions about the rigors of running for office, and they were a united front. They weren't sure where the election would ultimately lead them, but it didn't matter as long as they were together.

"I suppose," George Sr. said, "you'll want to meet George before the press conference."

George Sr. left Martha alone in the study. She had given dozens of corporate speeches, and she had played college volleyball in conference and NCAA tournament games without a hint of fear. For some reason, she felt an unfamiliar sense of anticipation waiting in the study.

George Sr. returned with a tall, handsome man with dark hair and blue eyes at his side. George Jr. looked a lot like Bill, except he was thinner, younger, and he didn't have twenty years of Congressional pressure tugging down at his eyelids, shoulders, and mouth. George Jr. was in the moment, and he greeted Martha with the brightest smile she'd ever seen outside of a commercial to sell toothpaste. He had seemed like an abstraction in the plan that she hadn't considered or taken too seriously—but if

George Jr. had wandered into a bar she was at, Martha would have figured out how to work her way over to his side for an introduction. George Jr. may have just wrecked her professional resume, but he'd look pretty good on her dating resume.

Martha composed herself and said, "George, it's so nice to meet you. Your father has told me a lot about you."

"Thanks. It's nice to meet you, too," George Jr. replied politely.

Then he bent down and gave Martha a bear hug. It was cute, like hugging a big puppy dog, but it was also the closest thing to foreplay that Martha had experienced for the past several months. The hugger was also the most gorgeous man who'd ever put the squeeze on Martha. She was in no hurry to try to pull away.

"This," George Sr. announced, "looks like a winner."

When Don called a second press conference, rumors began to swirl. Nobody had seen Bill since his illness had been announced. He was on leave from the Senate and sequestered on the Flowers family ranch. The press had contacted Dr. Gupta multiple times, but he obviously wasn't cooperating. He stuck to a story that he was still waiting to examine Bill. The information blackout coupled with Bill's haggard appearance at the press conference could only mean one thing. The one-time presidential frontrunner had passed away.

Maryann prepped Bill for a second time using her makeup bag. The people at McLintock and Hollister Funeral Home would have been impressed by her work. Bill almost looked as if he was still alive.

"It looks like his circulatory system has completely shut down," George Sr. complimented. "We should see some tears today. This is wonderful work."

Then George Jr. and Martha entered the waiting room, and the attention shifted. George Jr. was wearing a dark suit, his shiniest black shoes, and a silver tie. His hair was perfectly combed and sprayed into place. George Jr. and Bill were both made up, but George Jr.'s preparation could be done professionally and openly. It was hard to comprehend that George Jr. and Bill were members of the same species.

This was Martha's close-up too, and she looked like she was ready to walk the red carpet—except her dress was less like an evening gown and more like something a wealthy, conservative Republican fashionista would wear.

"I hope there are lots of cameras," Betsey commented to Martha. "You look lovely, dear."

Betsey hadn't offered Maryann a similar compliment on her appearance. George Sr. had promised Bill and Maryann they'd be an important part of George Jr.'s campaign, but it didn't feel that inclusive so far. Then again, saying one thing and meaning another was one of George Sr.'s primary talents. It was the same talent that had kept him in the Senate for decades.

When Don called the room to order and introduced Bill and Maryann as they walked out, the feeling was a mixture of relief coupled with renewed shock. Bill was still alive, but it looked like there were times when it seemed more merciful to just pull the plug and move on. If the event had been held outdoors, buzzards would have been circling the stage. As at the last press conference, George Sr. stepped forward to man the microphone.

"Thank you all for attending," George Sr. opened. "As you can see, Bill and Maryann are here. I think, under the circumstances, that Bill looks great."

There was polite but restrained applause, the same that would follow a terrible recital performed at a grade-school music program. The audience assumed God had thrown George Sr. a break. His eyesight had gotten so poor he couldn't tell his son had become a pale porcelain shell of a man.

"My last announcement was a sad one, and we still pray for Bill every day on his road to recovery," George Sr. continued. "But today I have better news. While Bill's illness has been a burden to Bill's wife and children, his mother and I and his brother and his fiancée, Martha, we also know it has deprived our citizens of Bill's services as a leader. Today I'm announcing that another man with the same qualities as Bill is willing to step forward and fill the leadership void that Bill's departure created. That man is my other son. George isn't a senator, but he brings tremendous intelligence, integrity, and experience in business and commerce to this election. We know another candidate just announced who also claims to have cornered the business experience market. Unlike Ronald Tripp, George brings a dignified, thoughtful determination to this contest. George will fulfill his brother's destiny and lead this great nation."

With that, George Sr. introduced George Jr. and Martha, who took George Jr.'s hand and led him to the microphone by his father. They'd practiced, and George Jr. did not disappoint.

"We will win," George Jr. announced.

This was the cue for the rest of the family to quickly join George Jr. so he didn't look lost in front of the microphone. Bill hugged George Jr., and George Jr. nearly squeezed the life out of Bill in return. Maryann and Martha eyed each other icily. The temperature was pleasant for Houston, but they could have easily dropped the room another ten degrees if they'd kept staring at each other. They gave each other the type of hug that women give when they don't want to smudge their makeup. Maryann was transitioning from symphony virtuoso to second fiddle, and she wasn't transitioning easily.

Don had orchestrated the perfect press conference and presented only one fact. George Jr. was running for president. The bonus was that Bill was still alive.

The press conference led to one negative repercussion for Martha. An hour later, her cell phone rang. She looked at the number and silently cursed to herself.

"Hello, Mom," she answered as cheerfully as she could manage.

"Martha, we've seen the news. It's all over the internet. You're engaged?" Martha's mother Peggy asked.

The engagement wasn't the big story, but Martha could see how her parents might think so. She knew she'd need to speak to them about it soon, but she thought she'd have a few more days. She wasn't prepared for her parents to be so connected.

"I am, Mom. I was going to call you and Dad tonight," Martha lied.

"You're engaged to a man we've never met?" Peggy asked. "Your father was hurt this Flowers fellow never even talked with us about it. You're not pregnant, are you?"

"No," Martha practically shouted. "We've never even done it. I've taken a vow of abstinence."

"Since when?" Peggy asked.

Martha had remained single, but her parents had no expectations that she was abstinent. Martha was still reeling that her mother thought she'd gotten knocked up at forty-two.

"Since I got engaged to a presidential candidate," Martha replied. "George can't have a pregnant fiancée. I'd have to wait until after the election before I could start to show. It would have to be the miracle baby."

"He's from Houston? We just saw you last week, and you didn't even mention him. Are you ashamed of us?" Peggy asked.

"No, Mom, of course not," Martha assured her. "We've just been incredibly busy, and I wanted the two of us to tell you together. Things just got out of synch. We'll be traveling, but you'll meet him when we get back."

"When is the wedding?" Peggy asked.

"We plan to wait until after the election. You'll be the first to know, Mom," Martha replied.

Martha got off the phone and shook her head. George Sr. had told Martha she was perfect for the assignment. He'd forgotten one other attribute for the perfect fake fiancée. She should be an orphan.

The Ronald and Malcolm watched the announcement with almost the same amount of interest as Martha's parents.

"Second-rate at best. Where are the dancers or the music? Where's the energy?" The Ronald commented. "The old man is a real conniver, though. He doesn't have any other sons after this, right? I want to know what happens after I make chopped salad out of number two."

"I did some research. This is the second and last child," Malcolm promised.

"He thinks he can ride my business-first coattails?" Tripp asked. "Find out about this George. He and the old man have the same name. I guess that makes him Junior. I'll have to give Junior a proper welcome to the senior leagues. He'll be gone before the first primary."

CHAPTER 10

EYE CANDY

The more Tripp and Malcolm researched George Flowers Jr., the less they knew about him. It was as if he had no history. The Ronald would have gladly traded places with him. Tripp had plenty of history, and part of that history included two ex-wives who tolerated him in the best of times and tormented him in the worst. Tripp knew they'd go off on him sometime during the campaign, and they knew things that Tripp would prefer they didn't share with potential voters. As much as he wanted to let sleeping bitches lie, he needed to prepare for stormy weather while the seas were still calm. Tripp had given his ex-wives a variety of reasons to hate him, but there was one particular thing The Ronald had done to both of them that made forgiveness or civility an impossible goal.

Men often love cars in the same way they love women. Many men use a car's odometer reading to determine when it's time to purchase a new one. One hundred thousand miles is a common odometer reading that signals the end of life to a car owner. The car may still run reliably, and the owner may be comfortable with, or even fond of, that old car. But if the owner can afford a new car, the lure of owning that newer model usually wins out over sentimentality.

The Ronald had no such prejudice when it came to his fleet of classic cars. He owned a Rolls Royce and a Duesenberg that had mileages well over a hundred thousand. The Ronald's version of a mileage bias applied to his women. Once each of his wives had turned forty, The Ronald traded them in for a newer and younger model.

There was one significant difference between trading in a car and trading in a wife. It was customary for someone, either a car dealer or a private buyer, to compensate the car owner for their used vehicle. It was The Ronald's experience that it cost the owner a handsome sum to discard a used wife.

The only positive outcome from his first two marriages was that he didn't have children with either. Children would have created significant complications when Tripp decided to move on. His ex-wives would have dutifully trained any offspring they'd created with Tripp in the art of paternal hatred. Children would also cause situations in which the Ronald would have had to see his ex-wives more often than he cared to, which was never. Finally, the cost of his divorces would have gone up even higher if there was child support on top of the spousal support.

Recently, Tripp had reconsidered the possibility of having children with Natasha. He realized the time may be about right. If they waited another five years, he could have children and enjoy them when they were young and cute. Then, with any luck, he'd die before they got older and turned into trouble.

The Ronald arranged to meet his ex-wives in order of difficulty, from easiest to hardest. That meant he'd meet first with wife number two, Illiana Tripp. Illiana was originally from Kiev. She met The Ronald at a charity fashion show in New York when she was twenty-eight and he was forty-eight. Tripp was in attendance to donate, and Illiana was in attendance to model and attract donations. The Ronald donated enough money through Illiana to keep Kiev in potatoes and vodka for a year. After the show, Tripp sought out and began to date Illiana. They were married and spent twelve years jetting around Europe and Asia and appearing on magazine covers. Illiana hosted many of The Ronald's foundations and charities, and they were in good standing in the New York social circles. They were like Cinderella and her older, balding Prince Charming.

When The Ronald turned sixty, Illiana threw an extravagant birthday party for him that was fully stocked with celebrities and tycoons. It was an event befitting a monarch. The Ronald seemed to have the time of his life, and he gave a truly heartfelt speech thanking his beautiful wife and soulmate. Then, a week later, he served her with divorce papers. This wasn't a reflection on Illiana's looks. She frequently made the listings of New York's most beautiful mature women. The problem was mathematical. If The Ronald was turning sixty, it meant Illiana was turning forty. She'd reached the magic number. The divorce was now in its fifth year, but Illiana still hadn't accepted that a husband who was twenty years older than her would dump her because she was too old.

Both ex-wives had managed to live, if not flourish, without The Ronald. Illiana founded her own successful corporation called Eye Candy Party Accessories. Eye Candy Party Accessories could only exist in a city like New York. The business model started when Illiana recruited a network of models and starving actors. Illiana wasn't an agent who could land them professional modeling or acting jobs. She was an agent would could arrange for them to be staged as guests at socialite parties that craved the "beautiful people" atmosphere. For those who desired more than just beautiful models, the actors gave the host or hostess a made-to-order option. You could review Eye Candy Party Accessories' specialized menu and sprinkle in a novelist, poet, or secret agent to your party as easily as you could cater the sushi.

Illiana had never remarried, but she was in a serious relationship with another Russian transplant named Ivan. Illiana had met Ivan through Eye Candy Party Accessories— he was one of her first models. Now Ivan helped Illiana manage the company. He also helped her use the car and the apartment and spend the alimony checks supplied by The Ronald. The Ronald never cared much for Ivan, or "Eye-von," as he insisted it be pronounced. The Ronald thought he was nothing more than a Eurotrash party boy who conspired to keep Illiana single so The Ronald's money kept flowing.

It was a distasteful mission, but The Ronald needed to either flatter Illiana into a state of neutrality or bribe her to stay quiet. She met him at his office in the Universal Hospitality Hotel, which was conveniently located a block away from her business's Fifth Avenue offices.

"Well, well, well. Look who wants to be president," Illiana greeted him. "Your self-delusion knows no limits."

The Ronald moved past what was sure to be a serial insult with, "Illiana, you look lovely."

"I love it when you flatter me," Illiana replied with a smile. "It means you need something from me. The last time you opened a conversation with a compliment, I got the bracelet."

The Ronald grimaced on the inside. He'd foolishly purchased a business under both their names when they were still married, and he'd needed her to cosign to sell it. Her signature had cost him a $200,000 diamond tennis bracelet. The Ronald always opened with flattery, but it always seemed to end with bribery. This was going to become an expensive meeting.

"My announcement was the reason I needed to talk with you," The Ronald continued. "I'm sure the press will try to talk with you about my campaign."

"You're too late, lover. My phone has been ringing off the hook. Everybody wants to talk to this old bag," Illiana said with an edge. "At my age, who knows if I'll remember that far back, but I'll do my best. I'll make sure to get my plugs in for Eye Candy Party Accessories."

"I'd appreciate it if you could focus on the good things about our marriage," Tripp requested.

"Are you asking me to lie or just tell them nothing?" Illiana replied. "That won't be good business. Have you taught me nothing? Take advantage of your opportunities, even if you have to step over a few dead bodies on the way."

"Let's talk about a different approach," Tripp said. "How much will it cost me to make you like me more?"

"I'll like you more for a quarter," Illiana clarified. "If you expect me to talk about you like you're human, five million would get me there."

The Ronald fought back the urge to scream and came back with, "I thought a million should rent your goodwill for the next twelve months."

"You know where you can stick your goodwill and your measly million," Illiana said indignantly. "You can't whore me out for that."

"Two million," The Ronald countered. "I can give you cash with no paper trail."

Illiana hesitated, then answered, "I can hold my tongue for twelve months for that."

"Thank you," The Ronald replied instinctively.

Tripp wasn't accustomed to thanking people who took his money and did little in return, but two million was a bargain. Illiana stated she wouldn't whore herself out for a million, but he knew she would for the right number. Two million was a right number for The Ronald. They sat for less than a minute more before Illiana stood to leave. They both knew their personal relationship had devolved to the point where The Ronald was little more to Illiana than her banker.

"You know, Ronald, 'Eye-von' asked me to marry him, but I told him we had to wait. I plan to collect alimony from you for the rest of your life," Illiana said as she leaned forward and looked closely at his face. "I love what politics is doing to you. I'll tell him I don't expect we'll have to wait more than a couple more years."

Tripp would have normally responded with a different two-word phrase that ended with "you," but he stuck with "thank you." Illiana could still get angry again and ask to renegotiate.

As men acquired wealth, many of them switched their rides from a domestic model to something foreign. This had been The Ronald's approach with women. Wife number one was a native New Yorker named Rhonda. But while domestic cars are typically cheaper than a foreign model, Rhonda had cost The Ronald plenty. Illiana thought she'd done a number on The Ronald, but he thanked his good fortune she never found out what he'd paid Rhonda over the years. The most discouraging thing was that it seemed like every dollar he gave Rhonda made her hate him even harder.

Tripp had married Rhonda when they were both in their early twenties. They'd stayed married for nearly twenty years, until she'd reached the magic number. During their marriage, Tripp had converted his father's money into a good deal of his current empire. He was already The Ronald when they'd gotten divorced. The Ronald had to pay Rhonda a fortune per the New York courts. He also had to pay her a second fortune because of their history. She knew about the early days of the Tripp fortune. There were the bankruptcies, the shady or even illegal business deals, things that The Ronald could protect himself from in later years when he had the money to operate in secret. He had effectively paid Rhonda hush money. Rhonda had remarried to a doctor just after Tripp married Illiana. The New York courts said Tripp could stop paying alimony, but Rhonda's private arrangement with The Ronald said otherwise.

Rhonda understood that The Ronald's latest venture increased the value of her silence. She met Tripp an hour after Illiana had departed.

"Hello, Ronald," Rhonda greeted him coldly. "Before we talk about whatever it is you want, I'm letting you know we need to change our terms. Now that you're running for president, somebody's going to take a shot at you. I can't take the chance that they have poor aim. I need to be named in your trust if something happens to you."

"I'm glad you heard the announcement," Tripp replied. "That's why we need to meet."

"We certainly do," Rhonda agreed. "I know some things you've done that aren't consistent with the Oath of Office. The price of my discretion just doubled."

"Double is obscene, but your birthday is coming up and I thought I'd get you something nice," The Ronald told her. "What's on your wish list?"

Rhonda thought a minute and told him, "I always loved the place in the Hamptons. I could use it as a hideaway to escape the press. Plus Roger could use a place to get away. Since I was married to you for so long, I never realized how hard an honest man has to work to be successful."

The Ronald ignored another barb and said, "I'll give you the house if you stay there and get a big dog to keep the press away. I expect you to be silent as a ghost."

"You mean a ghost of your past that doesn't wreck your chances," Rhonda corrected. "We have a deal. Remember the trust. Now if you excuse me, I have to go home and shower."

It was an expensive but necessary day. The home in the Hamptons he'd given Rhonda was worth ten million, and Illiana had walked away with two million. Again, Tripp was grateful Illiana would never know about his little talks with Rhonda. This was the price he had to pay for owning a late-model spouse and at the same time dabbling in politics. Natasha was about to turn twenty-nine, so she still had at least eleven more years of tread on her tires. The Ronald couldn't predict the future, but he'd likely turn her out when she reached her magic number. He'd only be in his mid-seventies, so he was sure he'd still covet that latest and greatest model.

CHAPTER 11

FX

Mounting a presidential campaign was a daunting logistical task. They needed manpower, transportation and facilities, research and polling, newspaper, radio, television and internet advertising, and a host of events. George Sr. suggested one other need, a special resource that none of the other campaigns would have.

"George needs to appear in ads and make speeches we can release on the internet," George Sr. said. "The more he says in private, the less he has to speak in public. The problem is that George may look like a president, but he doesn't sound like a president. I have an idea that will make this easier on all of us."

"We can't hide him until the election," Don pointed out.

"He has to do the debates and the public appearances," George Sr. agreed. "But why do the taped speeches and commercials?"

"They're usually more effective when the candidate is in them," Don replied.

"Maybe not if the candidate is George. The thing is, I know this guy," George Sr. began.

George Sr.'s guy was a world leader in animatronics. He wasn't from MIT or the government. He'd recently retired from Disney.

"They've nearly perfected it," George Sr. said enthusiastically. "He showed me some demonstration tapes, and if you put a camera about thirty feet back, nobody could tell them apart. I'll bet Betsey couldn't pick the real George more than half the time. We get a voiceover guy, and George will sound like George Will with a Southern accent."

As was the norm, Don thought the idea was half-cocked, but it wasn't worth trying to talk the senator out of it. He didn't think much more about it. It wasn't going to go anywhere. Then, three weeks later, George Sr. asked Don to visit the ranch. He indicated that he wanted Don to begin to prep George Jr.

When Don got to the senator's home, George Sr. led him upstairs to one of the guest rooms. In fact, it was the very room Don had stayed in on his first visit to explore Bill's campaign, except that when Don entered the room, it had been converted to an office. George Jr. was sitting behind a desk, and he must have been rehearsing for the first debate. He was wearing a suit and tie, and it looked as if his hair had been professionally done. The only thing that didn't fit was that George Jr.'s lips were moving, but he wasn't making any sounds. Don walked up to greet George Jr. and see why he was moving his mouth until he stopped and froze.

"Good Lord, he's a robot," Don uttered.

George Sr. let out a sizable laugh, and that's when Don noticed the older gentleman standing behind a control panel at the back of the room. George Jr. introduced Bruce Robinson, Disney animatronics genius, who had designed and built George Jr.'s doppelganger.

"He has hundreds of mouth-movement program options," Bruce explained. "He looks natural live, and he'll be undetectable on film."

"What do we plan to do about his voice?" Don asked.

"I know a lot of voice talent from animation," Bruce replied. "You can't believe the talent. I have some experience doing it myself. I'll have someone working with Virtual George soon."

"He understands what's going on here?" Don asked of George Sr.

He knew this must have already been discussed, but he needed to hear it himself. There was no way that spending a small fortune to create an animatronic George Jr. could seem normal.

"Disney was good to Bruce, but my retirement plan is even better," George Sr. explained. "This George will stay here, where I can keep an eye on him and filter who he meets. This room is about to become our campaign commercial studio."

"Better start writing those commercials, because in a day or so Virtual George is going to be ready to give you whatever you can imagine. Just like a day at Disney World," Bruce remarked. "He doesn't need bathroom or lunch breaks, and he doesn't throw hissy fits like real actors. He's so much better than a human candidate."

CHAPTER 12

THE DEVIL'S HUMOR

Next up, Don and George Sr. met with the publicity and advertising firm they'd selected. The firm sent their senior creative partner and two of his younger creative staff members to George Sr.'s Houston office. They were pitching potential television spot ideas and taglines.

"Mr. Flowers won't be joining us?' the partner asked.

"He's attending a campaign event," Don replied.

George Jr. was actually back at the ranch with Martha and Betsey. It was mid-morning, so some of his favorite daytime cartoons would still be playing. The partner began to pitch their first ad concept.

"There is a voter segment that fears the future," the partner began. "They support Ronald Tripp because he preys upon their fears. There's another voter segment whose greatest fear for the future is one where Ronald Tripp is our president. This will appeal to that group."

One of the creative staffers held up a series of storyboards with pictures on them. The second creative staffer offered the narrative. The first storyboard was a picture of a standard King James Bible.

"We Americans are a God-fearing nation," the narrator began. "God's word is in this book. The Bible speaks of love, hope, and salvation."

The next storyboard showed the Bible opened to the chapter of Revelation.

"Ronald Tripp claims he lives his life according to the Bible, but he's forgotten about the parts that speak of love," the narrator continued. "He only preaches about this chapter, and he implies that this is what lies ahead for America unless he's elected president. Maybe we need to examine the Book of Revelation a little closer."

The next storyboard took some liberties with the Bible. It pictured a page in Revelation with a heading, "The Seven Signs of the Apocalypse." It contained a list of seven items, which included plague, famine, earthquakes, and floods.

"Recently, biblical scholars have discovered an eighth sign of the apocalypse. Here's what the newest version of Revelation will look like," the narrator said.

The eighth line read, "Ronald Tripp is elected president of the United States."

The narrator closed with, "Don't bring on the apocalypse. Vote for George Flowers, Republican for president."

Don and George Sr. both laughed and applauded the presentation. Then they took a couple of minutes to confer. The concept was entertaining, but now they had to decide if it would win George Jr. votes. They made up their minds quickly.

"It's very funny. We also like it because we believe it's the truth," Don praised. Then he got a more serious tone. "The problem is that the religious right isn't known for their sense of humor. I can hear their response in my mind, and it has the word 'blasphemy' sprinkled through it. We'd better move on to the next idea."

They worked through a few more negative ads that poked fun at Tripp's wealth, his hairpiece, and his failed marriages. There was even old footage from his brief foray as a celebrity boxing promoter. He was standing between Mike Tyson and Don King, with bikini-clad ring girls rounding out the frame. The tagline went, "Can you pick the one who's qualified to be president?" The final message was, "We're sorry—it's a trick question. The correct response is none of the above."

"It may be too early to go this negative," Don explained to the partner. "In addition, there are three other candidates. It makes us look like we're only afraid of Tripp."

"Sometimes a campaign doesn't get aggressive until it's too late," the partner said, "and we believe Ronald Tripp is your only serious opposition. We understand your position, though."

The next pitch was for a straightforward candidate position piece. The partner read the narrative, which emphasized economic growth, military strength, and increased control in the hands of local government. The tagline was that George Jr.'s positions weren't too soft or too hard, they were "just right." They envisioned the piece and that tagline as part of what they had code-named the Goldilocks campaign. They felt it would appeal to moderate Republicans. The spot would end with George Jr. speaking to a cheering crowd.

"That's good," Don responded. "How do you plan to shoot it?"

"We thought we'd bring George to multiple locations, have him interact with different groups or talk with people in one-on-one situations. We'll have a segment with a factory worker, a farmer, a businessman, and a few others," the Partner explained.

George Sr. and Don looked at each other. They liked the narrative, but the visuals didn't line up with their strategy for George Jr.'s role in his commercials. They had to deal with getting George Jr. to the debates and rallies and controlling him as best they could. They had no intention of expanding their George Jr. exposure.

George Sr. advised, "We like the idea of these people expressing their support. We think it would work better if George were in a quiet setting, like an office, when he delivers his responses. It'll give it that personal touch."

"George is a tall, striking man," the partner reminded them. "The message will be more powerful if he's standing with other people. Plus, we'll take advantage of George's physicality. We don't plan to hire actors that are nearly his height. People equate height with leadership."

"We think he comes across as more casual and relaxed at a desk," Don insisted.

One of the creative staff knew some history and cracked to the other, "What's the deal, does he have polio?"

"What was that?" George Sr. asked the startled young man.

"I said he'd look even more casual if he wore a polo," the young man replied quickly.

The firm eventually yielded to Don and George Sr.'s wishes on the setting. The most important opinion always belonged to the hand that wrote the checks. When the partner told them he'd ask the firm's production crew to schedule studio time, he got some additional client feedback.

"We use our own production crew and studio," Don clarified.

"That's no problem," the partner responded. "Let us know where and when, and we'll have our people there for the shoot."

"We keep it small," George Sr. went on. "If you give us the script, we'll handle the rest. Don't worry about the money. We pay you for the idea, not for the appearance."

The partner gathered up their materials and his staffers and exited the strangest pitch meeting he'd ever managed. The clients seemed happy, so he'd call it a win with an asterisk next to it.

They met again with the agency a week later, and Don and George Sr. aired the finished product they'd shot. George Jr. was missing at the meeting again, although he'd at least had the time to shoot the commercial. He was obviously a very busy candidate. The partner gave them his mixed opinions.

"The set lighting was a little dark, which doesn't bring out George's features very well. We love the message content, obviously," the partner began. "George comes across as a little—well, a little stiff. We would have tried to get him to loosen up a little more."

"So are we looking at a reshoot?" Don asked apprehensively.

"I wouldn't go that far," the partner decided. "I suppose it'll do. Ask your director to work with George on his hand gestures and delivery techniques on the next one."

The meeting ended, and Don and George Sr. were alone. The mediocre response might have been discouraging under different circumstances. They'd shot a commercial with Bruce Robinson controlling both the animatronic Virtual George and the camera, and then adding his own voiceover to the recording. George Sr. and Don had just stood and watched and then reviewed the finished work.

"You heard it," George Sr. declared. "I suppose it'll do. He just gave an endorsement to a puppet with a voiceover."

"It may not be art," Don added, "but it must be better than a dubbed-over Japanese horror movie."

CHAPTER 13

DOG HEAVEN

George Sr. and Don weren't the only ones busy making a political ad spot. The Ronald and Malcolm were watching their first message of the campaign too. The angle was that the world had gone to the dogs, and it was raining Chihuahuas. The spot opened with a shot of a golden retriever and a yellow Labrador sitting side-by-side. In this dog's world, the dogs could talk.

"This used to be such a lovely neighborhood," the retriever said to the lab. "Just look at it now."

As the two dogs sat and watched, a herd of fifty Chihuahuas paraded by them. The Chihuahuas had been hand-selected by the production crew, and they weren't picked based on cuteness. Just as human actors are profiled into certain roles, these Chihuahuas were the bus station vagrants, bar drunks, or fat women on buses of the dog world. They had skinny legs, long boney tails, round bodies, bug eyes, and practically no hair. There was dubbed high-pitched, irritating barking and yapping as the mob passed by. Several Chihuahuas peeled off, ran past the two watching dogs, and attacked two food bowls set out behind them.

"Just look at that," the lab complained. "It's the same thing every morning. They come here and steal our food."

"The problem is they mate so often our breeds can't keep up," the retriever pointed out.

The next shot showed one Chihuahua starting to mount a second one. The camera quickly panned back to the two narrating dogs. They were looking down to divert their eyes.

"Oh, no. There they go again," the retriever said. "They don't even have the decency to take it to their own backyard."

"Looks like in two months, we'll have another half-dozen of them running around and stealing our food," the lab lamented.

"There are so many of them now, they've elected one of their own as a senator," the retriever went on. "Here comes Senator Ramirez."

A Chihuahua wearing a little shirt, tie, and jacket ran into the pack. The other Chihuahuas started to jump up and down in excitement. The Senator Ramirez Chihuahua walked up to a patch of tulips and lifted its leg on them.

The Ronald paused the commercial and said to Malcolm, "I still think it'd hit harder if it squatted and dropped a tiny log."

"That's true, sir, but it might be a little too crass for some of the audience we hope to reach," Malcolm tried to explain to his boss. "This is effective. Everyone knows that when a dog lifts his leg like that, it isn't doing aerobics."

They resumed the commercial, and the retriever said, "There goes my favorite corner."

"It looks like we'll have to move again," the lab told his friend. "I've already escaped them twice, but they just start showing up in the next neighborhood."

"Somebody has to do something," the retriever pleaded. "There's just too many of them, and it's only getting worse."

There was a cut to a new scene. The golden retriever and the yellow lab were sitting together on the banks of a river. The camera panned back from them, and the viewer saw the pack of Chihuahuas on the other side of the river, running around and barking at each other.

"Thank God for President Tripp's border protection water deterrent," the retriever said.

"I agree. Thank God for President Tripp," the lab agreed. "I feel safer, nobody steals our food, and life is just better."

"This must be dog heaven," the retriever closed the spot.

The spot ended, and Tripp repeated one of his creative inputs. Malcolm had respectably talked Tripp out of it until this point.

"I still think one of the Chihuahuas should try to swim across but not make it," Tripp said. "That would tell people the concept is sound."

"We can't harm any of the animals, even by appearance," Malcolm patiently told Tripp. "It has both legal and publicity downsides."

"They're like rats, for Christ's sake," Tripp fumed. "Who'd ever miss one of those? I'll see about those laws when I'm president. Overall, I think it's tremendous."

"We'll get it aired immediately," Malcolm pledged. "The response should be strong."

They moved on to other business. The Ronald may have been running for president, but that didn't mean he could let his companies slide to the wayside. Malcolm was always a source of counsel, but it was apparent Malcolm would have to directly manage more and more of the Tripp machine. Some of that was due to a lack of time, and some of it was because Tripp needed more separation between himself and some of the cellar dwellers. He'd just had a risky encounter with his West Coast film production unit. They'd mailed a shipment to Tripp directly without masking it with a conventional business logo.

"Harry, I don't care how you do it, but you can't send me samples in their original covers," Tripp scolded one of his faithful subjects. "If a tabloid intercepts my mail, they'll tag me as a deviate."

The voters might question a conservative proponent of family values who received two films titled *You Thank Me When You Spank Me* and *Mein Shaft.*

There were other projects Tripp needed to turn over to Malcolm. One of them was a real estate venture Tripp called his student housing aid project. The business model was simple. Tripp targeted a small college town and bought up all the rentals he could. Once he'd cornered the market, he doubled the rents.

"It's a captive market," Tripp told Malcolm. "Each school has twenty to thirty thousand students, and they have to live somewhere. Most of them have to deal with me."

"You're a true educator," Malcolm praised his boss. "They may learn math and chemistry from the university, but they'll learn their first lesson in business from you. Supply and demand is the basic tenet of economics."

The student housing project had been heating up lately. One of the student papers had gotten wind of the escalating rents, and there were some local government officials involved. Until Tripp could win the White House and squash these meddlesome do-gooders, he'd need to lay low.

The most lucrative business after the adult entertainment division was his counterfeiting operation. The availability of counterfeit jewelry, watches, handbags, wallets, shoes, and clothing was common on the streets of New York and other large cities. You could also purchase pirated CDs, DVDs, and every type of video game. All of it was a fraction of the price of the genuine, licensed articles. It was common knowledge that most of the knockoffs were produced in China. It was far from common knowledge that a high percentage of the merchandize was brokered through customs by one of The Ronald's importers and distributed through his vast distribution network.

"I sell more Gucci than Gucci," Tripp bragged to Malcolm. "My movies and video games are always early releases, and my Rolexxx may not keep as good time as your Rolex, but for what it costs, you could afford to buy a new one every week."

"You're truly a saint," Malcolm commented. "You make luxury brands affordable to the masses."

There had been a few unfortunate mishaps, which left the masses less than satisfied with the value of their purchases. Some of them were an irritation. One of the pirated DVD shipments was of excellent quality except for the sound. They had been produced for the Chinese domestic market and were all dubbed in Chinese. Some problems were more serious. A batch of counterfeit watches had wristbands of poorly processed leather that created severe reactions when the residual lye came in contact with bare skin. A similar problem occurred with a shipment of necklaces whose stainless steel promoted as silver was rinsed with a toxic organic chemical. A shipment of shoes fit perfectly until the nails that attached the sole to the body of the shoe began to migrate through the footpads and into the feet.

The Ronald's foray into the field of vision had been especially trying. One batch of contacts was poorly molded, leaving hard shards of plastic embedded into the lenses. A batch of saline rinse was formulated at too high a concentration, leading to precipitated salt crystals in the solution. Fortunately, neither issue led to any permanent sight loss—just a few scratched corneas.

Tripp and Malcolm reviewed the latest opportunities on the counterfeit table. As usual, there was no shortage of flawed products looking for inspired sales and marketing strategy.

"We've got the opportunity to purchase half a million cases of sterile bandages for under a tenth of the normal market value," Malcolm began.

"What makes them such a great value?" Tripp asked.

"They're actually not sterile," Malcolm admitted. "Some type of sterilizer failure."

"Buy them all," Tripp instructed. "We'll sell them through our nursing home distributor. Old people get infections all the time. Nobody will notice."

"Roger that. Next up, we've got cheap condoms," Malcolm continued.

"Do they break?" Tripp guessed.

"Micro pinholes," Malcolm clarified. "But not micro enough."

"I'm willing to bet my boys are too big to squeeze through," Tripp replied. "I get the picture. We're buying. We'll sell them to Planned Parenthood. I'll eventually defund them, and this will give me a second reason. The first reason is they're evil. The second is that they aren't doing their job."

It occurred to Malcolm that the micro pinhole specification might be focused on preventing AIDS rather than pregnancy. That was the premise of safe sex. The Ronald wasn't much of a scientist, so Malcolm didn't attempt to lecture him on the size differences between a spermatozoon and a virus. If Malcolm taught The Ronald too much science, it might have a negative affect when it came time to defend the party's position on global warming.

"I'll prepare the bid," Malcolm promised. "Finally, we've got four special cases of baby toys."

"What makes them special?" Tripp queried.

"Toxic level of lead," Malcolm told him.

"I'm not a monster," Tripp said.

He thought for a few seconds about how to make lemonade even if the lemons were poisonous. Then he brightened up. There was a home for the misfit toys.

"Call our pet distributor," Tripp commanded. "If a dog or a cat sucks a little lead and gets goofy, who can tell?"

Malcolm briefly wondered what would happen to toddlers who played with the family pet's toys. The Ronald wasn't very high on secondary scenarios.

"I'll lock them down," Malcolm said.

Malcolm admired his boss's steady focus and his lack of conscience. Tripp knew all the fringe markets.

"If you buy products out of a car trunk or off a dicey website, you already know you're gambling. This country has a gambling problem, which is great for repeat business," Tripp lectured.

"That's true, sir," Malcolm agreed. "They get the thrill of wondering if they got a deal or if they got ripped off. If they buy from us, they're always going to get ripped off. Maybe they occasionally buy from someone else where they don't."

CHAPTER 14

TASTES LIKE JELLY BEANS

George Jr. was scheduled to make his first major public appearance. He was going to visit a county fair in Iowa, but for Don Chambers they might as well be spending the day in Mogadishu. George Jr.'s motorcade pulled through the gate and stopped at the entrance to the grandstand. A committee of city and county politicians stood in a line to greet them. They all filed out of the black Tahoe and made their introductions. All eyes were on George Jr., but he seemed distracted. The midway was directly behind them, and the music, bells, and screaming children piqued George Jr.'s interest. He could see the Ferris wheel towering above the grounds.

"Welcome to the Polk County Fair, Mr. Flowers," the Mayor of Des Moines greeted George Jr.

"I like fairs," George Jr. informed them.

"You came to the right place," the fair's CEO boasted.

The public intent of the day's mission was to expose George Jr. to the citizens of Iowa. The private intent of the day's mission for Martha and Don was to make sure they didn't expose too much. Don had met with the fair's organizers to carefully map out George Jr.'s agenda. If George Jr. had a vote, he'd have chosen to spend the entire day on the carnival rides. George Sr. had advised Don that George Jr. would lose his lunch if he even looked at a Tilt-a-Whirl. That would make for a very poor photo opportunity for the reporters covering the day's action.

George Jr.'s first task was judging baked goods and other food. Don reasoned that George Jr. might not fare well judging art or sewing, but he certainly liked to eat. However, George Jr. wasn't involved in the official judging. The last thing they wanted was to have George Jr. try to explain his voting logic to another person, especially if that person was an expert in that event. If George Jr. picked their entry in this special ancillary judging, the cook would win a special ribbon called a Presidential Award.

The first category was pies. George Jr. was presented with a row of plates with a small slice on each plate. There were nearly two dozen pies represented. Martha stuck to George Jr.'s side like a baby whale stuck to its mother.

The first pie was apple, and Martha elected to pick up the plate, slice off a bite-size piece with the plastic fork, and feed it to him. George Jr. was a big boy and he could eat by himself, but he didn't pass up an opportunity to be fed by Martha. He took the bite and made a yummy sound. Martha put the plate back on the table and began to pick up the next.

"I'm not done," George Jr. protested.

"You're not supposed to eat it all, George," Martha mock scolded. She shot a look at Don and the crowd and told him, "You've got a lot more pies to eat, and there are cakes and cookies after that."

"But I'm in the clean plate club," George Jr. reminded her. "Besides, I liked that pie."

The crowd laughed, and George Jr. smiled at the attention. Martha convinced him to move on, and he got used to taking a single bite out of each slice. He made a yummy noise after every bite and was genuinely convincing that he enjoyed Iowa pie. There was a slight hiccup when he came to a slice of tart cherry pie.

"That makes my lips pucker," George Jr. said with a surprised look on his face.

Martha made a quick save. She took George Jr.'s fork, broke off a second bite, and ate it herself.

"You're right, George, this is delicious," she added.

The pie was very tart. She could have used a glass of water. George got to move on and wash the sour taste out of his mouth with a bite of a tempting glazed strawberry pie. He made quick work of the rest of the row, and it was time for him to judge.

"Show us which one was your favorite, George," Martha prompted.

Martha prayed that George Jr. didn't ask to sample them all over again. George Jr. got a serious look on his face. It was no act. Deciding which pie he liked best was a problem he could sink his teeth into. He looked up and down the row of slices and pointed to the only pie that was made of chocolate and whipped cream. It looked like a recipe from the back of a container of Jell-O Pudding or Cool Whip.

"Are you sure, George?" Martha asked him to reconsider.

"I like chocolate," George Jr. declared.

Martha couldn't very well show George Jr. the pie he was supposed to like the best. The strawberry pie looked amazing, and there was a pecan cream cheese and a blueberry streusel that Martha was tempted to sample herself. They'd have to hope they were properly rewarded by the regular judges.

They moved on to the cake and then the cookie categories, and they each had a similar outcome. George Jr. was a bit of a chocoholic.

The final category included a series of main courses, sides, and salads. None of them contained chocolate.

George Jr. enjoyed the meatballs, lasagna, a potato casserole, and a fruit salad. He tolerated several vegetable dishes and some other salads. One of the final dishes was a roasted Brussels sprout dish in some type of sauce. Martha scooped up a small sprout on a spoon and offered it to George Jr.

"No, thank you," George Jr. said quickly.

Martha immediately knew she had a problem. She wasn't fond of Brussels sprouts either, and she didn't possess the palate of a seven-year-old.

"Eat it, George. It's good," she implored.

She almost added that it was good for you, but any kid knew that was code for it didn't taste good. George Jr. kept his lips tightly locked. A woman stepped forward and accepted the blame for entering Brussels sprouts into a contest that was intended to delight, not defeat, the senses.

"Brussels sprouts are so hot right now, but I know not everyone likes them," she apologized.

"Nonsense, George loves them. He's just getting a little full. He isn't a professional eater," Martha tried to joke.

She knew she had to make George Jr. sample everything. She'd seen some of the world's most prolific amateur eaters at the fair. They wouldn't vote for someone that was too fussy about what he ate. She reached into her pants suit treats pocket and found a small round object. She discreetly placed it onto the spoon behind the Brussels sprout and showed it to George Jr.

"Look at it, George," Martha instructed him. "Doesn't that look too good?"

George Jr. spied the object next to the Brussels sprout, and his attitude immediately came around. He bowed down to accept the spoon, and Martha quickly delivered it to his lips. George Jr. tried to eat around the sprout, but Martha jammed the spoon into his mouth so he'd have to clean off both objects. She prayed he didn't spit it out in front of this crowd of people. George Jr. chewed the mixture slowly and swallowed it.

"How'd you like it?" asked the cook.

"It tastes like jelly beans," George Jr. answered.

"That must be the molasses," the cook told him.

The jelly bean wasn't sufficient to compel George Jr. to pick the Brussels sprout dish over the meatballs for the President's Award, but it at least got him through the rest of the category.

Their next stop was in the livestock buildings. They might as well have taken George Jr. to the zoo. He told Martha the names of every animal he recognized.

"Look, they have cows like we have in Texas," George Jr. said, an edge of excitement in his voice.

"I wish we had longhorns like you've got in Texas," the Mayor wished.

They were in the fowl building looking at the baby chicks. As George Jr. was watching, a rooster stuck his head through the bars on the top of his cage and looked into George Jr.'s eyes. George Jr. reached out and petted the top of the rooster's crown. Martha started to stop him, but the rooster didn't peck George Jr. It stood in place as he stroked his head.

"That's the damnedest thing," the rooster's owner told them. "He chases my wife clean out of the coop."

They gave George Jr. a minute to finish petting his rooster, but he was in no hurry to leave.

"I think George has found his vice president," Martha whispered to Don.

"We'll build a coop in the backyard of the White House behind the Oval Office, where George can watch it," Don promised.

They finally coaxed George Jr. to move on to their final destination. They were headed back to the grandstand where he would announce the start of the annual tractor pull competition. George Jr. walked onstage with the rest of the delegation, and they introduced him to that year's county fair queen. George Jr. shook her hand and noticed her sash. It had clusters of fruit and vegetables embroidered on it.

"You look good enough to eat," George Jr. told her.

The Mayor, a gray-haired widower, added, "I'll say."

The young lady stood for a second with her mouth frozen in an awkward smile. Martha jumped in and quickly clarified, "He's talking about the apples, pears, and tomatoes on your sash—they look good enough to eat. He's talking about the sash."

"Oh sure, the sash," the Mayor echoed. "I meant the sash, too."

Miss Polk County looked relieved and laughed at her mistake. She introduced George Jr. to the crowd, and he walked to the microphone and announced the start of the tractor pull.

"Ladies and gentlemen, start your tractors," he commanded.

The plan was that George Jr. and the rest of the group would watch a few heats, and then, during a break, George Jr. would leave the event to the thunderous applause of the crowd. The pull began, and George Jr. was fascinated by the tractors and the sleds they pulled.

"Why does the tractor stop?" George Jr. asked curiously.

"They redistribute the weights, so they get heavier and heavier," the mayor told him. "The sled can weigh up to 50,000 pounds if all the weights are shifted."

George Jr. didn't know what that number meant, but he knew it was a lot higher than he could count. Tractors were a lot of fun.

"I want to ride a tractor," George Jr. requested.

"It's too dangerous," Martha blurted, and then she realized she had said it a little too aggressively.

"That's true for the competitive tractors," the mayor agreed. "We've got that good old-fashioned stock John Deere over there that rakes the track. Henry could give you a spin around the track on the next break."

"That would be cool," George Jr. declared.

Don and Martha eyed each other nervously but didn't add anything. They couldn't insinuate they were afraid to let their candidate ride a tractor.

"I'm going to ride a tractor," George Jr. kept repeating every couple of minutes.

At the next break, Henry drove the John Deere to the front of the stage and helped George Jr. up onto the platform by the driver's seat.

"Does he want to drive it?" he asked the mayor.

"No," Don and Martha shouted back in unison.

George Jr. held the side fender and the back of Henry's seat as the tractor drove around the track. He was tentative at first and used both hands to hold on. He got more comfortable quickly, and he took his right hand off the fender to wave to Martha. She waved back, and the rest of the grandstand mimicked her. George Jr. noticed that everyone was waving at him, and he began to wave wildly at everyone there. He looked as if he was having the time of his life.

"When he gets off that tractor, it's time for us to get out of here," Don told Martha. "I hope this tractor doesn't do for George what that tank did for Dukakis."

"What did you expect, bringing him here? There's so much stuff for him to get into, and we got him started by feeding him about a bag of sugar in that pie-and-cake fiasco," Martha hissed back. "For our next stop, why not fill up a stadium with people and let George run an obstacle course? Or maybe you're planning on getting him onto an episode of *Celebrity Jeopardy*. He'll do fine as long as the categories are his favorite colors, foods, and animals. Look at him. He's way too overstimulated."

George Jr. was on a sugar and adrenaline high, and he looked less like the future leader of the free world and more like Gomer Pyle waving and riding on the back of the tractor. But the crowd loved it, and it played well in the Iowa media. At the end of the day it was politics, and when in Iowa, a candidate was expected to act like an Iowan. If that meant eating pie, petting roosters, and riding tractors, you'd better climb aboard and ride. Ronald Tripp might buy a company that makes tractors, but voters would relate better to someone who wanted to ride one.

Don and Martha were arguing, but they should have been congratulating each other for a brilliant day on the trail.

CHAPTER 15

L'ERUDITE (THE SCHOLAR)

Madame Fifi la Brousse was the *doyen des étudiants,* or dean of students, and owner of Paris's small but well regarded Université de Gosses de Riches. She was meeting with a gentleman who identified himself as a French government official named Jules Maigret. Mr. Maigret was asking Madame la Brousse an endless list of questions about one of the school's alumni, George Flowers Jr. Madame la Brousse had accepted Mr. Maigret's credentials at face value, provided him all the documents he requested, and freely answered all of his questions. Mr. Maigret was reviewing George Jr.'s transcripts.

"I see his lowest marks were honors, but the majority of his marks are highest honors," Mr. Maigret observed.

"*Oui,*" Madame la Brousse replied. "He was the most gifted student in his year."

"Your curriculum is entirely in French, correct?" Mr. Maigret confirmed.

"Mr. Flowers was fluent in French, German, and several other languages," Madame la Brousse stated.

"I would like to speak to some of his teachers," Mr. Maigret requested. "Is Dr. Follett still on staff?"

"I'm sorry to say Dr. Follett succumbed to a long illness," Madame la Brousse lamented.

"I see," Mr. Maigret replied. "Perhaps I could speak to Dr. Lafayette."

"Dr. Lafayette was an avid bicyclist," Madame la Brousse began. "Unfortunately, he was struck and killed by a lorry while he was riding to class."

"Dr. Dubois?" Mr. Maigret queried.

"Lab explosion," Madame la Brousse answered with sorrow.

"Perhaps we could save some time," Mr. Maigret decided. "Could you direct me to a *professeur* who taught Mr. Flowers and who is still of this world?"

Madame la Brousse surveyed George Jr.'s transcript carefully. Several times she stopped, paused in thought, and went on. When she finished her review, she handed the document back to Mr. Maigret.

"It is regrettable that all of Mr. Flowers' former teachers are no longer with us. I know personally that he kept in touch with many of them. We've already seen the letters he wrote me over the years. He must miss their counsel," Madame la Brousse sighed.

"Are there any former students or other employees you are aware of that might remember Mr. Flowers?" Mr. Maigret asked.

"None that come to mind," Madame la Brousse replied.

"So you are the only person at the school who remembers Mr. Flowers?" Mr. Maigret asked.

"*Oui,*" Madame la Brousse answered.

Mr. Maigret had exhausted his list of questions and saw no other interesting threads of questioning to explore. There were sounds of cranes and construction workers in the open area outside the administrative building.

"I noticed you have significant construction in process," Mr. Maigret commented just before he exited.

"*Oui,* we're expanding," Madame la Brousse told him. "The health of the school is strong."

Mr. Maigret phoned Malcolm from his automobile. While he asked Madame la Brousse to call him Jules, Malcolm used Henri. It was the name Henri's parents had given him.

"I have the transcripts and the diploma. They look authentic," Henri told Malcolm. "Madame la Brousse remembers him like he was there yesterday. It all seems to check out, except there's one thing that's very peculiar. Every teacher that taught Flowers is dead."

"All of them?" Malcolm asked.

"I'll confirm as many as I can, but if it's true, I can't do much more here," Henri told Malcolm.

Malcolm passed on the report to The Ronald, and they agreed that George Jr.'s teachers would ruin any actuarial table ever devised.

"I thought the red wine they all drank made them live longer," Tripp summarized. "Something is fishy here."

"It does seem rather incredible," Malcolm agreed.

They had already exhausted any leads on George Jr.'s education in the United States. All his tutors were well respected and deceased. While it was more likely the US teachers would be dead because of age, it was a frustrating and intriguing pattern. Unfortunately for Tripp, it wasn't a pattern he could turn into usable information.

"All this says Junior was a rich kid that was tutored or attended private schools. Public school wasn't good enough. That could work for us," Tripp pointed out.

"I don't know that it works if you try to insult a Republican by calling him rich. Besides, you attended Morgan Academy and Phillips. Then you went to Bennington. People might think you're insulting yourself," Malcolm reminded Tripp.

"Are you saying I'm not allowed to play the elitist card?" Tripp asked.

"It might seem a bit like the tiger telling the zebra he has too many stripes," Malcolm described. "How do you think that would play, sir?"

"So Junior's past is sealed. I'd hoped to have something we can use fall into our laps. It's back to good old-fashioned conventional warfare. Our espionage didn't pay off."

"We know more than we did before," Malcolm assured Tripp. "We know he's very smart, and we'll have to prepare for that. He seems to be squeaky clean. That tells me there's something big that we're missing. It might be right in front of us, if we can see it."

Madame la Brousse was on the phone at the same time as Henri.

"They sent a Frenchman to investigate," Madame la Brousse said in crisp English. "Telling him I only spoke French didn't shelter us much. He understood the French documents, too, obviously."

"Did he act like he questioned the documents or your answers?" George Sr. asked her.

"He asked to speak to some of the teachers," Madame la Brousse told George Sr. "Telling him they were all dead didn't go well."

"It's the truth," George Sr. argued.

"It's the truth they're dead, not that they were his teachers," Madame la Brousse clarified. "We constructed the transcript with deceased teachers."

George Sr. asked Madame la Brousse to contact him if any other visitors asked questions about George Jr. He thanked her and told her that her assistance would continue to be rewarded.

"Speaking of rewards, how is that new library coming along?" George Sr. asked her.

"Thank you so much again. It is lovely. It should be completed by the fall term," Madame la Brousse said. "I should mention that the Université is in urgent need of a new athletic facility, too."

CHAPTER 16

OUI, WEE, WEE

George Jr. had just toured a pig farm as part of his Iowa farm tour, and Don allowed the press a few minutes to ask questions in as tightly controlled conditions as he could manage. Don scheduled George Jr.'s appearances as close as he could to each other. It was always easier if he kept him moving so fast he didn't have time to stop and talk.

"George, what do you think of Ronald Tripp's statement that he'll mop the floor with you and the rest of the candidates at the first debate?" an AP reporter asked.

"Ronald Tripp should worry more about mopping the floors in his hotel's bathrooms," Martha answered. "I've been told their standards have fallen. Ronald is distracted, and his management style isn't high on delegation. I hope he doesn't think he'll be able to micromanage the US government. I've heard his hotels are disgusting. Right, George?"

"Disgusting," George Jr. echoed.

"What does the United States need to do to win the fight against terrorism, George?" another reporter asked.

"George will be tough," Martha promised. "How tough is tough enough, George?"

"Tough as nails," George Jr. remembered.

Another reporter was acknowledged, and he asked, *"Combien d'années avez vous étudier à Paris, monsieur Fleurs?"*

George Jr. smiled because the question sounded like a riddle or gibberish talk, and they were both a couple of his favorite things. Martha stiffened and immediately became alert. She knew George Jr.'s backstory, and part of it stated that George Jr. was fluent in French.

"Pouvez-vous repèter la question?" Martha asked to buy time. She told the rest of the crowd, "George's French is perfect, but I'm a little rusty."

Martha had taken French in high school, but she had to listen carefully. She recognized student, years, and Paris and gave her best answer.

"George graduated from the university in less than four years," Martha answered in English. For the benefit of the foreign press she answered, *"Quatre ans. Oui, George?"*

They were on a hog farm, so George Jr. replied appropriately. "Wee, wee, wee, all the way home."

The reporters laughed, and there were a few more cupcake questions for Martha to answer and George Jr. to acknowledge. The French reporter tried to ask follow-up questions, but fair play meant other reporters were selected first. On top of fair play, good campaign management meant the French reporter would remain invisible to Don for the rest of the campaign.

Once they were safely in the limo, Martha made sure Don was aware of her thoughts.

"You had to send him to school in France," Martha complained. "If you needed him in Europe, what's wrong with London? George can barely put together three to four words in English, but you made him fluent in French, and now I hear German too. This would have been good to know before I agreed to this."

"So you could brush up on your French?" Don asked.

"So I could have told you to pound sand," Martha clarified.

"We thought if the school was in France, it would be more difficult for the press to research it," Don tried to explain.

"Because you thought nobody can speak English and French?" Martha yelled back. "It isn't Klingon. Guess what? There are colleges in this country that hand out degrees in French."

"George did fine," Don dismissed her.

"Sure he did," Martha looked over at George Jr. while he gazed out the car's window. "The only word he knows in French is the same word he uses when he has to use the restroom."

Back in New York, Malcolm was delivering his report to The Ronald.

"So the only French word Junior used was *oui,* followed by a phrase from 'The Three Little Pigs'?" The Ronald repeated. "That must mean I'm fluent in German. I learned *jawohl* from watching *Hogan's Heroes.* Did the reporter ask a follow-up?"

"It was one and done," Malcolm replied. "When the press gets to ask questions, it gets competitive. It's like a rugby scrum."

"The debate is coming up," The Ronald said. "It was a shot, but it looks like Junior knows French after all. It looks like the only weapon I have going in is my tongue. I'll roast Junior and the rest of those clowns. This is where the American people find out who can cut it and who can't. I'm going to terminate some campaigns."

"Unleash hell, sir," Malcolm encouraged.

CHAPTER 17

OLD WITCH

It was midweek, and George Sr. and Betsey were home by themselves on the ranch. George Jr. was with Don and Martha on the road in Iowa. The phone rang, and as usual Betsey answered it. The senator had reached a point in life where he wouldn't answer a telephone unless he was expecting a call from someone he knew that he wanted to speak with. Betsey listened for a few seconds and immediately started to shout for George Sr.

"What happened?" he asked as he hurried into the study. "Is somebody hurt?"

"No," Betsey looked up in concern. "It's Consuela."

George Sr. sat down at his desk with a dazed look and told Betsey, "I assumed she was dead. She must be a hundred by now."

Consuela Hernandez had worked for the Flowers family decades ago. She'd started as a domestic servant, but she had raised three children. So when first Bill and then George Jr. were born, Consuela transitioned to caring for them. George Sr. and Betsey were often traveling to numerous campaign and political obligations and events. When George Jr.'s abilities began to manifest themselves,

Betsey needed Consuela to concentrate on George Jr. full-time. Consuela had practically raised him by herself.

When George Jr. got older, he became more self-sufficient. Part of Consuela's family still lived in Mexico, and she missed them. She'd finally decided to quit her job with the Flowers family and move back to Matamoros. While she was one of the only people alive to know everything there was to know about George Jr., she was loyal. She might have gossiped some, but it didn't get back to Houston. She was in her sixties when she'd quit, and they had only heard from her a few times after she'd moved back to Mexico. But now she was very much alive and, with George Jr.'s latest adventure, she possessed explosive information. George Sr. put her on speakerphone so they could both speak with her.

"*Hola,* Mister Senator," the voice on the other end of the line said.

There was no doubt it was Consuela. She sounded the same as she had thirty years before. They asked about her family before George Sr. cautiously asked what they could do for her.

"It's a miracle," Consuela said. "I pray and pray to the Blessed Virgin that Jorge get well, and I read my prayers they answered. He not idiot no more."

Consuela's English was limited and direct. They instantly realized she'd read some Mexican newspaper or seen a television piece covering the US election. She assumed that if George Jr. was running for president, he'd gone through some significant personal changes.

"George has been quite intelligent for some time now," George Sr. lied. "He must have just been a late developer. We'll give him your best."

"I must see him," Consuela insisted. "I must see Bill too. I read Bill, he very sick. I must see my boys."

"We wouldn't want you to have to travel all the way from Mexico," George Sr. told Consuela. "We'll set up a call for you to talk with them."

"Mexico?" Consuela asked. *"No esta en Mexico.* My family all in Houston now. I live with them."

That was just perfect. George Sr.'s mind raced to think of a reason Consuela couldn't visit them from thirty minutes away. His mind raced hard, but in circles. The only two reasons he could think of were that Bill, contrary to what they'd told the world, was healthy as a horse and that George Jr. had the same IQ as when Consuela had quit.

"We'll call you when George Jr. gets back from his trip," George Sr. said weakly.

"It will be so nice have grownup talk with Jorge," Consuela said.

After they'd hung up, George Sr. reviewed their options further. They could try to avoid Consuela forever, or at least until after the primaries. They could let her meet with George Jr. and hope she didn't realize he hadn't changed. It seemed unlikely these options would work. The final option was to show Consuela that George Jr. was the same but make sure she didn't tell other people about it. There only seemed to be one way to make sure that worked.

"We need to hire back Consuela," George Sr. told Betsey. "It's the only way we'll be able to keep an eye on her."

"How many people are going to have to work for you by the time this thing is over?" Betsey asked.

George Jr. returned from his latest trip to Iowa with Martha and Don. George Sr. and Betsey briefed them all on Consuela.

"George, do you remember Consuela?" Betsey asked George Jr.

George Jr. thought, and then grinned.

"Auntie Consuela called me Jorge," George Jr. remembered.

The next day, one of Consuela's grandsons drove her from Houston to the Flowers ranch. Bill and Maryann were on hand too. George Sr. told Maryann to apply Bill's death mask. When Consuela came through the front entrance and saw her boys all grown up, she cried and went to them and hugged them both. She looked at Bill, shook her head, and crossed herself. On the other hand, George Jr. looked in excellent health. Consuela needed to confirm George Jr.'s mental health for herself.

"So Jorge, you not idiot no more?" Consuela asked him.

George Jr. looked hurt and told her, "I'm no idiot."

"Is good," she told him and hugged them both again.

Consuela touched the side of Bill's face when she hugged him, and it felt sticky. She looked at her fingers, and they were white. Something was off, but Consuela kept visiting.

"Jorge, how you make up so much school?" Consuela asked George Jr.

"My mom taught me," George Jr. explained.

Consuela was surprised. Nobody could learn enough from the old witch to become president. She looked at the entire family and their new friends, and it didn't seem right. They all acted like they were afraid of her. They'd also told her Bill was sick, but he was just poorly made up. The only one who didn't act any differently was George Jr. Consuela could sense he was still an idiot. Her excitement faded. This visit was a poor idea.

"So nice see my boys, but *yo me voy*," Consuela told them.

"Consuela, please stay a while," George Sr. encouraged. "Seeing you here makes us realize how much we missed you."

George Sr. could see by Bill's smudged cheek, George Jr.'s simple responses, and Consuela's rapid change in demeanor that they had reached option three at supersonic speed. Consuela was back on the payroll before they saw her grandson's car back in front of the house. She came back the next day and every day after that from Monday through Friday. She helped Betsey with cooking and mainly kept George Jr. entertained. She needed a *siesta* in the afternoons but was good company for Betsey if everyone was traveling. She played with George Jr. on the rare days he wasn't away.

It was nice to take care of a child again. The rest of Consuela's great-grandchildren were too old for the games George Jr. enjoyed.

George Jr., Don, Martha, and George Sr. were all traveling to Dallas on a Wednesday to see some of George Sr.'s financial backers. Betsey and Consuela were home minding the ranch. It was midafternoon, and Consuela was down for her siesta. Consuela heard a car door and looked out her window. A man walked up and knocked at the front door. Consuela waited for Betsey to answer, but she didn't appear. Consuela walked to the door and greeted the man on the front porch.

"*Hola,* I'm Consuela," she told the visitor.

"Hello, Consuela. My name is Matt Johnson, and I work for TGC. I'd like to talk with George Flowers. I don't suppose he's available?" Johnson asked her.

Consuela looked back for Betsey, and when she didn't see her, she answered, "*Jorge no esta aqui.*"

Johnson asked Consuela if, since he had traveled all the way from the East Coast, she would mind telling him a few details about Mr. Flowers herself. Consuela didn't know that TGC stood for Total Gossip Channel or that they existed to dig up the dirt on every celebrity they could ambush. It wouldn't have mattered to Consuela if she'd known. She welcomed someone to talk with besides Betsey. Besides, Consuela had lived most of her life in

Matamoros. Compared to that, this man didn't look very dangerous.

"First of all, what do you do here?" Johnson asked Consuela.

"I Jorge's nanny," Consuela told Johnson. "He my boy."

"That's excellent," Johnson told her. "You can tell me about the young George Flowers. What do you do for the Flowers now?"

"I still Jorge's nanny," Consuela replied.

Johnson smiled at her answer. The Flowers could afford to keep Consuela even after she wasn't needed. It was a nice gesture to keep her around.

"What goes through your mind now that he's a strong contender for president?" Johnson asked.

"I hope Jorge win," Consuela told him. "No like Mr. Tripp. He send *mi familia* back Mexico or to prison."

"We know Ronald Tripp isn't popular with your people," Johnson replied. "Would you say Mr. Flowers is more accepting of people?"

"Si, Jorge like everyone," Consuela agreed. "He don't know no better."

"We hear he was a brilliant child. When did he start speaking his second and third languages?" Johnson asked.

This was news to Consuela. George Jr. had occasionally repeated a word Consuela said in Spanish, but his comprehension of the word's meaning was about as clear as a parrot's. He hadn't said a word in English until he was four or maybe even older. He might have said "Dada" or "Mama" when most children were starting preschool.

Consuela replied, "Jorge no say nothing until *cuatro o cinco años de edad.*"

"So he started to speak other languages when he was four or five years old," Johnson said as he wrote. "Just how smart was he?"

"He was simple *mente,*" Consuela answered.

"So he was an easy baby," Johnson repeated. "You hear how smart children are always into things. Does that describe Mr. Flowers?"

Consuela shook her head. She didn't mean George Jr. was simple to care for—he was just simple-minded. She was forming the same opinion about the visitor.

Consuela told him, "He just lay in crib *como una roca.*"

"What was Mr. Flowers' favorite game?" Johnson asked.

"Jorge like hide-and-seek," Consuela answered.

"You have a great memory, Consuela," Johnson encouraged her. "I'm sure it's been a while since you played games with Mr. Flowers."

"*No, justo ayer,*" Consuela tried to correct him.

Consuela had picked up with George Jr. just where she'd left off. It was sometimes disruptive, if not a little disturbing, for the rest of the household. Consuela and George Jr. played several hours of hide-and-seek and "I Spy" the day before.

"I bet he was walking at six months and toilet-trained at twelve," Johnson went on.

"*No, tres y cuatro,*" Consuela corrected again. "*Años.*"

Betsey finished her shower, toweled off, and went into her bedroom. She could hear voices and assumed Consuela had turned on the television. But one of the voices sounded like it was Consuela. She slipped on a robe and went into the hallway to find out what was happening. She saw Consuela at the door talking to a man holding a pen and a notebook. He looked like a reporter.

"Consuela, close the door and come here," Betsey yelled.

"Excuse me, I got go," Consuela excused herself. "*La vieja bruja* calls."

Consuela closed the door in the man's face. She hated to be impolite, but the old witch was calling. She didn't want to get fired. It was the best money she'd ever made in her life, not to mention the easiest. Plus, she'd miss George Jr. if they made her leave.

Matt Johnson regretted that his interview ended so abruptly, but he'd gotten some of that exclusive inside gossip he was paid to find. George Flowers was a wunderkind. That explained why he'd been privately tutored, accelerated through an exclusive French college, and immediately given a prominent role in his daddy's company. Most of Consuela's English and Spanish mix sounded like a magpie's chatter to him, but he'd gotten a story. Nobody at TGC had expected him to even get close to the house.

"Who was that?" Betsey demanded from Consuela.

"TGA, TGB, TGC?" Consuela tried to remember. "TGC sound right."

Betsey was shaken and immediately called George Sr. to tell him what had happened.

"How hard can it be to keep tabs on a ninety-year-old Mexican woman?" George Sr. scolded. "What'd she tell him?"

"I was in the shower," Betsey told him for the fourth time. "Consuela told me she told the reporter 'Jorge good boy.'"

"We'll be back in two hours," George Sr. told his wife. "Try to keep her away from reporters until then."

TGC told the truth when they bragged they had the world's largest news team. TGC's motto was "if you own a cellphone with a camera, you work for TGC." Part of TGC's *modus operandi* was to air their stories the same day they broke. The campaign team didn't watch it as a rule, but they did that night. They felt relief when George Jr. wasn't the top story. The top story did involve a nanny, but she worked for a well-known actor and actress couple. The general public might have felt the actress was super sexy, but that apparently wasn't good enough to keep the husband from frequently visiting the nanny's apartment.

The second story promised exclusive inside information on presidential candidate George Flowers.

"Sweet Jesus," George Sr. blurted.

"TGC has learned that presidential candidate George Flowers may not enter the race as one of America's better known candidates ever, but he might be one of the smartest," the show's anchor said. "The woman that cared for Mr. Flowers as a child told TGC that he knew multiple languages before the age the rest of us are in kindergarten. He was also walking when most of us are crawling, and let's just say Senator Flowers and his wife, Betsey, didn't have to spend too much on diapers. Mr. Flowers grasped the potty concept early."

The show's other anchor added, "He may have read the potty-training book to himself. My only question is this. If he's so smart, what's he doing in politics?"

Their apprehension was misguided. It couldn't have been a better publicity piece if Don had written it himself.

"That was a close call. The only reason they even aired it is because they got to say 'potty,'" Don remarked after the show had moved on to their next victim. "Why would Consuela lie like that?"

CHAPTER 18

ONE STEP FORWARD, TWO STEPS BACK

The first debate was scheduled months before the Iowa Caucus. There were five viable candidates invited to participate, and each of their teams were working day and night to research potential questions and outline the best responses. Most of the teams had a third step—practicing these responses with their candidate. George Jr.'s campaign team was no different in their approach to generating questions and responses, but their approach practicing those responses with George Jr. was very different.

"We're going to play a little game," Martha opened.

Martha was clearly George Jr.'s primary handler now, like the lead trainer of a specific killer whale at SeaWorld. They were hoping George Jr. possessed at least a fraction of a whale's ability for mimicking behavior.

"We're going to give you a toy so that you can hear a voice in your ear," Martha went on. "I want you to listen to what the voice says and then try to repeat it word-for-word in your captain's voice. I'll give you some candy for every word you get right."

Martha was over-promising a little bit; if she gave George Jr. a piece of candy for every word he'd have to repeat, their candidate would die of diabetes before the election.

The campaign had added a new vital insider to the mix. His name was Ted, and he was an electronics wizard that had worked as an information technology expert for George Sr. They had Bruce Robinson to run Virtual George, but they needed another set of hands for George Jr.'s road appearances. Ted had the personality of most information technology professionals.

"Hey," he said to George Jr. and Martha as he inserted a tiny device into the inner canal of George Jr.'s right ear.

They debated whether to design something that was hidden or make it look like a conventional hearing aid. They went with the concealed version because George Jr. did not need to appear to be physically disabled. They may need to emphasize George Jr.'s physicality if any of his true mental acuities were accidently divulged.

Martha then began to read George Jr. potential debate questions, and Ted transmitted the perfected response into George Jr.'s receiver while Martha followed along on a second copy. George Jr. was asked to repeat what he heard word-for-word as he heard it.

"Use your captain's voice," Martha reminded him.

George tried to repeat what he heard, and it was slow going at first. It sounded as natural as someone trying to relay a phone conversation in real time to a room full of people. He'd also stop frequently and ask the voice in his head to repeat itself. Martha worked with him on maintaining a natural pace and tone, and she eliminated scores of words written for somebody who had a college education. She had to work with Ted as well. George Jr.'s memory was limited to sentence fragments of five words at a time or less. Ted had to develop a rhythm in which he broke the answer into smaller logical fragments. Don thought it was sound because it aligned with his theories on the average American voter.

"Simpler is acceptable," Don decided. "George may give the only responses that most of the voters can understand."

George's captain's voice was his adult voice of authority, reserved for when he played war games or mimicked his parents. Martha had to make sure he didn't sound too theatrical, like he was playing Hamlet in a Shakespearean play.

"What if the other candidates start to attack him or want to debate him directly?" Martha asked.

"He'll finish whatever we tell him, and then we'll load the next response," Don said. "As long as he doesn't realize he's under attack, he'll be fine. We'll have to live with the timing issues."

"He probably won't even look at the right person," Martha worried.

"That's why we trained him to keep looking at the cameras," Don explained. "He'll connect with the viewers, and he'll appear to be stronger. He's not intimidated by the other candidates—in fact, he barely acknowledges them. The less he looks at Ronald Tripp, the better off he'll be."

The night of the debate, everyone was a nervous wreck except for George Jr. He was wearing the ear device, and that meant he was going to get some candy. The moderators were from a cable news network that was generally gentle to the Republican Party. The format of the debate was question-and-answer only, with rebuttals allowed if one candidate tried to spice up their position by denigrating a rival's position. Since denigrating was at the heart of most debates, numerous rebuttals were anticipated. Each of the candidates' teams, including

George Jr.'s, protested that the candidates should be allowed an opening and closing statement. Don and Martha silently thanked their good fortune when the network denied the request. George Jr. didn't need any more airtime than was absolutely necessary.

The five candidates looked their best, although George Jr. fared best under the bright lights. He looked willing, even eager, to answer some questions.

The Ronald brought his scorched-earth, winner-take-all mentality to the debate. Some candidates planned to outshine the others, some planned to pull down the others, and some planned to rise above the fray. George Jr. had no plan, although he appeared to rise above the fray. Tripp was the clear leader of the pull-down camp, and he wasted no time going after Elizabeth Martin, a female senator from Colorado.

Martin had an aspect of her personal life that was both tragic and, at the same time, priceless political currency. She was using some of that currency to explain her position on just how aggressively the next president should go after one of the alleged Middle East terrorist hotspots.

"I stand with our party, stating that terrorism is the number one issue facing America today. This is because our present leader in the White House has missed the mark in his duty to keep us safe," Martin began. "However, I would look at any and all options before allowing American troops to be sent to another potentially unwinnable conflict. As you well know, I take the concept of going to war very seriously. I know, better than most, the price that goes with it."

Elizabeth Martin's oldest son was a West Point man, handsome, intelligent, and patriotic. He was killed by a roadside bomb outside a small village in Afghanistan. She had experienced tremendous suffering and grief from the death of her son. On top of that, the stress of the loss damaged and eventually destroyed the relationship between the senator and her husband. Their divorce was finalized shortly before she'd declared her candidacy. The other candidates listened respectfully. There was no reasonable counterargument against a mother's loss or the turbulent aftermath. It was political kryptonite.

Ronald Tripp thought he was Superman, but that didn't stop him from eating kryptonite for breakfast. What he heard sounded to him like an excuse for showing weakness. The rules of politics told him to let Senator Martin say her piece and wait for the next question before attacking someone else. The temperature in the room could only get a little cooler than it was with Senator Martin's speech. But The Ronald believed the rules of politics had been written by the losers, who let human decency trump winning at all costs.

"We all know your history and respect your loss," Tripp jumped in. "But there is always a price to pay for freedom. And with all due respect to the senator, we all paid a little bit for your son. I mean, as taxpayers we put him through his military training and sent him to Afghanistan, and we didn't exactly get our money's worth."

The gasp in the audience could be heard on television. The moderators were supposed to designate who was sanctioned to speak, but they sat in stunned silence.

"How dare you," Senator Martin fumed.

"I'm just saying," Tripp weathered on. "One of our greatest generals, George Patton, said real heroes don't die for their country. Real heroes make the enemy die for their country. That's the army you'll have if I'm president. Our enemy's mothers will be crying for their sons."

Elizabeth Martin looked as if she might charge The Ronald's podium and rip off his hairpiece. The cameras caught her look of rage before it melted to sorrow and then grief. Her eyes began to water, and the tears came.

"My son was a good soldier, and there is nothing he or any other soldier could have done to prevent what happened to him," Senator Martin sobbed. "Excuse me, ladies and gentlemen, but I can't share a podium with this man. I'm embarrassed for these other fine candidates, I'm embarrassed for our gracious hosts, and most of all, I'm embarrassed for the Republican Party."

Then Senator Martin noisily pulled off her microphone and stormed off the stage.

The other candidates were still silent, although not out of respect. Politics were a dirty business and they were veterans of it, but they were unprepared for The Ronald. As usual, The Ronald was always prepared.

"You know, they say that if you can't stand the heat, you'd better stay out of the kitchen," Tripp said, lining up his kill shot. "I say, if you can't stand the heat, maybe it's time to go *back* to the kitchen. Maybe if she'd spent more time there, she might have been able to keep her husband. It takes big balls to lead this country, but it looks like any balls are a good start."

There was hissing and catcalls now in the audience. Don and Martha knew George Jr. should say something, but they hadn't drafted a response Ted could use for this. There was no way George Jr. was equipped to get into this kind of off-the-charts dust-up with Tripp.

Then they heard George Jr. clear his throat and speak.

"Bad boys make girls cry," George Jr. said with signs of anger.

The Ronald was a little surprised at the source, but he looked at George Jr. and told him, "I am a bad boy, George, because that's what it takes to lead a business empire, and that's what it takes these days to lead a nation. I'm a bad boy because I tell the truth."

"Bad boys tell lies," George Jr. declared.

He had seen Elizabeth Martin cry, and he naturally assumed Tripp had pulled her hair. He hadn't noticed any other fighting or yelling, so what else could it be?

"Bad boys pull girls' hair. I'd rather be a good boy," George Jr. pledged.

"That's why you're too weak to lead this country, George," Tripp countered.

George Jr. was looking at Tripp, not the cameras, and his next move was something that sometimes happened in world politics but never happened in US presidential politics. George Jr. took a step toward Ronald Tripp, and it wasn't the kind of step that implied he was getting closer so Tripp could hear him better. It implied physical violence. The next event would become the talk of the debate. Tripp and George Jr. were next to each other on stage, and Ronald Tripp instinctively took two steps backward.

With those steps, one forward and two back, Ronald Tripp's aura of invincibility evaporated. He wasn't America's flamboyant model for tough love anymore. He was a bully with poor manners. The debate continued, George Jr. recited his lines passably, and the tone became markedly more civil. Ronald Tripp argued some of George Jr.'s positions, but he never went after him personally. George Jr. had put him in his place.

CHAPTER 19

MOVES LIKE BUCKNER

The typical television post-debate analysis is as exciting as watching paint dry or listening to a Kenny G song. But tonight, the analysts couldn't get enough of the Tripp two-step.

"Up to now, everyone tried to stay out of Ronald Tripp's way," analyst one remarked. "The strategy has obviously been that if I concede little things to him, he'll leave me alone. That hasn't worked for any of Tripp's competitors. In fact, some pundits have compared Tripp to Hitler and his opponents to Neville Chamberlain. The more they concede, the more Tripp perceives them as weak, and the more he expects from them in the future. Tonight, George Flowers let Tripp know that he won't back down. Tonight, Ronald Tripp met his Winston Churchill."

"I thought George Flowers' approach to Ronald Tripp was brilliant," another analyst said. "He made the country see Ronald Tripp as a classic grade-school bully. 'Bad boys pull girls' hair, bad boys tell lies.' He's making moderate voters decide if they're comfortable voting for a self-confessed bad boy."

"It was a shock to the Republican Party when Bill Flowers announced he was ill and couldn't run. They ended up with his brother instead, someone who's an untested political unknown," yet another analyst said. "Now it looks like the party may have gotten the most capable Flowers brother."

"I'm sure there were times when each of the candidates wanted to give Ronald Tripp a sock on the nose," a network newscaster summarized. "For a moment tonight, it appeared that George Flowers might do more than just think about it."

"I wish he'd done it," a Republican insider remarked. "It would have represented the entire party."

The debate talk filtered through the hard news media and trickled out into the sports and entertainment media. ESPN's SportsCenter did a segment that was perfect water-cooler fodder. They didn't just replay George Jr.'s advance and Ronald Tripp's retreat—they analyzed it in context to other significant moments in sports.

"What did you think of The Ronald's form, Kevin?" sportscaster one asked.

"It was obviously the move of a seasoned boxer, Jack," sportscaster two replied. "The Ronald went right to the rope-a-dope."

"Are you sure it was good strategy to retreat?" Jack asked. "Here's what happened when they went to commercial."

The next scene showed two Rock 'Em Sock 'Em Robots inside their toy boxing ring. One of the robots wore a tiny orange-blond toupee. The other robot landed an uppercut, and the Ronald robot's head popped up as his orange-blond toupee flew out of the ring.

"Ouch," Kevin grimaced. "Ronald has two ex-wives who'd love to do the same thing."

"So where do you think The Ronald's retreat ranks on a list of the all-time less-than-cool moves?" Jack asked.

"Let's take a look. There's this one," Kevin said.

They proceeded to show a series of sports clips. Some of them were famous, but not because they were championship moments. These were the moments that made the athletes involved wish they'd chosen a different line of work. The clips were all authentic, except for one minor alteration. The network superimposed Ronald Tripp's face and hair over the image of the athlete's. The first was a replay of Ronald Tripp as Chris Weber in his infamous NCAA basketball finals timeout clip.

"The debate is heating up, and Ronald Tripp just called a timeout," Jack announced.

"Wait a minute—he's out of timeouts," Kevin said in mock horror. "He's going to be penalized heavily for that. He doesn't get to answer any more questions."

The next clip showed Ronald Tripp as a bull rider being tossed from and then trampled by a two-ton bull. Next was Ronald Tripp the bicycle road racer, flipping over his handlebars onto the pavement and setting off a twenty-bike pileup that buried him. Then there was Ronald Tripp the hockey player who lost control on the ice and smashed face-first into the side of the rink.

"We're down to the two most humiliating moments in sports, and it looks as if we've got ourselves a tie," Jack said. "We've reviewed these two clips over and over, and we can't tell them apart."

Then they replayed Ronald Tripp's retreat side-by-side with Bill Buckner's 1986 World Series error. They put it on an endless loop, first with the correct faces and finally with Ronald Tripp's face and hair on both images.

"You're absolutely right, Jack. I can't tell them apart," Kevin agreed. "All we know is that one of these images is from an important event that affected millions of lives and the course of human history, and the other is from tonight's Republican debate."

Don, Martha, and George Jr. were in their dressing room inside the theater watching the post-debate coverage.

Don and Martha were as excited as the television analysts, while George Jr. sat calmly watching himself on television.

"George, you were brilliant," Martha gushed.

"Thank you," George Jr. answered politely.

"Maybe we're going about this all wrong," Don told Martha. "Maybe we're holding George back. We should turn our boy here loose."

Martha looked at Don, and they both laughed. There was a knock on the door, and an aide stuck his head inside the room. Senator Martin was outside, and she'd asked to speak with George Jr. They didn't let George Jr. speak to anyone, but they couldn't think of an excuse to deter Senator Martin. George Jr. had been ready and willing to fight for her less than an hour ago. They got George Jr. off his chair to greet the Senator. They prayed he wouldn't be too chatty.

Senator Martin entered the small room and immediately walked up to George Jr. and clasped both his hands in her own. Martha looked on nervously, hoping George Jr. didn't start swinging their arms in unison and signing the words to "Ring Around the Rosie."

"George, I wanted to personally thank you for coming to my defense tonight against that heartless blowhard. You were the only one on that stage with enough guts to do it," Senator Martin said.

"George was just telling us how he couldn't stand by and watch what was happening," Don offered. "He was glad to do it."

George Jr. recognized the woman in front of him. "He made you cry. That was bad."

"Maybe he'll think twice next time," Senator Martin said. "I won't be the one calling him out, though. I was mad when I walked off, but I've had enough of this race. I was a long shot anyway, and I'm not happy with the company we're forced to keep."

"You'll be missed," Don said graciously. "I'm afraid there'll be even less opportunity to have a civilized discussion of the issues if you're not in the race."

"The other thing I wanted you to know," Senator Martin told George Jr. "I'll be throwing you my support immediately. You're a good man who can restore some dignity to our party."

"I'm a good boy," George Jr. concurred.

"That's right," Senator Martin laughed. "I forgot—you're a good boy."

The Ronald's dressing room was also watching the post-debate analysis, and they were excited too—but not in a positive way.

"I can't believe Junior torpedoed me that way," Tripp fumed. "I underestimated him. He seemed stiff and disengaged but there's fire in his belly. He's devious too, and I know devious."

"Maybe we should direct a little temptation his way. We'll see if his brain is located in the same organ as his brother's," Malcolm proposed.

The Ronald liked the idea. Men that were intelligent weren't always that intelligent when women were in the mix. Good things usually happened for Tripp every time he paid a woman to remove their clothes. His adult films and Miss Fontaine's encounter with Bill Flowers were two good examples. It was when they got naked for free that the outcome was less favorable. His two ex-wives were proof of that.

"Do it before the next debate. Keep digging for dirt, too. If Bill Flowers were still in the race, we'd be posting a new picture of him at a frat party or strip club every day of the campaign. We don't have any of that on Junior. It's as if he lived in a monastery his whole life. We're missing something," Tripp said.

"Nobody goes to college in France and escapes clean," Malcolm agreed. "But I can't find out any more than he lived in a dormitory and went to class. I have documentation he was there, but I can't find eyewitnesses who saw anything he did. I haven't gotten anything from Flowers' company, either. That makes sense for the current employees, but the ex-employees aren't telling me a thing."

"The next debate is two weeks away, and Super Tuesday is right after that. I'll tear him apart at the next debate, but I need ammunition," Tripp demanded.

"I'll get it. No man can live his life like a ghost," Malcolm promised.

CHAPTER 20

LINCOLN

Don was planning George Jr.'s New Hampshire campaign appearances. There were a number of invitations from schools on the list, as there were in every state, and Don thought one of them might offer the campaign a safe but productive stop. He reviewed the choices with George Sr. and Martha.

"First of all, do we want a high school, a middle school, or an elementary school?" Don asked.

"Elementary school," Martha insisted. "High school is like dragging George in front of a bunch of immature adults with attitude. Middle school is even worse. They're a bunch of punks, and they know they can't be tried as adults. Go with an elementary school, the younger the better."

Don settled on an elementary school in Lincoln, New Hampshire. He needed the media in attendance, or else George Jr.'s attendance would be like the age-old question as to whether a pine tree falling in the New Hampshire forest really made a sound. Without the media on hand to document and publicize it, George Jr.'s appearance never really happened. Because it was an orchestrated event, Don could set the ground rules. He'd allow a single local television film crew with no live audio to film the event, and they had to agree to share it with the other networks. George Jr. would visit a single lucky third-grade class with teacher and students only, no parents.

"That sounds harmless enough," Martha thought aloud. "Why can't you negotiate the same terms for the next debate?"

"I have connections," Don told her. "But I don't think they'll pull the plug on the audio."

The day of the appearance, George Jr., Don, and Martha arrived with two members of the Secret Service. It struck Martha as comical that the Secret Service was on hand to protect George Jr. from a class of third graders. Then she thought about recent events that made some elementary schools famous. It was a sad state that an elementary school was more dangerous than most other public places.

The film crew was already at the school. The Secret Service checked their credentials, and the cameraman and his producer introduced themselves. The school's principal met the party at the front entrance. Mr. Worley had been at the school for decades, and he told the group it was the school's first visit by a presidential candidate. Because of New Hampshire's size and early primary importance, most schools had been visited at least once. He walked the group down the single hallway to the third grade class. It was supposed to be a normal school day, but the classroom doors were all open, and the teachers and students stopped and stared when the group passed each room. Even if they hadn't known who their visitors were, the sight of the camera would have created a stir. George Jr. wanted to stop and gawk at several of the rooms, but Martha kept him moving.

Mr. Worley introduced them to Miss Snow. Miss Snow was in her mid-twenties, and she wore a new dress for the occasion. Mr. Worley took his leave, and Martha relaxed a little bit. The film crew was benign, and Miss Snow was a young and inexperienced hostess. Don reviewed the plan with Miss Snow.

"We really just need some footage of George interacting with your students," Don told her.

"I've seen the President and First Lady reading to a classroom," Miss Snow told him. "We'd be honored if Mr. Flowers wanted to recite one of his favorite books. It would have to be age-appropriate, of course. We have a number of children's classics."

"I think it would be even better if one of your students read to George," Don quickly answered.

George Jr. would certainly enjoy hearing a good children's book; he just couldn't be the one to read it. Don explained that a student explaining their work to George Jr. would also be compelling footage. Don didn't add that the student needed to imagine George Jr. was their younger brother or sister when they explained it.

"We'll start with some spelling," Miss Snow decided.

The class went around the room spelling what would be simple words to a literate adult. George Jr. was attentive to, if not fascinated by, all the information that was flying past him.

"Maybe we should ask Mr. Flowers to spell a word," Miss Snow suggested. "Mr. Flowers, will you spell potato?"

There was no audio rolling, but Martha didn't want George Jr. to pull a Dan Quayle. George Jr. would miss the mark by more than an E.

"Now George, don't you add that E," Martha joked. "Stop at P-O-T-A-T-O."

Miss Snow frowned and said, "Class, Miss Wilson didn't let Mr. Flowers spell his word. What do we tell her?"

"Wait your turn," the class answered in unison.

Martha saw Miss Snow smile at her. She'd underestimated her. She was already a professional teacher. She may not make much money or carry much weight outside her classroom, but inside it she was the empress of her domain. These third graders were her little serfs and oafs, and by extension, so were any adults that wandered into her kingdom.

"Please excuse me," Martha responded as she fought to smile.

The class went on to some simple arithmetic. Martha was relieved Miss Snow didn't call on George Jr. again. She'd already been scolded once. If she'd answered for George Jr. a second time, Miss Snow would have probably had her stand in the hallway with her nose pressed against the wall. Then Miss Snow offered Don the photo opportunity he'd originally asked for. She asked one of her students, who happened to be her prize teacher's pet, to show George Jr. their history board.

"Daniel, show Mr. Flowers our New Hampshire history wall," Miss Snow instructed.

Daniel stood up, and Martha immediately did the same and prompted George Jr. to stand as well. Miss Snow looked surprised, but she didn't ask the class to tell Martha what happened when someone stood up without permission. Daniel led George Jr. and Martha to a bulletin board that was labeled "New Hampshire History" and began to describe the pictures of its people and places. The camera crew positioned themselves so they could film Daniel talking and George Jr. and Martha attentively listening. Daniel told them about New Hampshire's president, Franklin Pierce, and its poets and authors. There were pictures of Nathaniel Hawthorne, Robert Frost, Sarah Josepha Hale, and John Irving. He showed them a picture of an early New Hampshire lumberman.

"I don't know his name," Daniel admitted.

"That's Paul Bunyan," George Jr. informed him. "He has an ox named Babe the Blue Ox."

Daniel hesitated, looked up at George Jr. uncertainly and continued. He showed some more pictures of Franconia Notch, the Flume, and an iconic natural wonder.

"This is the Old Man in the Mountain," Daniel told them. "He's not around anymore."

George Jr. squinted up at the picture. The old man didn't look very healthy when the picture was taken.

"Did he die?" George Jr. asked.

"He fell, George," Martha quickly responded. Then she realized she probably hadn't cleared up all of George Jr.'s confusion and added, "It's a rock formation. The rocks fell down the mountainside."

"That's too bad," George Jr. replied.

"This is a picture of Abraham Lincoln," Daniel soldiered on. "Everyone thinks Lincoln was named after him, but it wasn't. I guess they think that because he's so famous."

"Mr. Flowers is a Republican, and he's running for president," Miss Snow informed the class. "Abraham Lincoln was a Republican too. He's the most famous Republican president ever. Wouldn't you say so, Mr. Flowers?"

"Abraham Lincoln is famous," George Jr. concurred. "He freed the Negroes."

George Jr.'s answer brought Don out of his seat. Miss Snow didn't reprimand Don when he didn't ask permission. She was standing in front of her class with her mouth open. The cameraman was peering around his camera at George Jr. The lens might occasionally distort what he saw, but it couldn't affect what he heard. The producer just stood there and didn't say a word.

"George, look," Martha cried in desperation. "They have goldfish."

Nobody commented on the manner in which George Jr. described Lincoln's defining achievement. George Sr. and Betsey had tried to educate George Jr. as best they could, but some of their teaching materials were no longer endorsed by the National Education Association. Adults understood that you sometimes needed to self-correct things you were taught back in the day when different cultural standards ruled. George Jr. didn't possess these same powers of recalibration.

Mr. Worley met them again on their way out of the school. He thought that, outside of George Jr., the group was subdued. One of the students must have done something that was inappropriate. When Miss Snow wouldn't talk about it later, he knew he was right. The film crew delivered their work but otherwise had no comments on what Mr. Flowers was like. They'd signed on to find good footage, not find trouble.

The last thing Don said to Miss Snow was, "Thank you for having us. We learned a lot about New Hampshire."

"It was a pleasure to meet all of you," Miss Snow returned the pleasantry. Then she added, "My class learned a few new things too."

When they were in the safety of the limo, Martha told Don, "That was a ton of fun. That reminds me, I'm due for a Pap smear. That's my new definition of fun."

"It's going to be hard for a Republican presidential candidate to avoid images of Abraham Lincoln," Don commented.

They received their customary call from Houston. George Sr. called them after practically every appearance. Don told Martha it was because he wanted a head start toward Mexico if the whole thing came down. George Jr. was sitting right next to them, but he was in his own world, watching a mountain stream that flowed beside the roadside.

"A class of third graders," George Sr. said. "That should have been easy."

"Mostly good," Don answered. "It got a little rough at the end."

"For God's sake," Martha fired out as she grabbed the phone. "Senator, I hate a tattler, but your son said the N word."

"He said what?" George Sr. yelled. "He must have learned it from you. Betsey and I don't use that word."

"OK, first off, I haven't taught George any bad words. I may have taught a few new ones to Don. As for the big N word, I won't go all Fuhrman and say I've never used it. I sing along to hip-hop sometimes. But I would never use it to describe another person. Despite growing up in Texas, I'm no racist. I enjoy swimming upstream," Martha spewed. "George used the other N word. He told the class that Lincoln freed the Negroes. I believe it came from you or something you showed him. It might have happened thirty years ago, but it stuck."

George Sr. thought for a few seconds and replied, "Oh God, we used to read this old history primer to him. I'll see if we still have it."

"I'd tell you to burn it," Martha said, "except it's too late to do anything about it. We go to California in a few weeks. You'd better check this primer for the term it uses to describe the people who built the railroads."

"I don't think the term Asian-American was invented before it was written, either. You've got to help George avoid these situations," George Sr. implored.

"Senator," Martha broke to him. "All situations run the risk of becoming these situations."

CHAPTER 21

ZIP IT

The fundraiser was at the White Mountains retreat of a wealthy New Hampshire lumber executive. George Jr. sat next to the man at dinner, and, as usual, Martha sat on the other side of George Jr. Getting a seat as George Jr.'s wingman wasn't easy, though. The executive's wife was a self-taught expert on parties, and she had read that splitting up couples at dinner parties encouraged mingling and enhanced the overall experience. When Martha noticed that she and George Jr. were seated at different tables, she had to act fast.

"I'd really prefer to sit next to George," Martha told her hostess.

"You think you would, but I've read that a good dinner party pulls people out of their comfort zones and causes them to have a better time than they would have ever imagined," the hostess explained eagerly.

"This might sound silly, but George and I have eaten together every meal since he announced his candidacy, and I'm afraid if I break the streak, it might jinx him and cost him the election," Martha explained.

It did sound silly, but this woman could run her social experiments on her own time. The hostess was also a self-taught spiritualist, and she didn't want to risk costing her husband's candidate the election either. George Jr. and Martha sat side-by-side, where Martha could track George Jr.'s every word.

The lumber executive tried to make small talk with George Jr. before he transitioned into his expectations of a good president. Several of his expectations were very specific.

"The American lumber industry is under some severe pressure from the north," the executive began, referring to Canada. "I'm sure you're aware of the subsidies they get from their government. We feel those subsidies allow them to play an unfair game when it comes to costs."

"We should all play nice and fair," George Jr. emphasized.

"That's exactly right. We should all compete on equal ground so the industry is nice and fair," the executive repeated, pleased with George Jr.'s response. "This means we need a combination of tariffs on imported lumber and subsidies for American lumber."

"Lumber builds houses," George Jr. explained.

The lumber executive became a little more guarded. The point was well taken that if Canadian lumber was cheaper, it could benefit the overall US homes market. After all, builders went to Canadian lumber to keep home prices lower and more affordable and to keep their profit margins higher.

"You've made the connection with the housing market," the executive admitted. "But we think we can drive growth in the US lumber industry while sustaining growth in the housing market."

"I want to drive someday," George Jr. replied.

That was Martha's cue to step in and help steer the conversation for a while. The executive wasn't quite sure what George Jr. wanted to drive, but he hoped it was American lumber. Martha assured him that George Jr. was a friend of all American industry and that he understood it was important to balance the considerations of both the overall housing market and the lumber industry.

After the dinner, George Jr. and Martha walked the room and rubbed palms with the New Hampshire economic elite. George Jr. was always pleased to meet new people, and he was never afraid to show them. His energetic handshake was always followed by an enthusiastic, "Pleased to meet you."

They had one near miss when an older couple walked up and introduced themselves as Mr. and Mrs. Butz. The husband was Kevin, and his wife's name was Sylvia. Martha shook their hands, but George Jr. just began to laugh. Martha might have been as clueless as Kevin and Sylvia a few short months ago, but she had gotten to know George Jr., and he had just been told a naughty word. You used the word "butts" to insult someone. He'd never heard someone refer to themselves as butts.

"Oh, George, now I get it," Martha recovered. "George said something funny, and I just got it. He has such a complex sense of humor. George, be polite and say hello to Kevin and Sylvia."

George Jr. got a serious look on his face. It was important to always be polite, even to a pair of butts. George Jr. gave them a hearty handshake and a "pleased to meet you" and all was well again with the world.

Martha was a superhuman watchdog, but she was still human. She'd had several glasses of water and had allowed herself a glass of wine, and now she needed to use the powder room. There were hours of fundraiser to go, so she couldn't hold out. She told George Jr. she had to use the bathroom, and as part of their routine, she made sure to check if he had to go too. George Jr. had never had an accident in her presence, but Senator Flowers and Betsey told her it was always a good idea to periodically check with him. George Jr. seemed to appreciate the suggestion, and he followed Martha to the bathroom. Martha let George Jr. use it first, and she gave him detailed instructions when he finished.

"Wait for me here," Martha ordered. "Don't go back to the party without me."

Porn actress Lola Fontaine, AKA political groupie Dorothy Landers, had been shadowing Martha and George Jr. all evening. She felt pretty clever after she'd bribed one of the waitstaff fifty dollars to seat her next to George Jr. at dinner, but when she went to the table to seat herself, the name card had been changed to Martha Wilson. She didn't try to get her money back. Her sponsor, whoever it might be, had already paid out five thousand to get her a plate somewhere in the room. She'd have to find another opportunity to make contact. When Martha went into the bathroom, Dorothy saw her first opportunity. The Wilson bitch clung to George Jr. tighter than a dryer sheet on a polyester pant leg. Dorothy walked up to George Jr., reached over to touch his arm, and smiled up at him like she was saying yes to a three-way in one of her films.

"Are these the restrooms?" she asked.

George Jr. was thrilled to receive a question he could readily answer. He'd just flushed the toilet a minute ago.

"The bathroom is there," George Jr. pointed at the closed door. "My friend is in there."

"Your friend is in there?" Dorothy asked coyly. "I understand she's more than a friend."

"My best friend," George Jr. clarified.

"I can be friendly too," Dorothy purred.

Her hand slipped down George Jr.'s arm and brushed along the top of George Jr.'s belt. George Jr. immediately took notice.

"My fly is zipped," George Jr. informed her. "I always check."

Dorothy laughed, and George Jr. laughed with her. "Why don't we take a walk?" Dorothy suggested. "I can help inspect your fly somewhere that's a little quieter."

"That's a good idea," George Jr. agreed. "It falls down sometimes."

Dorothy couldn't believe how quickly things were moving. George Jr.'s older brother had been a testosterone-infused horndog, but he'd been cagey for at least the first hour. If she could steer the younger brother into an empty bedroom, mission number two might be accomplished in the next ten minutes. But then the mission turned sour.

Martha opened the bathroom door and saw George Jr. standing next to an enormous pair of fake breasts wearing a low-cut gown, bleach-blonde hair, and too much makeup and perfume. The pair of breasts had their hands all over George Jr. Martha's hunches were always good, and she formed an immediate first impression. Even if this was some wealthy donor's trophy wife, the trophy couldn't exactly tell her husband why Martha was less than pleasant when they first met. Besides, the campaign didn't need the money this badly.

"I'm all set," Martha said coldly. It really was difficult staring into the woman's eyes without letting her gaze stray lower. "We don't want to keep your husband or date waiting, do we?"

Dorothy's smile evaporated. She'd needed to move George Jr. upstairs faster. There just wasn't enough time. A full sex scene might be less than a minute's worth of film time, but there was a lot of preparation and editing that went into the final product. Dorothy stuck with her favorite line.

"So nice to meet you, Mr. Flowers," Dorothy said politely. "You've got my vote."

On the way back to the main room, Martha asked George Jr. some simple questions about the woman he was talking to. She wasn't happy with his answers.

"I showed her the bathroom," George Jr. said proudly. "Then she helped check my fly."

Martha kept a watchful eye for the enormous pair but the look in Martha's eye had spooked Dorothy. Dorothy snuck out of the bathroom and called her ride. A rented Mercedes pulled up to the entrance of the retreat, and a doorman ushered Dorothy into the vehicle's backseat.

"It's early," the deliveryman greeted her. "Don't tell me he cashed in his chips this fast. Did you do him in the bathroom, or what?"

"His girlfriend sticks to him closer than the Secret Service," Dorothy complained. "She's a lot scarier, too. I could've done him in the bathroom, except she was already in there. This may be a two-person job. You'll have to do her so I can do him."

"It might be easier to kill him," the deliveryman speculated.

"Sorry, that's not my area of expertise—unless I count that old guy who bought it when I was working the geezer-with-hot-young-girl genre," Dorothy said. "I just need five minutes of alone time with him. The setting doesn't matter. He was ready to drop them and rock them. He kept talking about how I could play with his fly. He's worse than his brother."

"I'll let my people know it didn't work out tonight but that the problem was logistics, not a lack of interest," the deliveryman explained. "You'll get another run at him."

"Five minutes is all I need," Dorothy repeated.

That was less time than it took for a sound and lighting check in the industry. She just needed a thirty-second segment with George Jr.'s face, and anything else she could shoot that was under his clothing.

CHAPTER 22

LIVE FREE OR DIE

The Ronald was also in New Hampshire, delivering his vision for America's return to its rightful place as the world's undisputed military power. The audience was a friendly gathering of military veterans and their spouses. The Ronald was dressed for the occasion. His wardrobe included an American flag patterned tie, an American flag lapel pin, American flag cufflinks, and an American flag belt buckle. If the speech had been scheduled in a locker room, The Ronald would have worn American flag boxer shorts.

He had just run through an abbreviated version of America's illustrious military history. That history left behind a wake of dead Frenchmen, Englishmen, Mexicans, Spaniards, Germans, Italians, Japanese, Chinese, Koreans, and Native Americans crushed under the wheels of our military machine. It might have been easier to list major countries we *hadn't* fought at one time or another. The audience was northern, so the Civil War was mentioned briefly. If The Ronald had been in the South, he would have referred to it as the War of Repression. Korea was tricky, but The Ronald counted it as a win. We'd ultimately saved South Korea from communism and had kept them communist-free for more than half a century.

"We were the world's only undisputed, undefeated champions," The Ronald continued, "until we discovered a worthless, crappy jungle in Asia called Vietnam. I know a number of you were there, and you've got even worse things to say about it. You're angry, and you should be. It's not one of America's best moments. You served your country faithfully, and in return you were sold out by your government and some of its citizens."

The Ronald received vigorous applause. Some of those Vietnam veterans might have once been young hippies that fought with peace signs on their fatigues, but they were grandparents now. The Baby Boomers had grown up and grown gray.

"There was a man of vision in 1964 who some call the father of the conservative movement. He lost his bid for president, and it couldn't have happened at a worse time," Tripp continued. "I was too young to vote, but I remember that election. What we ended up with was Lyndon Johnson and his communist social agenda and his mismanagement of the war. I won't speak of the social disaster he caused in the 1960s, but we're going to roll back a lot of those laws and policies he saddled us with. I will speak of the war, though. If Barry Goldwater had been elected president, Vietnam would still be a democracy, and America would still be undefeated."

The veterans were more accustomed to cheering for Eisenhower or Reagan, but they could cheer for the concept of victory in Vietnam.

"The difference between Goldwater and Johnson is the same difference we have today between my primary opponents and me," The Ronald explained. "Goldwater understood that once you're at war, you have to win. He was willing to use all our resources to do so. I promise not to pull America into an unnecessary war. But if we fight, we'll always fight to win. This country needs a president who isn't afraid of the price of victory."

Tripp was subtly referring to Goldwater's willingness to use America's nuclear arsenal against a foe that did not possess nuclear capabilities or pose a nuclear threat. It could be argued that Truman established a precedent, but it didn't seem fair to compare the situation at the end of World War II to the situation in Vietnam. The American people decided they'd rather not find out whether or not Barry Goldwater would actually go ahead and nuke North Vietnam until its jungles became a desert. There is a belief he might have, especially as the war grew more prolonged and more unwinnable.

Tripp was telling the crowd he was offering the country the same choice it had turned down when Goldwater was defeated. Total war in the era of nuclear weapons was a crazy man's game. There had been plenty of crazy men who had tried to provoke the United States even though it was a nuclear power. The problem was the United States hadn't elected a second crazy man as president and put him in charge of our nuclear arsenal. The Ronald was making it clear that he didn't plan to come in second in any contest for crazy. If he were provoked, he'd launch first and ask questions later.

"There are countries in the Middle East today that remind me of Vietnam," Tripp told his audience. "They're small, insignificant wastelands, but somehow they're a thorn in our side. They sponsor terrorism and destabilize the entire region, if not the world. They make Americans unsafe. They hate our guts. We need to stop talking about this problem and start fixing it."

The crowd stood and applauded. The Ronald was edging toward fighting words, and Americans were always ready for a good fight. They had no problem if The Ronald took a bite out of the Arab world. Some were better than others, but who could tell the good guys from the bad?

"New Hampshire has a motto, 'live free or die,'" The Ronald told them. "I propose we adopt a new motto, 'if they die, we'll live free.' If we erase terrorism, we'll live in a freer world. These places already look like the nuclear test zones outside of Las Vegas. We shouldn't be afraid to scorch a little desert."

The Ronald was always mindful of economic impact. He had developed a policy he called his military-economic synergy plan. It was a combination plan to rebuild the military and eliminate welfare.

"I'll double the conventional military because sometimes you need a hammer, but sometimes you need more directed tools," The Ronald opened. "As our military gets healthy again, I'll eliminate the blight of welfare. I'm not talking about cutting off the old or the sick, but if you are a citizen of this country and you're fit for duty, don't expect the federal government to take care of you for free. From now on, if you expect a government paycheck, you'd better be willing to march for it."

The crowd loved the sound of it, especially since they were all past the point where they were fit to march. If a slacker grandchild or two was impacted, they could live with that. In a way, Tripp was modeling an army similar to the one that lost in Vietnam. The wealthy stayed in college and got deferred. The poor who couldn't go to college got drafted. Some of their names ended up on a monument wall in Washington.

"Live free or die" was a motto that was intended to be a battle cry for personal choice over tyranny. It wasn't intended to be a motto for an outside power that demanded the world operate under its definition of democracy or perish. By changing the order, The Ronald had altered its use and meaning. Terrorism had become such a bogeyman that some of democracy's finer points were turning into luxuries and not rights. If slogans could get the American people to endorse Tripp's vision of the practical dirty work that was necessary, he could come up with a hundred more.

CHAPTER 23

USING THE BED

Secret Service Agent Webster stood outside George Jr.'s Iowa hotel room. It was almost midnight, and the candidate was inside for the night. Webster could faintly hear the sound of the television. This wasn't unusual. Webster was frequently on the 10 p.m. to 6 a.m. watch, and Mr. Flowers slept with the television on all night, every night.

The girlfriend was asleep in her room to his right, and the campaign manager was in the room on the left. Webster was aware that the Flowers campaign insinuated that the candidate and his girlfriend didn't sleep together. From what Webster witnessed, this wasn't just conservative abstinence rhetoric. Webster didn't know what they did off the campaign trail, but on it, Martha Wilson and Mr. Flowers always booked separate rooms, and there was no late-night wandering back and forth between them.

The Secret Service enjoyed guarding George Jr. He was always friendly, and he acted as if they were just as important to him as everyone else he met. He was guarded, though—he didn't share any of what had to be an endless stream of deep insights and thoughts. And

Don Chambers and Martha Wilson seemed to go out of their way to isolate George Jr. from his protectors.

The phone in the room rang and awoke George Jr. from his deep sleep. He hesitated. If a phone rang at home, his mother, father, or a servant always answered it. Recently, Don, Martha, or a staff member answered. George Jr. knew how to answer a phone, though. He'd seen other people do it. George Jr. decided to pick up the phone and deliver a hearty hello.

"Well, hello there," he heard a female voice say. "This is Dorothy from New Hampshire. I'm the one who helped you with your zipper. Are you alone?"

George Jr. was a little slow to recognize the voice, but he remembered a lady who kept talking about his zipper. She smiled a lot and smelled nice. George Jr. told her he remembered her and that he was alone.

"I'm at the hotel. I was hoping I could come up and visit," Dorothy explained.

"I'd like that a lot," George Jr. told her.

He was alone, and he was wide-awake now. It would be nice to have a friend to play with.

"You'll need to tell the Secret Service agent I'm coming up, or else he won't let me in," Dorothy instructed George Jr.

"You mean the man at the door?" George Jr. asked.

"If that's what you call him. I'll be up in five minutes," Dorothy said.

George Jr. did as Dorothy asked. He went to the door, opened it, and peeked outside. The man in the hall was standing where George Jr. thought he would be. Webster heard the door and looked back to see what George Jr. needed.

"My friend Dorothy is visiting," George Jr. told Webster and began to close the door.

"Should I allow her in the room, sir?" Agent Webster asked for confirmation.

"Yes, please," George Jr. answered.

Webster arched his eyebrows but otherwise remained fixed at his post. This assignment had just gone from routine to spicy. Political infidelity was not unique in the annals of Secret Service history, but Webster had never heard an account where the candidate's girlfriend was asleep in the next room. If Martha Wilson walked in on George Jr. when he was messing around with another woman and she lost control, was he supposed to protect the candidate and shoot the girlfriend? Maybe Dorothy was an unlucky campaign staffer who was being summoned to practice campaign speeches because the candidate was experiencing insomnia.

Webster heard the elevator bell sound from down the hallway, and he turned for a visual on the intruder. The woman he saw approaching didn't look like she was visiting to rehearse any speeches, unless it was an acceptance speech at the Adult Film Awards. This was one of those times where it was difficult to maintain that "just the facts, ma'am," Jack Webb neutral expression.

"May I help you, ma'am?" Agent Webster queried the woman as she approached.

"My name is Dorothy," she said. "Mr. Flowers is expecting me."

"Yes, ma'am," Webster replied.

With that, Dorothy was in the room. The television was on, and George Jr. stood to greet her, wearing a pair of striped pajamas.

"Hello, Dorothy," George Jr. said a little too loudly.

"*Ssshhh,* let's not wake the neighborhood," Dorothy cautioned. "We don't want any company."

"Sorry," George Jr. said in his inside voice.

Dorothy took off her brooch with the camera in it and placed it on the dresser facing the bed. In a few minutes, she'd have a new video to add to the Flowers family collection. George Jr. was younger, a little taller, and fitter than Bill, but they both had male-model good looks. These were things that made the job a little more enjoyable. Dorothy walked over to George Jr., stood on her toes, and kissed him on the lips.

"Why don't you take your clothes off and get more comfortable?" she suggested.

George Jr. thought a kiss meant a peck on the cheek from his mother. The request to take his clothes off was also foreign to him. There was only one reason he ever got naked.

"Do I have to take a bath?" George Jr. asked apprehensively.

"Why, are you a dirty boy?" Dorothy asked. "I'd suggest we take a shower together, but it's late and it might get too noisy."

"I like baths better," George Jr. informed her.

"I like the way your mind works, but let's use the bed instead," Dorothy said.

Dorothy took George Jr. by the hand and led him toward the bed. He followed her obediently. For a man who publicly pledged his love to Martha Wilson at every opportunity, he didn't waste much time on foreplay. Dorothy began to roll down her dress straps so she could peel it off before crawling in with him. Rather than ogle Dorothy or help to undress her, George Jr. took a running leap and jumped up onto the middle of the bed. For a second, Dorothy imagined she was in for some type of sexual gymnastics. But then George Jr. started to bounce on the bed like it was a trampoline.

"What are you doing?" Dorothy said a little too loudly herself.

"I'm using the bed," George Jr. said with a broad smile on his face.

Dorothy held up her hands, motioning George Jr. to stop jumping. He slowed but he didn't stop. Instead, he jumped off the bed and landed on the room's floor with a loud thud.

"For your sake, you'd better be here to steal something," said a loud and angry voice from the doorway.

Martha was already upset that George Jr. had woken her up. The awkward conversation with Agent Webster before she got into the room didn't improve her disposition. When she saw the bleach-blonde with the large breasts from the fundraiser with her dress straps down, ready for action, it was code red.

"I'm sorry, I must have the wrong room," Dorothy muttered as she pulled her straps up and shuffled toward the door. Martha was planted in her path.

"Where are you going?" George Jr. shouted to Dorothy. "I thought we were going to play on the bed."

"You have the wrong room, all right," Martha seethed. "First I see you in New Hampshire, and now you're here in Iowa. Are you some kind of political groupie skank?"

"I made a mistake," Dorothy apologized.

"You bet you did," Martha went on. "This is two strikes. For the third strike, I either sock you myself or have you arrested. Maybe we'll do both. Are we clear?"

"You won't see me again," Dorothy promised.

Martha stepped aside, and Dorothy practically ran down the hallway to the elevator. By this time, Don had joined them. He was speaking with an uncomfortable Agent Webster to find out what had happened. Martha made it clear to George Jr. that he couldn't let people into his room without their permission. George Sr. and Betsey were his parents, but Don and Martha were like parents when the senator and his wife weren't around. Martha walked into the hallway and interrupted Don to let Agent Webster know that she was putting the Secret Service on notice.

"Tell your fellow agents that unless they want to transfer from this detail to monument protection, you'd better keep strangers away from George. He was"—Martha hesitated. "He was teaching this person tonight a lesson, but it could be dangerous. I'm not talking about guarding the Lincoln Memorial or the Washington Monument, either. If you're not careful, you'll find yourself keeping pigeons and crack addicts off the statues in Lafayette Park."

Don directed Martha back into George Jr.'s room. There were guests on the floor trying to sleep. George Jr. was sitting solemnly on the bed. An adult was angry, so he knew he'd done something wrong.

"Look at this. That whore left her jewelry behind," Martha shouted. She lifted the piece to examine it and said to Don, "Feel how heavy this is."

Don took the piece and was surprised by its bulk. He looked at the odd design in the middle of the brooch. Small petals surrounded a single large glass centerpiece. Don looked at the centerpiece more carefully.

"Interesting," Don said to Martha. "I need someone I know to look at this."

The deliveryman picked up Lola, AKA Dorothy, in front of the hotel. He'd been sitting in his car parked across the street, watching the monitor attached to the receiver that was attached to the CD recorder. When he saw Dorothy fleeing the room, it was time to go.

"So, we got a grown man jumping on a bed and the schnoz of his campaign manager after he discovers the camera you left behind," the deliveryman commented. "I gotta tell you, Lola, it ain't your best work."

"When that crazy bitch showed up, I panicked," Dorothy admitted.

"They're going to figure this out, and we didn't want that to happen until they got the DVD," the deliveryman added. "I think we're done here."

"I'm done here," Dorothy told him. "I'm not finding out what happens if there's a third time."

Malcolm and Ronald had another tough session. They had been optimistic that Lola Fontaine would bring down a second member of the Flowers family. That hadn't happened, and now the Flowers campaign knew George Jr. was a target.

"It's like he knew what Lola was up to and humiliated her to have some fun," Malcolm lamented.

"It was too easy. You should have known something was wrong. He's too smart for this. He isn't like his brother," The Ronald shot back. "Can he pin this on us? He's like Sherlock Holmes."

"There's no way to prove it," Malcolm assured Tripp. "We've decommissioned Lola, and we obviously can't do the same thing with somebody else. He's bulletproof."

"I'd hoped Lola could strip the petals off two Flowers," Tripp complained.

Don's technical advisor examined the brooch the next morning and quickly got back to Don.

"It's a camera, pretty standard model," he told Don. "It has a wireless feature, so the signal was probably picked up by a receiver somewhere else and recorded."

Don had a hunch. Martha watched as Don loaded a DVD into the DVD player. Don had convinced Bill that they shouldn't destroy the disc he'd gotten from the deliveryman and that Bill couldn't keep it at his houses in Houston or DC. If Maryann ever discovered it, all their lives would be affected. Bill had given the DVD to Don, as long as Don promised Bill he'd destroy it after the election. Don was glad they'd kept it.

The screen came on, and it showed Bill in an apartment bedroom fully clothed. A second later, a woman with big blonde hair came into the picture and kissed Bill. When the woman turned back to the camera, it spared Martha the prospect of seeing more of Bill than she'd cared to.

"That's her," Martha affirmed. "She didn't even bother to come up with a second fake name. She's one heck of a secret agent."

"George Sr. said all along that her talents wouldn't work on George," Don said. "Let's hope he's this right about the election."

"George let her into his room," Martha reminded Don. "That's still dangerous. If she had gotten naked, we'd have had some explaining to do. Is the Secret Service up to speed on unauthorized visitors? If we can't depend on them, you and I will have to take turns sleeping in his room. Then we'll have a scandal without Dorothy's help."

"He won't be alone again," Don promised her. "If all else fails, I'll take the camera we found and put it in his room. It'll be like the panda cam at the zoo."

CHAPTER 24

BUILDING BLOCKS

Martha put off visiting her parents as long as she could. The team had flown back and forth from Texas to Iowa and New Hampshire, but she had been back in Houston for several two-to three-day periods. Martha always told her parents via email that she was out of town. As much as she wanted to, though, she knew she couldn't avoid them until after the election. Martha always knew it would take a special man to spend a day with Chuck and Peggy. George Jr. was extra special, though, and Martha needed to make sure her parents didn't see it. She arranged a visit for Sunday lunch at her parent's house. She lied when she told her mother they had to catch a plane to Des Moines at Houston International at three.

Transportation was always the easy part. George Jr. had a limo and two Secret Service agents to bring him anywhere he needed to go. The Secret Service might have anticipated a routine drop-off and pickup, but when they turned down Martha's parents' street, it looked as if they were throwing a block party.

"My mother invited all the neighbors," Martha shook her head. "George, it looks like you're getting a welcome party."

"A party for me?" George Jr. asked. "Is it my birthday?"

Chuck and Peggy were standing in their front yard surrounded by nearly everyone in the neighborhood. They were having a dispute about the location of a new fence with the Johnsons next door, so they weren't invited. Some of the neighbors were holding signs that read "Congratulations Martha and George" and "Welcome President Flowers." The Secret Service pulled in front of the house, opened the car door to let George Jr. and Martha out of the car, and watched the crowd for weapons.

"Mom," Martha greeted Peggy. "I thought we talked about a quiet lunch so you could meet George. Look at this mob. I'm surprised you didn't invite the press."

"We called the *Evening Courier,* but they didn't believe me," Peggy complained. "We'll send them some of our own photos."

Martha had no choice but to introduce George Jr. to the neighbors. He gave each a hearty hello and a hearty handshake. Martha supposed George Jr. could always use the practice on live subjects. Martha recognized Bucky Bristol, the neighbor from across the street. Bucky owned a large car dealership in Houston. It was a nice neighborhood, but when Martha was young, Bucky had ruffled some feathers. He took advantage of Houston's lax zoning laws and showed his overflow car inventory on his front yard. Martha had another memory of Bucky. She'd caught him lurking outside her bedroom window when she was in high school. Martha told Chuck, and when her father confronted Bucky, he claimed he was looking for his lost dog. It was a credible excuse, except Bucky was the only man in Texas who'd never owned a dog. Bucky was never one of Martha's favorites.

When Martha tepidly introduced George Jr. to Bucky, Bucky told her, "You be sure to invite old Bucky to that White House wedding."

Martha took a deep breath, smiled, and promised, "Sure, Bucky. You'll get one of the first invitations."

Bucky would receive that invitation to George Jr. and Martha's wedding the same day he won a free trip aboard a flying pig and got to play ring toss onto a unicorn's horn. These events all had equal weighting in the probability table inside Martha's head.

They finally got inside the house, and the crowd outside dispersed and returned to their homes.

"So, George, can I fix you a drink?" Chuck asked his future son-in-law.

"Do you have any iced tea?" Martha quickly answered her father. "I'll have some too."

Chuck looked at his daughter to make sure he'd heard correctly. Chuck had been a solid engineer before he'd retired from NASA, but bourbon had gotten him through some difficult projects. Martha usually helped him damage a bottle of his best when she visited.

"So, George, are you a drinker?" Chuck wondered.

"I like milk and soda pop," George Jr. answered cheerfully.

Chuck recognized the manic cheerfulness of a where-fun-goes-to-die religious nut. He felt as if he was being judged. A drink now and then didn't make someone a bad person. As long as you could make it to work by the next business day and didn't break any major commandments, what did it hurt? A simple no would have been a sufficient answer.

Peggy poured four iced teas, and they proceeded to the part of the visit that Martha was dreading. They adjourned to the living room to chit-chat.

"We want to know everything," Peggy began. "Tell us how you two met."

Martha couldn't tell her mother everything, but she could tell her everything she had made up with Don. The news that George Jr. was Martha's boss was news to her parents. It conflicted with some of what they thought they knew.

"We're not trying to cause trouble, but we thought your boss was older," Peggy said. "You always referred to him as the old man, or the senator."

"George is a few years older than I am," Martha struggled. "The senator is George's dad. I worked for him when George and I started to date."

"You must have worked on some great projects," Chuck told George Jr. "You're the biggest commercial real estate builder in Houston."

"I like building blocks," George Jr. answered. "Big blocks. I make tall buildings with them."

This just sounded like bragging. Chuck could have used a bourbon.

Peggy made them sandwiches to go with the iced tea. They were prosciutto and cheese with arugula. George Jr. preferred bologna and cheese, and his mother usually cut off the crusts. Martha nervously eyed George Jr. as he looked at and then sniffed the sandwich before he took a bite out of it. Martha was worried he'd spit out the arugula, but he ate it without incident.

"So when is the wedding?" Peggy demanded.

"We'll wait until after the election. We haven't decided on the exact date. There's obviously a lot of uncertainty in George's schedule until we find out if he wins," Martha explained.

"Well, I hope you invite the whole family," Peggy told Martha. "You've got a lot of cousins, and it isn't fair if the guests are all heads of state and famous people."

Martha had a brief picture of some of her hillbilly cousins in the White House spitting chaw into a Ming vase or handling some artifact from George Washington. She shuddered—then remembered it was all fantasy.

"Mom, when George and I get married, you can invite anyone you like," Martha assured Peggy. Peggy could travel to Washington for the wedding next to Bucky on the same flying pig.

Martha's mother asked about wedding colors, invitations, and a number of other irrelevant wedding details. Surprisingly, Chuck wanted to talk about the wedding too.

"You know, the bride's parents traditionally pay for everything," Chuck said. "I don't exactly know what we're in for here, though. We have some money put aside, but I don't know that we've got a White House wedding budget."

The truth was that Chuck and Peggy had planned to spend Chuck's retirement savings on themselves. They'd long since assumed their forty-something daughter was either never getting married, or she'd go the city hall route if she did.

"Relax, Dad," Martha told Chuck. "I promise you won't have to pay for a thing."

Chuck and Peggy didn't learn much about George Jr. He was a great listener, but he didn't talk as much as they thought a politician would. George Jr. liked milk and soda pop, he enjoyed lunch, and he liked their horse picture in the living room. The time passed quicker than Martha could have hoped.

"George, Martha's father and I enjoyed meeting you today so much. You've got our blessing, and you've got our vote," Peggy said as they were leaving.

"Vote for George," George Jr. replied automatically.

"Always campaigning," Martha added with an awkward laugh.

"I hope you come back often," Peggy said. "I can't believe my little girl is getting married."

Peggy started to cry, and George Jr. noticed it.

"I'm sorry," George Jr. told Peggy.

"Don't be silly, George. You've got nothing to be sorry about," Peggy laughed as she cried. "These are tears of joy."

George Jr. didn't really understand tears of joy, but he smiled and shook Chuck's hand again. Peggy hugged her daughter, hesitated, and hugged the potential future president. Peggy didn't realize she was hugging a hugger until George Jr. squeezed her back harder.

Chuck looked on, and his opinion of George Jr. softened. George Jr. was affectionate, and he'd never seen his daughter put so much effort into making somebody else look so good in front of her parents. Martha's fiancé was richer and smarter than they were, and he knew it. But he was a good man once you got to know him. He wasn't the kind of son-in-law that drank beer with you at a barbeque, but he was the kind that took good care of your daughter.

Martha was becoming famous, but it looked like she was a winner even if George Jr. didn't win the election.

CHAPTER 25

LEGALLY STUPID

The campaign team spent more time in Iowa and New Hampshire than they did back home in Texas in the month before the Iowa caucus and the New Hampshire primary. They celebrated in Des Moines with their supporters when George Jr. beat Tripp by a narrow three-point margin in the caucus.

"Those two steps back were all we needed," George Sr. boasted to Don.

George Sr. was referring to the debate that demonstrated The Ronald wasn't as unflappable as he tried to make the public believe. In addition to being a master debater, George Jr. had shown considerable skill at riding tractors, petting roosters, and calling hogs. These skills must have impressed Iowa Republican voters, because they felt it meant George Jr. possessed the skills necessary to be their next president.

"It's important to be the frontrunner," Don lectured George Sr. "Momentum builds on itself, and losing collapses on itself. I've seen an early loss kill a campaign before it even gets rolling."

George Jr. delivered what might have been the most succinct victory speech ever delivered in presidential politics.

"Thank you, Iowa," he managed.

Don and several prominent local Republican politicians followed George Jr. with more thanks and predictions of the great victories ahead. If George Jr. was proclaiming victory, it left three other candidates with the unpleasant task of conceding defeat. Senator Ramirez and Governor Hastings weren't as celebratory as George Jr., but they optimistically thanked the Iowa voters and their local campaigners. Ronald Tripp also eventually conceded, but in his own special manner.

"I'm disappointed, not in myself, but in the voters of Iowa," Tripp stated. "You'll have a chance to redeem yourselves in November."

The Ronald was much more complimentary to the voters of New Hampshire a week later. His rhetoric about dying and living free made the Granite State a piece of Tripp's rock collection. He won by nearly five points over George Jr.

"It's a conservative state, and it's near Tripp's New York base," Don rationalized. "We shouldn't get too excited."

"We've got almost ten days until the next primary and almost three weeks until Super Tuesday. That's a long time for voters to dwell on this," George Sr. reminded him.

Super Tuesday was when over a dozen states were scheduled to hold their primaries and caucuses. The only events before then were in South Carolina and Nevada. They needed to be everywhere at once, but they started in South Carolina. George Jr. and Martha gave speeches in Columbia and Charleston. Tripp was in South Carolina the same day, holding a rally in Myrtle Beach. George Sr., Don, and Martha caught Tripp's speech that night on the news.

"South Carolina is a state that understands federal government oppression better than most," Tripp declared. "You took the most aggressive action against it, too. I applaud you for it. I don't think the government has the right to dictate our lives for us."

The Confederate applause was strong. The Republicans of South Carolina felt the same way as the Republican voters of New Hampshire. This promise of personal freedom sounded promising.

"The federal government can't tell us what the colors of our flag should be that we fly above our own capitol. That extends to our individual freedoms, too," Tripp continued.

The defense of the flying of the stars and bars above the capitol building drew a tremendous cheer. African-Americans might not have agreed, but they weren't in attendance.

"Let's talk about laws that rob us of our personal liberty," Tripp said. "They tell us you can't ride a motorcycle without a helmet or drive a car unless you wear a seatbelt. You can't text or use a phone when you drive. These are choices that should be up to you. These are the laws I'll overturn when I'm president."

"Am I the only one hearing this?" Martha asked.

"He wants to make sure it isn't a crime to be stupid," George Sr. clarified. "He must be afraid he'll be arrested unless he figures out how to decriminalize it."

"We're the only country that doesn't allow promising medical treatments because the government forbids them," Tripp went on.

"That might actually be a valid point," Martha conceded.

"And what right does the government have to poison our drinking water? We've got to stop fluoridation," Tripp implored.

"And he's back," Martha sighed.

"I'm not sure anyone under sixty is even going to know what fluoridation is," Don stated.

"It's a communist plot," George Sr. said. "Watch *Dr. Strangelove* again."

The Ronald continued to explain to the masses the many ways in which the government systematically ruined their lives. The speech would have been longer if Malcolm hadn't talked Tripp out of a couple more examples. He had planned to tell the group moonshining was a right and that the government shouldn't interfere if a feller wanted a little taste of shine or to share a favorite recipe with a friend, a neighbor, or a stranger who paid the right price. Malcolm pointed out it would be difficult to advocate moonshine but condemn marijuana.

"Moonshine is American," Tripp argued. "Marijuana is subversive."

"There's a fine line," Malcolm argued. "Some would claim marijuana saves eyesight, but moonshine takes it away. Leave it alone."

Tripp also wanted to take issue with the new laws that required adult film actors to wear condoms.

"The actors don't want to wear them, and I sure as hell don't want to see them," Tripp complained. "Plus, it's costing me money. I'm losing ground to the markets where the sex flows free and easy."

"I don't know that the voters of South Carolina are going to sympathize with a bunch of porn actors from LA," Malcolm told Tripp.

"You'd be surprised how much business I do in South Carolina," Tripp explained.

"What they watch in private and what they say in public could be very different," Malcolm said. "Leave that alone too."

Malcolm had also advised against reviving the attack on fluoridated water. He explained most Americans had moved beyond that fear and that white, cavity-free teeth were socially desirable now. Malcolm hinted that he had no desire to advocate crooked, rotten teeth that would mimic his fellow Englishmen back in the United Kingdom. Tripp wasn't willing to leave this one alone.

"Forget it," Tripp dismissed Malcolm. "I'm banning fluoridation. It's my tribute to Barry Goldwater."

CHAPTER 26

COOTIE GERM

The morning campaign stop was at a rally outside the Alamo in San Antonio. George Jr. had a comfortable lead in Texas, but it was a Super Tuesday state. The mayor made a speech in which he swore the city's allegiance to its native son, George Milhous Flowers Jr. Don followed with a brief speech and introduction that mixed one part political science professor with one part cheerleader. When the time came for George Jr. to stand up, walk to the microphone, and acknowledge the applause, he wasn't alone.

"George, have you ever seen such a fine-looking, excited group of Americans?" Martha spoke into the microphone. She and George Jr. stood on stage holding hands. "George normally does all the talking, but he's a true gentleman and he's graciously allowed me a turn. Now, y'all are smart enough to know that a man can be smart and strong and still be a true gentleman. That is one thing that differentiates George from at least one of the other candidates."

The crowd roared with this thinly veiled slap at Ronald Tripp. Tripp's wife had that European accent, and she had probably never eaten barbeque or drank a Lone Star beer. Martha was pure Texas, and she was on friendly turf.

"We appreciate this turnout and all your continued support," Martha continued. "There are people out there who are asking why we're even here. They tell us we've got Texas sewed up. Spend your time up north in, say, New York, where it might be closer. Believe me, we'll spend plenty of time in New York. In fact, we've got a big rally planned next week across the street from the Tripp Universal Hospitality Hotel. But we're here today to say that we'll never forget Texas. When George gets elected, get ready for lower taxes, lower unemployment, and the greatest wedding the White House has ever seen."

The crowd cheered for each promise, and the women in the audience exploded at the mention of the nuptials. They could already envision this country's version of a royal wedding, and they wouldn't have to stay up all night to watch it take place in a European time zone.

"George, we're going to get married in the White House," Martha prompted. "How good is that?"

"Better than Christmas," George Jr. instinctively responded.

Martha's nod told him he'd given the correct answer, and he looked down at her pockets expectantly, waiting for his piece of candy. Anyone that noticed assumed he was so in love he was always checking out his future bride. The crowd continued to applaud and cheer. George Jr. had only said three words, but they had enough information already. Lower taxes and unemployment and a wedding ticked all their boxes. They were such a handsome couple.

Don walked out with George Jr. and Martha and thanked the audience for attending. He motioned them away from the microphone and delivered some news to Martha.

"There's a car meeting us on the street. These people aren't going anywhere until we leave, and we're going to have to walk through them to get out of here," Don explained.

"My God, that's a suicide mission. The press and other people are going to try to talk with him and ask him questions. If he doesn't say anything, it looks bad, and if he does, we're dead," Martha answered, trying to stay calm.

"The police and Secret Service are making a corridor for us to pass through," Don said. "We've got no choice. We have the flight to Dallas, and we can't stay on this stage for hours and hours."

"That might be better," Martha hissed, but she began to move off the stage holding George Jr.'s hand. He could walk and smile at the same time, but she wasn't as sure he could stay silent.

George Jr. quietly surveyed the crowd, a content, confident smile pasted on his face. Martha looked at him and saw him as a striking figure, someone who stood out and demanded attention. Martha tried to think of the right description for him when the term "presidential presence" came to her.

Martha and Don looked around nervously as they entered the gauntlet between the stage and the street. The crowd was awfully close—close enough to interact with George Jr. Under normal circumstances, the primary concern would have been George Jr.'s security. Robert Kennedy had shown the world that you didn't need to be elected president to be an assassin's target. Granted, Texas was friendly to George Jr. But if a candidate could be shot in the wimpy, liberal, anti-gun state of California, what were the risks in Texas? Carrying a gun was considered a civic duty, and even brandishing it in public was considered potentially awkward but acceptable. They wouldn't know if it was a crime until the first bullet flew in George Jr.'s direction.

The handlers weren't thinking about guns, though. Their greatest fear was that George Jr. might try to do more than smile and wave.

Suddenly a woman holding a baby stepped out of the crowd and approached them. In the Middle East, the baby could be wearing a bomb vest. As it turned out, this situation was much more dangerous.

"Would you please give my little Marvin a kiss?" the woman requested. "We'll be able to tell everyone we know he got hisself kissed by the president."

It wasn't an unreasonable request, even if it was a little clique and dated. Nobody had explained political baby kissing to George Jr., though, because it passed beyond the wildest possibilities of their emergency planning. If George Jr.'s response were any indication, telling him in advance wouldn't have helped. He might have just refused to go out in public.

"What a cootie germ," George Jr. muttered as he recoiled from the child.

Martha's reaction time was worthy of a Secret Service agent shielding their target. She immediately positioned herself between George Jr. and the baby-wielding mother.

"Oh, what a precious little button you are. George, just look at those eyes. We can't wait to have kids of our own," Martha gushed.

Don Chambers looked on with held breath. Marvin's mother was delighted to get so much attention from the First Lady-to-be, but Don wondered if she or others heard what George Jr. had said. Then there was Martha, declaring she wanted kids. George Jr. and Martha were both in their early forties. He might have to devise an entire press release about how the Flowers planned to adopt once they were married. Marvin's mother looked happy and confused at the same time. That couldn't be good. Then there was George Jr. He didn't look confused. He looked as if he had just stepped in something revolting.

"What did Mr. Flowers say?" the mother asked.

"He said what a cute girl," Martha clarified.

"Marvin is a boy," the mother said. "I thought I heard the word germ."

A few people listening nearby laughed, and one even rolled their eyes at the woman. It didn't seem likely they'd heard George Jr., but Martha needed him to say something that was germ-free.

"George, what's your favorite color?" Martha asked him.

"Blue," George Jr. answered with an eager smile. He was back in his comfort zone.

"We love blue eyes, don't we, George?" Martha asked, feeling lucky.

"Blue is my favorite color," George Jr. repeated.

Martha leaned over and kissed the little brat herself. "That's right. We love this little blue-eyed angel. He's so cute, George just assumed he was a girl. It's so hard to tell at this age."

The mother smiled and Martha moved George Jr. down the gauntlet before the mother could realize she still hadn't gotten her baby kissed by a future president. Don pointed out that the car was just up ahead waiting for them.

"Get him inside before something else happens," Don instructed.

"If you schedule another walkthrough like this, I'll ram the point of my shoe so far up your ass, you'll have to spread my toes apart to eat," Martha said through the ever-present fake smile.

"Funny, that's exactly what Nancy Reagan used to say," Don said as he held the door of the limousine open.

Martha said to George Jr., "They want us to ride in the car. Wave goodbye to the nice people, George."

George enjoyed waving, almost as much as he enjoyed ice cream or getting his face licked by a puppy. The smile on George Jr.'s face got even bigger, and he waved enthusiastically. The crowd sensed his genuine affection, and the cheers got louder as he got into the car. They all planned to vote for him anyway, whistle stop or no whistle stop, but he'd gone that extra mile and shown them he didn't take Texas for granted.

George Jr. would need to win Texas—just after his Texas stop, The Ronald won South Carolina and Nevada. Don told George Sr. they were two more small, highly conservative states that were Tripp strongholds, but the campaign was getting nervous. If Tripp continued his streak on Super Tuesday, they might not be able to stop him.

CHAPTER 27

A ROTTEN APPLE

The rally was at Rice Park in the middle of downtown St. Paul. The Minnesota primary was part of Super Tuesday, and it was only a few days away. Fortune rained on the Flowers campaign. It was late February, but there was no blizzard, the temperature was a balmy thirty-four degrees, and the turnout was good.

They followed the winning formula they'd used for each rally. A local politician opened with a speech and an endorsement for George Jr., Don delivered an introduction spiced with rhetoric and exultations, and Martha and George Jr. took the stage together. Martha delivered her remarks on George Jr.'s behalf and gave a wedding plan update. They had reached the point where Martha played the role of Edgar Bergen and hoped George Jr. could deliver a passable Charlie McCarthy.

"George, people told us the weather was good for this time of year. What do you think?" Martha opened. "Isn't this cold compared to Texas?"

"It is cold," George Jr. agreed.

George Jr. was wearing mittens, but it didn't keep his teeth from chattering. The crowd laughed that their candidate was pretending he was cold, and they cheered.

Martha had promised George Jr. hot chocolate, and he couldn't wait to go inside where it was warm to have some.

Suddenly there was a disturbance in the crowd, and a man stepped forward with an object in his hand.

"Vote for Jackson," the man shouted as he threw the object toward the stage.

Martha saw it coming, and she instinctively ducked behind George Jr. for protection. George Jr. didn't seem to notice until it whizzed by his right ear. He calmly turned his head and watched as an apple that had naturally progressed to applesauce splattered into the center of the American flag that was the backdrop.

George Jr. turned to face the rotten apple chucker and said, "Apples are to eat, not to knock down flags."

George was about to stick out his tongue and taunt the attacker for missing him, but the Secret Service had already gathered the man up and was escorting him out of the crowd. George Jr. calmly waved goodbye to him. The man who tried to share his apple was taking a trip somewhere.

"Thanks for saving me, George," Martha said as she nervously surveyed the crowd. You could never tell if there was a secondary apple-throwing sniper.

"I'll always save you, Martha," George Jr. replied with a smile.

Cameras or no cameras, Martha couldn't help herself. She grabbed George Jr. and hugged him. The crowd was in a frenzy. They'd gone to a political rally expecting dry speeches, but instead they'd witnessed an assault with deadly fruit. George Jr. wasn't only handsome, brilliant, and humble. They had just witnessed the bravest American since John Wayne. Some crackpot had tried to take him out with an apple, but George Jr. looked death in the eye without flinching, said his piece, and hugged his girl. That's just what the Duke would have done.

Later, Martha told Don, "I didn't sign up to get hit by a rotten apple. I'm not some kind of carnival knock-down doll. Don't they screen these people?"

"It's an open-air public rally," Don pointed out. "Besides, even if we did screen, an apple wouldn't register on a metal detector."

"Maybe from now on we should campaign from inside the popemobile," Martha suggested. "Why does an Andrew Jackson supporter throw stuff at us? He's got a whole bunch of Democrats to work through before he should care about George."

"The Senator and I are asking ourselves the same thing," Don answered. "The Jackson campaign has already contacted us to assure us they didn't sanction this. The man was either a lone wolf, or it was a cover."

"Someone needs a cover to throw rotten fruit? Politics really is vaudeville," Martha concluded.

The reaction from the eightieth floor of the Tripp Universal Hospitality Hotel was frustration.

"You swore to me that an apple to the face was just the ticket to knock Junior off his high horse and make him look like a fool," Ronald Tripp yelled at Malcolm. "Who's a fool now?"

They were watching a cable news network where the apple-throwing incident was playing every fifteen minutes as the lead story. The cameras showed George Jr. nonchalantly watch as the apple flew past his face and hit the American flag. They included George Jr.'s response to the attack. Rather than dropping George Jr. off his high horse, that horse had grown another couple of feet higher.

"It's obvious the attacker didn't intend to hit the flag, but Mr. Flowers' remark was perfect, I think," the commentator said. "He shielded his girlfriend, Martha Wilson, didn't back away an inch to the object that was thrown at him, and scolded his attacker for desecrating the flag. If Don Chambers wasn't his campaign manager, I'd wonder if his own campaign didn't orchestrate this. It's a magical moment for George Flowers."

The Ronald turned off the television with disgust and yelled at Malcolm some more. "You either hit the man in the face, or you don't throw it. This near miss is a direct hit for Junior. Where'd you find that guy, with the Mets?"

"The Mets aren't the Mets anymore. They have great young pitching," Malcolm reminded The Ronald. "He ensured our man he could do it."

"If by 'do it' he meant throw it, he did it all right," Tripp yelled some more. "The only good thing is he believes he did it for Jackson."

"Absolutely," Malcolm replied. "The Flowers and the Jackson campaigns can fight it out. We're the only people who know any different."

"I'm glad, because if people knew I paid somebody to make Junior more popular than he already is, they'd think I was a fool," Tripp complained.

CHAPTER 28

THE LONGEST DAY

Don arrived at the Flowers campaign Houston headquarters before dawn on Super Tuesday. He could bank on staying up well past midnight Central time monitoring returns in Colorado, Oklahoma, and Alaska. Early results began to arrive from Virginia, Vermont, Georgia, and Massachusetts almost as soon as he choked down his first of many cups of coffee.

It was no mystery where George Jr. and his team would spend the day. Texas was a major participant in Super Tuesday, so George Jr. would ultimately join Don at the Houston headquarters for the almost certain home state victory speech. Since Georgia was holding their primary, Governor Hastings also didn't have to pick a travel destination. He would stay in Atlanta, although it wasn't as certain his day would end as well as George Jr.'s.

The Ronald and Senator Ramirez didn't have a home field on Super Tuesday, so they had to decide where they wanted to be seen in primetime. This was particularly difficult for Ramirez, because he wasn't projected in the top two in any of the Super Tuesday votes. It wasn't much better for Tripp. He preferred Virginia because he could be staged right across the Potomac from DC. The problem was he had to be in a state he won, and Virginia was a toss-up between him and George Jr. Boston would have been a convenient helicopter ride from New York, but Massachusetts was just as tentative. Minneapolis and Atlanta were major cities, but he was neck-and-neck with George Jr. in the Gopher State and had to compete with both George Jr. and Governor Hastings for the Bulldogs vote. He told Malcolm to get him to Nashville if Tennessee looked favorable, or Oklahoma City if it didn't.

"This is garbage," Tripp complained to Malcolm. "Junior is anchored in Houston, but my best case is going to Nashville. Do I just give my usual speech, or do they expect me to talk while I play a banjo? I want Arlington, Virginia, but the numbers don't work."

"I know it's an inconvenience, sir, but we don't want you to end up as a wallflower," Malcolm tried to assuage his boss. "If you end up sitting in your hotel room all night waiting for a win that never happens, you'll be absent on the entire day."

"If I lose Virginia, can't we just say I'm in Nashville?" Tripp inquired.

"I'm fairly certain the press will announce where you are, sir, and your Virginia supporters aren't exactly going to be raucous for the cameras if you lose their state," Malcolm pointed out.

Don anticipated this would be the longest day of the campaign until they made it to the general election. He wasn't disappointed. It wasn't just the sheer number of primaries and caucuses being held that day; it was the multiple time zones. The kicker was that four of the largest states were too close to call the entire day and well into the evening.

There were a couple of early, easy calls. The Ronald said a lot to please Texas Republicans, but ninety years of Flowers political machinery couldn't be toppled by a

New York interloper. Texans didn't want their salsa or their nominees to be made in New York City. Texas was the most lopsided victory of the day. The second runaway was more of a surprise and demonstrated the power of the home field. Governor Hastings hadn't finished higher than third in any of the previous contests, but his state machine delivered Georgia. Tripp was a distant second in both Texas and Georgia.

"This is the beginning of our march to the White House," Governor Hastings declared.

The Georgia faithful were exuberant, but The Ronald wasn't as impressed.

"I may shift my focus from Junior and Ramirez to Hastings for a couple of weeks," Tripp told Malcolm. "I know we're supposed to be kindred spirits and all that crap, but he's starting to get on my nerves. Plus, our policies overlap to the point where I think he's stealing some of our support. It's no wonder he won Georgia. He isn't that great a governor, but he looks like a bulldog. We should check his birth certificate to see if he's part human and part canine. They voted for their goddamn mascot."

Over the course of the day and night, the churning in each state slowed and the outcomes were revealed. George Jr. made up for his earlier loss in New Hampshire in the northeast by winning Massachusetts and Vermont. Don wasn't as excited about these wins as he might have been.

"We'll take their delegates, but we aren't going to spend much time touting Massachusetts and Vermont," Don told George Sr. and Martha. "They aren't really GOP states. Next thing, Tripp will hit George with the L word."

"I obviously haven't checked to make sure, but I'm pretty certain George isn't a lesbian," Martha quipped.

"L is for liberal," Don clarified for Martha. "It's the most heinous word in the Republican dictionary. If this were the eighteenth century and Tripp called George a liberal, George would have no choice but to defend his honor by challenging Tripp to a duel. If Tripp called *you* a liberal, George could just shoot Tripp in cold blood and be commended for it. We must never speak of the L word again and hope nobody else brings it up."

Tripp secured solid wins in Alabama, Oklahoma, Alaska, and North Dakota. Arkansas was a neighbor of Texas, but Tripp secured a razor-thin win there too.

"I don't like this pattern in the South," Don told George Sr. "Did I miss something? I didn't see any appearances where Tripp dressed up in a white suit and a white beard and mustache and bragged about his chicken. Why are your people electing a carpetbagger?"

"My people?" George Sr. retorted. "Are you referring to rich, white Protestants? The man is vermin, but he knows how to find common ground."

The other state that was a solid victory for George Jr. was Colorado. He wouldn't have normally had any advantage there, but Senator Martin had done more than talk about her support for him. She would have likely won her state if she stayed in the race, and she parlayed that support into a win for George Jr. When Colorado was declared for George Jr., the campaign headquarters received a call from Senator Martin. She wanted to speak to George Jr. directly. It was an unexpected risk, but George Jr. seemed to always tell Senator Martin the right thing. They put him on the phone.

"George, congratulations on Texas and Colorado," Senator Martin told George Jr.

"Thank you," George Jr. replied.

"I'm proud of my people and my state," Senator Martin went on. "We worked hard for you here, and I'll continue to work for you inside the party."

"Can I come to the party?" George Jr. asked.

"You're always invited, George," Senator Martin told him. "Good luck the rest of the night."

"See you at the party," George Jr. promised.

Don, George Sr. and Martha weren't sure what party George Jr. meant, but the senator might have been jumping ahead to the convention. They wouldn't let themselves move ahead quite so fast.

As the evening progressed, Malcolm's advice to The Ronald proved to be wise. Virginia and Minnesota didn't go Tripp's way. Minnesota was an especially narrow win for George Jr.

"That was a close one. We won Minnesota by an apple," George Sr. told Don.

Tripp committed to Nashville, and his plane arrived at six o'clock local time. He sweated it out as he cooled his heels at his campaign headquarters until after nine o'clock waiting for the margin over George Jr. to grow wider or the counting of votes to slow down or stop. When Tennessee was finally called for him, Tripp reapplied his swagger and headed down to the press conference and supporter victory rally.

"Thank you, Tennessee, for being smart. There are some other smart states tonight, and a few others we'll have to educate by November," Tripp declared. "Now let's roll through the rest of the primaries."

George Jr. had given his typically succinct victory speech for the Texas Republican Primary hours earlier. He had his father, mother, and Martha nearby, but Bill and Maryann were missing. It was too early yet for the miracle.

"Thank you, Texas," George Jr. got out before he was swarmed by his family, his girlfriend, and his campaign manager.

They didn't dump Gatorade on George Jr.'s head like in the NFL, although that would have been a handy excuse to take him out of circulation. Near the end of the night, they appraised George Jr.'s position. It was clear they had to keep winning.

"The American people have spoken," Don told the group. "They've given us a firm 'definitely maybe.' We may need to accept that we're in a fight where living to fight another day is good enough. Tripp is in the same position we are. Hastings and Ramirez would sure trade with us."

"If it's this tight at the convention, we're in," George Sr. pointed out. "It may or may not be fair, but Tripp has to clinch before the convention to win. We're like the house in Vegas. We win the ties."

"As long as they don't decide it by interviewing George," Don speculated.

"They don't need interviews," George Sr. countered. "Tripp has already said more than enough."

The Ronald wasn't satisfied with a stalemate, either. He hadn't totally accepted that he could be hated, but he was aware he wasn't a favorite inside the party. Part of that was by design and fueled his popularity, but it was fuel that was tainted if he needed the Republican mainstream's endorsement.

"If we don't win by some type of large margin, we'll lose in the long run," Tripp admitted to Malcolm.

"It could be worse. Hastings only won his own state, and Ramirez is last everywhere," Malcolm said, trying to cheer The Ronald up.

"Don't compare me to the losers," Tripp reprimanded Malcolm. "Ramirez is a waste of ballot paper, and we've already established Hastings is a mongrel bulldog. They don't matter. It's always been about Junior and me. Nobody remembers second place. Junior has hung around too long."

"What can we do?" Malcolm asked.

"Hit harder. We do what it takes to take him down," Tripp declared.

CHAPTER 29

WHITE KNIGHTS

Don had met with his campaign staff to map out the agenda for George Jr.'s trip through Mississippi a few days before the state primary. There had been a handful of primaries and caucuses since Super Tuesday, and they hadn't offered much to resolve the race. Tripp won Kentucky and continued a strong Southern showing by winning Louisiana. George Jr. stayed strong in the Northeast by winning Maine and added a win in Kansas. Now they were focused on Michigan, Idaho, and Mississippi. In Mississippi there were rallies scheduled in Jackson and Gulfport, but there was time for a few more stops in between. Elvis Presley's birthplace in Tupelo and Ole Miss in Oxford would have been excellent stops, but they didn't work geographically. Don was reviewing the other options with George Sr. and Martha. Before they discussed places to visit, George Sr. made sure another issue had been resolved.

"Have you straightened out that flag nonsense with Governor Smith?" George Sr. asked.

"He agreed that they'd only display the stars and stripes," Don assured George Sr.

The Mississippi state flag contained an embedded image of the old Confederate flag. While it was popular with the locals, George Sr. and Don didn't want to see a picture in the New York Times showing George Jr. making a speech with something that looked like the rebel banner as his backdrop.

"If Smith double-crosses us, you make sure George doesn't even get out of the car," George Sr. ordered. "I wish we could stick Smith in the same closet as his flag. I know he'll say something stupid."

"Whatever it is, I'll make sure George doesn't repeat it," Martha told them.

They began to review their list of potential stops. They passed on several for obvious reasons.

"Here's a request to visit a gun factory outside Jackson. They'll show George how they make them, then they'll take him to their range to let him shoot a couple of them," Don read. "They think it'll close the gap between George and some of the other candidates with gun owners."

"What could possibly go wrong?" George Sr. deadpanned.

They placed that option in the reject pile and went on to the next proposal.

"We're invited to Beauvoir, and it's located right outside of Gulfport," Don went on. "Guess what that is?"

"I'm a Southerner, remember? It's the Jefferson Davis Presidential Library," George Sr. answered. "Next."

"This one is interesting," Don said. "George got an invitation to speak to the Knights of Columbus in a small town called Columbus. It isn't between Jackson and Gulfport, but they promise a large turnout."

"That does sound encouraging," George Sr. agreed. "Let me see the letter."

George Sr. looked at the letterhead and said, "Don, did you look at this closely? It's from something called the White Knights of Columbus."

"I thought it was a typo," Don replied. "Is there a problem?"

George Sr. read further and said, "It's signed Roscoe T. Hawkins, Imperial Knight of the White Knights of Columbus. It isn't a typo."

"It says White Knights twice? Maybe he copied and pasted the same mistake," Don reached.

"This is why you can't leave the South solely in the hands of a Yankee campaign manager. You're ignorant of some of our great southern heritage. Haven't you ever heard of the Klan out there in California?" George Sr. asked.

Don looked at the letter again and said, "So the White Knights of Columbus is a KKK den? I suppose this goes in the reject pile."

"I won't say it might not help us in Mississippi, but visiting a KKK den would represent a significant shift in your campaign strategy," George Sr. pointed out. "It would make the risk of alienating minority voters by appearing in front of the Mississippi state flag a moot point."

"Is this a trip we even want to make?" Martha asked.

"George is from Texas," George Sr. reminded them. "We need another win in the South. We'll be fine. This is the reason we plan."

Back on the eightieth floor of the Tripp Universal Hospitality Hotel, Malcolm informed The Ronald that the Flowers campaign had declined the Imperial Knight's invitation.

"That's unfortunate," Tripp declared. "I thought it was camouflaged well enough to lure the fly to the web. I would have loved to see the look on Junior and Chambers' faces when the Klansmen marched out in their white robes. I planned to have every news outlet in Mississippi on hand."

"I agree—I thought we had a chance," Malcolm agreed. "It's no surprise they turned down Beauvoir. It's easy to research. I thought they might fall for the Knights of Columbus."

"Junior has a sixth sense, but we'll keep trying," The Ronald encouraged. "This is like gambling. If you've got the money, you keep playing. Even if you don't always win, it's still fun to play."

CHAPTER 30

THE MECHANICS

A Ronald Tripp rally was becoming the definition of the term "conflicting opinions." The majority of those in attendance were supporters who were his fanatical devotees. But there was a smaller but equally fanatical group of protesters from a number of the demographics that The Ronald had targeted. As he targeted more of those demographics and his criticisms got harsher, the protesters' numbers swelled, along with their passion.

"It doesn't make me happy when I'm talking to my supporters and some radical is raising some stupid sign and yelling at me. One of our people even got Maced at the last rally," The Ronald complained.

"That was unfortunate, but it shouldn't happen again," Malcolm said. "We've retrained each one of our security people on the correct way to hold the can."

"That doesn't make the protesters go away. I need you to do something about them," Ronald commanded Malcolm.

"We've removed many of them from the auditoriums," Malcolm reminded his leader. "I promise you, several of them woke up the next morning with quite a headache."

"I enjoyed watching that," Tripp agreed. "But then they get onto television and become minor celebrities. I see them back again at my next stop. We're reacting. I need you to come up with a plan that prevents them from showing up to begin with."

"I'll put the specialists to work on it right away, sir," Malcolm promised.

Malcolm's corporate security force was mostly composed of individuals he called security technicians. These were employees that guarded the hotels and offices and provided routine security for his companies. A small portion of them worked on Tripp's personal security detail before the Secret Service became Ronald's official protectors. Tripp still kept some of his own people in the mix because he could divide their roles between security and personal servitude. Malcolm also had his cybersecurity group, which protected the company's computer and information systems. The final group was a smaller, hand-selected group Malcolm called security specialists. These were his inner-circle people, used for black operations and special projects. Convincing a large group of organized protesters that free speech really wasn't that important to them was a special project.

Like the cybersecurity team, the specialists were all experienced men with unique talents. The majority had worked as private security contractors for the US government in Iraq or Afghanistan. The contractors enjoyed rules of engagement that gave them more freedom and individual discretion than was afforded the average GI. Most of those that Malcolm recruited left their firms to work for The Ronald. He had deeper pockets, and Malcolm didn't believe in any rules when it came to engaging the enemy.

Malcolm considered himself a man of the world, so he targeted the hiring of a handful of specialists from outside the United States. He might have searched for a top mercenary from his native Britain, but he ended up finding three team members from other countries.

Bern was originally from South Africa. He'd served his apprenticeship enforcing apartheid and trying to stem the social tidal wave that eventually freed Mandela and made him South Africa's leader. He left South Africa and became a legend because of his role in a series of other African conflicts. He was the man you hired if you were an African dictator with a pro-democracy problem.

Dov was formerly with the Israeli special forces, but he left the military because of the political swings between its ultra-hardline and merely hardline policies. He went private and developed a reputation protecting some of the remotest Israeli settlements. His rules of engagement stated that if an Arab over the age of twelve got too close to the settlement, he probably needed to be shot. His second rule was that if the Arabs take out one of ours, we'll take out ten of theirs. Whether or not Dov selected the correct ten was of minor concern to him. When he got too hot for Israel, he went into business as a for-hire one-man strike force against Islamic extremists. Malcolm hired him permanently, and Dov got to keep the same rule book he was already using.

Some of The Ronald's rhetoric was anti-Jewish, but Tripp had always clarified there were times when having a Jew around was just part of the price of doing business. Dov and Ronald had some compelling common ground. They both shared a strong distaste for Muslims.

The last and most dangerous of the three was Ours. Ours had started his military career in the French army, but he found the job boring. The French didn't do much fighting, and he didn't see the next Napoleon anywhere on the horizon. After he was discharged, he made a career protecting French interests in Central Africa, in countries such as Mali and the Central African Republic. He earned the nickname *le Stabilisateur,* or the Stabilizer, because when he entered the picture the situation went from impossible to stable. French corporations discovered their problems just disappeared, along with the people that caused them.

The three foreigners had several things in common. Each of their names meant "bear." Bears were one of nature's more imposing animals, but the odds of survival were much better for the person that was attacked by a real bear. Each of them had stopped placing value on human life decades in the past. And each of them was conditioned to serve their current master unconditionally.

"Should I put the bears on it?" Malcolm asked.

This wasn't a question to be passed over lightly. It was the equivalent to the decision a president needed to make before he pushed the big red button. The blast radius could be considerably wider and the fallout considerably heavier if the bears were assigned.

"This is my current number-one problem," Tripp decided. "Turn them loose. We need to convince these college kids that keep showing up to stay in school. As for the rest of those misfits, they need to learn we don't want them at my rallies or in this country. Make sure your guys don't do anything that gets back to us or riles up the media. I don't want to read about this somewhere."

The next scheduled appearances were in Michigan. The first was in Lansing. The core team of protesters came out in force and booed Tripp outside as he entered the auditorium where he was speaking. A portion of the protesters managed to work their way into the building, and they booed and harassed Tripp through his entire speech. In past rallies, some of Tripp's people would attempt to quiet or remove the protesters, but instead they were allowed to express themselves.

After the Lansing rally, the protesters manned their vehicles and hustled to Tripp's next stop in Ann Arbor. The rally was a repeat of the one in Lansing. The protesters that got in to hear the speech yelled and screamed, and nobody tried to stop them. They had gone in expecting trouble, but it was really getting too easy. The next speech was down the road in Detroit, and the protesters planned to be there when it started. They left the auditorium to find their cars and hit the highway.

Four young protesters walked from the auditorium to their car, but as they approached it, they noticed it didn't look right. All four tires were flat.

"*Excusez-moi,* it looks like you gentlemen have a problem, no?" they heard a man with a French accent say.

The voice belonged to a large man with a dark beard. He was with a friend, a friend that looked like he was a member of the Detroit Lions.

"Somebody slashed our tires, man," one of the students explained.

"Is a shame, no?" Ours sympathized. "Do you have four spares?"

"Four spares? Who carries four spares?" another student asked.

"Someone who goes to one of Mr. Tripp's speeches and acts, well, not so nice. They should probably carry four spares," Ours observed. "You are lucky it was just tires. A person who does this could do so much more. They could do more dangerous things, such as severing a brake line. They could direct the emissions into your car. You pass out while you're driving, and then, who knows? You can even make a car explode if you have just a little knowledge."

Ours held up his pointer finger and his thumb to show them what a little looked like. The students didn't say much. These large, scary men didn't look like good Samaritans.

"Who are you guys?" the bravest in the bunch asked.

"Us? Today we are auto mechanics," Ours answered, "although my life's work has been more about pest control."

Other protesters were having similar experiences with a shortage of spares and large men who knew a lot about automobiles. A group of four young Latinos had attended the Lansing and Ann Arbor meetings to protest Tripp's immigration policies. They had a surge of machismo and tried to stand up to the strangers who told them their car looked unsafe and would likely crash if they tried to attend another Tripp rally.

"Hey, buddy, are you threatening us?" one of the Latinos said to Dov. "Didn't you notice there are four of us and two of you?'

"You have a point," Dov replied calmly. "We've got all day. We can wait for you to round up some more of your friends."

"I don't think they look like they know enough friends to worry us," said Dov's partner, a former security contractor that had run convoys in Iraq.

A third group of protesters consisted of old white Michigan Democrats who disagreed with Tripp's policies and were following him around to harass him and have a little fun. Now the rims of their Mercedes were kissing the pavement, and they were about to call AAA. Two large men appeared and started to explain the real inner workings of their Benz. Despite the company's advertising, it didn't sound like the world's safest car. The speaker sounded credible because he had a German accent.

"Do you work for Mercedes?" one of the old men asked.

"Ach, no, I'm originally from South Africa," Bern answered. "In my country, old men play golf or find other sources of amusement. They don't shout down politicians. I suggest you find another hobby."

"That might be a good idea," another of the old men agreed.

After Bern and his partner left, his friends were calling the old man a traitor.

"Look, even if Tripp wins the primary, he'll lose the election. I don't know what we're doing out here. We should want him to get nominated," the old man explained.

Bern had the easiest assignment that day, but there were many more discussions with many more men, and sometimes women, about many more cars. Nobody called the police or tried to stop Malcolm's specialists, and the number of protesters at each rally started to decline. The specialists had a particular look that compelled obedience. They could back up their talk with action, but their talk made the action unnecessary.

"Malcolm, I've noticed the dramatic change at the rallies," Tripp said. "Protesters are few and far between."

"We can't stop all the local first-timers, but you shouldn't see any repeat offenders," Malcolm replied.

"I don't," Tripp assured him. "Did we have any problems?"

"Nothing physical. A few came back because they didn't take us seriously the first time. That was more ignorance than defiance. We never had to tell anyone more than twice," Malcolm said.

"Tell your people they did an excellent job. I have a rally in LA, and I plan to reward them there. Talk to Dominic and arrange for some actresses. I'll cover all the costs," Tripp offered.

Dominic ran Tripp's adult film enterprises. Some of the actresses transitioned between film and prostitution, depending on their current career path. Using baseball jargon, Tripp often referred to prostitution as his adult film farm system.

"Thank you again, sir. It's fortunate the most dangerous people at your rallies are typically your own supporters.

These protesters were mainly just kids, minorities, and liberals. I'm surprised your supporters didn't drive them off without my help," Malcolm replied. "I know my men appreciate the gesture. I personally wouldn't have unprotected sex with southern Californian prostitutes, but my men do have a natural affinity toward danger."

"Especially thank Ours, Dov, and Bern," Tripp requested. "The bears showed remarkable restraint."

"I know—initially I wondered if their use was necessary," Malcolm confessed. "In hindsight, they were perfect for this job."

CHAPTER 31

WORSE THAN A TUMMY ACHE

That night's debate included opening and closing statements, but George Jr. was getting so good with the earpiece that the team felt he could handle it. Their optimism wasn't misdirected. He delivered an opening remark that gushed sincerity. He really did seem to be honored, pleased, and blessed to be in attendance. There were only four candidates, though, which meant George Jr. was required to share a great number of his carefully considered positions.

The Ronald had compared Governor Hastings to a bulldog, but he actually looked and sounded more like Arthur Godfrey, which made him a favorite with senior voters. Unlike Arthur, the governor wasn't sponsored by Geritol. He was the darling of the National Rifle Association, and their sponsorship was worth considerably more in hard and soft money.

It was public knowledge that the governor owned more than two hundred guns, many high-capacity automatic weapons. He was the most avid hunter-politician since Teddy Roosevelt. He claimed he had hunted and killed every worthy animal that roamed his native state. While this made him a spokesman for the NRA, it wasn't without controversy.

Told that he had just shot one of Georgia's rare southern flying squirrels, the Governor responded, "I do hate to hear that. I'd like to get me another. It was one helluva lot more fun than shooting skeet."

There was also some negative publicity when he was photographed holding up a dead Appalachian cottontail by its ears. When he was told by a reporter that the animal was considered one of Georgia's rare species, the governor claimed that he shot the Pomeranian-sized animal in self-defense. There were some jokes about the killer rabbit, and several reporters asked if he was hunting for the Holy Grail. The jokes went right over the governor's head, along with those of most other Georgia Republicans.

This was a Republican debate, not a bleeding-hearts club, so the governor was aggressively stumping for the Second Amendment.

"I am the one candidate who doesn't just promise you the right to bear arms," Governor Hastings said with a raised fist. "I live it."

The governor's wife had also lived it a few years back. Governor Hastings was cleaning one of his rifles when a cartridge he had left in the chamber discharged. The bullet went through the bedroom wall, shattered the bathroom makeup mirror while his wife was applying her eyeliner, and came to rest in the governor's walk-in closet after it had passed through about a dozen of his suits. In hindsight, he regretted his decision to alert the authorities about his near miss. Once the press got ahold of the story, they found it both newsworthy and ironic. The governor was never a big fan of irony.

Senator Ramirez tried to join the Second Amendment discussion, and he chimed in about his opposition to all forms of gun control. Florida had more concealed weapons licenses than any state in the country, and taking a rifle into the swamps to shoot a wild boar, alligator, or the occasional bass that swam too close to the surface of some pond was a time-honored tradition. Ramirez didn't mention the equally impressive rate of unlicensed concealed carries in Miami, Jacksonville, and Tampa. These were used in gang warfare, holdups, and crimes of passion.

George Jr. was from Texas, and George Sr. and Don knew he couldn't afford to idly stand by and listen as his foes wooed the gun vote. Ted fed him his pro-gun snippet.

"I've always been for guns," George Jr. repeated from his earpiece. "I'm an owner too."

George Jr. was telling the truth. He owned a Colt 45 that made a loud popping noise whenever he pulled the plastic trigger. When he really wanted to impress somebody, there was his full size plastic M-16. It held a gallon of water and could squirt over one hundred times without reloading.

Ronald Tripp weighed in last, and he wasn't about to concede any core Republican voting block, especially one as fanatical as the NRA. Tripp's chances were dependent on fanatical voting blocks. They would blindly focus on a single divisive issue, and The Ronald was running a divisive campaign. Governor Hastings could have the geezers, but The Ronald wanted the NRA.

"I've made my position on gun control clear, as have my colleagues. I'm the only one who has taken it to the next level, though. When I'm elected president, I'll establish a federal tax deduction for gun ownership. You currently get a deduction if your kid gets done with school and still lives at home. Who the hell wants that? Now you'll get a deduction for something that can actually help you," Tripp declared.

Don and Martha looked on as the crowd cheered. They knew what was coming next.

"It makes perfect sense because we all know higher gun ownership makes our streets and homes safer. We don't need tax dollars for more cops—we need more guns in the hands of law-abiding citizens," Tripp shouted over the clapping. "When I'm president, the only ones that'll still need police protection are the criminals."

Don and Martha knew every reputable police commissioner in the country cringed every time they heard The Ronald's plan, and it wasn't because they were afraid they'd be out of a job. But asking George Jr. to point that out wasn't good primary politics. George Jr.'s pro-gun stance was already far right of center, but far right wasn't even close to the middle in this crowd. Martha wondered if Mrs. Hastings thought that the hundreds of the governor's guns had made their home a safer place. If the governor had been cleaning one of his automatic weapons rather than a single-shot rifle, he might be campaigning with wife number two.

The next question was on immigration, and The Ronald was sharing his solution to illegal immigrants.

"God has given us at least half the solution to stem the invasion of our borders, and it's called the Rio Grande. The problem today is that the river has shallow spots. As your president, I'll commission the dredging of the Rio Grande as my highest priority civil engineering project. There are other rivers that we can use in addition to the Rio Grande. We can connect the American Canal, pieces of the Colorado River, and other rivers to create a natural and effective barrier to Mexico. I've developed a plan to exchange territories with Mexico to use waterways which are north and south of the current Mexican border. Finally, we'll create canals to connect these natural barriers. This doesn't just address the national security problem. We all know there is a severe drought in the southwest. These canals and rivers will also help us bust this and any other future droughts. It's all part of my Border Security Water Deterrent Plan," Tripp explained.

Senator Ramirez immediately protested. "This is his 'build a moat' plan," Ramirez shouted. "Every civil engineer in the country has pointed out how crazy this plan sounds. The Big Dig cost taxpayers fifteen billion dollars, and Egypt has estimated a forty-mile Suez Canal project would cost four to five billion. We're talking about five hundred to a thousand miles of digging and dredging. The estimates for this are easily fifty to a hundred billion dollars. Then he says Mexico will pay for it. We're talking about a third of Mexico's annual infrastructure budget. It's delusional."

"I'll get your relatives to dig it with shovels," Tripp shot back. "It'll practically be free."

"We need to keep out bad people," George Jr. repeated. "But not with moats or fences."

"I know we're all worried about losing our cheap Mexican labor," The Ronald continued. "Let me assure you, I have an Asian gardener and an Asian cook and housekeeper, and they're far better domestics and their rates are competitive. It's not like we're going to lose the taco—it's like we're going to add in a little sushi and pad Thai. We need to think ahead. Those Asian kids are going to end up as our future engineers and scientists. A school system full of Mexican illegals means you get gardeners, best case, but most likely drug dealers and gang-bangers."

"I resent the implication that Mexicans aren't intelligent," Ramirez fumed.

"I'm sure some of them are," Tripp conceded. "Unfortunately, none of the smart ones seem to find their way into politics."

"When I'm president," George Jr. pronounced, "our school system will work for all."

Ted was struggling to feed George Jr. with timely, relevant remarks whenever the debate heated up. Governor Hastings jumped on George Jr.'s segue into education.

"I support local control of education," Hastings opened. "We need school vouchers, and I believe it is despicable that federal school funding is only available for schools that demonstrate a lack of a spiritual education."

The Ronald saw his opening to transition to an appeal to the religious right.

"I agree with the governor," The Ronald confirmed. "In fact, I've reviewed the Constitution, and I believe we've lost the ability to interpret it in its historical context. Many of the people who came to this country before the Revolutionary War came here to escape religious persecution, but this was a time when Catholics and Protestants persecuted each other, and some Protestant groups persecuted other Protestant groups. My point is, they were all Christian. Since when did it become about Muslims or atheists? We've broadened the concept of religious freedom since the original words were written. You might even say we've corrupted the concept, and I'm not so sure it's a good idea."

From George Jr.'s dressing room, Ted was preparing a response from Don's religious position notes for George Jr. to share with the crowd. It was a conventional defense of the inclusive nature of the freedom of religion. Ted was sipping a bottle of water to keep his throat lubricated so his voice would stay pure and clear. This was critical because George Jr. repeated everything he heard, and a hoarse voice might lead to an embarrassing answer. What wasn't a good idea was placing the water bottle between Ted's elbow and the transmitter. Ted knocked it over, spilling water onto the transmitter box. It immediately shorted out with a loud pop and a faint smell of ozone. George Jr. was flying solo.

"The founding fathers never pictured us worshipping some guy wearing a turban," The Ronald ranted.

"Aladdin wears a turban and rides a magic carpet," George Jr. said.

Don and Martha looked at each other with alarm, and Don looked at his phone. He'd just received a text from Ted, and it was the worst possible scenario. Ted was down. Don showed Martha the message, and they both looked on with apprehension.

"Are you saying we should worship a Disney character, or is this your abstract way of saying freedom of religion is broad and that you're all right with mosques and men with turbans in your neighborhood? Sometimes you're too smart for your own good, George," Tripp went on.

"Aladdin is a hero," George Jr. replied.

"Many Muslims are dangerous, and some have said they wish to kill us," Tripp argued. "I believe we have to view the Constitution with a practical mindset."

"Killing is bad," George Jr. agreed.

"Do something," Martha hissed.

"What can I do?" Don whispered back. "Tell the moderator we need a break because our transmitter is out?"

"I don't know, you're the campaign manager," Martha whispered back. "Do something."

Don surveyed the situation and decided there was only one course of action available.

"Oh no," Don said loudly. He stood up, clutched his hands to his chest, crumpled to his knees, and rolled onto his back and into the aisle.

Martha looked on initially in shock and surprise, which had nothing to do with good acting. She didn't anticipate Don's choice of solution, but she started to contribute in a few seconds.

"Oh, my God," Martha shouted. "He's having a heart attack."

Martha leaned over Don and grabbed his hand. Don was sweating, and his pulse was racing. "This isn't real, is it?" Martha said quietly.

"It isn't a heart attack," Don whispered. "I may be on the verge of a panic attack, though."

"He says he's having chest pain," Martha told the first responders.

The moderators, the audience, and the other three candidates stopped debating and looked on at the spectacle. George Jr. continued to stand at his podium, smiling and staring at the camera. It was fine, because the network went to commercial as soon as the disturbance started. People crowded in to help, and several were doctors. Martha left Don's side to work her way to George Jr. She motioned him to join her.

"Don is sick," she explained to George Jr.

"Does he have a tummy ache?" George Jr. asked.

"Worse than that, George," Martha replied.

George Jr. acquired a more appropriately serious expression. He didn't like tummy aches, and he couldn't imagine what could be worse. An ambulance was onsite in ten minutes, and Don was on the way to a hospital only a couple of minutes after that. The debate would not resume. George Jr. and Martha had to follow their fallen comrade.

Ronald Tripp walked over and spoke to George Jr. and Martha before they left.

"I hope Don is all right. I really mean that," Tripp told them.

"Thank you, Ronald," Martha responded.

It was odd Ronald felt the need to affirm he really meant it. There was no reason he should wish their campaign manager ill will. Then again, who knew what The Ronald was actually thinking?

"It's worse than a tummy ache," George Jr. informed Ronald.

The Ronald gave George Jr. the once-over. This guy was either incredibly cool under pressure, or he was as much of a wise-ass as The Ronald.

George Jr. and Martha waited in the emergency room waiting area for about an hour before a physician met them and briefed them. Don's EKG and blood tests were normal, so it probably wasn't a heart attack. They'd hold him for observation and more tests and decide whether to release him in the morning. The doctor emphasized that Don needed rest, even if he was discharged. The doctor let them visit Don briefly.

"I'll be on my back for a few days, and I'll try to convince people I'm a sane and responsible person for the next week until I get cleared to come back. This solution isn't without consequences," Don complained. "I'm going to be as big a news story as George. Anyone suspicious?"

"I don't think so," Martha said. "Tripp even wished you good health. He was about as sincere as a mortician with an empty parlor, though."

"So what happened?" Don asked.

"Ted learned the transmitter isn't water resistant," Martha said. "We should replace him, but then we'd have to kill him, and we never know how trustworthy his replacement would be."

"We only have one more debate. We'll get Ted a sippy cup," Don decided.

"I'm sorry you're sick," George Jr. offered.

"I'm feeling better, George," Don said. "I'll be back real soon. I'm thinking this was just a simple case of food poisoning."

"Don't blame shellfish," Martha reminded him. "We're in Florida, and that'll anger some of the voters."

"Good point," Don responded. "I'll tell the press I tried my first falafel, and it was just too beany. It was gas, not the big one. It can't hurt us with the Middle Eastern vote. Who else are they going to vote for, Tripp?"

CHAPTER 32

MAKE OUR DAY

Don Chambers' run as a media whore was a short one. He wasn't the big post-debate story anymore. The dynamics of the election had suddenly shifted.

Ronald Tripp made a strong impression on Second Amendment supporters during the debate. They all agreed his were the greatest words ever spoken next to Charlton Heston's "cold, dead hands" speech. Tripp made sure he threw the competing NRA suitor under the bus.

"Governor Hastings claims to be a Second Amendment advocate, but the only guns he really cares about are his own. I don't see him getting more guns into the hands of the good guys who need them," Tripp implored.

The NRA agreed, because that week they endorsed Ronald Tripp for president. This created several immediate problems for Governor Hastings. He was relying on the NRA's endorsement if he was going to be a serious contender. He also relied on the NRA's overall support when he ran for governor, but now he was competing with the candidate the NRA had endorsed. Hastings met with his NRA contacts, hoping he could win back their support. Instead, they strongly confirmed that Tripp was their candidate. They also suggested Hastings drop out of the race so they could consolidate their members' support behind Tripp.

The next day, Hastings announced he was suspending his campaign. He spoke eloquently about his supporters and the things his campaign had accomplished. He knew there would be pressure on him to endorse another candidate. He also knew the Republican Party was becoming increasingly concerned that Ronald Tripp might actually win the nomination. They would expect Hastings to endorse either Flowers or Ramirez. Hastings had carefully considered this political landscape and his future prospects before the press conference. The course of action was clear to him.

"In addition to suspending my campaign, I have another important announcement," Hastings went on. "I am offering my endorsement to, and implore my supporters to offer their vote to, our next president, Ronald Tripp."

Then The Ronald walked onto the stage carrying a rifle in each arm. He kept one and handed the second one to Governor Hastings. Each man raised the rifle over their heads, and the pro-Hastings crowd was won. They applauded their new hero, Ronald Tripp. If the men had sported dark beards and berets, they could have passed for Che Guevara and Fidel Castro.

Governor Hastings had been handed a choice between serving the Republican Party or serving the NRA. It wasn't that tough a choice in his mind. The Republican Party would twist, turn, and change over time, but the NRA would ultimately stay the course and pull the conservative strings.

George Sr., Don, Martha, and George Jr. sat in the Flowers' ranch study. George Jr. watched the horses playing in the corral outside the window. The others watched the latest Tripp television ad. It opened in a dark urban alley with a police siren blaring somewhere in the distance.

"America is falling apart. Crime, drug use, and illegal immigration make it so we don't feel safe walking down the street in front of our own homes. But if you can hold out just a little bit longer, America, help is on the way. There's a new sheriff in town, and he's packing some heat."

The alley image transitioned to Ronald Tripp and Governor Hastings on stage together brandishing their rifles. The caption under them read, "Make Our Day. Ronald Tripp for President."

George Sr. was less than impressed by the image of The Ronald with a gun.

"Look how he holds that rifle. Make our day? It looks more like a classic suicide pose. He's got the barrel pointed right up toward his own chin," George Sr. observed. "I hope somebody who knows his rifle from a hole in the ground checked to make sure it wasn't loaded. I don't mean Hastings, either. He knows guns, but he's proven to be unreliable about seeing if they're loaded."

"If they do more of these spots together, it might help our case," Don agreed. "For now, we have a problem. Tripp just got stronger."

"We've got Senator Martin's endorsement, and she's a lot stronger than Hastings," George Sr. pointed out.

"She is with moderates and mild conservatives, so George has solidified his position in the middle. Ramirez is still pulling some of it away from us, though, and Tripp owns the ultraconservatives. Hastings had some of it, but now Tripp reigns the far right," Don said.

"We've got the mainstream party's support," George Sr. thought. "We can afford to go further right."

"We've got to be careful," Don said. "If we go too far, it'll be payback time in the general election. The Democrats will hang the crazy card on George."

They all took a look at George Jr., obliviously watching the horses. The campaign was already in crisis mode, and nobody had figured out yet that George Jr. couldn't have passed a basic legal competency assessment. They didn't want anyone playing a crazy card that they'd have a difficult time passing along. They went on to review their basic campaign performance.

"We carried Texas, but the rest of the South is going with Tripp. Southern voters care more about what Tripp has to say and less about where he comes from. A New York billionaire talks smack about immigration and holds up a rifle, and all of a sudden he becomes Beauregard Jefferson Davis Tripp. George is polling higher in New Jersey than he is in North Carolina," Don complained.

"We need to advertise more in the south," Martha agreed. She found campaign research and business market research were similar, and she had some feedback on their surveys. "The survey data and focus session data rated what people thought of George in several different scenarios. They categorize it by personal appearances and his debate performance, then by the television, radio, and internet ads and position statements we did using voiceovers and Virtual George. Guess what?"

"I think I know, but I'm not going to like it," Don replied.

"Probably not. George makes a far better impression in person than he does through the commercials and other media," Martha confirmed. "The George we created isn't as popular as the George we're trying to hide."

"It's a delicate balance," Don warned. "His ad libs won debates, but each one of them took years off my life."

"We know," George Sr. agreed. "The public and the press think you almost died."

They began to shoot commercials with George Jr., but they limited his lines. They couldn't use enough big words to shoot any of the position summary pieces. Those all stayed with Virtual George. They were running a strong campaign, but Ronald Tripp was matching them dollar-for-dollar and vote-for-vote.

Senator Ramirez aimed to stay in the race until after the primary in his home state of Florida. While this would hurt George Jr. in the long term, in the short term Don welcomed it. With the NRA and the Hastings supporters on Tripp's side, Tripp was a strong candidate in Florida. Ramirez was the only person who might prevent a Tripp victory there. Tripp and George Jr. were systematically splitting the delegates everywhere else.

George Sr. and Don had hoped to have more separation at this point in the campaign. Separation between George Jr. and the next candidate would have meant they could back off on campaigning. Backing off meant George Jr. could make fewer appearances, and they'd be taking less risks that someone would truly understand the candidate. Many candidates had a skeleton or two hanging in their closet. George Jr.'s skeletons were hanging out in the middle of his living room if somebody could get inside his head and look around for them.

CHAPTER 33

MEMBERSHIP HAS ITS PRIVILEGES

The Christian Coalition of Saved Souls convention was held each year on the campus of the University of Enlightened Angels in Tulsa, Oklahoma. It was a forum where fundamental Christian conservatives absolutely defined good and evil. It was truly a come-to-Jesus meeting for Republican presidential candidates who didn't want to end up on the evil list.

Don called George Sr. when George Jr.'s invitation to speak at the convention arrived. Ronald Tripp was also a featured speaker. Don was told that Senator Ramirez hadn't made the cut.

"That's no surprise," George Sr. responded. "Ramirez may think he's a Christian, but the coalition is closed to Catholics. We won't be running into too many Mormons there, either."

"We'll tick that box before the Utah primary," Don told him. "There are too many rules these days for my taste. All we had to do in Ronnie's day was throw in the occasional 'God bless America' and vote against abortion."

"This convention will be our biggest challenge yet," George Sr. announced. "We'll have to be careful. Nobody does backstabbing hypocrisy better than a band of evangelicals."

"I understand you and Jim Bob Bunker have not always seen eye-to-eye," Don said.

Jim Bob Bunker was the president of the University of Enlightened Angels and had founded the convention. He was the country's leading televangelist and the most politically active.

"Catholics are taught to kiss the pope's ring," George Sr. said. "If you want the evangelical vote, you have to kiss Jim Bob's ass. The son of a bitch knows it, too."

"Should you be calling a man of the cloth a son of a bitch?" Don asked.

"Man of the cloth," George Sr. snorted. "Remember, the devil was a fallen angel. It never made sense how the devil could have once been an angel. Then I met Jim Bob, and it made sense."

They wrote George Jr. a special speech that focused solely on conservative social issues. Martha began to practice the transmit-and-repeat process with Ted and George Jr.

"Has it occurred to you that we're deceiving thousands of people at a Christian conference?" she asked Don.

"Are you asking me if I've considered that a lie on this scale could be a mortal sin? Or that, given George Jr. doesn't know any better, all God's wrath will be directed to me alone?" Don asked her back.

Martha thought for a second and answered, "That's about it."

"If God sends me to hell for eternity," Don told her, "it'll be an improvement over the past couple of months."

The day of the conference arrived, and the delegation of George Jr., George Sr., Don, Martha, and Ted arrived at the stadium. They were greeted by the Honorable Reverend Jim Bob Bunker. Jim Bob and George Sr. immediately started to relive their history.

"Senator, you old scoundrel," Jim Bob greeted George Sr. "I'm so glad to see you. You aren't getting any younger, and I was worried I wouldn't get a chance to talk with you again. Given your history, there's no guarantee we'll meet again in the hereafter."

"Don't worry, Reverend. I'm sure you've still got time to turn your life around," George Sr. fired back.

Jim Bob laughed and stepped over to meet George Jr. "Welcome to the convention, my son."

"Thank you," George Jr. answered. "I'm his son too."

George Jr. meant George Sr., but Jim Bob assumed George Jr. was referring to Him. He brightened up at this unsolicited acknowledgement of George Jr.'s faith.

"I can tell you are with us, George," Jim Bob replied. "I've got some hope for the next generation of Flowers."

"I'll give you flowers," George Jr. promised.

"This conference is willing to accept you too, George," Jim Bob said. "Your dad was a five-term Republican senator, but for some reason we never managed to mesh together like I'd have expected."

"I'm a Christian, but I admit I'm also a sinner," George Sr. explained. "All Christians are, but some of them don't seem to want to admit it. When I join any club, I make sure I take advantage of that club's benefits. The best benefit in Christianity is God's forgiveness. If you don't sin a little, you leave a lot of God's forgiveness on the table. I believe membership has its privileges."

"At your age, I'd advise you avoid carrying too high a negative balance," Jim Bob retorted.

George Sr. and Jim Bob spoke a few minutes about the convention. George Sr. was especially interested in the other invited speakers.

"So Ronald Tripp is here tomorrow," George Sr. commented. "It's funny how he found Jesus the same day he found his urge to run for president."

"He's very popular here," was all Jim Bob said.

"Remember there was only one Messiah, and there can never be a second one," George Sr. reminded Jim Bob. "The most Ronald Tripp can be is a disciple. If Jesus could manage twelve disciples by himself, the coalition should be able to afford at least two. I'd even say three, except I noticed Senator Ramirez wasn't on the program."

"Ronald has created a platform that addresses all of our beliefs," Jim Bob told George Sr. "We like George, but we'll need to wait until we see what the candidates have to say. As for Senator Ramirez, if he wants to speak at a religious conference, he'll have to wait for an invitation from his pope."

"Tripp may tell you what you want to hear, but it's too bad we can't see into his soul to see what's really there," George Sr. went on. "The hate he spews against some of our citizens and half the world's population doesn't have too much of Jesus's love mixed into it."

"Jesus loves me, this I know," George Jr. added.

"You may have a point, George," Jim Bob replied to George Jr. "Stick to the Bible basics. We'll endorse a single candidate, just like we do every election. Ronald Tripp is not a lock; not yet. You've got a chance."

George Jr.'s speech covered all the coalition's wants and needs. He told them that when he was younger, he'd wrestled with whether to go into business or go into the clergy. He told them that the reason he was running for president had nothing to do with power or his ego; it was to honor his poor sick brother and God. He told them that every decision he made would be made in a Christian context. Don wasn't merely lying to people at a Christian conference by having George Jr. use a transmitter. Nearly every sentence was actually a hollow or outright lie. If lying at a Christian conference was a mortal sin, the forecast for Don's eternity was hot, followed by more hot.

George Jr.'s speech was sincere, fundamental, and simple. He smiled and waved at the end, and Martha came out and joined him at the podium. It wasn't on George Jr.'s curriculum vitae, but George Sr. and Don made sure that part of the buzz in the stadium included the word that George Jr. and Martha had vowed to abstain from premarital sex. It was accompanied by word that George Jr. didn't drink, smoke, or use foul language. Since these things were all true, it might help offset whatever other eternal punishments Don had earned on the day. The crowd responded enthusiastically, and in an average year George Jr. would have just earned their endorsement. But with The Ronald in the race, this election was far from average.

"Nice job, George," Martha praised him when they had finished.

"They're nice people," George Jr. told her.

"From the mouths of babes," George Sr. commented to Don.

The Ronald took the pulpit the following day. It was like a Christian rock concert to George Jr.'s violin recital. The energy level in the room started at high and progressed upward to a near riot. The coalition already knew they were God's chosen people, but that didn't mean they didn't enjoy having it reinforced by a presidential candidate. The Ronald didn't have to modify or customize any of his messages for this audience.

The first topic was education, and he enhanced his viewpoints with some props. He held up a book with the words "Sex Education" on the outer jacket. The stadium was large, but there were multiple video screens to share the image. The crowd immediately began to boo robustly. They didn't want any strangers teaching their children about sex. It was a vulgar and disgusting topic. Some of the mothers might have a brief and painful talk with their daughter a few days before their wedding, but the majority preferred to let their offspring figure it out with their husband or wife once they were married.

"When I'm elected, the first thing I'll do is replace this," Tripp shouted and tore the sex education book in two. Then he held up a King James Bible and finished, "With this."

The crowd noise increased another twenty decibels.

"We know that abstinence is the only thing our children need to understand on that topic. That's what they'll teach in health classes under my administration," Tripp promised. "But I don't think abstinence is anything to brag about for two adults that should know better. And frankly, I don't want to hear about it."

This was an obvious reference to George Jr. and Martha. His people had analyzed every word of George Jr.'s speech and the messages floating through the building from the day before. The bar was high, but it was always best to go last. Tripp knew exactly how high he had to jump.

"We know drugs and alcohol are the enemies of abstinence and a huge problem in general," Tripp went on. "My plan is to put a box like a suggestion box in every school. I call it a narc box, and I don't believe 'narc' should have the negative image that the liberal media has given it. I promise we'll investigate every name that ends up in the narc box. We'll drive the drug users and drugs out of our schools."

Tripp's audience responded like an Oprah Christmas show audience that had all just won a new car. Christmas had arrived early for the religious right.

Tripp held up a second imitation book. This book said "Evolution" on the cover. The evolution book suffered the same fate as the sex education book as The Ronald ripped it in two.

"That's my view of evolution," Tripp told the cheering crowd. "This is another education issue that sets me apart from the other candidates. When I'm president, evolution won't be taught in our schools. Did you hear

George Flowers make that promise? He told you he's a Christian conservative, but underneath he's just another liberal intellectual. The intellectuals expect us to believe we descended from monkeys. Are your ancestors a bunch of monkeys?"

The crowd assured The Ronald they were not.

"The only case where evolution is valid is Senator Ramirez," The Ronald continued. "His grandfather was a howler monkey from the Yucatan."

The Ronald had taken a shot at Senator Ramirez that the Senator wouldn't be able to return. Since Senator Ramirez wasn't invited to the convention, he wouldn't be able to either confirm or deny his grandfather was a monkey or retaliate by calling Tripp's relatives a bunch of baboons.

"My ancestors and yours began with Adam and Eve," The Ronald told them. "In fact, if you look close, you'll see I have Adam's chin and Eve's hair."

Donald turned sideways to show the crowd his profile. If Adam had a block jaw with a cleft chin, The Ronald was part of his lineage. As for the hair, The Ronald's piece was blond, human, and from a single source. It's possible the source was named Eve. The crowd cheered The Ronald's chin and hairpiece.

"This is another reason we need school vouchers," The Ronald insisted. "You can't teach what they call creationism in public schools. They call it creationism, but I just call it the truth. It's illegal for our teachers to teach your children the truth."

And they all said amen.

"It's so illegal to teach your children the truth, teachers have been put to death for doing it," The Ronald informed them.

The crowd was outraged by this news. The Ronald had not exactly fact-checked this statement. His first draft had read "fired." He'd changed "fired" to "terminated," and then finally he'd changed "terminated" to "put to death." It was the right choice of words for this particular audience.

"I propose we acknowledge our heritage and adopt a literal interpretation of the Constitution," Tripp moved on. "Just as I believe English is the only language that we should accommodate in this country, I believe that Christianity should be declared our national religion."

He had to pause for several minutes to allow the cheering and applause to dial back to a volume he could speak over.

"This is a fundamental pillar of my immigration policy," Tripp enhanced. "I believe we have to limit new immigrants to Christians. We may have to look at some specific exceptions for economic reasons, but otherwise we don't need to add to our existing problems. I've already stated that when the founding fathers wrote the Bill of Rights, freedom of religion meant diversity within different Christian religions. I know Jesus was born a Jew, but he died a Christian. Even Jesus was a convert."

The crowd was chanting "Tripp, Tripp, Tripp" now. Women in the audience were swooning. Ronald Tripp was moving the entire convention toward the rapture.

"I plan to do this in a perfectly reasonable and logical manner," Tripp explained. "Non-Christians that are already legalized citizens will be grandfathered in. We all know that I'm the smartest businessman on the planet, and I know people will try to beat the system. You won't be able to just mark the Christian box on the application and waltz on in. I plan to implement a three-year waiting period for recently converted Christians. We're working up the requirements for demonstrating a pattern of Christian worship."

Tripp transitioned into his plan to stack the Supreme Court with conservative, moral judges who would strike down the abominations of abortion and gay marriage.

"I won't go as far as to suggest gays belong in prison," Tripp told the conference. "But from what I understand, they'd enjoy certain aspects of the prison lifestyle. I've also come up with a solution to all the restroom controversies. I propose we create a third restroom option. From now on, the choices will be men, women, and hybrid. If you need to use a restroom and you don't like the sandbox you were born into, hybrid is the room for you."

George Jr. had pleased the Christian Coalition of Saved Souls, but he couldn't wow them the way The Ronald could. Don had his eye on the general election, and he wouldn't pass words through George Jr. that he'd need to retract or modify later. The Ronald wasn't looking past the nomination. The Ronald had not only wowed the coalition, but he'd told them about things they didn't realize they'd wanted until he told them they did.

The day after his speech, The Ronald was back in his New York suite enjoying an afternoon of downtime before he hit the road again. Natasha was out of town, so he was watching the latest from his ghost-owned flagship San Fernando Valley adult film production company, Hard Entertainment. The video was named *Five on Five,* but it had nothing to do with basketball. Watching his studio's output wasn't work-related. Ronald had no input into what his people called the development of creative content; in fact he only interacted with one of his employees there. He just enjoyed pornography. It pained him that he was never able to take credit for making up the studio's advertising slogan: "If you can't get a woman, get Hard."

The phone rang, and Ronald recognized the number and put the video on mute to answer it.

"Tell me what I want to hear," The Ronald greeted the caller.

"The coalition endorsed you before I said my final amen," Jim Bob Bunker told Ronald. "I did my part to speed it along."

"And I'll do mine. You'll be my Secretary of Education after I'm elected," The Ronald promised.

"To be honest, we would have endorsed you either way," Jim Bob confessed.

"That doesn't matter," The Ronald told him. "I'd name you to the job anyway. You're one of my key appointments for establishing the Tripp presidential legacy."

CHAPTER 34

REPUBLICANS YOUNG AND OLD

The day's campaign stops were in Florida. Senator Ramirez might be on his home turf, but The Ronald and George Jr.'s current Sunshine State numbers were better than Ramirez's. Don would have loved to win Florida or see Ramirez win it as the next best option. If The Ronald won Florida, the race would remain a dead heat.

They typically would congregate in George Jr.'s room before starting each day. Martha was a few minutes late.

"I was stressed, so I ordered a massage through the hotel," Martha told Don. "I feel like a million dollars."

"I could use one," Don thought. "You didn't ask George?"

"I didn't even think of it," Martha told Don. "He'd probably giggle the entire time."

The first stop was at the Young Republicans Club luncheon at the University of Florida. The agenda didn't sound too complicated. The luncheon was being held to initiate new members. All George Jr. had to do was hand them a piece of paper and join them afterward for lunch. There were no speeches, and Martha would actually hand out the certificates and make nice while George Jr. just shook hands. They'd worked with George Jr. on his handshaking. He'd moved past the bone-crusher, the arm jerk, and the wet shake.

When they arrived at the luncheon, Martha was impressed by the large hall, the white tablecloths, and the floral arrangements. The college men wore jackets, and the women all wore dresses. The dominant color scheme was orange and blue. They were introduced to the club's officers, and George Jr., Don, and Martha sat at the head table with them. The omnipresent Secret Service stood on each side of the table and surveyed the students. The students were as intent on watching the Secret Service as they were on watching George Jr.

The club president stood up, called the meeting to order, and gave a brief speech. This was an important moment for him. A man with his title was interested in a political future. He was being given the opportunity to audition in front of a man who could become the world's top politician.

After the speech was delivered, it was time to welcome the new members. The club president stood up in front of the table, and George Jr. and Martha joined him. He picked up a certificate, called a name, and handed the certificate to George Jr. Martha immediately snatched the paper from George Jr. and handed it to the new member.

"Congratulations," Martha told the first student.

"Thank you," George Jr. answered automatically as he shook the student's hand.

"Tell them good luck," Martha whispered to George Jr.

They delivered the rest of the certificates to the new members, and George Jr. remembered to say good luck to all of them. After the last recipient was announced, the club president turned to the audience and told them that Mr. Flowers was staying for the traditional post-initiation party. The audience cheered.

Martha looked at Don and raised her eyebrows. There was no sign of a luncheon. Instead, a set of doors were slid open on the side of the room, and an enormous bar appeared. The Young Republicans Club wasted no time retiring to the bar for their favorite beverage.

"Could I get you a drink?" the club president asked George Jr., Martha, and Don.

Martha asked what they could choose from and was told, "Beer, wine, or Gatorade, of course."

Martha asked for water and told him, "Mr. Flowers will have Gatorade."

She didn't feel it was necessary to explain that they had another stop and they didn't want to be plastered when they got there. She also didn't feel it was necessary to tell him that alcohol was foreign to George Jr.'s metabolism and that the results might be unpredictable if he experimented. Martha didn't normally let George Jr. drink sugar during a campaign day, but a little sugar and the chemicals that went with it probably wouldn't harm him. The club president went to the bar and came back with a water and two yellow beverages in plastic glasses.

George Jr. took a drink and told them, "Hmmmm. Tastes like lemonade."

Martha left George Jr. for a second to walk over to where Don stood. She wanted to give him her assessment of the Young Republicans Club.

"Nice appearance," Martha told Don. "You got our boy invited to an underage frat party. I haven't seen so much beer since the halftime commercials at the last Super Bowl."

"This isn't like the club at Stanford," Don agreed.

"Did you think the Young Republicans Club at Florida would be just like the Young Republicans Club at Stanford when you went there in—what was it, 1940?" Martha asked.

"We'll move on before the police arrive," Don promised. "George looks like he's enjoying it. Just look at him laughing with those two students. You'd better get over there and check out what he's saying."

Martha looked around the party and noticed how many club members were coeds.

"This is one of the times you're lucky George is your candidate," Martha commented. "Bill could get himself into some real trouble here."

When Martha walked toward George Jr., the two students he was talking with saw her coming and walked away. They looked back at Martha with grins on their faces. Martha was concerned with what George Jr. might have said. It turned out the grins weren't because of George Jr.'s words.

"They just told me," George Jr. informed Martha, "you have a nice pair. Are they talking about eyes or ears?"

Martha shot the young men a dirty look and told George Jr., "I'm sure they're talking about my eyes. They're hazel."

The club president came back with two fresh Gatorades and handed one to George Jr. At least *he* was a responsible student.

Martha had finished her water and decided to get a second one. Don was with George Jr., so it was safe for her to wander into the bar area. As she walked up to the bar and looked for the waters, someone bumped her hard from behind. It wasn't a shock, considering how much alcohol was flowing. She turned around to see who rear-ended her, and she was face-to-face with the club's sergeant-at-arms. He had sat across from Martha at the head table.

"We meet again," he opened. "That was just my way of saying hello. Don't call me Rodney. Everybody calls me Gator, for obvious reasons. I kind of sneak up from behind, and then—*snap*. It's a shame we aren't in a pool."

Martha wondered how many University of Florida Casanovas were named Gator. At the University of Texas, the guys had all bragged about their longhorns.

"I had alligator for the first time last night," Martha told him as she leaned forward, nose to nose. "It tasted just like chicken. Get out of my way, or I'll have the Secret Service Taser your gator."

Rodney backed off, and Martha returned to where George Jr. and Don were standing. George Jr. saw her approaching and started to laugh. It was always nice to see George Jr. happy, but he couldn't stop himself. Don looked around nervously, hoping no one would notice George Jr.'s giggle fit. The club president saw George Jr. laughing and started doing it himself. Martha didn't know what was happening until she took a fresh look around the party. Most of the Young Republicans Club was drinking a glass of Gatorade now too.

Martha snatched George Jr.'s glass and sniffed its contents. She could have preserved a dead alligator with what was inside it.

"Does this have vodka in it?" Martha asked the club president.

"No, it's Everclear and lemonade," he answered.

"You said it was Gatorade," Don protested.

"We call it Gator Aid," the club president tried to defend himself. "That's what we call Everclear and lemonade."

When he saw the looks on Don and Martha's faces, he joined George Jr. in an impersonation of two men inhaling nitrous oxide.

"Mr. President," Don told the student, "It's time for us to leave for our next appointment."

In the meantime, Martha had to remove another Gator Aid from George Jr.'s hand. Someone had left it sitting on another table. Nobody had thought to count George Jr.'s consumption, but they estimated he'd drunk four Gator Aids.

"If George gets sick on the ride to the next stop, these Secret Service guys are going to be real pissed off," Martha told Don.

The second stop seemed mundane, until George Jr. got tipsy. They were visiting a senior living center to participate in their weekly bingo game. Again, there were no speeches to give. They'd never tried to rehearse a speech with George Jr. after he'd had a lot of Everclear, so it was best there wasn't one on the agenda. George Jr. was supposed to call the numbers, although Don and Martha had already decided Martha would actually do the calling. Now they were worried if George Jr. could pull out the balls or even stand up.

"We could always cancel," Martha suggested.

It was the easier road, but they decided to honor their commitment. If they didn't win the seniors, they couldn't win Florida. The director of the center showed them the bingo hall, full of little old men and women wearing big glasses and black socks and sandals and riding an assortment of electric wheelchairs.

"It's almost three o'clock," Martha commented. "Shouldn't they be at supper?"

"Supper?" Don responded. "I think they're so excited George is here they decided to stay up past their bedtime."

If the first bingo ball didn't drop at three, the seniors' universe would unravel. The director introduced George Jr., and the residents applauded for him. Martha showed George Jr. how to retrieve the ball from the sophisticated airflow ball machine. He'd pull out the ball and hand it to Martha, and she would call the numbers.

The first ball appeared, and George Jr. managed to pry it out of the air tube before he proceeded to drop it on the tile floor. The ball bounced, and George Jr. and Martha bent over simultaneously to pick it up and bumped heads. The seniors were being treated to some *Three Stooges* with their bingo, but they were too intent on their cards and the numbers to notice the show. Martha finally flagged down the errant ball and read the number.

The process was much smoother after that. They didn't have to verify winning cards, but although Martha felt she could speak loudly, she was asked on numerous balls to speak even louder. It was fortunate the seniors were a little hard of hearing, because George Jr. belched often and got the hiccups twice. He told Martha he didn't feel good several times, and she prayed he didn't get sick. He was not his clear-eyed and bushy-tailed normal self.

After they'd finished bingo, the director told them there was a cocktail hour before dinner. Don told her they'd have to pass. They had another event to attend. He didn't mention the next event was the next day.

As they left, one of the seniors walked up to George Jr. and said, "We really enjoyed having you select the numbers."

"You're welcome," said George Jr. "I like ping-pong."

George Jr. slept all the way back to the hotel. He didn't want dinner, so Martha and Don took turns watching him while the other one went to the coffee shop for food. Don ended up with the worse shift. That was when George Jr. finally got sick to his stomach.

"I gave him some 7-Up," Don told Martha. "I think at first he was a little afraid of it."

George Jr. slept late the next morning and still looked terrible. They had stops in the afternoon and had to hope they didn't have to cancel. If they claimed their candidate was under the weather, it would be the truth.

"I have a tummy ache," George Jr. told Martha meekly. "And my head hurts."

"It's a hangover, George," Martha tried to explain. "It's God's way of protecting us. You drank something that wasn't good for you, and God's reminding you not to do it again."

"I didn't mean to," George Jr. told her.

"Nobody ever means to get a hangover, George," Martha explained. "God works in mysterious ways."

CHAPTER 35

COLONIAL TIMES

The Ronald was enjoying his own senior moment at a community center in Clearwater. He could use parts of his Christian coalition speech, but not all of it. He was told the community was partially Jewish. He eased off the religious accelerator but put the pedal to the metal for age-related phobias. He also turned the room's sound system up loud enough to cause hearing loss for those that could still hear.

"You all know my position on welfare," Tripp said. "Why should your generation foot the bill for all these lazy bums that are young and can still work? But when it comes to Medicare and prescription drug coverage for seniors, I'm your ally."

The Ronald had done his homework, and there was no public assistance for this community.

"One of the reasons yours is the greatest generation is that you take your citizenship very seriously," Tripp went on. "The right to vote is your best opportunity to be heard. When I'm president, I'll ensure your generation is heard, not undermined by the flaws in our system."

The audience was captivated and anxious to hear what the system was doing to their generation.

"We know immigration is a problem," Tripp said. "But there's another problem for your generation. The legal voting age is way too young. We used to allow eighteen-and-nineteen-year-olds to legally drink alcohol. We realized, tragically too late for many, that children this young are not mature enough to make the right decisions about alcohol. We now mandate that the legal age to purchase and consume alcohol is twenty-one. I ask you, which is more dangerous? Allowing someone who's eighteen to drink, or allowing someone who's eighteen to decide your future? You wouldn't let your grandchildren make all your decisions for you. They don't have your experience and wisdom. So why should we let them vote? As president, I'll introduce legislation to increase the legal voting age from eighteen to twenty-one."

The seniors liked this idea. Tripp wished somebody had already made this happen. He was getting killed with younger voters. It would have helped his chances as much if women had been disenfranchised too, but he couldn't risk proposing that and losing the few women evangelicals or other ultraconservatives he had. Tripp had another voting proposal to add. His research told him the community consisted entirely of resident-owned condos, with no rentals.

"Another tradition we had in this country dating back to colonial times has also tragically been lost," Tripp told them. "We used to reward our citizens who owned property and paid taxes. That reward was the right to vote. As president, I'll ensure we limit voting rights to tax-paying property owners."

Tripp was a real estate tycoon, so anything that created a demand for property ownership was good for The Ronald. The proposal would also play well to this group of white, conservative property owners. The proposal was the opposite of communism, because true communism dictated that property was owned by the state. It also went against the grain of most current democratic ideals, though. What Tripp really needed to win was a feudal system with a small group of powerful landowners. He was at the top of that food chain.

As Tripp surveyed his audience, he saw a number of them wore white shirts, white socks, white belts, and white shoes. What was more important was that they all had white hair and white faces. He could use his entire toolbox, except for his Jewish hammer.

"The concept of affirmative action is killing this country," Tripp continued. "Your grandchildren are going to end up living with you because they can't go to college or get a job unless they're black, brown, red, or yellow."

The Ronald didn't provide his audience with an ethnic color wheel, but they understood he meant people who weren't like them. What really scared the seniors was the idea they'd have to support their grandchildren someday from their fixed Social Security or pension checks. It was time for The Ronald to move on to his concept of good people. The Ronald had a slide projector to lend some visuals.

"I talked about how your vote is being undermined by the punks. Here's the average eighteen-year-old voter. Does this look like a good person?" The Ronald prompted.

He flashed an image of a teenager with orange spiked hair and a safety pin through his lip. The audience told The Ronald that it didn't look like a good person. They didn't recognize the picture of Johnny Rotten or realize he was now old enough to meet the community's "fifty-five or above" requirement.

"Does this look like a good person?" The Ronald asked.

He showed them a picture of an African-American prisoner who had escaped and terrorized a white suburban Tampa family for a day before he was recaptured. The audience told The Ronald he didn't look like a good person, either. Most of them didn't recognize the picture or know he was an escaped prisoner who'd terrorized the family. His appearance just scared them.

"Does this look like a good person?" The Ronald asked.

The picture showed a popular Latina singer who was performing while wearing nothing more than clear, yellowish plastic wrap. The naughty parts were tastefully obscured by black rectangles. The audience didn't think she looked like a good person. The old men in the audience came to that conclusion after an exceptionally thorough examination.

The next person The Ronald showed them was a Middle Eastern terrorist holding a rifle. The audience could quickly decide they didn't think this met their definition of a good person.

"With our current immigration policies, this guy is going to end up behind the counter at the corner quickie service mart selling you your lottery tickets. Is that what we want?" The Ronald asked.

The audience all agreed they'd rather not buy lottery tickets from a terrorist.

"Does this look like a good person?" The Ronald asked as another image came on the screen.

It was a man with dark hair, wearing a sombrero and western wear that made him look like a mariachi. The audience instinctively answered he didn't look like a good person. Then they realized it was a picture of Senator Martinez. There was a murmur from the audience as they recognized him. The picture was from a Cinco de Mayo celebration in Florida during his first run for the Senate. Senator Ramirez was about to pay for this attempt to celebrate his Mexican heritage.

"I got you," Tripp smiled at the audience. "I know many of you voted for Senator Ramirez because you thought he would represent Florida. I think this picture tells you where his interests lie. He's a smart little sneaky man. If he can bring enough of his countrymen into our country, and if they get to vote, he'll eventually steal the presidency. I'm trying to keep that from happening now, but it'll only get worse. If he brings his Mexican friends to Florida, they won't just steal your vote—they'll steal your money and your possessions. These people can even do worse things than that. I'm concerned for your safety. Think about which candidate is trying to keep criminals out of this country and which candidate is trying to bring them into this country. Thank you, and God bless America."

Many in the crowd might have voted for Senator Ramirez in the past, and just as many might not have been able to remember it even if they did. But the Florida primary was under a week away, so they'd be able to remember whom they planned to vote for. They might have made a mistake in the past, but they could make up for it by voting for the man who promised to make them safe. They could show the punks, the color wheel of minorities, and these criminals invading their borders who was in charge. A vote for The Ronald could eliminate part of that feeling that getting old was hell. The new feeling was that getting old meant getting even.

CHAPTER 36

WHAT WOULD JESUS DO?

After the second Super Tuesday primary results were counted, Ronald Tripp and George Jr. were still locked in a near delegate draw. Wins in North Carolina, Illinois, and Ohio gave the advantage in number of states to George Jr. Florida was the biggest story of the night, though. The Ronald won the Sunshine State, and with its winner-take-all rules, he edged out George Jr. for the most delegates on the day. Not only did Ramirez lose to Tripp in his home state, he came in third behind George Jr. Ramirez called a press conference as soon as all the major networks had called the results.

"The voters have spoken and, unfortunately, they have not spoken for me," Ramirez started. "We ran a strong campaign, which matches my strong faith. The strength of my faith and the justness of our cause made me consider whether I should continue to fight for what I know is right. I prayed and asked Jesus to help guide me through this difficult decision. He spoke to me. He told me that I'm a good man and that we ran a fair and just race. He also told me that it is time to step aside so that the voters can find another just and good man to lead this country."

There were some moans from Ramirez's supporters. They apparently felt that Jesus wasn't as perfect as advertised and that Ramirez should seek a second opinion. Ronald Tripp and Malcolm watched on television from Tripp's Florida campaign headquarters. Tripp had spent the day circling the country in his G5 watching election results, and when it was clear he would win Florida, he told the pilot to get him to Palm Beach. He landed just before the networks called it, and he was in front of the cameras eviscerating Ramirez at the top of the six o'clock news hour.

"It's a shame he's dropping out," Tripp remarked. "He reacts so emotionally to everything I say. Now there's just Junior, and he's not nearly as much fun."

"You crushed Ramirez in his own state," Malcolm pointed out the obvious. "Plus Jesus told him to quit."

"I'm sure he did," Tripp said. "All Ramirez's friends, neighbors, and relatives are named Juan or Jesus. He was probably talking with a cousin."

"You don't suppose the just and good man he was referring to was you?" Malcolm queried.

"Very funny," Tripp shot back. "It's an obvious reference to Junior."

"Flowers will likely get his endorsement and pick up a lot of his delegates and voters," Malcolm pointed out.

"Ramirez's numbers were as weak as his nerve," Tripp said dismissively. "Junior can have Ramirez's weak little dicks and pricks, along with the handful of Republican Catholics and spics. It doesn't hurt us that badly."

"It's a close race," Malcolm reminded Tripp. "Every vote counts."

"I like the odds of me and Junior, mano a mano. He has no idea what he's in for," Tripp promised.

George Sr., Don, and Martha were also watching the press conference at George Jr.'s headquarters in Chicago. The news wasn't a surprise, given the day's results, and they'd already reviewed the implications for hours and hours.

"Losing Florida might help us win the war," Don summarized. "Our polls show well over half of Ramirez's supporters favor George Jr. over Tripp. Tripp's camp is very loyal, but it is also very narrow."

"We should pick up most of his existing delegates, but I don't know how much it helps us for the rest of the primaries. Did our polls include the option Hispanics may just vote Democrat if Ramirez dropped out?" George Sr. asked.

"No, they did not," Don admitted.

"So they could just vote Democrat," George Sr. concluded.

"Or they could vote Democrat," Don agreed.

CHAPTER 37

THE BLACK LIST

The beginning of the campaign had been an exciting time for The Ronald and Natasha. But the new adventure and the novelty of constant attention had worn off for Natasha. She and Ronald had lived like rock stars before the election. Now they lived like Republicans.

"I miss friends," Natasha complained. "Kim and Kanye, Jay-Z and Beyoncé, Derek and Hannah."

"We've talked about this," Tripp explained for the twentieth time. "We have to avoid some of the people we used to hang out with until after the election. Once I'm president, nobody can tell us what to do or who to see. I used to go to President Smith's fundraisers, but you don't see me there now, do you?"

Natasha didn't need to point out that The Ronald wasn't avoiding the president by choice. When Tripp found political religion and started to constantly attack President Smith, the White House invitations just naturally went extinct.

"I want party, no Republicans," Natasha requested.

"We constantly go to fundraisers already," Tripp reminded her.

"I say party," Natasha shot back. "Not fundraising. You give speech, I look watch and pray to go."

"Make a list of who you want to invite, and I'll look at it," was all Tripp would promise.

Natasha left but was back again in less than thirty minutes. She handed Tripp a list of names. The Ronald read the list and handed it back to Natasha.

"This would be an excellent list," The Ronald said, "for Vice President Jackson's next event. I'd forward it to him, except I don't want to introduce him to every nonwhite celebrity we know. He'd make a killing."

"Who can I ask?" Natasha wanted to find out.

"Look at your hands," The Ronald commanded her. "If someone is the same color as you, we'll talk about it. My supporters don't want to see me before the election with any of our old friends. That can change after I'm elected. It's too dangerous right now."

"I thought," Natasha told Tripp, "you going turn Republicans on nose. Now whose nose turning?"

Tripp couldn't tell Natasha that, with a little translation, she was right. He had conceded some of his "love me or leave me" philosophy in order to win conservative Republican voters. He couldn't very well ignore the conservatives now because they were all he had. He didn't want to describe to Natasha all the hard scheming, conniving, and manipulating that he'd put into the race so far. He couldn't stomach throwing away so much perfectly planned deception on a party with a few friends. But he knew his wife, and he knew he'd either need to appease her or divorce her. The idea of asking for a divorce seemed a little harsh and was about a decade premature. He thought of an alternative.

"We go to California in a few weeks," Tripp told Natasha. "Why don't you go to LA now, and I'll meet you there. Look up some of your friends and have a good time. All I ask is that you join up with me again when I get out there."

"No rules?" Natasha asked.

"Do what you want," Tripp assured her.

Natasha's boredom had her on the Gulfstream to LA the next day. She booked a room at the Beverly Wilshire and called her friends. She was in town and looking for fun. LA was the right town, and her friends were the right people. Word spread, and social media chronicled Natasha's whereabouts like a documentary on the lifestyle of a rare migratory mammal. Tripp heard about some of that lifestyle all the way in New York.

"Your wife is in Los Angeles, but she doesn't appear to be there to campaign for you," a reporter told him.

"She's taking a break from the campaign for a few days. She's relaxing with friends," Tripp answered.

"Some of the places she's going and the people she's meeting are pretty far outside the mainstream," the reporter continued. "She was at a series of clubs in West Hollywood and is with a group of artists and actors that can't possibly be Republican."

"My wife is an artist herself, and we don't restrict ourselves to who we're friends with based solely on their politics," Tripp expanded. "I support my wife and her right to see who she pleases."

"Even if it hurts you with Republicans?" the reporter persisted.

"This won't hurt me because they know they can count on me. Who I know doesn't influence how I think or act," Tripp finished. "I love my wife, as I love all women."

The Ronald smiled as he wrote his next petty partisan speech. Natasha's trip was a brilliant idea. It kept Tripp in the news, yet it gave him a platform to affirm his conservative loyalty. It brought him as close as he felt comfortable with thumbing his nose at the Republican establishment. Nobody would forgive him if he kept company with liberal fornicators and heretics, but he could forgive his wife for doing it. Nobody could blame him for that. It was one thing if she was ugly, but hot women like Natasha could always earn that pass.

CHAPTER 38

CLOSED CLUB

"So it's already shaping up like it'll come down to New York, Pennsylvania, and California," Don briefed George Sr. and Martha. "Don't get me wrong—they're all important, but those are the three monsters, and they're all in a dead heat."

"I don't understand it," George Sr. groused. "Our polls say that if the election were held today, George would destroy Jackson. The same polls say that Jackson would do the same thing to Tripp. Yet we're in this dogfight to win the nomination."

George Sr. understood the differences between the nomination and the general election, but Don explained the landscape of primary politics for the umpteenth time.

"That advantage over Jackson is our reward for taking the moderate road," Don began. "The Republican primaries are a different story. All three of these states have closed primaries for registered Republicans only. If this race has taught us anything so far, it's proven that around half of registered Republicans adhere to what we believe are ultraconservative viewpoints. They're the half that will vote for Tripp."

"The Democrats run an open primary in California. How many registered moderate Republicans do we expect to lose to Jackson?" George Sr. asked.

"Very few," Don answered. "Jackson's got a large lead. We're the ones having all the fun, and Tripp is certainly continuing to generate headlines. The Republican primary turnout is going to be large."

"I don't get it," Martha chimed in. "The Republican Party is hell-bent on stopping Tripp, but their primary system is at least partially to blame for his success."

"Our leadership has always been focused on preventing Independents, or even worse, Democrats, from polluting our primaries," Don lectured. "In hindsight, we were afraid of the communists but forgot about the fascists. The Democrats really don't have the same problems we do. The Socialist Party used to be an option for those who were so far left they nearly fell off the table. Now they can vote for the Green Party. The far right doesn't offer any similar options. If someone is too right-wing for Ronald Tripp, they don't vote at all. They're too busy marching with other skinheads or plotting to blow up a post office somewhere."

"Where do the Libertarians fit?" Martha asked.

"Their platform is a potpourri of ideas from the two mainstream parties," Don continued. "I can't imagine a single American who can honestly swear they support their entire menu. They aren't even the best ideas. It's as if they went to the Republican and Democratic diner and ordered the dishwater from one and the used fryer grease at the other."

"It makes me glad I'm a Democrat," Martha declared.

George Sr. and Don paused and looked at each other. They'd just learned another in the long list of the campaign's dark and unmentionable secrets.

"You're a Democrat?" George Sr. repeated.

"That's right. We've never talked much politics before our arrangement," Martha said with a chuckle. "It isn't illegal to be a Democrat in Texas. It just gets you thrown out of a lot of clubs and organizations if you go around advertising it. Given my career choices, I'm the most discreet Democrat you'll ever meet. You all assume I'm a Republican because I'm white, educated, and not so poor. You forget I'm a woman. If you haven't noticed, I'm not one of your strong demographics."

"Did you ever vote for me?" George Sr. asked curiously.

"No offense, Senator, but the only way I could have voted for you was if they dropped the voting age requirement to sixteen," Martha answered. "I voted for George in the primary, though. He isn't like the rest of you middle-aged Republican men. He offers me ice cream all the time. Of course, he's probably hoping he'll get some too."

They all knew a little bit more about each other, but that wasn't going to win George Jr. any additional registered Republican votes. George Sr. went back to his bread-and-butter plea to Don.

"I still think we should appeal harder to the far right," George Sr. declared.

"It's almost tax day. George can join Tripp's protest march in front of the IRS building," Don answered sarcastically. "I'd better cancel all those May Day rallies I committed to. Where do we stand on Cinco de Mayo? I'll make sure any events we do with Mexican-Americans includes a pre-rally citizenship screen."

"I'm sure Tripp will be at some anti-immigration rally that day," George Sr. speculated. "I get your point. If we can edge out the nomination with our current strategy, we should cruise through the election."

"George is doing well with our current strategy," Don reminded George Sr. "We could have never envisioned where we are today when we started the whole concept that George should run for president. George continues to surprise and help us. That rotten apple is an example. The rumors that Jackson's campaign was behind it have evolved into a rumor that Jackson threw it himself."

"There are eyewitnesses who saw the other guy throw it, and Jackson was in Washington at the time," Martha pointed out.

"A Republican can believe in Jesus based on faith, but I guess they need to witness an apple being thrown firsthand," Don tried to explain.

"Are our people being asked about it?" George Sr. asked.

"My people will neither confirm nor deny what happened. We're referring questions to the Jackson campaign," Don clarified.

"Let me reinforce my previous statement," Martha said. "I've always voted Democrat."

CHAPTER 39

SWEET DREAMS

George Jr. was about to make a speech during a campaign stop in Fargo, North Dakota. Don was trying to remember when or why he had scheduled Fargo. Public appearances by George Jr. were parceled out selectively to the states with the greatest number of voters. The crowd was large and raucous, which was a surprise, and they all had Brooklyn accents.

Martha suddenly appeared at Don's side, and she was wearing her old college volleyball uniform. She was normally a couple of inches taller than Don, but today it seemed as if she was seven feet tall. She was wearing eye black and sporting a heavy five o'clock shadow. Don did a full body inspection, and there was a defined bulge in her uniform trunks. This is when Don realized his current position in the campaign pecking order. George Sr. had always been the alpha dog, but Martha had climbed up to the beta position. Don's position gave him an excellent platform for viewing their derrieres.

"Hey pipsqueak, I just spoke to George, and he doesn't need Ted anymore. When he woke up this morning, he'd turned into a genius. He even explained Reaganomics to me, and it made perfect sense," Martha told him.

"We removed the earpiece. Get ready for some George uncensored."

The message was strange, but the way it was delivered was even stranger. Martha sounded just like Ronald Tripp. Don looked back, and Martha had disappeared. Then the lights dimmed and signaled Don it was time to do his introduction. He wasn't comfortable about what was about to happen, but the show must go on. Don walked out on the stage to the microphone, but it was two feet over his head. He couldn't lower it, and he had to shout up into it to use it. Had Martha grown, or had Don shrunk?

"I'm here today to introduce a man I admire so much I would kill for him," Don began. "In fact, if it would get him elected president, I'd kill you all right now."

Don knew this wasn't the introduction he'd planned, and he tried to make himself stop talking. Yet he heard himself as he continued to speak.

"After you've heard this man's visions, you'll realize you miserable lumps of carbon matter aren't worthy to be in the same room, nay, even the same planet, as this man," Don continued. "If you don't kill yourselves in shame, we'd really appreciate your vote in this week's Republican primary. You worthless wretches, I give you George Flowers, your next president and a god who walks among you."

The second Don stopped talking he was back on the side of the stage and George Jr. was at the microphone. This didn't look like the George Jr. Don knew. He wasn't the enthusiastic, happy George Jr. It was more the self-satisfied, arrogant George Jr. His attire had changed, too. He wore a red jacket, white bowtie, and red checkered shirt. An oversized campaign button that read "Vote for Gorgeous George" was pinned to his jacket. The most striking part of the ensemble was the pants. Today's selection was a pair of red checkered boxers that complimented the shirt. The crowd reacted to George

Jr.'s look with laughter. Don reacted to the look in horror, but the real horror for Don began when George Jr. spoke.

"Welcome, fools," George Jr. opened, "to my vision for the new Reich. I have some important policy changes to talk about today. I'm sure you'll love them all because I'll tell you to. I also know you'll love them because you look like good people."

Don had a start when he heard "good people." George Jr. hadn't woken up a genius; he'd woken up as Ronald Tripp. He had to stop George Jr. from talking, but when he stepped toward the microphone, his movement was obstructed. He looked at his leg, and there was a large iron clasp around it attached to a thick iron chain. The other end of the chain was attached to an iron cleat buried into the stage floor. He looked around for help and spied Martha on the opposite side of the stage. But she didn't come to help him. Instead, she held up George Jr.'s missing trousers and laughed at him.

"Let's talk about immigration," George Jr. continued. "Everybody tells me what a perfect plan it is to use rivers and canals to create a physical barrier between us and Mexico. Everybody agrees this will make us safe. I call it the WWDS plan. That stands for 'wet wetback deterrent system.' Today I'm announcing a modification of the WWDS that will affect California. We should have implemented my plan before it got to this, but we've already lost San Diego. Do you realize there's an immigration checkpoint in northern San Diego County to try to stem the flow of illegals heading north? This makes no sense because we know they're still getting through. Pretty soon, you'll have as many illegals in North Dakota as they have just north of Tijuana. As your *führer*, which means president, I'll elect to fall back and regroup. I'm afraid we won't be able to save San Diego."

The crowd stopped laughing and started cheering. Don struggled harder with the clasp and tried in vain to break the chain.

"I'll use the same principle a gardener does to save a diseased tree. You don't just cut off the dead, you prune back to where it's still alive. Camp Pendleton is a natural buffer zone between San Diego and the rest of the country. The Marines are already there, and everything south turns into open territory. Of course, my plan will contain a provision to relocate wealthy San Diego white people to a location of their choosing."

Don thought about chewing his own leg off like a rodent, but George Jr.'s speech would be over by then, and he might bleed to death before he was free.

"Long-term, I have a plan for the immigration problem I call the final solution," George Jr. continued. "All US-born babies who are naturalized citizens will have a tracking chip implanted. We're still researching the exact location for the chip. We'll also implant them during the next census into all legal citizens. The same goes for any adults or children who obtain citizenship legally. We're working out a plan for tourists, work visas, and the like. Then we install scanners at airports and on highways entering the country. It's a proven technology in supermarkets and tollways. We're also working on the action plan. Do we arrest or vaporize?"

Don was getting more and more desperate. He was actually hurting himself trying to get free.

"Let's move onto the homosexuals and my plan to register them as sex offenders," George Jr. continued.

Suddenly Don was free and on the stage with George Jr. He tried to take the microphone, but George Jr. just held it over his head and toyed with Don like he was a small child. The crowd was laughing at Don, but it wasn't because he couldn't reach the microphone. Don looked down, and he was completely naked. He looked around, and the crowd, George Jr., and Martha were pointing at him and laughing.

Don gasped and sprang up in the bed. The room was dark, and as he gathered himself he remembered he was in a hotel in Wisconsin, not North Dakota. He was fairly certain the speech he'd just heard had never taken place. It was a pretty crazy rant—or just another speech, if you were Ronald Tripp. Don felt relieved until he remembered George Jr. was scheduled to give a real speech in Milwaukee later that day.

Don had to admire the diversity of his own psyche. In just the last week, he'd woken up falling off a cliff, falling into a pit of snakes, and having endless dream sequences where he brought George Jr. to the wrong venue at the wrong time. Some of the dreams were reality-based. There was the dream where George Jr. kissed, or more precisely, didn't kiss the baby. There was the dream where George Jr. was riding the tractor, or the dream where Ted told Don that George's earpiece was dead. Tonight's was the first dream where Don pulled a full frontal.

Don could only laugh and try to fall back asleep. Given his age and the amount of exercise a campaign manager got, full-frontal action on his part would translate into nightmares for a lot of voters. Don was certain George Jr. was the only member of the campaign team whose dreams were sweet.

CHAPTER 40

MORE THAN TWO WEEKS

The story broke in *The New York Times,* just edging out a *Washington Post* reporter who was a few verifications away from the scoop. George Sr. heard it from an old connection from the *Times* a few days ahead of the chaos. Theirs was a symbiotic relationship built over years. The reporter gave George Sr. priceless early warnings, and George Sr. shared whatever inside information he could in return. This information might have been the most important early warning George Sr. had ever received. The *Times* had discovered a deep, dark secret concerning a central character in the election. George Sr.'s pulse raced and his spirits sank during the first few seconds of the phone call. By the end of the call, he had to laugh out loud and pour himself a stiff drink to calm his nerves.

When the blockbuster edition of the *Times* came out, the headline read "Natasha Tripp Illegal Alien," with a subhead of "Ronald Tripp Denies Connection Between Wife and Russian Mafia."

"Natasha has an uncle in Russia named Boris Popov," George Sr. explained to Don and Martha. "He's where all the family money came from, including her father's fortune. Boris's business cards say he's an importer and exporter, but Boris's real occupation is Russian big-time organized crime figure. Natasha's father Dimitri runs the US side of the import and export business. That is potentially legitimate, but most of the money he got likely isn't."

"So there's the organized crime piece," Don said. "What about the illegal alien piece?"

"The Department of Justice ran a sting in Immigration. Some of their people fast-tracked citizenships for pay. Natasha was one of them," George Sr. explained.

"Did Tripp know?" Martha asked.

"Unlikely," George Sr. said. "He isn't being investigated directly, but Natasha is in the middle of it."

"What'll happen to her?" Don asked.

"She'll probably cooperate and help the Feds clean up their internal issues. Boris is in Russia and isn't about to come here and get involved. His people who set it up are long gone. Her father just went back on business and probably won't return. Natasha's married to Ronald Tripp. I don't expect the Feds will handcuff her, put her on a bus, and drive her to the border," George Sr. said.

"It makes Tripp look like a total hypocrite, though," Don pointed out.

"He looks like a hypocrite, a fool, and a number of other unflattering things if you're a presidential candidate. His constituents won't like this at all," George Sr. allowed with a grin.

Ronald Tripp was also contacted by the *Times* before the story broke, but this was an official call to offer him an opportunity to issue his and his wife's side of the story. Tripp replied emotionally and in haste, and his response did not douse the flames. It added a few glasses of lighter fluid.

"If this is coming from a government employee, you can't trust them. They're all liars. Besides, why would Natasha need to pay to become a US citizen? Her family had money. She would have gotten it in due time," Tripp stated.

The Democrats owned the government unions, but some unionized professions, such as the police and the firefighters, were split. Labeling all government employees and civil servants as liars was not going to win voters. When the details of the case became clearer and the government employee was one of the people being prosecuted the hardest, Tripp's remarks seemed totally out of context.

The second comment was by far the most damaging. Despite the fact he was a multibillionaire, Tripp had managed to attract a large segment of the low-income to no-income voters based on his policies and positions. The comment about Natasha's income wasn't part of his previous policies and positions on illegal immigrants. Tripp seemed to be saying that there was not an equal playing field among illegal immigrants. Some began to question whether Tripp's immigration policies were motivated by a desire to defend the nation's citizens, as Tripp claimed, or if they were motivated by a desire to reduce the number of lower-income inhabitants.

"So what happens if I divorce her?" Tripp asked Malcolm.

"You might as well admit she's guilty," Malcolm advised. "It isn't the time for that."

"What about this uncle?" Tripp asked.

"My sources in Russia wouldn't talk about him," Malcolm explained. "That makes him as dangerous as Stalin, and it's another reason not to divorce Natasha."

The Ronald had the conversation with Natasha that he should have had before responding to the *Times*. Her answers didn't solve any of their problems.

"When you came to this country, how long did it take you to become a citizen?" Tripp asked his wife.

"It was long time," Natasha assured him. "More than two weeks."

Malcolm and Tripp looked at each other, and Tripp just nodded his head. They had done their due-diligence prenuptial screening and had verified citizenship, marital status, and finances, but that hadn't offered a picture of any of the history of how it came about. Tripp wasn't sure how he would have done a deeper dive, but he'd needed to dive much deeper.

"Uncle Boris is very important man in Russia," Natasha elaborated. "He so important, he know man in this country who I give application. I give money, he give papers. He tell me I skip ceremony, and he swear me US citizen at my apartment."

"Is your uncle a criminal?" Malcolm asked Natasha.

"My uncle wonderful man—always give me and my brother presents. He give my father his business. He not criminal. He is like governor, except he not in government. People all over give him money," Natasha explained.

Tripp and Malcolm were disheartened how easy it would have been to research Boris Popov, if only they'd known he was important. There were plenty of news stories in English, and they weren't flattering unless you were an admirer of large-scale criminal enterprises.

The scandal hit just before the New York primary. The Ronald wasn't in any mood to talk with anyone, and the phone was constantly ringing. His assistant told each caller that Mr. Tripp was in a meeting.

His assistant paged him and told him a caller insisted he speak to Ronald. The caller claimed to be part of Tripp's campaign. Tripp recognized the number before he picked up the phone. The area code was from Oklahoma. The news must have reached the Honorable Reverend Jim Bob Bunker. If Tripp had to choose between speaking with Jim Bob and speaking to a tabloid, he'd have flipped a coin. But he had to speak with Jim Bob eventually, and he was already in a foul mood, so he had nothing to lose.

"Ronald, what happened?" Jim Bob greeted him.

"This is a technicality," Tripp assured Jim Bob. "We'll be fine."

"I hope so," Jim Bob sounded relieved. "I've been focusing all my time in anticipation of the Secretary of Education post. I'm working on a series of history books to replace the current garbage they teach. The ancient history edition covers creation through the crucifixion. The modern history edition covers the apostles through to the founding of the University of Enlightened Angels."

"I see," Tripp said with disinterest. "Did you write anything about American history?"

"I covered the Pilgrims and the Puritans, the temperance movement, and I already mentioned the University of Enlightened Angels," Jim Bob explained. "So are you worried about the nomination? Am I still going to be Secretary of Education?"

"I don't see a problem," Tripp assured him. "It wasn't a sex scandal. That's for people in your line of business. Nobody will care. My supporters are loyal."

"I hope you're right," Jim Bob told Tripp. "I'm ready to print the ancient history edition."

Tripp shook his head. Everyone wanted to assume the worst. The other half was only concerned with what it might do to them personally. Jim Bob was a little of each. Tripp had already heard from Governor Hastings. Hastings kept begging Tripp to name him as his running mate. The Ronald may have hinted at it before Hastings dropped out of the race and supported Tripp, but Ronald had really only been interested in getting Hastings' supporters. The man Tripp had his eye on for his vice president was Arnold. Arnold was a former Republican governor of the largest and most liberal state in the land. He had that thing with that maid, but he'd made some new movies, so the public had likely moved off that by now.

"Jim Bob," The Ronald said. "In twelve months, your textbooks will be in every school, and the graduates from your school will always be able to find a teaching job. I'm pretty sure we'll have lots of openings. Don't worry about this immigration nonsense. We're solid."

If Tripp had said they were solid like lead, he'd have predicted his future. His numbers sunk faster than a lead weight in a shallow pool. Tripp had been ahead of George Jr. in New York by five points a week before the primary and ended up losing to George Jr. by ten. The Tripp bandwagon went from an Indy car pulling ahead to a useless box with no wheels. The publicity was so bad, Ronald Tripp couldn't have been elected dogcatcher in his own building. He had sold his supporters on the importance of the immigration issue. Now he was suffering for that sale.

The Ronald got a text from Rhonda right after he lost New York. It read, "If you'd stayed married to me, you'd be on your way to the White House. Thanks for the house in the Hamptons, asshole."

The Ronald didn't care about the money or the insult, but he wished he still owned that house. It would have been a good place to go hide from the vultures after he announced he was suspending his candidacy.

CHAPTER 41

FOOL'S GOLD

When Ronald Tripp asked to meet with George Jr. after he'd quit the race, George Sr. and Don were hesitant. They eventually agreed to meet and invited The Ronald to their New York campaign headquarters. They would have preferred to leave George Jr. in Houston, but Tripp had specifically asked to meet with George Jr. Tripp had dropped out of the race, but that didn't mean he wasn't still dangerous. It was Tripp's choice whether he would help, harm, or compete against George Jr. in the general election. There were rumors that Ronald might still run as a third-party candidate to stir things up some more. Meeting with Tripp was like cutting the head off a rattlesnake. Just when you thought you'd killed it, the head could still strike and the venom flow.

They met Tripp in the headquarters' modest meeting room. George Sr., Don, Martha, and George Jr. greeted Tripp when he entered the room. His bodyguard waited outside the room, so he was alone. There was a marked change in his demeanor compared to the brash, cocky man they'd experienced at the debates. Either the scandal had driven the swagger away, or he was acting humble because he wanted something. Defending Natasha had taken a toll, but Tripp also wanted something.

"First of all, congratulations, George," Tripp offered to George Jr.

George Jr. was going into the convention unopposed, so he was the nominee. He wasn't sure what had happened, but it was the type of greeting that typically was followed by a cake or a present.

"Thank you," George Jr. beamed.

"Look at this guy. He's already won, but he's still got that motor running. I admire your energy and focus," Tripp complemented George Jr. "Everyone wants to know what's next for Ronald Tripp. Am I going to run as a third-party candidate? I thought I should let you know first. I'm disappointed I didn't get nominated, but I'm also a realist when it comes to the results. I agree with the pundits. If I run, it's as good as handing Jackson the election. I don't want that, George. I know we've had our differences, but I believe you'll be a great president. You might even be almost as good as me."

The last sentence showed some signs of the old Ronald. George Sr. was struggling to be civil, but he reminded himself that this man had garnered nearly half the Republican votes during the primaries. For George Jr. to beat the Democrats, he'd need his own votes, Tripp's votes, and Ramirez's votes from the primaries.

"We appreciate that you told us first," George Sr. said.

"George, you'll get endorsements from Governor Hastings and me this week," Tripp added. "I want to offer more before the convention than just an endorsement. I want to offer my services. This election has given me a taste for public service, and I feel I can help your administration. I admit it's a big change for me, but I could even learn to live with a job title that begins with the word 'vice.'"

George Sr. took a long, deep breath. Don and Martha sat with a stunned look on their faces. They were looking to the senator for guidance. George Jr. was looking at a pencil he was slowly rotating.

"That is an intriguing thought," George Sr. said slowly. "It would meld some powerful forces. Of course, George has a list of possible running mates, but under these circumstances, there's no reason your name shouldn't be on it."

Tripp looked over to George Jr. and said, "I appreciate the consideration. How about it, George? Do you think we can bury the hatchet?"

"I like to throw hatchets," George Jr. replied.

"I guess we did throw hatchets at each other, but all's fair in love, war, and politics," Tripp continued. "If you give me the chance, you won't be sorry. I'll follow your vision."

"I don't need glasses," George Jr. said.

"No, you don't," Tripp agreed. "It's your plan all the way. Speaking of plans, I'm offering all my policy positions and papers. I think these will help you in the next phase. This is how serious I take our collaboration."

"That's a splendid offer," George Sr. gushed. "We'll look through this carefully and incorporate it, won't we, George?"

"Yes," George Jr. added.

The Ronald had accomplished his mission, and he thanked them again and left. His bodyguard and his limo were waiting. All in all, it had gone splendidly. Even when the chips seemed down, he was still the world's number-one negotiator.

"My God, he wants to be vice president," Don said as soon as the conference room door closed. "The scandal with Natasha killed his presidential hopes, so now he's trying to carry his burden into our race."

"Can you picture him as a second banana?" Martha asked. "Who hires someone who's unmanageable?"

"We need his supporters," George Sr. reminded them. "We may have to offer him something. Maybe we give him an ambassadorship. Are there any countries we really don't like?"

"There are, but we don't want them attacking us. How about Antarctica?" Don proposed.

"I don't think we have an embassy there," Martha said.

"We'll hire some American Eskimos to build a giant igloo for him," George Sr. decided. "It's a perfect setup—a government contract with a minority-owned business."

Don walked over to the table and picked up the policy book. He thumbed through it and scanned a few pages.

"Jesus, it all sounded so crazy when he said it. Seeing it all systematically organized and rationalized in print is surreal," he said for everyone's benefit.

Don handed the book to George Sr., but he didn't bother to look at it. He reached behind him and flipped Tripp's bible into a nearby trash receptacle.

"What's that?" George Jr. asked curiously.

"It's fool's gold, George," George Sr. told him.

"I thought gold was shiny," George Jr. said.

"You're right, George," George Sr. corrected himself. "It's just trash."

CHAPTER 42

UNITED WE STAND

Most of the Republican Convention was easier for Don to manage than an average day on the campaign trail. The role of the nominee at the convention was similar to that of a bride at a wedding. George Jr. didn't have to mingle with the other conventioneers prior to the big ending. He wasn't expected to make an appearance on the convention floor until his nomination was officially announced. All the Republican Party heavyweights naturally wanted to arrange a meeting with George Jr. before then, but he was impossibly busy. Don discreetly avoided divulging to Senator Joe that George Jr. was already tied up in a meeting with Senator Blow. Don didn't want Joe and Blow to talk with each other and figure out George Jr. hadn't met with either of them.

As soon as it was clear the nomination had been settled, George Sr. and Don began to discuss the one other item on the agenda at the convention. George Jr. needed a running mate. The Ronald had already done more than hint he'd wanted that role, and if George Sr. and Don wanted Tripp's cooperation at the convention, they had to convince him they had an equally spectacular but different role in mind for him. Don called The Ronald to break the news.

"Ronald, we wanted to make sure to talk with you before the convention," Don opened. "We spoke about vice president, and we agree you'd be a fantastic fit. Then the senator and I spoke some more, and it hit us that we'd be wasting your talents. The VP gets lost in administrative activities, while we really need you to be part of the cabinet core. We're looking for something huge for you."

"You do have a rare opportunity that somebody with my talents is even willing to work in government," Tripp concurred. "What do you have for me?"

"This is going to take time," Don explained. "We don't want to blow this."

"We want to get it right. So you'll tell me at the convention?" Tripp asked.

"After the convention," Don promised. "We'll have the whole picture by then."

Don and The Ronald were beginning to forge a bond. Don flattered Tripp, and Tripp let him do it. They had The Ronald on ice, but they still needed a name. It was already a challenge to select a Republican who would support George Jr.'s platform, solidify the mainstream Republican voter block, and draw in more moderate voters. The bigger challenge was that the vice-presidential nominee would be the first person outside the inner circle to have more access to George Jr.

Bill was a low-risk option for minimizing George Jr.'s exposure to an outsider, and he was popular with Republicans and moderates. The public believed Bill was seriously ill, but a miracle was on the horizon. If they'd opted for a spectacle, Bill could have bounced back to good health and made a grand appearance at the convention. But all the low-risk elements were offset by one high risk. They knew The Ronald had a collection of Bill on film, and he could still release it to the public whenever it suited him. They had placated Tripp with promises of a prominent role, but he might go off again if he found out they'd selected Bill instead of him. If Tripp released the films now, he couldn't damage George Jr. too badly if Bill was just his brother, but that would change if Bill was part of the ticket.

"It's a shame," George Sr. commented to Don. "Vice president is a good job for Bill. He's good with people, and the VP is like a glorified public relations man for foreign governments. We'd just need to make sure he doesn't try to hit on some foreign leader's wife or daughter."

"We can't take the chance that Tripp turns Bill into an internet joke," Don reminded George Sr. "Bill isn't viable for the same reason he isn't the nominee instead of George."

The most familiar set of names were George Jr.'s rivals for the nomination. They had already ruled out Tripp. Governor Hastings was almost as divisive as The Ronald, and George Jr. didn't need stronger conservative support. The other negative with Hastings were some of the things he said about George Jr. when he had dropped out of the race in support of Tripp. Senator Ramirez would help garner the Latino voters that weren't locked down by the Democrats, but he hadn't made much of a showing in the primaries. That left Senator Martin.

"She's from Colorado, and George Sr. is from Texas, so the demographics don't help us in the East," Don pointed out.

"She's a woman," George Sr. countered.

"Normally we'd be addressing a Republican vulnerability," Don agreed. "I don't think it applies to George, though. We initially joked about how George's looks would win the woman vote. It isn't a joke anymore. His numbers with women are strong, and his interactions during the campaign were perfect. Besides, George already has a woman on the ticket. Her name is Martha. The wedding update bit is killing it with women voters. The situation with Senator Martin's son makes her a sympathetic figure, but she can be a little abrasive."

"Are you saying Martha isn't abrasive?" George Sr. asked.

"She's smart enough to limit it to you and me," Don reminded George Sr. "She must really want to be CEO. She's altering her entire personality. The public actually describes her as sweet."

"Let's consider this, then. Senator Martin knows George Jr., and she likes him," George Sr. described. "She doesn't seem to notice all there is to notice about George. Is this the right time for George to try to make a new friend?"

Don took a second to consider George Sr.'s argument before he answered, "I'll call her this afternoon."

When Don spoke to Senator Martin, she told him she had hoped to be asked to run with George Jr.

"I told George I'd give him my full support," Senator Martin explained to Don. "I look as this as the fullest level of my support."

Don thanked the senator and nervously promised to set up a meeting with George Jr. at the convention. He also told her they could use her immediate help. He didn't tell her just how much help they needed, but as the convention approached, Senator Martin was meeting nonstop. She didn't know it, but she was trying to manage a meeting load intended for two people.

The challenge for Don at the convention would come during the thirty-minute interval that would start when they announced George Jr. as the nominee and end when he got off the podium and back among his inner sanctum of Don, George Sr., Martha, and Betsey. By that time, George Jr. would have delivered an acceptance speech that was witnessed by tens of thousands at the convention and millions more on television. It was a speech that had to dazzle and energize the party and jumpstart his run to the presidency.

George Jr. had made tremendous strides using the transmitter. Don knew the convention speech would be different than the debates, though, because of the size and the raucous nature of the crowd. The conventioneers would sound just like the fans at a professional sporting event or a large Amway meeting. The more noise you generated, the more it proved you were a true red Republican. They set about preparing George Jr. for the experience.

"Okay, George. We're going to practice a speech like we usually do, except we're going to make some noise," Martha instructed him. "Concentrate very hard on the words and try to block out the noise."

Don had rented a PA system and a series of live rock concert DVDs. Ted played them at nearly full volume while George Jr. practiced. The results were not stellar.

"I stand before you, ready to serve as your nominee," Ted recited into the transmitter.

"I stand to pee," George Jr. partially repeated.

"That's not quite right, George," Martha advised patiently.

"It's hard to hear. That's very loud," George Jr. informed her.

"Listen closer, George. You have to understand the words," Martha coached.

"I'll be better if you turn that off," George Jr. promised.

"You'll need to be able to hear and repeat things when it's this loud," Martha tried to explain.

"I'll just wait for it to get quiet," George Jr. explained.

Martha was never going to be able to explain to George Jr. why it was necessary for him to be able to hear the transmitter during the middle of a rock concert.

She doubled his treats and powered on, and George Jr. improved.

"We're going to fix America. We'll be great again," Ted recited.

"We're going to fit America. We'll be eight again," George Jr. heard.

"Better," Martha said wearily.

There had been some pre-convention campaign stops, but given the decisive turn the primaries had taken, they could back off on the schedule. George Jr. had time to prepare. They went into Kansas City with as much confidence as they could hope for.

Once they were at the hotel, they had to allow George Jr. to meet again with Senator Martin. She was his choice for vice president, so he couldn't easily avoid her.

"George, thank you so much for this honor. I'm not the first woman to ever be a candidate for vice president, but thanks to you, I expect to be the first one to win," the senator opened.

"Winning is fun," George Jr. said.

"It will be fun." Senator Martin smiled. "I'm so lucky to be working for a person who appreciates that what we do isn't all about work. You can make it fun at the same time."

"I hope you've read the platform proposals," Don jumped in. "We'll need your help with the platform committee. We feel this is such a good fit. You're already aligned with George on nearly every issue. We're closer to the party line on foreign policy, but we think you'll find our approach very moderate, like your own. We're spot-on with economic and social policies."

"I agree completely," Senator Martin replied. "We don't have time for fighting, do we, George?"

"You get in trouble if you fight," George Jr. replied earnestly.

"Amen to that," Senator Martin agreed. "We've got enough of a platform fight ahead with the far right."

George Jr. heard Senator Martin say she might get into a fight and asked, "Is Mr. Tripp still bothering you?"

Ronald Tripp was still a sore subject with Senator Martin, but she assured George Jr. that she hadn't gotten into any further altercations with him since the debate. Don saw an opening to discuss The Ronald further. He wouldn't break the news about his status in the administration just yet. That was something he could postpone until after the election, assuming George Jr. won. There was another small matter that was more immediate.

"There's one logistical item during the nomination I'd like to talk about," Don began delicately. "After George and you have been nominated and after you've each delivered your speeches, we plan to bring all the primary candidates on the podium for a show of party unity."

"You're telling me I'll share the stage with Ramirez, which is fine, and Hastings, which is distasteful but tolerable," Senator Martin said. "But you're also asking me to share the stage with Ronald Tripp, which makes my stomach turn. The man is human garbage, but right now he's political garbage, too. Why bother with him?"

"He's still got supporters, and we want those supporters to switch their allegiance to us with no second thoughts," Don explained. "Remember that Ronald could have run as a third-party candidate, split the Republican vote, and handed the election to Jackson."

"The party would be better off without some of his supporters," Senator Martin argued. "But I'll do it for George. You have to promise me George will stand between us. If I'm too close to him, I might forget where I'm at and kick him."

Don promised the senator she'd have her separation. The meeting went perfectly, just as the entire convention seemed to purr along without incident. The harmony was in stark contrast to the often acrimonious primaries, and it made for boring television. Ronald Tripp joined the New York delegation, and he was as bland as delegate Joe Schmo from Peoria. The networks all got a brief floor interview with The Ronald, and his message was nearly identical in each interview.

"I'm excited and honored to be part of the great Republican convention tradition," he said. "I'm here to support our next president, George Flowers."

The reporters exhausted their book of tricks to get Ronald to open up and repeat some of his negative remarks about Senator Ramirez, Senator Martin, George Jr., or even the Democratic nominee, Vice President Jackson. His responses were as interesting as an Eagle Scout altar boy's. Natasha was still laying low, but if the press asked about Natasha and her immigration status, he just told them his wife was studying hard to retake her citizenship test.

George Jr. recited his acceptance speech nearly flawlessly over the roaring crowd. One of his lines implored Republicans to get out in November and goat, but with the noise, most people didn't notice anything. Don, Martha, George Sr., and Betsey were on pins and needles and at the same time they were as captivated as the rest of the audience.

Senator Martin was a polished speaker, and her praise of George Jr. matched any of the superlatives assembled by Don and his speechwriters during the campaign. Martha caught herself wondering if Senator Martin might have her own designs on George Jr. Then Martha remembered that she and George Jr. weren't a real thing. The story sounded so real, she was starting to believe it herself.

The convention ended with George Jr. and Senator Martin standing side-by-side on the podium as the crowd went wild. Then it got even crazier. Senator Martin announced that they had invited some good friends to come up and join them in their celebration. Senator Ramirez, Governor Hastings, and The Ronald filed out onto the podium. The tagline belonged to George Jr.

"We are the Republican Party," George Jr. announced. "And we came here to win. United we stand."

George Jr. was in the middle, with Senators Martin and Ramirez to his right and Governor Hastings and The Ronald to his left. They clasped hands, held them above their heads in a victory salute, and did a stage bow to the convention in unison. It was the night's money shot.

"This has to be the least contentious Republican convention I can remember," a news anchor declared. "There are no poison pills or dissention in the social platform or splits in the economic platform. George Flowers may have done the best job of unifying the party since Ronald Reagan."

As they bowed, Senator Martin glanced down the line at The Ronald. He looked back at her, gave her his lizard-like debate smile, and winked. The Ronald had been on his absolute best behavior for over a week, and he couldn't control himself much longer. He couldn't help it.

Bill and Maryann didn't make it to the convention, but they watched all the coverage. Maryann was more than through with the long campaign, and she stopped talking with Bill every time George Jr. was on the television. Maryann's message was clear. She was letting Bill know it should have been Maryann and him on the convention stage, not George Jr. and Martha.

Late that night, after they'd gone to sleep, Bill heard Maryann tell him, "I don't believe you."

Bill tried to act as if he was asleep. There were an endless string of possible things that Maryann didn't believe, and none of them could be good for Bill.

"I know you're awake," Maryann said louder. "The floor isn't shaking from your snoring. I don't believe that stupid story from when you were at Princeton. There's some other reason you dropped out of the race."

"You heard my father and Don," Bill protested. "I don't want to talk about what happened again. We already talked about how embarrassing it is."

Maryann gave her husband a "Fine," which meant things were anything but fine, and rolled over to try to get some sleep. She knew he was lying, but he seemed to be resolved to stick to the story. She could only imagine how bad the truth must be.

Her life had been turned sideways ever since the meeting at the ranch. When Bill announced he was ill and dropped out, Maryann began to receive letters, phone calls, and even personal visits of condolence. Bill was supposed to be too ill to talk with or see anyone, but Maryann couldn't avoid them. She had to endlessly lie for Bill and accept falsely placed sympathy and well-wishes. It was as draining as it would have been if her husband were actually dying. The guilt was the worst part. She'd channeled a large part of that guilt into resentment against Bill.

The illness wasn't all of it, though. Once Bill dropped out, George Jr. dropped in. She had always been both fond of and sorry for George Jr. But knowing who George Jr. was and then seeing him contend for the most coveted and difficult job in the world was insane. On top of all of that, they'd found *that woman* to be his copilot. Maryann and Martha didn't see each other often, but when they did, it was a battle of wills.

The day George Jr. announced he was running, or more precisely George Sr. announced George Jr. was running, Maryann had taken a second shot at making Bill look like a sick man. Everyone had commented negatively about Bill's appearance, but she took the greatest offense to Martha's comment.

"I've seen him before," Martha said. "Bela Lugosi as Dracula."

Everything Martha said aggravated Maryann. The thing that aggravated her the most had nothing to do with what she said, though. Maryann caught Bill watching Martha bend over to lift a pile of papers off the floor. Martha was younger than Maryann and had never had children. Maryann knew her husband's tastes, and attractive blondes were some of them.

Lately, Bill had talked with Maryann about a run at Senate majority leader. The Republicans would likely hold the Senate, but the incumbent majority leader was in a dogfight for re-election. Bill had no such worries on the horizon. He'd been popular in Texas, and the illness raised that popularity even higher. If Bill became majority leader, he'd be the most successful Flowers ever. Of course, that accomplishment would be dwarfed if George Jr. managed, by some miracle, to go the distance.

Maryann listened to Bill's grand plans, but she couldn't muster any enthusiasm for them. Bill's popularity might be peaking in Texas, but it was waning with his wife. The Republican Party united at the convention, but Maryann felt far from united with Bill. She'd have to hold out until he recovered from his phony illness, but once she didn't risk public condemnation for leaving a dying man, she planned to vote him out of office.

CHAPTER 43

QUID PRO QUO

Lola, AKA Dorothy, smiled at the Secret Service agent in the hallway as she quietly closed the hotel room door. Her mood was considerably brighter than it had been the last time she'd scurried out of a room with Martha yapping at her heels. This time, she'd accomplished her mission. She clutched her small purse, containing the camera, under her arm that was opposite from the agent.

"We finished our meeting, and Vice President Jackson was so tuckered out he went straight to his room and went to bed. I think he's already sleeping," Lola informed the agent. "He looked awfully tired."

"Yes, ma'am," the agent responded.

"He's got my vote," Lola said as she briskly walked down the hallway.

The deliveryman was waiting for her at the curb in front of the hotel. Lola hopped into the front seat of his nondescript midsize sedan, and they drove off.

"Lola, that was your best work yet," the deliveryman complimented her. "The positioning of the camera was perfect. You could see his face the entire time. I've got to tell you, when you did that move where you spun around while your feet were planted on the mattress, that was some cinematography. I've got to try that with my girlfriend."

"Thank you," Lola chattered. "I got that move from the best director in the business. We made *Hot for Teacher III* together. Be careful, though. It isn't easy. Remember, I'm a professional."

"We'll be careful," the deliveryman solemnly promised. Then he got down to business. "There'll be a hundred grand in your account by tomorrow morning. This will be the last time we work together. By this time tomorrow, you'll be the most famous woman in America. I'd say 'person,' but that title will belong to the vice president. When this hits the press, you'll be able to star in every skin flick ever made."

"I've been thinking, and my movie career might be over," Lola informed the deliveryman. "I've been doing movies for years, but my family still doesn't show me any respect. I've decided a new career is in order. I'm going to become a daytime talk show hostess."

"Nice," the deliveryman agreed. "Just remember this once you're famous. We've never met, and nobody asked you to sleep with the vice president. You've had an affair going for months. You have no idea how you ended up on tape or who released it. You're angry because you've been embarrassed and humiliated too. The vice president's people will deny it, but people won't know who to believe. The tape shows he's a two-timing adulterer."

"With a tiny wee-wee," Lola added. "Don't worry about me. I'm an actress. I'm ready for my close-up, Mr. DeMille."

"Nice try, but that ain't my name," the deliveryman replied. "Here's the hotel. You'll be on your way back to LA on the first flight tomorrow. Good luck, Lola. It's been fun working with you."

"I'll miss working with you too," Lola returned the compliment. "You have an interesting job. Call me when you retire, and I'll invite you onto my show as a guest. You could tell some pretty good stories."

"Sorry, Lola," the deliveryman said. "My stories follow me to my grave. That comes with the job."

The Ronald and Malcolm were in the New York suite watching their latest short film project. The action in the beginning and the middle was their best yet, but the ending needed some reshooting.

"When campaigning got to me, I always used a stiff drink and a warm shower to relax," Tripp commented. "I guess Lola had the same effect on Jackson. He was snoring before she even finished dressing."

"It is curious," Malcolm agreed. "She was the one who did all the work."

"So the torpedoes have been fired, and they're all running hot and straight?" Tripp asked.

"Affirmative," Malcolm confirmed. "This is like hunting a sparrow with a bazooka. Copies of the DVDs are being delivered at the *Post*, the *Sun*, *National Enquirer*, the *Star* and Total Gossip Channel before ten this morning local time. We've sent a blind email to each of their management teams in case their mailrooms are lethargic. It won't be a business-as-usual day in the media."

"When will lovebird number one return to her nest?" Ronald asked.

"Lola arrives at LAX by eleven Pacific and should be at her apartment by noon," Malcolm replied.

"I wish I could be there when Mrs. Jackson finds out," Tripp laughed. "I love a good drama-action story."

Later that day, George Sr., Don, and Martha were watching cable news trying to keep pace with the Vice President Jackson scandal story. The story was a real roller-coaster ride. When they first heard there was a tape of the vice president in an intimate setting with a porn star named Lola Fontaine, there was a high-energy thrill associated with the fact that the election could be decided early for George Jr. The Democrats had just nominated Jackson at their convention less than a month ago, and there was no way for Jackson to quit the race at this late date. He'd need to weather the scandal and hope registered Democrats were really the godless heathens the Republicans imagined they were. George Jr. was currently ahead in the polls, but it wasn't a commanding lead. This could be their big break, albeit a break at the expense of their foe.

"The Democrats hoped Jackson would be the next Kennedy," George Sr. told Don. "I've got to admit, he's got some of Kennedy's style. The problem for Jackson is he got caught."

"They were running a strong campaign," Don complemented the competition. "You notice how he was Andrew Jackson except when he did some inner-city rally? I thought it was smart how he went by Samuel Jackson in African-American neighborhoods."

"What do you think happened when Samuel L. Jackson didn't show up?" George Sr. asked.

"He was fine," Don noted. "Morgan Freeman was usually there."

They had undercurrents of apprehension because this sounded very familiar. The networks couldn't show the video, but TGC was the first to post an image of a heavily censored Lola from a still frame of the video. When they saw Lola's face, euphoria was out and fear was in.

"It's the same woman who trapped Bill and tried to seduce George," Don stated out loud. "We know who she works for. The question is why Tripp did this."

"Maybe he set it up when he was still in the race," Martha proposed.

"Are we saying he forgot to call it off? This isn't like canceling a newspaper for a week," George Sr. declared. "He's up to something."

As if on cue, an aide interrupted them and informed them an important Republican was on the phone and he desperately needed to speak with Don.

"Don," Tripp greeted Chambers. "It's shocking news about the vice president, terribly shocking."

"I couldn't agree with you more," Don said cautiously. "I'm with the senator, and we're both flabbergasted."

"This could be great news for George," Tripp stated. "But I've also heard some disturbing reports. There's a rumor that Jackson had never met this Fontaine woman before the tape was made and that this is some type of Republican smear job. One of my people heard it was being linked back to your campaign."

"One of your people heard that?" Don repeated in a monotone.

"That's right," Tripp went on. "So this will hurt Jackson, but if these rumors persist, it could also hurt George."

"I can assure you this campaign wasn't involved in this," Don argued.

"I'm sure you weren't," Tripp replied. "At least I'm pretty sure. If one of your people did do something, I'm sure you weren't aware of it personally."

"We're in control of our people," Don reiterated.

"I'm sure you are," Tripp conceded. "But we don't want any surprises. I could help you manage this. We don't want any loose details to get blown out of proportion."

"I don't know what those details could be, but your help is always appreciated," Don offered. "I'm sure you'll do the right thing. Ronald, I'm going to need to run to another meeting."

"I understand," Ronald said. "I have just one more thing. If I can head off these vicious rumors or help set the record straight, I feel it's only fair that my contributions are rewarded. I'd like us to finish our discussion about my role in the Flowers administration."

"We do need to finish our conversation," Don agreed. "Give me a few days to deal with this Jackson mess, and then we'll get together."

The call ended once Tripp's objectives were satisfied. George Sr. had been listening carefully.

"The last conversation we had with him, he wanted some crazy bastard named Ronald Tripp as George's running mate," George Sr. explained. "That job's been filled. What does he want now?"

"We need to come up with a position for Tripp that we can all live with," Don replied. "Jackson may have been the one on the tape with the porn star, but we're the ones getting the blackmail note. I'm not saying George would trade places with Jackson, but I'm beginning to think Jackson was collateral damage and we're the real targets."

"That's some collateral damage," Martha pointed out.

"So the question is whether to deal with the devil or make a deal with the devil," George Sr. pondered. "If this bounces back to us—and we know Tripp can make it look any way he wants it—George will have a lot of explaining to do."

The implications if George Jr. had to explain it were clear.

"I'll come up with a list of positions we can live with," Don volunteered.

CHAPTER 44

PAY UP OR ELSE

George Sr. and Don arranged to meet with Ronald Tripp a week after the VP scandal broke. Given The Ronald's implied threats, they were ready to welcome Tripp into the Flowers administration family. They had carefully considered their role for The Ronald; in fact, they'd put more thought into it than any other position. Before they could offer their post, they had to listen to a number of other ideas from Tripp.

"I know it had to be obvious, but with my experience I'm a natural for secretary of commerce or secretary of the treasury," The Ronald began. "They're the money jobs, and very few people have handled more money than I have."

George Sr. and Don glanced at each other. They didn't anticipate an easy time of it, but this was a necessary meeting, just as it was unpleasant but necessary to unstop a clogged sink or toilet.

"We considered commerce," Don went first. "But we feel some of your statements during the election wouldn't play well with the rank-and-file there. Do you recall your pledge to overhaul the commerce department?"

"I pledged to overhaul everything for the greater good," Tripp responded.

"The greater good is always a matter of opinion," Don continued. "Your exact pledge was that you'd start firing at commerce the day you became president, and you'd keep firing until they were invisible. You added something about how the only way to keep their meddling mitts off businesses was to eliminate them."

"I do think they do more harm than good," Tripp agreed. "What I said was motivational. You'll need to work harder to stick around."

"Some might feel that if they work hard enough to get noticed, they'll be fired," George Sr. took over. "Then there are your policies on free trade. You promised to ban trading with any country whenever we hit a negative trade balance with them. This sounds like a policy that says if we can't compete, we'll quit."

"I feel it would save American jobs," Tripp argued.

"We feel it hurts our economy by isolating ourselves from the rest of the world," George Sr. replied. "On top of that, see how Americans react when everything costs more. We can't appoint someone to head a department they've vowed to destroy. Commerce isn't the right fit."

"Then I guess it's treasury," Tripp concluded.

"Again, some of your previous statements might get in our way," George Sr. pointed out. "You advocated a return of the gold standard, which most economists disagree with. Do you know China is the world's leading gold producer?"

"I'd like to know my money has more behind it than paper," Tripp countered.

"Fair enough, but your statements about countries that owe us money are more problematic," Don continued. "You said during the primaries that you'd present countries that owe the United States money a 'pay up or else' ultimatum. You said if they didn't settle their debt in currency or goods in ninety days or less, we'd invade them and take what they owe us. It sounds a little like what Nazi Germany did, except they invaded countries they owed money to so they wouldn't have to pay them. The countries that owe us money are our allies, or we're trying to help stabilize or protect them. A loan now is a hell of a lot cheaper than military intervention later."

"I'm a huge advocate of debt reduction," Tripp explained.

"We appreciate that about you," George Sr. jumped in. "But a secretary of the treasury has to think about more than not spending. It should be one of the least political positions in the administration. We feel that would go against your nature."

The Ronald was disappointed, but now he was curious. They'd ruled out what he had suggested, but maybe he'd aimed too low. They still hadn't announced who would be secretary of state. After all, The Ronald was the self-proclaimed number-one negotiator in the world. Don quickly ended the suspense.

"We have the perfect appointment," Don announced. "We are looking for a strong, dynamic ambassador for the world's most critical country. We need a man that represents America's power but who also can improve relations and trade. This country has been our historical adversary, but in the future they could be an important ally in the world's economic race with China."

"Are we talking about England?" Tripp guessed.

Don was knocked a little off-stride by Ronald's answer, but he recovered and told him, "No, Ronald. We're talking about your post as ambassador to Russia. You're the perfect man for the job, plus you have a natural connection through your wife. The time she'll be able to spend with her family is the added personal bonus in this."

For once Ronald stopped talking and just thought. He was personally happy that Natasha's family had moved back to Russia so they would stop bothering him all the time. It was possible that Natasha might miss them, though. The Ronald would be the most important and powerful American in Russia, and by his book, where America was always number one, that made him the most important and powerful person in Russia. Russia wasn't exactly a tropical paradise, but that could be said of all the world's truly important places. Then there was the caviar. Ronald did enjoy caviar.

"We need someone to watch the Russian bear and keep him in his cage," George Sr. added. "If you can tame that bear a little bit along the way, you'll be a true patriot."

"I see what you mean," Tripp replied. "I could end the Cold War."

George Sr. and Don looked at each other again. President Reagan had already received the W on that account, but if agreeing there was still a Cold War put Ronald's keister in an Aeroflot seat to Moscow, they'd rather be dead than red. They had turned The Ronald onto the notion of becoming the Russian ambassador, and as soon as they were sure the excitement would stick, they ended the meeting. Once Tripp was out the door, they assessed their prospects.

"All we have to do is invest a few minutes into sucking up to him, and we can get him to do anything or go anywhere," Don marveled. "I was right. We should have gone for Antarctica."

"Russia is perfect," George Sr. said. "He's more than an arm's length away from George, and he can't do any real damage. We're barely on speaking terms with the premier as it stands. The important statements on US-Russian policy come from Washington, not the embassy. I think it sends the right message to the premier: 'We sent you a pain in the ass, not somebody we care about. Let us know when you want to sit down and have a serious talk.

Until then, screw you and have fun talking with Ronald. We're through.'"

"It's not like we have military bases in Russia. All we have there are the embassy guards. I don't think he can start a war," Don agreed. "I guess that makes it better than if he were in some NATO country."

"Remember Natasha is still resolving that citizenship issue. Before we send Tripp and her to Russia, we need to verify that if Natasha leaves the country, they'll let her back in," George Sr. instructed. "We may be mean, but we aren't that mean."

CHAPTER 45

LOS MELONES

After the scandal hit the media, Lola Fontaine cashed in on it as best she could. She did interviews with everyone that would have her and sold a slightly different angle on her story to every one of the tabloids. She received a healthy sum from a book publisher, and she didn't have to write a word of the book herself. They hired a professional writer who recorded interviews with Lola and produced a wonderfully entertaining account that bore some resemblance to the real story. Through it all, Lola faithfully followed the deliveryman's instructions. She told all about her dalliance with the vice president, but she said nothing about her two separate encounters with the Flowers brothers.

She'd also realized her penultimate dream, almost. She was a regular on a daytime television talk show. The show was very popular, especially in Mexico and along the US-Mexico border. The show was called *Sexo Despeja La Mente,* or *Sex Clears the Mind.* The show was in Spanish, and it was produced by the Televisión de Baja network. Lola wasn't the hostess. That job was filled by the hottest sex therapist in Mexico. "Hot" described Dr. Merida Jimenez in both appearance and popularity. Lola played her daffy and well-endowed sidekick. Dr. Merida would take a pointer, for example, and remind the audience of the exact location of a woman's erogenous zones by pointing out their locations on Lola. Dr. Merida would tell the audience that the average woman might have fifteen zones of various intensities. Then she'd add that Lola had thirty-five and that they all led to instantaneous climax.

Lola got the role because of a host of qualifications. She'd become famous because of her sexual encounter with a presidential nominee, and she was an adult film star. While an adult film background might be a negative for an actress trying to break into mainstream American television, it was a résumé booster on Televisión de Baja. It made Lola a non-certified sexual expert in her own right. Lola wasn't a sex therapy PhD, but nobody could argue she wasn't sexually experienced, and she possessed one of the clearest minds on the planet. An American wouldn't typically land a role on a Spanish language station because of the obvious language barrier, but Lola was an exception. Over the course of her life, Lola had used an assortment of different names. She'd settled on Lola Fontaine as her acting name, but she had been born Lola Perez. Although she had grown up in East LA, she would have preferred to appear on a show that was in English. When that opportunity didn't materialize, she was more than qualified to perform in Spanish.

The show took advantage of Lola's claim to fame during the US presidential race. They featured Lola in a daily segment called "What's New with Vice President Jackson." They would show a clip of the vice president campaigning, and Lola would comment on it. For example, one of the clips showed a strained appearance with Jackson and his wife.

Lola commented in Spanish, "I offered them a three-way, but she told me she'd prefer it if she could sit this one out. She looks angry because I'm not there to help."

On another occasion it was, "The vice president looks tired. I hope he isn't cheating on me. Oh, pardon me. I meant on his wife."

The day of the election, Dr. Merida did an entire show on why powerful men like Vice President Jackson cheat on their wives.

"Excitmen, aburrimiento, powe," Dr. Merida began. Excitement, boredom, and power.

Lola interrupted the doctor's professional dissertation.

"Lo sé," Lola interjected. *"El Vice Presidente goza de los melons."* I know. The Vice-President enjoys the cantaloupes.

Lola received the biggest laugh of the season. She had considered leaving Televisión de Baja and returning to the San Fernando Valley to resume her film career. The deliveryman was right when he told her she could pick her roles and they'd all sell. She'd make more money in porn than she was on Mexican television. But *Sexo Despeja La Mente* was growing on her. Besides, she couldn't disappoint her fan base. Her fans just loved *los melones.*

CHAPTER 46

THE ANOINTED

After the sex film was released, the polls rapidly tilted in George Jr.'s favor. Unless the world discovered George Jr.'s inner character, he might coast to victory. George Sr. and Don were doing serious planning now for the Flowers cabinet and other agency appointments. They disagreed on one key appointment.

"I don't want to be chief of staff," Don vehemently told George Sr. "I agreed to make George president, not keep George president. The campaign has been hard enough. I'm counting the days until this becomes someone else's problem."

"You don't understand," George Sr. explained. "The club that truly knows George is a small one, and it's permanently closed to new members. The chief of staff is the one person who has to constantly interact with the president. They'll have to make it look like all the key decisions are coming from George. They won't be popular, because the rest of the cabinet won't have access to George. It'll make the politics inside our administration difficult, but it beats our other alternatives. That means it has to be you or me, and I'm too old. Hell, I might not live through his first term."

"If I take the job, I might not *want* to live through the first term," Don replied. "What about Bill?"

"I love my son," George Sr. said carefully. "He's a good senator. But Bill needs someone to advise him. Besides, he still has the same problem as when we talked about him as a possible vice president. He could be linked to the same woman who took down Jackson."

George Sr. had spent decades wearing down opposing senators until they agreed to his legislative proposals. Don never had a chance.

"I can't believe I'm going to do this," Don said solemnly. "If I pull this off, I'll be the greatest presidential chief of staff of all time. Nobody will ever know, but I'll be the greatest. You'd better live forever. I'll need at least one person I can brag to after this is over."

George Sr. and Don had done a masterful job of dodging the Republican Party hierarchy at the convention, but now that victory seemed inevitable, they clamored to meet their new leader. They'd held out as long as they could, but the day of reckoning had arrived. George Sr., Don, Martha, and George Jr. flew to Washington to meet with senior Republican congressmen. They brought one additional traveler along for the trip.

"I'm going to bring Bill along," George Sr. explained to Don and Martha. "It's time for the miracle. We need Bill's help promoting George. The other reason he's coming is that having him with us will create one hell of a distraction. A distraction is always a good plan, as long as the one doing the distracting isn't George."

The party landed at Reagan and drove to the Capitol for the meeting. Even though his father and brother had spent a good part of their lives in Washington, it was George Jr.'s first visit. He had always stayed behind in Houston with Consuela or, as he got older, with his mother. George Jr. had seen picture books, though, and he recognized the major monuments and buildings.

"Look, that's the Washington Monument," George Jr. pointed out to Martha.

"Yes, George. It's very tall, isn't it?" Martha encouraged him.

George Sr. asked the driver to get as close as he could to the White House for George Jr.'s benefit.

"Look, it's the White House," George Jr. told the group.

"That's going to be your new home," Martha told George Jr.

"Really?" George Jr. answered. "Does the president know?"

"You'll be sleeping in his room, George," Bill explained to his brother.

"I hope he doesn't snore," George Jr. told them. "Where are Mom and Dad going to sleep?"

Bill looked very senatorial in a dark power suit. George Sr. was energized to be back in his second home, too. Don looked at George Jr. He looked as powerful as his father and brother, but when he thought of all the amassed Republican firepower, he shuddered.

"Martha, this is one meeting you won't be able to attend," Don reminded her. "The first lady doesn't accompany her husband when he's talking business with Congress. That means the first girlfriend shouldn't, either."

"You mean we can't tell them George and I are inseparable?" Martha kidded Don. "They should understand that there's a difference between being married and being single. George hasn't reached the point yet where he's trying to get away from me for a few hours."

"Enjoy the artwork and statues in the rotunda," George Sr. advised Martha. "We'll be done as soon as we can, believe me."

When they got into the Capitol building, Martha assumed the role of a tourist, and the rest of the party met the powerbrokers in one of the House committee rooms.

The senators and representatives all stood to meet their candidate for the first time. As George Sr. had predicted, Bill's presence was the initial focal point. Several senators immediately walked directly to Bill to welcome him back. George Sr. wasted no time announcing the miracle.

"I'm so thankful to be able to give you good news about my older son's presence here today. Bill is in remission, and in fact, he's back to where he was before the illness," George Sr. spread the good news. "He'll be back in the Senate full-time starting next week. Our prayers have been answered."

The congressmen clapped and cheered, and Bill humbly bowed his head in thanks.

"Bill, how are you feeling?" Bill's friend Senator Brown asked him. "We'll have to play some golf as soon as you're up for it."

Bill had been going out of his mind from boredom during his alleged illness. The ranch had a lot of open land around it, so on the bright side his short game had improved considerably as he pitched and putted for hours in the back ninety. He'd only lost a couple of balls and disturbed one rattlesnake.

"I'm ready to play next week," Bill insisted.

"Don't push yourself," Senator Brown quickly replied. "I don't want you to take any chances with your health. I won't try to take advantage of you until you build up your strength, either. We won't play for money until you're a hundred percent."

"I can play next week, and we're absolutely playing for money," Bill informed Senator Brown. "We'll get a drink afterwards, too. The doctors are fine with it. You'll be buying."

Bill had always relied on his weekly winnings from Senator Brown to cover some of his bar tab. Since they played for cash, it gave him some spending money that Maryann couldn't trace. Bill realized just how much he'd missed the Senate. There was the golf, the drinking in every bar in town with lobbyists and cronies, and all those young, eager female interns. It was the best job in the world. It took some of the sting out of botching the presidency. He wasn't sure what it would do to his style if his brother, mother, and father were in town full-time. He might attract even more unwanted attention as the president's brother.

George Jr. looked at all the men and the couple of women standing in the room and immediately recognized two of them. Senator and vice-presidential nominee Martin was in attendance, along with Senator Ramirez. Senator Ramirez might not have been invited to such an event the year before, but his role as a presidential candidate and Ronald Tripp's number-one trash receptacle had raised his profile and notoriety.

"Hello, George," Senator Ramirez greeted George Jr. formally. "It's so nice to see you again."

George Jr. was in peak handshake conditioning, and he gave Senator Ramirez a firm but not painful grip and replied, "Nice to see you too."

Senator Martin would have been in the congressional welcome wagon, but her role today was stronger as a member of George Jr.'s administration. She had George Jr. to herself, although Don tried to stay as close as good manners would allow.

"George, just seeing you here in Congress for the first time is a thrill," Senator Martin opened. "I'll miss the Senate, but we're starting a true adventure together. The next time we're in Washington, we'll be meeting in the White House."

"Are you sleeping with the president too?" George Jr. wanted to know.

Senator Martin smiled and looked around the room to make sure they weren't being overheard. Her new boss might not be worried what was overheard, but it always seemed to be harder if you were a woman that was perceived as being on the prowl. Don was close, as he always seemed to be, but not too close if she spoke quietly.

"Your arrangements with Martha are none of my business," Senator Martin clarified. "But I've always wanted to check out the rooms in the White House. Like I said before, I'm looking forward to new adventures. All you need to do is ask."

Don moved closer, and Senator Martin squeezed George Jr.'s arm and gave a "So nice to see you" for Don's benefit and walked back to join her colleagues.

Don hadn't heard the conversation, but he knew more than two short sentences from George Jr. could never be a good thing. Don guided George Jr. to the congressional reception line, and they sandwiched George Jr. between George Sr. and Bill as they introduced him to his potential allies and enemies, depending on what lay ahead. George Jr. gave his top-shelf handshake and a hearty hello to each member. Then he was guided to a seat at a table facing the group. The Senate majority leader was the first to welcome George Jr. to the Capitol. This was the man that Bill had thoughts of replacing if he lost his re-election bid.

"In opening, let me tell you how exciting it is to see our party in such a strong position to reclaim the White House," the majority leader told George Jr. "We'll get our paddles moving in the same direction again once you're in office."

"Like a boat," George Jr. guessed.

Don was sitting next to George Jr., but he was on the edge of his seat waiting to jump into the conversation if George Jr. led it wayward. So far, paddles and boats were consistent with each other. Martha had been George Jr.'s filter throughout the campaign. As a filter functions to trap unwanted or unpleasant substances, Don was discovering that the job of a filter for George Jr. meant constant vigilance to prevent unwanted remarks. If the filter couldn't prevent the remarks, they'd have to filter away the damage once they got out. Don would be George Jr.'s new filter when George Jr. was on the job as President. Don might have to consider finding a cabinet post for Martha so she could help manage George Jr. full-time.

"We love your platform and your positions," the House minority whip told George Jr. "We hope you stick to your guns once you start feeling the daily pressures of office. You'll be under a great deal of non-conservative pressure to back off some of our beliefs."

"George will stick to our beliefs," George Sr. promised. "Won't you, George?"

"Stick like glue," George Jr. promised.

They had worried about the meeting, but it went quickly and smoothly. George Jr. hardly had to speak because the large number of congressmen present were focused on standing out and making a favorable impression. By the time each one had congratulated George Jr. on his nomination, expressed their support and optimism for his election, spoke of their commitment to work with him, and told him what was important to their state's constituents, the meeting was over.

"We feel," the majority leader told George Jr., "like we really got to know you in the last hour."

The best way to get into good graces with a congressman was to let him or her do all the talking. Senator Martin told George Jr. goodbye before he left with the rest of the group.

"George, I'll see you election night," Senator Martin said. "I also look forward to seeing you soon in the White House. I look forward to seeing you all over the White House."

"We'll explore," George Jr. proposed.

"I'm sure I'll like what I find," Senator Martin promised.

They met Martha in the rotunda looking at the *Baptism of Pocahontas.* An hour was hardly enough to make a dent on the Capitol's splendor.

"How was the meeting?" Martha immediately asked.

"I don't know how you did it all those months," Don told her. "I'm a wreck."

"It was fine," George Sr. assured her. "They talked and we listened. Congress loves George—at least the Republican piece. How was your tour?"

"It was educational, but I didn't get too far," Martha told them.

"You'll get a chance to see the rest," George Sr. assured Martha. "We'll be back soon, and we'll stay longer. If things go as planned, you'll have time to see all the artwork in the Smithsonian if you want to."

"I'll see about that," Martha told him. "Too much culture might make Martha a dull girl."

CHAPTER 47

V DAY

The campaign released the location of the Flowers ranch polling place to the press so that they'd be set up when the candidate arrived. Two limos arrived at the ranch at six in the morning. One held the Secret Service team, and the second would transport George Jr., Martha, George Sr., and Betsey. Given Bill's condition, he and Maryann had voted absentee. Consuela was at the house, but she told them she wasn't registered to vote.

"I wish Jorge good luck," Consuela told them. "Make sure he vote for he-self."

Don wouldn't be joining them either. He'd voted absentee as well, so he could spend the day at the Houston headquarters. They wanted to get to the polling place early so that the press could show George Jr. voting when other voters were rising to vote or go to work. The other advantage was that early meant smaller crowds for George Jr. to navigate.

"Are you excited, George?" Martha asked. "You get to vote to elect yourself president."

"I have to vote," George Jr. urged, "to win."

"I don't think we have to worry about carrying Texas," George Sr. said.

They arrived at the polling place, the local middle school, and the television crews were camped out waiting. They wanted a statement from George Jr. before he went into the building to vote. Martha sprang into action, taking George Jr.'s hand and stepping him forward toward the press.

"Mr. Flowers, the polls show you're ahead by a sizable margin, and there are predictions of a landslide," a reporter asked. "How confident do you feel today?"

"George is always confident," Martha answered. "You feel good, right George?"

"Feel good," George Jr. confirmed.

"Today Ronald Tripp told a New York reporter that he'll have a prominent role in your administration," another reporter asked. "Do you have a cabinet post in mind for him?"

George Sr. swore to himself quietly and fielded the question. "We are discussing some role for Mr. Tripp, but we haven't discussed a cabinet position."

The rest of the questions were powder puffs. Martha informed the press that George Jr. was happy with the campaign they had run, he was ready to lead, and they would go to the Houston campaign headquarters later in the day when results began to come in. George Jr. did an acceptable job of acknowledging each of Martha's answers.

"Thank you, ladies and gentlemen, but it's time for George to exercise his democratic right," George Sr. announced.

They entered the polling place, and the volunteers were star-struck. They processed the VIPs, and it was time for George Jr. to vote for the first time in his life. He hesitated when it was his turn, but Martha and Betsey simultaneously egged him on. They made sure he was clear on the booth he was supposed to use and hoped for the best. They had rehearsed every aspect of voting with

George Jr. They had constructed a booth at the ranch, and George Sr. had managed to procure an older model voting machine. George Jr. may have practiced more than any other voter in Texas, but his finished ballot was the most gently used. He cast a single vote for himself in the least number of available steps. On their way out of the polling place, a reporter asked George Jr. the oldest line in the history of democracy.

"Who did you vote for, George?" he asked.

"I voted for me," George Jr. answered sincerely.

The way George Jr. answered earned him another round of laughter from the press. A clip of George Jr. arriving and one of him answering the voting question were carried nationally. The voters must have enjoyed them, because most of them voted the same way George Jr. had.

They drove back to the ranch and watched the network election coverage the rest of the day. By midafternoon, states were being called for George Jr. George Sr. stayed in constant contact with Don. Don gave them the word at three in the afternoon.

"That was Don again," George Sr. told the group. "He says we'd better get to the Hyatt, or we'll miss out on the party."

The drill was the same as in the morning, except Bill and Maryann joined them and the ride was further. Consuela's grandson came to the ranch to pick her up and drive her home. Senator Martin had voted early in Colorado and caught a charter jet to Houston to meet them at headquarters. The process on election day would mimic the process at the convention. George Jr. and his entourage would steal away to a hotel suite, while Don and others managed the reception room crowd and stoked their fire. George Jr. was expected to show his face when it came time to celebrate victory or acknowledge defeat. Unless every network's election coverage had been hijacked by a madman, the only speech in George Jr.'s immediate future was a declaration of victory.

Senator Martin was already at the suite, and she greeted George Jr. when he arrived.

"I'll call you George one last time. The networks are calling it. Thank you again for making me your vice president, Mr. President," Senator Martin told him.

Martha stuck even tighter to George Jr.'s side. She got the feeling Senator Martin would have switched roles with Martha if she was given half a chance. Don came up to the room as soon as he was told they'd arrived.

"Senator, old-timers like us are going to enjoy this election. We won't have to stay up late to find out what happened. We might hear from the vice president before the ten o'clock news, and I'm talking about the East Coast edition. I haven't had a night like this since Reagan was re-elected," Don gushed.

Don had been running ragged all day, but he was as excited and emotional as they had ever seen him. George Sr. was less stern or scary and more the genial old man himself.

"They loved George," George Sr. declared. "I suppose part of this is an opposite reaction to Jackson."

Don agreed. "George didn't need help with the female vote, but the exit poll numbers he has on female voters are crazy. The first female president we elect won't touch George's numbers. The footage of Jackson and that girl just destroyed the women's vote for him. When you spurn one, you spurn a bunch."

"So we'll wait for the call," George Sr. said.

"When Jackson's concession call comes, come down to the banquet hall right away. I'll stay in touch with Jackson's people and try to give you advance warning. I hope George is up for his victory speech. It's going to get loud, maybe as loud as at the convention. I'll talk to

Ted again and remind him to talk slow," Don offered as final instructions.

Don's remark about an early evening was on the money. Jackson called to concede just before nine Central. George Sr. greeted the vice president and gave him his best wishes. Protocol said that George Jr. had to speak to the VP, and there wouldn't be an intermediary. The upside is that whatever was said would be man-to-man, and Jackson was in no position to talk out of school. George Sr. slowly handed the phone to George Jr.

George Jr. seemed to listen for a long time. He said yes twice, and thank you, and he handed the phone back to George Sr.

"Senator, you must be proud," Vice President Jackson said. "George will be a great leader. I wish you both well. If there's anything I can ever do, do not hesitate to contact me."

They made the journey from the suite to the reception area, and everyone they met stopped, stared, and then applauded. The future president was in the house. Martha was glued to George Jr.'s side, her place through the entire campaign. They entered the ballroom, and the applause started spontaneously even before Don realized they were in the room. Don wasted no time in calling George Jr. to the stage. They had discussed sending Martha with him, but this was a job a president had to do alone. Besides, he wasn't truly alone. He had Ted on the other end of the transmitter. Don was right about the noise level, too. But George Jr. had become a much better listener.

"I have just," George Jr. repeated in fragments, "talked with the vice president. He told me congratulations. We ran a fair race."

Congratulations sounded as if it had fifteen syllables when George Jr. pronounced it, but otherwise he was doing fine. George Jr. waited with an impatient look for the next line, but Ted waited until the noise died down. It made George Jr. look excited, and maybe he was showing signs of emotion for the first time. It was a look that worked. He finally went on, thanking Vice President Jackson for a fair and honorable fight. George Jr. didn't comment on how honorable the vice president was from where Mrs. Jackson stood. He thanked his supporters and told them he meant every word he told them during the election. He told them he didn't just give speeches as a way to win; he gave them to tell the country his plans. None of those plans would change just because he'd won.

George Jr. concluded with, "I need to thank the people who made tonight possible."

Then he introduced Senator Martin, and they had their winning twosome moment. Next he introduced Don, George Sr., Betsey, Maryann, and Bill. He gave Bill another tremendous public hug, and the crowd loved it. Then he introduced Martha, and the noise peaked. The White House wedding had gone from fantasy to reality— the election win was the last step. George Jr. had finished his job. The only thing left was to stand on stage smiling, waving, and enjoying their supporters' energy and love.

Consuela was watching the event from her son's house with the rest of her family. She had tears in her eyes. Little Jorge was going to be President of the United States.

"America some country," Consuela told her family. "You can be *simple mente* and still be *presidente*. And they call Mexico third world."

Back in the banquet hall, George Sr. and Don were congratulating each other.

"Remember that announcement Tripp made when he came out as a candidate?" George Sr. shouted to Don. "He ramped up too early. This is the time to celebrate."

"He might be the one doing this if he'd paid closer attention his wife's citizenship papers," Don shouted back.

Martha took George Jr.'s hands on stage, and they danced to the music. Martha led as discreetly as she could manage. George Jr. wasn't a bad dancer, considering he'd never had a chance to do much of it. He had that natural rhythm that came from not overthinking it. This went on for a while, and the party showed no signs of ending. George Jr., Martha, and the others waved and made their exit as Don announced to the crowd that the next president was leaving. They were heading back to the sanctuary of the ranch. Don had a longer night ahead of speaking to the press in multiple time zones and countries.

The day caught up with everyone on the ride back to the ranch. Even George Jr. nodded off. Martha was the only one too keyed up to sleep. George Jr. was sleeping on her shoulder. She looked at him and felt as proud as she would have if he were her actual fiancé. What he had accomplished was remarkable, especially considering how he had accomplished it. A lot of the credit went to a crazy old man, the world's best political strategist, and Martha herself. But they couldn't have done it without George Jr.

She looked over at him and whispered, "Sleep tight, George." Then she reconsidered and corrected herself. "Sleep tight, Mr. President."

CHAPTER 48

BALL-BUSTER

The convention and election night had been two of the greatest thrills of Martha's life, but at the same time, now that they were over, they were two of her life's most anticlimactic moments. She'd spent more than a year focused on a singular goal, and that goal had just been realized. It was time to consider the next one.

She understood her fairytale goals. She'd move to Washington to be closer to her president-elect fiancé, and they'd have that White House wedding sometime during his first year of office. As first lady, she'd visit hospitals, shelters, and foundations raising awareness against all the ills of man. She'd be at George Jr.'s side during all the White House dinners and accompany him on exotic and monumental foreign junkets. There would be buildings, bridges, and roads named after George Jr., but there might be a few named after Martha too. When a poll was given asking American girls who they admired most, Martha would be at or near the top of the list. Even after George Jr. was done serving his terms, they'd remain part of America's history. They'd still attend presidential inaugurations, state dinners and, sadly, state funerals until the day came when one of those funerals was in their honor.

That was the fairytale future. When Martha tried to picture her real future, her mind went blank.

They spent a few days after the election at the senator's ranch, except Don, who was back in California with his family. Martha was getting a little tired of the ranch's surroundings, but it was George Jr.'s only home and safe haven. Where George Jr. went, Martha must follow. She realized she couldn't appear anywhere in public alone. She'd be hounded by the press and asked endless questions about George Jr.

It was late in the afternoon, and Bill and Maryann were visiting the ranch with Justin and June. Maryann, Betsey, Justin, and June decided to go horseback riding on the ranch. George Sr. and Bill elected to stay behind and crack open a bottle of George Sr.'s bourbon. George Jr. and Martha didn't ride, so Martha joined the drinkers in the study and George Jr. watched television in the den. George Sr. was still on a post-election high, and a few fast glasses of bourbon fueled his energy further.

"Can you imagine, Bill?" George Sr. kept saying to his elder son. "Your brother is going to be President of the United States."

Martha was interested in Bill's reaction, and she noted a slight cringe every time George Sr. drove home the message. Bill had some other things on his mind.

"I still don't understand why I shouldn't be a part of the cabinet. If I were secretary of state, I'd be better positioned to run for president again at the next election," Bill complained and then corrected himself. "I mean, after George is re-elected."

"We've talked about this," George Sr. said with an annoyed look. "That video is still out there, plus you're still supposed to be recovering from your illness. Besides that, we think you can help George more in the Senate. He'll need your help negotiating Capitol Hill."

"George doesn't even know what Capitol Hill is," Bill pointed out.

"His administration needs your help, then, if you want to get technical about it," George Sr. answered.

Martha sat, watched, and sipped her bourbon. Bill sipped faster and got himself several refills. George Sr. sipped the fastest and matched Bill refill for refill. Just when it looked like they might have to crack open a second bottle, George Sr.'s age and recent activity level caught up to him. He stopped sipping and started snoring.

The election had been hard on Bill too, mainly because he wasn't in it. He spent most of it pretending he was gravely ill. At the same time, Bill's lifestyle had experienced alterations that weren't to his liking. He couldn't philander if he was supposed to be gravely ill, and, after Dorothy, sex with strangers was too dangerous. That didn't mean that his urges had disappeared. In fact, things had gotten so bad he'd resorted to sleeping more often with Maryann.

Bill liked what he saw the first time George Sr. had introduced Martha. He knew the relationship between Martha and George Jr. was a charade and that she wasn't a blackmailer. A few glasses of bourbon and an opportunity alone, and Bill was back to his old form.

He picked up the bourbon bottle, walked over to Martha, and refilled her nearly empty glass.

"I didn't ask for another," Martha pointed out.

"You looked like you wanted something," Bill came back. "If it isn't a drink, maybe it's something else."

Martha glanced over at George Sr. His head was back, his mouth was open, and he sounded like the automatic swimming pool skimmer when it got too close to the surface. There were times when Martha had wished the senator would stop talking and fall asleep, but this wasn't one of them.

"You know I have a thing for strong women," Bill kept coming on. "I know my way around this house. Maybe you'd like to see my old room."

"I don't think that's a good idea," Martha replied.

"My father is passed out, and everyone else is out riding for hours," Bill said and paused. "Then there's George. We know about George, and George won't mind. There are things I can give you that we know George can't."

"I'll bet there are," Martha started in a husky voice. Then she went from sexy to angry. "Three things come to mind. You can give me a sense of self-loathing, a lifelong hatred for men, and venereal disease."

Bill got angry in response. "You're a real ball-buster, aren't you?"

"Damn right, I am," Martha spat back. "The next time you come onto me, I'll give you the literal version. I played volleyball at UT and was good at spiking. I was even better at the two-handed digs. If you make me have to dig you, you'll sound a lot younger the next time you make a speech."

Someone needed to leave the room, and Bill wasn't going to abandon the bourbon. Martha walked out and joined George Jr. in the den.

"Hi, Martha," George Jr. said with a smile.

His happiness made Martha feel a little ashamed. They were all too fast to abandon him because he didn't share their interests or participate in their intellectual conversations. It wasn't fair to George Jr. He couldn't spend his time with children, and he wasn't treated like an equal by adults.

"Hi, George," Martha answered. "What are you watching?"

"It's about dogs," George Jr. told her, happy to have someone to talk with. "Dogs are man's best friend."

George Jr. hadn't learned that a woman was man's best friend when he got a little older. Martha reached over and held George Jr.'s hand, and he squeezed it in return. Then Martha leaned over and gave George Jr. a kiss on the cheek.

"Thank you," George Jr. told her as he blushed.

Martha leaned over farther. Her intended target was George Jr.'s lips. She began to close her eyes instinctively, but she noticed George Jr.'s eyes were opening wider as hers were getting smaller. George Jr.'s expression reminded her of the day the mother at the Alamo asked George Jr. to kiss her baby. He was in his early forties, but he wasn't ready for his first real kiss. Martha caught herself and recoiled back to her spot on the couch.

"Got you," she said as she reached up and tickled George Jr.'s ribs.

George Jr. giggled, and everything was back to normal. Martha realized what she'd just tried to do, and now it was time to feel some real shame. She didn't think highly of female teachers who seduced their fourteen-or fifteen-year-old students. George Jr. may look like Cary Grant, but he had the mind of Beaver Cleaver. She wasn't any better than a pedophile.

At that moment, coming off Bill's pass at her and her pass at George Jr., she realized she'd lost her way. She had a clear picture of her future. It was anything other than what she was doing now.

CHAPTER 49

PLAUSIBLE DENIABILITY

Martha didn't say anything about her thoughts the rest of the day. She was quiet and moody, but not so moody she got into any altercations with Maryann. The next morning, she told the senator she needed to meet with him in private.

George Sr. didn't go into the meeting with any major fears, but he thought it was a meeting where Martha would ask about the next leg of his plan. He'd been working to write that screenplay himself, and he still had some rough patches to work through. Martha's news would lead to some significant rewrites.

"This has been a scary and an amazing ride, but I feel I need to get off," Martha opened.

George Sr. wasn't ready for the direction the conversation was headed, but he'd worked with Martha long enough to know when she was serious.

"Why leave now?" George Sr. asked. "It's just getting to the good part."

"It's getting to the insane part where George Jr. is the most scrutinized person in the world," Martha said.

"Is this a renegotiation?" George Sr. asked suspiciously. "I thought CEO was enough, but I'll do what I must to keep you. You've done a great job."

Martha did something she hadn't done since she was a girl. She started to cry.

"It isn't a renegotiation," she sobbed. "You're a real asshole sometimes, Senator."

His tone softened, and he said, "I apologize. It's an occupational hazard that goes with being a congressman. Nobody but my wife can call me that, though. Last night it was because I picked on her favorite show. I'm not sure what it'll be for today. You can use it just this one time. So what is this really about?"

"It's hard to be around George all the time. I don't want to confuse him," Martha said.

"George isn't confused about this," George Sr. replied. "He's the most consistent person we know."

"I have inappropriate feelings for him, okay?" Martha said emotionally. "There, you made me say it."

"You've got some variant of the Florence Nightingale effect," George Sr. told her. "He is a handsome devil. He looks just like I did at his age."

"Nice try, but that isn't enough to cure me," Martha laughed.

George Sr. realized this was a problem he couldn't solve with money or filibustering. It was really over.

"So I lose my make-believe daughter-in-law, but at least I get back my best employee," George Sr. acknowledged. "It isn't like we can talk to a lawyer, but if we did, they'd tell me you held up your end of the deal. You got him elected."

"I'm sorry, Senator, but I can't go back to work for you at all," Martha informed George Sr. "Part of it is that everyone at the company thinks all my ideas were George's, but the main reason is it's too close. I've got to make a total break."

"This isn't my day," George Sr. lamented.

They saw no reason to put off telling Don. George Sr. called him and gave him the news.

"What else can we offer?" Don said desperately.

"It isn't a renegotiation," George Sr. told him.

"I'm sorry, Don," Martha said sincerely. "I enjoyed working with you. I even planned to learn CPR for around the White House. With your job, you may need it."

"I'm hoping the Secret Service is trained in it," Don answered. "Are you afraid we're going to implode?"

"I can't believe the two best political minds in the world have come up with a plan that's earning them four or more years of hell," Martha said. "I've asked my investment guy to buy stock in the companies that make Maalox and Xanax. You'll make them growth stocks. But that isn't my reason."

"You may be the smart one," Don told her.

"If someone figures it out, say it's something you've just started to notice. George must have a rapid-onset neurological disease," Martha said. "They can call it Flowers Syndrome."

"I like it," George Sr. replied. "It has to work better than the truth. I'm still considered a trusted public official, but I've done things in my past I can't talk about. I need to make sure none of them catch up to me. Where are you going?"

"Initially, I was looking outside the US. Then it occurred to me that if I'm recognized, I might be kidnapped. I'm going to look at California," Martha replied.

"I wish I could join you," Don said. "Tomorrow is your first day of plausible deniability."

CHAPTER 50

BYE, GEORGE

Don cut his visit home short and flew back to Houston. The breakup of America's fairytale couple would be the biggest news event between the election and the inauguration. George Jr. might announce his cabinet choices or an assortment of policies that were wildly popular or unpopular, but that would pale in comparison to calling off the engagement. A firestorm of media attention would rain down and burn both sides of the relationship. Don and George Sr. could shelter George Jr., but Martha would not be afforded the same protection.

"I don't care where you go, the media will hunt you down and dog you," Don warned Martha. "We need to think about what you'll tell them."

"I think it's simple," Martha replied. "I'll tell them I had womanly needs, and George insisted we honor our vow of abstinence. The religious right is to blame for breaking up our engagement."

George Sr. and Don listened and paused to think. They looked as if they might accept Martha's idea.

"Oh my God, I'm kidding," Martha said in an exasperated tone. "I don't want the world to think I'm a nymphomaniac. That's what Jim Bob Bunker calls his wife if she tries to have marital relations with him more often than once a month."

"I'm glad to hear you're kidding, because I wasn't in love with the idea," Don told her.

"I suppose telling them to mind their own goddamn business is out of the question, so I'll tell them I got a taste of the pressures and chaos of being first lady during the campaign and decided I couldn't handle it. I'll tell them that other first ladies must have had similar fears, but since they were already married they felt they didn't have a choice. They loved their husbands too much to crush their dreams. I felt I could still make a choice, and I made this one. I'll tell them it had nothing to do with anything George said or did. I still love George, and I feel he's the greatest man I'll ever meet for the rest of my life. Then I'll confirm a hundred times that we never did the dirty deed. No matter how many reporters ask, I'll say the same story over and over again, nearly word for word, until the press gets bored with me and leaves me alone," Martha recited. "Then, if there are still a couple of jerks who persist and won't leave me alone, I'll eventually kick them in the balls."

"Most of that was nearly perfect," George Sr. told her.

George Sr., Don, and Martha broke the news to the rest of the core team in the study. Bill, Maryann, and Betsey were in the room. Betsey already knew, but she hadn't spoken about it to Martha. George Jr. was in the den watching television. Martha would speak to him alone. The group waited as Martha began to speak. She told them her relationship with George Jr. was coming to an end and she would be leaving for California the next day. She thanked them for their friendship and their support. Bill was in the room, but Martha didn't bother to stipulate any exclusions.

Betsey stepped forward and said, "We all knew your relationship with George was never going where we told the public, but it still makes me sad to see you leave. We'll all miss you, George included. It would be wonderful if George could marry someone like you, but that was never part of God's plan for him. I feel like you're the daughter I never had."

Martha was touched and thanked Betsey at the same time she watched Maryann out of the corner of her eye. Martha was relieved that Maryann's anger at Betsey's remark looked to be directed toward Betsey.

Bill stepped forward and acted as if he was about to give Martha a hug goodbye. Martha quickly stuck out her arm for a polite handshake. Bill's handshake in return was about as personal and familiar as the one he gave random Capitol visitors from Abilene or Plano who wanted to shake their senator's hand.

"I guess if you're moving to California, I'll have one less vote in Texas," Bill commented.

"We both know who I'd have voted for if I stayed," Martha shot back.

Bill clumsily moved aside to let Maryann say her goodbyes. From the first time they met, Martha and Maryann had gone together like tiramisu and chili powder. Martha expected a minor hug or a handshake that was even more tepid than Bill's, but Maryann surprised her.

"Can I speak to you alone?" Maryann requested.

The group watched as the two routine combatants walked out into the hallway.

"If I take a page out of Betsey's book, I'd call you the sister I never had," Maryann started. "It's a lucky thing I didn't have a sister because I never wanted one. But I'll miss you too. I hated your guts at first, but I realize what things will be like when I'm back to just Bill, his parents, and George. Right now I like George better than the other three. You were good for him, although he can't tell you just how good."

"I apologize for coming on so strong, but you're an imposing group," Martha tried to explain.

"No apologies necessary," Maryann told her. "So, is George getting a new girlfriend right away, or is he taking some time to get over it?"

"I didn't even ask, but I think Don has his hands full without adding another player," Martha speculated. "George will have to play the field on his own."

"I don't know what they told you about Bill dropping out, but I don't buy what they told me," Maryann went on. "I knew Bill wasn't husband material when I married him, but I tried to force him into the position. If you, George, and Bill were in Washington together, I was ready to move there too. I know Bill had a notion about you."

"Maryann, you would have had nothing to worry about," Martha promised her. "I have too much respect for you to go there. For that matter, I have too much respect for myself."

"You and about three and a half billion other women on the planet seem to have something Bill needs," Maryann explained. "I feel like I'm the only one of us who's missing whatever it is. If a surgeon could lobotomize that need from Bill's brain, I'd tell them to start cutting. They might have to keep shaving until his head's empty, though. What would you do in my position?"

"I can't say," Martha told her. "I'm not Dear Abbey."

Martha wanted to leave as cleanly as possible, and repairing or wrecking Maryann's marriage wasn't leaving clean. Maryann gave Martha a genuine hug and returned to the study. The preliminaries were over, and it was time for the hardest part of the assignment. George Jr. was waiting in the den.

Martha walked into the room, sat on the couch, and greeted George Jr. He looked at her and smiled and returned the greeting. It was the same response she received every time they saw each other. Martha thought about getting up and leaving. That way, she wouldn't be spoiling his day. Then she realized that option was being easy on herself, not easy on him.

"George, I have something important to tell you," Martha said.

George was usually distracted when the television was on, but he recognized that important news should be given his full attention. He turned slightly to face Martha and waited to see what could be important.

"I have to leave," Martha told him.

"Okay," George Jr. answered. "When are you coming back?"

Martha thought a second and replied, "I can't come back, George."

"Why not?" George Jr. asked. "Won't my parents let you?"

"I have a job, and I have to get back to my life," Martha struggled to explain.

She couldn't tell him it was because she'd started to love him in the wrong way. Love was good, so in what way could love be wrong?

"I don't want you to go," George Jr. told her.

George Jr. didn't realize the television was even on now. He was starting to comprehend what was happening, and he was showing that he wasn't always the happy child. His feelings were beginning to show themselves in the form of tears and silence. He'd had enough experience with adults to know that asking more than once rarely changed their minds. Martha's demeanor told him it was her final decision. Martha had started to cry too, for the second time that week.

"You can't go," George Jr. took a last hopeful try.

"I have to, George," Martha sobbed. "I have to."

George sat a few minutes as they both grieved and then said, "I'll miss you."

"I'll miss you too, George," Martha managed to say.

She stood up, and George Jr. stood beside her, towering over her like he had on the stages and podiums during the campaign. She hugged him, and he hugged her back tightly, also like he did at every campaign stop. Betsey appeared at the door, and Martha waited for George Jr.'s bear hug to subside before she broke away and walked out of the room.

"I love you, Martha," George Jr. promised.

"I love you too, George," Martha promised in return.

Betsey was crying now, too, but she had to focus on comforting George Jr. for the rest of the day and however long it took for him to accept that Martha was gone. Martha gave Betsey a hint of a smile and a nod as she walked out. She went straight out the front door of the ranch house, got in her car, and drove away for the last time.

CHAPTER 51

AS SEEN ON TV

President Smith and his chief of staff agreed to meet George Sr., Don, and George Jr. the week after the election to formally kick off the transition of power. The transition teams would be much larger, but George Sr. and Don planned to manage the process so that George Jr. would only attend one or two smaller meetings with the president. The risks of George Jr. getting to know President Smith's cabinet and his cabinet getting to know George Jr. were too great. They also needed to gradually introduce George Jr. to his own cabinet.

"This is the Super Bowl," George Sr. cautioned Don. "The president is a smart cookie, and the only other person in the room that's supposed to be his equal is George. We won't be able to cover for him the entire meeting. President Smith is going to be sizing up his successor."

"I can't fake another heart attack," Don said. He looked like a candidate for the big one. "George needs a full-time chief of staff."

They rode the limo to 1600 Pennsylvania Avenue. Protocol dictated that President Smith greet heads of state at the front entrance of the White House, and

George Jr. was an officially elected head of state. The press was on hand to document the first meeting of the current and future leaders of the nation. The transfer of power had officially begun.

As elder statesman, George Sr. exited the limo first and greeted President Smith. They exchanged pleasantries, and then the president greeted Don. Don was a political legend, even if he did serve the opposing party, and he earned similar pleasantries. George Sr. and Don briefly greeted the president's chief of staff, but they were clearly distracted by George Jr.'s first interactions with President Smith.

"Welcome to your new home, Mr. President," President Smith greeted George Jr.

George Jr. looked momentarily confused and responded, "No, *you're* Mr. President. I've seen you on TV."

President Smith laughed and replied, "So it's true what they say about your sense of humor. That's going to serve you well. After this election, the country can use a little levity. I think we're close enough to the Inauguration that the title fits you."

George Jr. was buoyed by the president's laughter, although he didn't have a clue what was so funny. He also didn't know what levity meant. He followed the group into the White House foyer and walked the center hallway to the West Wing and the Oval Office. George Sr. and Don made small talk with the chief of staff and the president, but George Jr. was busy admiring the artwork and the general grandeur around him. This was nicer than the ranch. When they entered the oval office, George Jr. couldn't continue to contain his enthusiasm.

"Look at the eagle," he instructed.

"I remember having to wrap my mind around working in the same office as some of the greatest men this country has ever produced," President Smith contemplated. "The presidential seal still stuns me every time I see it."

They sat on a couch and chairs in front of the president's desk. President Smith wanted to create a mood of collaboration.

"Have you picked out your office furniture yet?" President Smith asked George Jr. "I'll be putting most of this in my library when it's built. The desk stays, of course. The resolute desk is a presidential institution."

George Jr. glanced at the president's office and told him, "It looks like a library. My mom will get me furniture."

"George has been kind enough to include Betsey and myself in a lot of the details," George Sr. quickly added. "We'll look at options together."

"It's got to be a thrill for you, Senator Flowers. You know this city better than anyone alive, and now you're back here to help your son, our new president, get settled. It certainly has been a wild twelve to eighteen months for your family," President Smith went on. "I anticipated this meeting way back then, but I thought I'd be meeting with Bill, not George. How is Bill these days? I know he's back in the Senate."

"He's doing much better. He couldn't be happier to get back to work," George Sr. replied hastily.

"That is excellent news. At the end of the day, the health and well-being of the people we care about is really what is important, right, George?" President Smith commented.

"Excellent news," George Jr. repeated.

"Before we get down to business, I want to compliment you, Don, on the campaign you ran. You stayed on message, and George's image was untarnished in frankly the most vicious election this country has ever known. I certainly don't mean the contest between George and Vice President Jackson. Your party's primary was high on entertainment but at times low on dignity. That had nothing to do with you. I feel confident entrusting the keys to this residence and to the country to your care."

Don, George Sr. and, belatedly, George Jr. thanked the president for his kind words.

"I supported Andrew out of party loyalty, of course. He was my running mate, after all. But this election ultimately gave the American people two strong choices," President Smith continued.

"Will the vice president be joining us?" George Sr. asked.

"Andrew and his wife are taking some time off after the election. You know better than anyone how grueling the campaign can be, and it takes an extra toll if it doesn't go your way," President Smith explained. "He and his wife are at a resort."

There were stories in the tabloids that the vice president and his spouse were at some undisclosed location that specialized in marriage counseling and couples therapy. This was an improvement over some earlier articles that claimed the marriage was already over. The Jackson's leave of absence told George Sr. the tabloids were probably right about the counseling camp. George Sr. tried to picture Andrew Jackson in a group therapy session.

It might go something like, "Hello, my name is Andrew."

"Hello, Andrew."

"Well, I'm here because I should have been president, but I slept with a blackmailer, there were pictures, and I subjected my wife and me to the greatest public humiliation in political history. I know I did wrong, and I'm here to change."

George Sr. imagined a room filled with dead silence and a few awkward coughs. It was a relief the vice president wasn't in attendance at the transition meeting. It would have made the meeting more stressful for everyone in attendance but George Jr. It was President Smith's turn to ask about another potential attendee.

"I halfway expected Mr. Tripp to join you," President Smith commented. "We understand he's part of your administration."

"We have a role for Mr. Tripp," Don advised. "But not as a member of our transition team. I don't anticipate he'll accompany us on any of our visits to the White House during your term."

"That's good to know," President Smith answered. "This job takes very thick skin, but it would be one of my greater tests to shake the hand of a man that called me a liberal helping of human excrement. That's one of the few quotes I saw in full. The press typically had to censure words when I was his topic, and I refused to directly read what was in his Twitter account. I'm getting close enough to the end of my term—I could probably withstand the fallout if I punched a billionaire in the nose."

"I hope you get the chance to someday, Mr. President, but it won't be with us," George Sr. answered tactfully.

President Smith had one final subject before they talked policies.

"George, I'm sorry the election cost you so much personally," President Smith said. "You were engaged to a wonderful woman, and now you're facing this enormous job with that void in your heart. My wife has been an invaluable resource to me in this office. You need a spouse or someone special to confide in. I hope you find that person. I'm sure you miss Martha."

George Sr. and Don looked on with concern. George Jr. was still sensitive, and Martha was an emotional trigger word they'd done their best to avoid.

"I miss Martha," was all George Jr. said.

"You have to keep all of it inside," President Smith advised. "But figure out your special outlet because you'll need to let some of that quiet fortitude bubble out. Let's take a tour of your living quarters. I'll show you where the president sleeps, and some of the other rooms."

"Good," George Jr. replied. "We can pick out my parents' room."

President Smith laughed again and said to George Sr., "I'm sure you and your wife are going to want to spend a night in the White House."

George Sr. smiled and nodded. He didn't tell President Smith that Betsey was busy working out the logistics of their move to Washington. They'd be using the bedroom that historically belonged to the first lady. It was the closest one to George Jr., and they planned to stay close to him every waking hour. Don would be with him most of the workday, but George Jr. only slept seven or eight hours a day. They had more time to cover than Don could give.

President Smith sized up George Jr. and smiled openly to himself. This man matched what he'd heard. He didn't drone on endlessly like so many of the windbags that were drawn to politics. He interjected quick, poignant comments that made his point with humor but also an underlying sense of authority. Even his father and Don, a veteran politico, seemed captivated and attentive to his every word. This man would weather the office better than most.

Then he looked at his chief of staff, Don Chambers, and a sense of concern replaced his sense of ease. Don looked like he'd just stepped on a landmine and was waiting for a sapper to wander by the area and disarm it. He hoped Don could survive the job.

CHAPTER 52

VICE

George Jr.'s transition team was working in synergy with President Smith's lame duck administration. As George Jr.'s chief of staff, Don was involved with every cabinet post transition. He needed support, so George Sr. had become as politically active as he had been during his days in the Senate. Since they couldn't expose George Jr. to his cabinet or the current administration, Don asked Vice President Martin to step into situations that would normally involve the president. Don told people he was relaying information to the president. The only person Don was actively communicating with was George Sr.

They had one less lame duck to deal with than planned. Vice President Jackson never returned to his position after he lost the election. He wasn't a lame duck—he was a dead duck.

Vice President Martin wasn't pleased that Don was managing all the communications with George Jr. directly. She wanted to discuss her own transition tasks with George Jr., but she also wanted a bigger role in overall communications with him. She also had a handful of pet policies and programs she wanted to discuss privately. She might have dropped out of the race, but the benefit of accepting the VP position was that some of her platform could survive under George Jr.'s administration.

"I need to meet with George," Vice President Martin said to Don as soon as he got into the office. "We need to review my proposal for tax code reform."

Vice President Martin wasn't as high maintenance as Ronald Tripp would have been, but Don was beginning to think they should have asked Senator Ramirez instead. Don had put her off daily, and he took one last shot at managing her.

"Why don't you and I meet this afternoon?" he suggested.

"It really isn't the same as if George and I met on it," she protested. "You can sit in, of course."

Vice President Martin was correct that it would be a very different meeting if George Jr. attended, but Don had put her off too many times to make up another excuse. Vice presidents weren't supposed to feel irrelevant until sometime late in the first year of their first term. Don scheduled the meeting and held his breath.

The three executive branch leaders met the following day. Vice President Martin was cordial to Don, but she practically lit up when she saw George Jr. She had been friendly with him ever since the "two steps back" debate where he had defended then-Senator Martin's honor against the scoundrel Ronald Tripp. Her excitement seemed to escalate to the next level when she greeted George Jr. before the meeting. When Vice President Martin began to speak, Don felt as if she didn't even know Don was in the room. She told George Jr. about ways she would simplify capital gains, cut unfair inheritance taxes, and modify qualified tax-exempt retirement plans. George Jr. appreciated the brightly colored charts and graphics and listened politely. Don listened too, but he also watched more than the charts. Someone in the room had a crush, and it wasn't Don and it absolutely wasn't George Jr.

Don wondered if it had anything to do with the presidential factor. George Jr. was about to be sworn in, and there was something about the most powerful man on the planet that turned a girl's heart to mush. If George Jr. had the whim, he could turn the world into a charred piece of cinder. But the vice president hadn't acted nearly so star-struck on election night, when George Jr. had become that powerful man. Something was different since the election.

Then Don realized what was so different between then and now. George Jr. was with Martha on election day, but Martha was out of the picture now, at least from the vice president's perspective. George Jr.'s status was single.

"Are there any areas I should change?" Vice President Martin asked. "I'll redo any part of it you ask me to."

George Jr. looked at the multi-colored pie charts and bar charts and told her, "It's very pretty."

"Thank you, George," the vice president said as she blushed like a ten-year-old girl at the compliment.

Don didn't say anything because nobody asked for his opinion. She'd gotten the only opinion that mattered to her. Don had formed a different opinion, one he shared, as it was his turn to act like a ten-year-old girl. Don had gossip and he couldn't wait to share it with George Sr.

"We have a situation with the vice president," Don began.

"Oh no, does she know?" George Sr. asked with concern.

"I don't think the vice president would notice if George Jr. sucked his thumb and called her Mama," Don explained. "She seems to be smitten by your youngest son."

George Sr. initially dismissed Don's pronouncement as a joke and then as a misread by a man that had been married too long to be able to tell. But Don persisted, and George Sr. understood it wasn't out of the question. They were two consenting adults thrown together in the work environment. It happened all the time, except it had never happened in exactly this way before.

"At least this time someone's hitting on the son that's not married," George Sr. replied.

"I wonder if there's anything in the Constitution that forbids excessive fraternization among members of the executive branch," Don wondered.

"That would have been inconceivable to the Constitution's authors," George Sr. reminded Don. "They would have never pictured a woman as president or vice president, and they'd have an even harder time imagining two men in a relationship."

"You skipped the third option—a relationship between two women in office," Don pointed out.

"Remembering the two men scenario is good for a Republican," George Sr. defended himself. "If my sexual diversity score gets too high, I'll test at a Democrat level. They'll make me switch parties."

The relationship wasn't good news. They wanted to limit George Jr.'s interactions with his staff. Now the highest-level person on his staff wanted to interact with George Jr. all the time. The ways she wanted to interact with George Jr. were also the fastest ways to expose him for what he was. Then George Sr. brought up another troubling point.

"Let's say Martin tries to work her spell on George, but he rejects her, probably by accident, and she gets angry," George Sr. speculated. "Then let's think about what would happen if she finds out why he isn't interested. What happens if George is forced to quit?"

"Vice President Martin becomes President Martin. The person most likely to find out about George also has the most to gain if she exposes him," Don said. "My God, I feel as if I'm having labor pains."

"That's impossible," George Sr. told Don. "You're too old to even have children."

Don ignored him and asked, "What do we do?"

"We let her flirt with George and hope she's happy to do it for eight years with no results," George Sr. answered. "In the meantime, if she gets too misty around him, we'll have to put seat covers on all the conference room chairs. If it gets to a certain point, we follow Martha's advice and tell her George just had a stroke."

CHAPTER 53

THE CORONATION

Martha sat in an open-air Laguna Beach bar watching the television. She'd transitioned seamlessly into her new job, and she loved her new condo with the ocean view. It was a Friday, but she wasn't working. The bartender approached, and she got to use a line she'd been saving for just such an occasion.

"It's almost noon somewhere," Martha told him. "I think I'll have a drink."

It was almost noon in Washington DC, which meant it was just shy of nine in the morning in Laguna Beach. The bartender didn't bat an eye. He made some gender-influenced suggestions.

"We have a killer drink called an Early Riser, with vodka, OJ, grenadine, and soda," the bartender suggested. "Our martini menu is the best in town. I'd suggest a Lemon Drop."

"A Lemon Drop martini?" Martha questioned, making a sour face. "Does that come with a candy straw and a Midol chaser? I'll have a double Four Roses neat."

Martha helped the bartender by pointing out the bourbon she'd ordered. She didn't have to pour it herself. She hadn't been especially kind to him, but she was having an emotional day and was still adapting to certain aspects of California life. She knew what a Lemon Drop was, and she had some friends that drank them back in Texas. The transition was that in California, she'd met more men who drank Lemon Drop martinis than men who drank bourbon.

Martha had received one phone call commiserating the end of her relationship with George Jr. The call came as soon as the Flowers campaign released the announcement of the breakup. Martha grimaced as soon as she saw the number on her cell phone.

"Hi, Mom," Martha answered. "Do you and Dad sit around the house all day and watch cable news?"

"Martha, we're so sorry," Peggy said, ignoring the question. "What happened?"

Martha hadn't thought to tell her parents she was engaged to George Jr. because it was never real. She had the same lapse when the phony engagement ended. She realized now that her parents didn't have that insight and that Martha had contributed to their state of mind by bringing George Jr. to their house and pretending they were in a real relationship. She hadn't really thought about what she would tell Chuck and Peggy, so she used what she had practiced with Don and George Sr. She told her Mom the pressures of the campaign made her realize she didn't want the responsibilities that came with the title of First Lady.

"You're telling me you don't want to live like a queen? Your Father and I were so looking forward to the wedding and visiting you in the White House," Peggy pleaded.

"I never thought of that," Martha answered. "I'll call George and tell him I was joking."

"You'll do that?" Peggy hoped.

"No, Mom, it's over. Have I taught you nothing about sarcasm?" Martha corrected her.

"Martha, I can't believe you'd get cold feet because you're afraid of becoming First Lady. You've always been fearless," Peggy said. "Are you sure you like men? I always worried that we pushed you into all that volleyball. You spent a lot of time in women's locker rooms."

The conversation made Martha miss the days when her mom thought she had to get engaged because she was pregnant. Martha assured her that sports had not made her gay and that nobody could judge her unless they'd lived the rigors of a presidential campaign. She didn't add that the campaign was especially rigorous if you had to deliver all the speeches for the candidate yourself. They'd talked some more, and Martha broke the news that she planned to move to California. This was another blow to her parents. Martha had lived in Houston her entire life, except for the brief period she'd attended graduate school.

"I guess your father and I can visit you in California instead of the White House. That'll be nice too," Peggy offered. "Let us know if you get engaged again."

The bartender delivered the drink, and Martha went back to the television. George Jr.'s inauguration was about to begin. Martha watched it in a near-trance, and before she knew it, the double Four Roses was little more than a glass full of smoky-smelling vapor. It did improve her disposition on the bartender's return trip to pour her a second round.

"This may seem strange, but I'm traveling from Europe," Martha felt compelled to lie. "This is a nightcap."

"You sound like you're from the South," the bartender commented.

"I'm from all over," Martha decided. She pointed up to the television and said, "I was supposed to be there."

"You're better off here. It looks like a lot of people," the bartender commented.

"My seat was good, and I would have gotten a ride there," Martha informed him.

The bartender asked Martha if she needed a food menu, and she told him she was fine for now. He went to fill other orders while Martha continued watching the ceremony. The weather wasn't as nice as in Laguna Beach, but it was mild and sunny by DC standards. George Jr. looked regal, and Martha could spot George Sr., Betsey, Bill, Maryann, and Don around him. In fact, as Martha looked closer, she could see they formed an almost perfect square around George Jr. Vice President Martin sat next to Bill and Maryann. The other person on the podium that Martha recognized was Ronald Tripp.

Don acted as if he expected some juvenile delinquent to toss a pack of lit firecrackers onto the podium at any moment. It was common to document the physical transformation of a US president from the day he took office to the day he left it. The pressures of the position seemed to exponentially accelerate the aging process. Martha was confident that George Jr. would prove to be the exception as he aged normally. On the other hand, Don was going to age faster than a vampire exposed to sunlight.

Martha understood the disappointment Don and George Sr. had felt when she told them she was leaving. They had grown close during the campaign, and they worked well together. But they also could have used her help to manage George Jr. She tried to imagine the logistics of tracking him 24/7 and doing damage control for every errant remark or unorthodox act. As she watched George Jr. speak, it was difficult to comprehend he didn't understand any of it. She had to compliment herself on the job she'd done perfecting George Jr.'s ability to recognize and repeat speeches he heard through his earpiece.

"I want to make America," George Jr. repeated Don's speech in fragments, "the land of opportunity. Look at me. My first public office is President."

Martha was among the handful of people who knew just what an opportunity George Jr. had been given. The camera showed a shot of Vice President Martin gazing up at George Jr. as he spoke. She had an intent look on her face and seemed to hang on every word from the president's mouth. It wasn't the look a subordinate gave her boss. Vice President Martin looked like the type that would try to block Martha's fake reconciliation to maintain the fake split of her fake engagement. Martha had no such plans, but Martha felt a flurry of jealousy rage through her veins.

Martha told the bartender, "I hear Vice President Martin is a real C-U-next-Tuesday."

"Oh, really?" the bartender answered awkwardly. "I hadn't heard that."

He wandered over to the opposite side of the bar and pretended to wipe out perfectly clean glasses. It was clear to Martha he was afraid of powerful women. He was afraid of drunken, crazy, jealous, powerful women.

As Martha watched the inauguration, a man walked into the bar, surveyed the land, and walked over and sat next to her. He looked like a local. He wore shorts, a Hawaiian shirt, and sandals, and he had bleached hair. The bar was nearly empty, so there was obvious intent in his seat selection. Martha was attractive, alone, and had a glass of whiskey in front of her. He didn't know it was her second, but that would have been all the better. She might as well have placed a "solicitations welcome" placard on the bar in front of her.

"Hello, there. My name is Brice, and I must say, don't you look nice," the man delivered his standard opening line. "That looks good. I'll have the same. Let me know when you're ready, and I'll order you another."

Brice was looking for a nooner, and he wasn't worried if its quality was diminished by too much alcohol. Martha thought she might struggle with a response, but as she watched George Jr. it came to her easily. George Jr. enjoyed spending time with Martha, and it had nothing to do with sex. He was the only man that Martha could be certain genuinely liked her because of her personality. She already knew what Brice liked about her.

"I'm sorry. I'm coming off another relationship, and I'd prefer to be alone right now," Martha informed Brice. "It's nothing against you."

Brice was a veteran of the mean streets of Laguna Beach, and he wasn't about to go down without a fight. He didn't have any more rhyming pickup lines to go with Brice. Once, when he was drunk, he rhymed Brice with "name your price" and ended up with a black eye.

"Sometimes the best way to get over a breakup is to get right back up into the saddle," Brice persisted.

"I've got this theory," Martha told him. "In my experience, all the good men are married, gay, or simple."

"I'm not any of those," Brice clarified.

"So that gives me more data to support the theory," Martha concluded.

Martha turned her back on Brice and continued watching the Inauguration. Brice moved over to the opposite side of the bar, ordered a beer, and did his best to avoid eye contact with Martha. It was early, but more fish would swim into his pond over the course of the day. At closing time, some of them practically jumped into his boat.

Martha felt a pang of guilt when she realized she'd indirectly called George Jr. simple. She hadn't meant it in a negative way, no more than she was negative on men who were gay or married.

She had no second thoughts about taking a pass on the strange trip that would be the Flowers presidency.

At the same time, she'd always feel close to George Jr. It might be the bourbon, but Martha realized she'd just completed a life experience. Before she met George Jr., Martha would start a potential relationship by examining a man's job, his appearance, and his intelligence. It seemed shallow now, but she knew it was the truth.

She couldn't go back and relive it, and she wouldn't go back and change it. Someday she'd meet another man that was as kind to her and as happy to see her as George Jr. had been. If she could find a man with George Jr.'s personality and an extra hundred IQ points to go with it, she'd be set for life. He might not be intelligent enough to be elected president, but he'd be able to treat her as his wife and not as his nanny.

CHAPTER 54

SERVING TIME

For Bill Flowers, it was as if he had slipped right back into his old routine. He worried at first that Washington might shrink for him if his brother was in the White House and his parents were always in town watching George Jr. Fortunately, they left him to his own business. There were times when it might have been nice to be included in more presidential politics, but otherwise Bill was generally satisfied with their arrangement. George Sr. only asked for Bill's help if George Jr. needed to work with Congress. Otherwise, George Sr. was too busy maintaining the delicate balance of George Jr.'s presidency to worry about his eldest son.

Having to drop out of the election was still a bitter memory for Bill. It was made even harder by the realization he would have won the election, and he had fits of jealousy that his predicament had made his brother president instead. Bill could still dream, and although he couldn't run against his brother, he could aim for the next election after that. George Jr. would either be through his two terms, or there would be a first-term incumbent Democrat to defeat. Either way, the Republicans would be looking for a new nominee. Despite the jealousy, Bill needed George Jr. to be at least a modest success. A loss in the next election would be acceptable, but if George Jr. sullied the Flowers name too badly, Bill's reputation would be sullied with it.

While Bill's parents had for all practical purposes moved to Washington, Maryann had remained in Houston. The months Bill had spent with her during his phony illness reinforced that Maryann was an amazing woman. She was a good mother, incredibly intelligent, and still attractive. Other than a swing and a miss with Martha, Bill had been on his best behavior when they were together. Maryann also hadn't bought up the blackmail story again. They seemed to be back to their old, comfortable, familiar roles. Bill was a cheating bastard, and Maryann pretended as if she didn't know about it. Bill's admiration of Maryann wasn't enough to make him stop cheating on her. It just reaffirmed to Bill that he must be something special.

Bill had sworn off female interns and lobbyists while he was running for president, just like a responsible expectant mother gives up booze and cigarettes while she's pregnant. The election was over now, and Bill was back as Washington's nastiest senator. His current fling was with another intern, but Bill felt as if he'd matured and learned from his previous experiences. This intern was from Senator Brown's staff instead of his own.

After his run-in with Dorothy and the deliveryman, Bill considered the staff apartment to be bad luck. He rented his own place now for his extraneous relationships. Bill had just entertained Tina the intern at the apartment before she had to leave to attend one of Senator Brown's staff meetings.

There was a knock on the door that startled Bill. Unpleasant memories flashed through his mind, but this knock wasn't nearly as unexpected. Tina had just left, and she must have either forgotten something or wanted to deliver some silly twenty-something's message of love.

Bill was so sure it was Tina, he didn't bother to see who was there. He'd had enough of Tina for one day, but he put a smile on his face and whipped open the door. He suddenly felt as if a little more of Tina would have been just fine. Bill found himself staring directly into the eyes of his father-in-law, T-Bone Simmons.

"Howdy, Bill. I hope you don't mind a visit. I didn't want to be rude, so I waited until your guest left. I'm surprised you opened the door to me. People would say that means you're either very brave or very stupid," T-Bone smiled at Bill. "I know you, and it ain't because you're brave."

Bill thought about trying to close the door, but getting physical with T-Bone would have to be his last resort.

"T-Bone," Bill said, trying to think. "What are you doing in Washington?"

Bill had a pretty good idea, but he wasn't sure what else to ask. T-Bone had found Bill at the apartment, and Bill certainly hadn't given the address to Maryann. T-Bone was carrying a satchel. Bill worried about what was in that satchel.

"I'm here for Maryann," T-Bone explained. "It has to do with this."

T-Bone let his gaze circle around the apartment.

"It also has to do with that filly that just left and dozens of others like her," T-Bone went on. "And that."

T-Bone pointed, and the "that" was Bill's crotch.

"I use this place for work whenever I'm in the office late," Bill tried to explain.

"That's a good excuse," T-Bone commented. "Except if you're going to use that excuse, you should have thought about getting an apartment that's closer to the Capitol, not farther away than your home."

"That woman shuttles paperwork to me," Bill tried to explain.

"You get that much from Senator Brown's office?" T-Bone asked. "If she shuttles paperwork, she must have a photographic memory. All she brings with her are raging hormones and the morals of a tramp."

"These young kids today are really smart," Bill attempted.

"Shut it, son," T-Bone threatened. "I told you a long time ago what would happen if you weren't a good listener. I knew you weren't the first time I said it, and I've known it plenty of times since then. I gave you a lot of passes, but I got news for you. Your time is up."

T-Bone reached into the satchel, and Bill turned his back and grabbed his ears. Bill wasn't sure if T-Bone planned to pull a knife or a gun, but he knew better than to face either head-on.

"Hey, son, you might want to look at this," T-Bone told Bill.

Bill glanced back, expecting to see a high-caliber handgun. Instead, T-Bone was holding a large envelope. Bill felt foolish as he turned back to face T-Bone and his papers. T-Bone handed Bill the envelope, and Bill accepted it with relief.

"Son, you just got served. If you come back to Houston, you better be campaigning. Maryann is done with your lying, cheating ass," T-Bone said.

"Is that it?" Bill asked hopefully.

"Son, I'm not stupid enough to shoot or dismember a senator," T-Bone shook his head at Bill's response. "There's more than one way to castrate an ornery bull. Maryann is going to have the house and, at the very least, half your money."

Bill just stood there thinking about the fallout to his image and the sum he'd have to pay his wife. It wasn't Ronald Tripp money, but then again, Bill didn't start with Ronald Tripp money.

"I know everything," T-Bone told Bill. "Maryann told me you faked cancer and dropped out of the election because you were blackmailed. We both know that lamb-sucking story was nonsense. I told her you got caught with another floozy. The details don't matter. It's all part of the same reward you're holding there in your hand. Before I go, I've got one more message, but it isn't for you. Maryann told me about your brother, and based on what she said, he can't be running the country. Tell your daddy that as of now, we're partners. Tell him I'll be calling him real soon to talk business."

After T-Bone departed, Bill thought about what he had to do. He needed a lawyer, but the first thing he'd need to do was talk with George Sr. Bill didn't have to fly back to Texas this time, but it wouldn't go any better than the worst meetings in his father's study.

T-Bone's lawyer had insisted they could have used a conventional process server to deliver Maryann's divorce papers to Bill for a fraction of what it cost T-Bone. T-Bone insisted that he should do it himself.

"That sounds so impersonal," T-Bone told the lawyer. "Bill will take it much better if it comes from me."

CHAPTER 55

THE AMBASSADOR

Ambassador Tripp and Natasha left the embassy for a dinner with her mother, her father, and her uncle Boris at her parent's house. It was late March, but the Moscow weather was subzero, and the limo's seats felt like cement blocks. Natasha was decked out from head to toe in sable, both for fashion and for warmth. The Ronald never wore a hat during his winters in New York because they wreaked havoc with his toupee, but he sported a sable hat for the occasion too.

Before The Ronald had left for Russia, he received good luck messages from both his ex-wives.

"Just because you're on the other side of the world doesn't mean you can get out of your alimony payments," Illiana emailed Tripp. "My lawyer is on standby if you're late for even a single payment."

Rhonda called Tripp directly and offered her regards. Her comments were as direct as her method of contact.

"I'm thrilled to get you out of town so I don't have to see your bloated face or read about which party you and your latest whore attended," Rhonda told Tripp. "Just remember to pay me my damn money. Your ass belongs to me, and your assets are still in the US. I hope you get frostbite so severe your dick turns black and falls off. Protect your hands, though. You'll need your fingers to sign the checks you'll keep sending me."

They arrived at the mansion, and Natasha greeted her family. They all had a couple of rounds of vodka to warm their bones and limber up their tongues. Tripp was seated next to Boris at dinner.

"What you think Mother Russia?" Boris asked.

"The people and the culture are magnificent," Tripp answered politely. "And it's cold as hell."

"Cold as hell is what I think you Americans call oxymoron," Boris pointed out. "My brother and his wife so happy Natasha back in Russia. We should talk about other benefits of your position."

"I'm an official of the US government," Tripp reminded Boris. "I have to be careful to avoid even the appearance of impropriety."

The Ronald had no issues with impropriety with people he trusted. He didn't trust someone who could drink a fifth of vodka standing on his head.

Boris chuckled and said, "In Russia, even premier stays clear of my business. Nobody give us any trouble here. They call me Russian gangster. My sources tell me we have a lot in common."

The Ronald was paying close attention, and he detected the aroma of a side of blackmail with his caviar. His ambassadorship could turn out to be a long and dangerous appointment. He wished he had one of the bears, preferably Ours, at the embassy to keep the Russians away. Unfortunately, none of his mercenaries could weather a US government background check.

When The Ronald and Natasha returned to the embassy after the dinner, it was early enough for them to launch into their nightly argument.

"I hate it here," Natasha yelled. "It's cold and dreary, and this embassy is slum compared to our apartment.

There's no clubs or galas or parties like in New York. My parents want visit all the time. These are reason I go New York. Now you drag me back."

"We've been here less than a month," The Ronald argued. "Give it a chance."

Tripp always found that the toughest negotiation was the one where you had to argue one position when you agreed with the opposing position. He had to argue the positives of being the Russian ambassador because for now he had no choice. The Ronald was beginning to feel as if he'd been hustled by George Jr. The dinner tonight with the mobster was another in a string of unpleasantness that was Russia. He didn't see how he was going to have any effect on US strength if he went hardline or US-Russian relations if he went softline. He'd already called Don Chambers twice to complain and had gotten nowhere.

"Ronald, we're right in the middle of the transition, and we have our hands full," Don explained. "We don't think now is the time to hit the premier with a change in direction, as long as he behaves himself. Work on building a relationship with the man."

"The man has cancelled our first three meetings," The Ronald complained. "If I'm just supposed to conduct business as usual, why am I here?"

"You're there because Russia is the second-most powerful country on the planet, and it could become critically important at any time," Don told him patiently.

"Until that happens, bring me back to Washington," Tripp pleaded. "I'll work domestic, economic, foreign policy, you name it."

Don had a hundred things to do, but he knew the call was important. As much of a nuisance as these constant calls had been, he had The Ronald safely tucked away on the opposite side of the globe. This call wasn't so much a waste of Don's time as it was an investment of his time.

"We feel that the Russian ambassador should be in Russia," Don ordered. "Things could heat up at a moment's notice."

"You just want me here if we decide to drop the big one. I've seen *Fail Safe*," Tripp said in frustration.

"The Cold War is over, Ronald," Don announced. "If the premier gets frisky in some small Eastern European or Asian country, this administration will deal with it diplomatically."

The idea of dropping an atomic bomb on The Ronald's head didn't bother Don too much, but he had to consider how many innocent Russians would meet the same fate. Don hadn't managed to placate The Ronald, but he'd managed to keep him in Moscow.

The Ronald knew what it felt like to be exiled in Siberia. There was nothing The Ronald liked to think about more than The Ronald, and he had a lot of extra time to think sitting in his embassy office day after day. A thought came to him, and he called Malcolm. In contrast to Tripp, Malcolm had his hands full managing their ongoing enterprises in The Ronald's absence.

"I need you to get the band back together," The Ronald informed Malcolm. "I'm running for president again at the next election."

Malcolm was a little slow to understand, partly because the request was unanticipated and partly because it was two in the morning New York time.

"You're going to run in the primaries against Flowers?" Malcolm asked for clarification. "You're in the same party, and you're part of his administration. How does that work?"

"No," Tripp answered impatiently. "I'm running as a Democrat. It looks like Junior has his ticket punched for two terms unless I beat him. I'm not waiting that long to run as a Republican. I'll resign this bogus job before the primaries start."

"Do you expect the Democrats to welcome you with open arms, given your policy positions in the last election?" Malcolm asked delicately.

"I'm a good businessman, the best, and a good businessman adjusts with the market," Tripp lectured. "The primaries are three years away. By the time they roll around, the only difference Democrats will see between me and FDR is that I can stand on my own to give a speech."

"Politicians have switched parties in the past and been successful. They usually go from Democrat to Republican. It's a natural byproduct of the aging process," Malcolm reasoned. "This is unusual, but if anyone can get away with pretending the last election never happened, you can."

"The American people can't keep straight what they heard yesterday. They won't care what I said four years ago," Tripp agreed.

"What do you want me to do?" Malcolm asked.

"I need to kiss and make up with all the groups that hate my guts," Tripp began. "I need to improve my image with all the blacks. Call Magic and Snoop Dogg's people, and get them on board. I need to win back the Hispanics, so get George Lopez on the team. I need gay friends, and I need them fast. Get me on Ellen's show. I might have rubbed a lot of female voters the wrong way, too. Get me on *The View.* I'll have those bitches eating right out of my hand."

"You'll do fine as long as you don't call them bitches," Malcolm remarked.

"I need to be around poor people. When I get back to the States, I want to visit ghettos—with the proper amount of personal protection, of course. I'm deeply disturbed about the economic disparity in the country," Tripp went on.

"There are going to be people who point out that you're one of the most disparate," Malcolm said.

"I'm going to solve that," Tripp said. "I have a couple of ideas already. I'm going to buy everyone that's homeless an old high school band uniform, a folding chair, and a coin jar. People are a sucker for that routine. For the second idea, we all know I was the best boxing promoter ever. I'm going to start the UHF."

"The UHF?" Malcolm asked as expected.

"The Ultimate Homeless Fighter. You take homeless guys right off the street and have them fight in one of those cages," The Ronald explained with excitement. "I'll need to explore whether we can do women too. Any woman that's hot enough for the UHF probably isn't homeless, though. I even thought about this angle during the introductions. The referee tells the two fighters the rules, and then he looks into the camera and winks. Rules? We don't need no stinking rules. The most famous moment in boxing over the past twenty years was some fighter biting off another fighter's ear. We'll have that every night."

"So it won't be staged?" Malcolm played out his interest.

"Hell, no. We let them beat the crap out of each other. We'll hold all the matches in Vegas and Atlantic City," The Ronald went on. "The gambling revenue will be huge."

"And it all goes to the homeless?" Malcolm questioned.

"A percentage will, after expenses, taxes, and a decent profit," The Ronald explained. "At least they're off the streets."

Malcolm heard an endless stream of The Ronald's creativity. If there were a god, these would be two of the many ideas that never went any further than a single psychotic rant.

"There will be a lot of people, some of them powerful Democrats, who will question your motives," Malcolm pointed out.

"I've got skin thicker than an alligator's," Tripp said. "I don't care about the party mainstream as long as I can convince voters the color of my spots has changed. I'm an outsider, a radical. I'll be like Eugene McCarthy, except less of a loser. Power to the people, baby."

"I suppose it's the same drill as last time, with a different set of facts," Malcolm thought aloud. "It doesn't matter what we believe, it only matters what voters believe."

"I'll make them believe whatever we want them to believe," The Ronald bragged. "This is why they call America the land of political opportunism."

Malcolm knew that wasn't what they called it, but part of Malcolm's success was that he never contradicted The Ronald on any of his Ronaldisms. It was one of Malcolm's strongest assets, but he wasn't alone. George Flowers Jr. seemed to be the only person left in America who had the nerve or the strength to try to fight The Ronald. Malcolm couldn't predict the results of the next election or whether it would help or harm the American people, but he knew it would be entertaining.

CPSIA information can be obtained
at www.ICGtesting.com
Printed in the USA
FSOW02n0842221016
26435FS